Sadie Pearse

sphere

SPHERE

First published in Great Britain in 2018 by Sphere

1 3 5 7 9 10 8 6 4 2

A CIP catalogue record for this book is available from the British Library.

ISBN 978-0-7515-6378-8

Typeset in Baskerville by M Rules
Printed and bound in Great Britain by
Clays Ltd, Elcograf S.p.A.

Papers used by Sphere are from well-managed forests and other responsible sources.

Sphere
An imprint of
Little, Brown Book Group
Carmelite House
50 Victoria Embankment
London EC4Y 0DZ

An Hachette UK Company
www.hachette.co.uk

www.littlebrown.co.uk

To F and M, my sun and moon

Part One

SPRING

Prologue

Riley moved like mercury.

Sally's had been a childhood spent sitting still – making a fairy door in the hollow under a tree, putting flags in sandcastles, arranging flowers in her press. Her daughter was different; Riley was born restless and whippet-quick.

'Hold this, Mum,' Riley said, passing Sally her orange ice lolly. Sally bent to catch the drip heading southward down the stick.

Riley ran across the garden and swiftly climbed towards the top of the apple tree. Her slim body, in jean shorts and a T-shirt, became partially obscured by the blossom, but Sally could see her feet reach a high branch. Riley stepped over to her bedroom window ledge, teetering for one heart-stopping moment between the sill and the branch, which bowed a little under her foot. Sally's breath caught. Riley jumped back to the tree, clutching the trunk to cement her hold.

'Time to come down,' Sally said.

She watched her seven-year-old daughter navigate the network of branches. A slender one snapped and Riley lost her footing. Sally heard her scrambling to regain a foothold and her heart began to thud.

Riley held tight and repositioned herself, and Sally exhaled. Her pride was mingled with anxiety at her daughter's adventurous nature. *I wish you wouldn't do this.*

'Come down, now, Riley,' Sally said, more firmly. She heard Theo's voice in her mind: Let go. Let her take a few risks. She always comes back to us, doesn't she?

'No,' Riley called out. 'I'm not coming down.'

As Riley moved, disappearing behind the leaves for a moment, a shoe bumped a path down the trunk, hitting the ground near Sally's feet. Sally picked it up – purple, Clarks, size twelve, with scuffmarks on the toe.

She remembered the day they'd bought those shoes together, at a shoe shop in London, just before they'd moved here to the outskirts, to Penville. New shoes for Riley's new school, Elmtree Primary. Sally remembered the trip, seeing her daughter try on the shoes over stripy tights. They'd stood in front of the shop mirror and Riley had tilted her head before giving a nod of approval – as enthusiastic as she got about clothes. Sally had asked the assistant to box them up – these were the ones.

'I lost my shoe!' Riley called out. The words carried on the wind, pure sing-song, detached from any visible body.

'Hey,' Sally called, waving the shoe in the air.

Riley's face, pink-cheeked, appeared through the leaves. 'You've got it!' she called out, laughing.

'I have, Cinderella.'

Riley came down to the ground and, with one sock-clad foot, ran over to her mother. She allowed Sally to hold her for a moment while she put her shoe back on. Her girl. As close to her heart now as she'd been as a newborn – closer. Sally took in the honey scent of her. Stroked the nape of her neck, gently.

'I'm not Cinderella,' Riley said. Then she got to her feet and ran back to the tree again. 'I'm Riley.'

Chapter 1

Theo walked down Addison Road, the day working in the café still buzzing in his mind. He saw their house towards the end of the cul-de-sac, 1950s semi-detached, a little boxy, but with enough room for the three of them. From the outside, it was just like the others in their patch of suburban London – the bay window bright. But then, a couple more steps to the hedge, up the path, and he saw what made this one different. What made number twenty-eight home.

He saw Sally first. Her dark-blonde hair was up in a loose top-knot and she had her glasses on. She was on the sofa, legs crossed, in jeans and a sweater printed with tattoo hearts, her arm draped around Riley's shoulder. They were watching something on the iPad. *Danger Mouse*, Theo guessed. Sally glanced up at the window, saw him and smiled.

It had been eleven years since the two of them had met, in their mid-twenties. When Theo had got the letter calling him for jury service, his first thought had been how to get out of it. He'd been working for an advertising firm back then – the café he ran now no more than a doodle on his notepad – and with an important pitch to deliver he really hadn't wanted to take the time off. But he'd gone, and as soon as he walked in through the courtroom doors, there was Sally – she'd looked up and smiled, as if she already knew him.

In the court, they'd agreed, unanimously, to deliver a verdict of not guilty, and as they'd walked out on that last day, Theo had asked for Sally's number. It wasn't where he'd expected to meet the woman who'd change his life – on a wooden bench, holding another man's future in his hands – but that week, the long waits and chats over vending machine coffee had shown him enough to know he didn't want to let Sally slip away.

Riley spotted him and jumped to her feet, then dashed over to the window, pressing her face up to the glass. Her smile was broad, her brown curls loose, darting in different directions. He pressed his face up to the other side of the glass and for a second they were almost touching. Then she disappeared, dashing around to the front door to let him in.

At the front door, Theo grabbed Riley and swept her up into a hug. There was a faint smell of biscuits clinging to her. Theo squeezed her tightly and she laughed, a big, loud, belly laugh. He relished that laugh; it made him whole.

'Hey, Sal.' He kissed her. 'You guys have been eating Hobnobs.'

'How do you always know?' Riley said.

'I have my ways.'

'Chocolate ones,' Sally said. 'Last ones in the packet. Sorry.'

Sally Pieterson. The light at the end of his day, each day.

'I like you in those glasses, you know,' he said.

'Ah, no,' she said, wrinkling her nose. 'Yes, I can see. And that's nice. But finding out I'm long-sighted and moving out to the suburbs in the same year is making me feel pretty middle-aged.'

'Happens to the best of us, I've heard.'

She laughed. She hadn't changed much, or at least not that he really noticed or cared about. Neither of them was standing still, and why would they want to? For a second, looking at Sally, he wasn't in their hallway, surrounded by family photos, Riley's scooter, discarded welly boots. They were on the sand dunes of a Norfolk beach, both of them in their twenties, their cheeks wind-burned and their lips raw from kissing after a weekend trip that had made them solid. Sally had shown him what it was to feel you had everything you needed, right there, in your arms. She'd shown him how to forgive himself for the things he'd never achieved and strive for the things he still could.

'Marble run, Dad,' Riley said, tugging at his hand. 'Let's make one. Up in my room.'

Theo pulled away, caught Sally's smile, and ruffled his daughter's hair. 'Sure. Let's do that,' he said.

She thumped up the wooden stairs.

'We should carpet those stairs,' Sally said, half to herself. 'Get a runner, maybe.'

Theo followed Riley upstairs. Things had changed for good when Riley was born. They'd got noisier. Busier. Messier. But better. She'd arrived after two years of trying. He'd done all he could to keep Sally feeling positive, even when he started to wonder himself if it would happen for them – then along came Riley. He would never forget the sunlight in Sally's smile the first time she held their daughter in her arms. His wife's hair mussed, cheeks pink, in that hospital gown, more beautiful than he'd ever seen her look. And then his daughter. Sally had passed their little girl to him and his heart had started to thud. He had been scared to hold her – she seemed so fragile, her hands tiny. Her head – he wasn't even sure how to support it. But when he did hold her, he became someone new. His feet were more firmly rooted to the ground, his arms grew stronger, and he knew, from somewhere deep within, how to keep her safe.

While Theo got Riley ready for bed, Sally went upstairs and into the box room that was now her studio. On the desk were

Sally's laptop, her sewing machine, design book and folder of sample fabrics – her tools for designing and making her range of children's clothes. She needed to tie up some ends that were loose after the school run called an end to her working day.

She and Theo had loved their flat in Islington, and the buzz of the city – weekends filling easily with activities and visits to friends. Riley was settled and happy in her primary school, St Michael's, and Sally had a good network of local friends as well as those at her office. But as Riley grew, so did their collection of things; their bikes and her scooter clogged the hallway and the flat began to feel cramped. They both realised they were only fighting the inevitable: their urban family needed more space.

So, they'd talked with estate agents and looked at houses further and further up the underground line, eventually finding Penville, and their new house, right at the end. The décor throughout had been caught in the 1970s, but they'd seen potential there. Riley had been reluctant to move and leave her friends, but once she saw the garden and the nearby park, she decided she could get used to it. They'd started work just before their first Christmas in the house, and had now updated most of the rooms, decorating them one by one. In this room, her studio, they had kept the original wallpaper, with deer and rabbits on it, and the window framed the apple tree in the garden that Riley had climbed that afternoon. Here was where Sally found peace.

She went through some new material samples and put a couple up on her pinboard, lingering over one with a Mexican-inspired flower print. She pictured it on a toddler – perhaps it was something she could fit into a summer collection. She pinned the sample next to her sketches and photos of children's clothing designs at various stages of production – spiked dinosaur hoodies, sugar-skull-print dresses, skirts with dachshunds running toe-to-tail around the hem. From these daydreams came finished products, more each week, and the floor was stacked with packaged-up orders ready to take to the post office.

Sally could hear Riley's laughter through the closed door. Yes, Riley's arrival had thrown so much of their ordered lives into chaos, but having her daughter had also brought energy and inspiration. Sally had enjoyed working as a graphic designer, but had always wondered what it would be like to work for herself. With the new house came the beginnings of her clothing business and the start of a new career.

Since they'd moved, Isabel, her ex-colleague, coffee buddy and confidante, would sometimes ask if she missed the magazine offices where they'd worked together for almost a decade. Sally missed their Thursday-night cocktails, and the water-cooler chats about Isabel's dates. But she didn't miss the office. It was invigorating to be doing something for herself, and anyway the move hadn't been for her as much as for Riley. Life had changed, and her daughter had started taking priority a long time ago. She would never look back. Their family had been too hard-won.

The day, nine years ago, when Theo had asked if they might start trying for a baby, excitement had mingled with trepidation, but underlying it all was the certainty that this was going to be their future. She'd started to form a picture of the three of them in her mind. They knew what they wanted and where they were headed.

But then, month after month of hope, and hopes dashed. There were times she'd wondered if opening up that space in their lives, only for it to stay empty, was worth all the pain. Theo had helped her to stay positive, but she could see it in his eyes too. The uncertainty, and the fear that wanting wasn't necessarily enough. The rollercoaster of hormones, emotions and hope. One Sunday morning, those two blue lines had shown up – an exhilarating jolt. Their future was beginning.

In the following weeks, Sally's body felt weighed down with

a tiredness that seemed out of all proportion with the tininess of the foetus inside her. She'd expected to feel nothing but happiness and gratitude, but a hundred nuanced emotions came through instead, and in those first twelve weeks she'd told no one but Theo and Isabel. She wanted more than ever to have her own mother there, to share the secret with. She longed to be able to tell her mum, see the delight on her face, and feel the comfort of a hug. Twenty years could do a lot to heal, but the wound was still there.

After three months of pregnancy, Sally relaxed a little, and started to trust that the baby she was carrying would arrive safely in her arms. She started to trust in herself, and that she and Theo could do this. One day she stood with Theo in the bathroom and looked at the two of them in the mirror, and saw that they really were ready for their lives to change.

Riley's room fell quiet, and Sally stayed at her desk answering emails until the smell of Theo's cooking drew her out. Her day had been full of thoughts of food – an apple for school pick-up, a snack bar during their trip to the park, a fish pie and peas for Riley's dinner – but she'd forgotten to eat anything herself for hours and her mouth was watering. Now Riley was in bed, the evening was hers and Theo's. Passing her daughter's room, she peeked in at Riley and watched her sleeping. That day, like most days, had been full of noise – demands, raised voices, stubborn refusals, warm hugs, the shriek of a grazed knee, the frustration of waiting for shoes to go on, teeth to be brushed. But now there was only silence, and maternal love flooded back so quickly it almost overwhelmed her.

Downstairs, in their open-plan kitchen, the white walls brought to life by their daughter's paintings and drawings, was Theo. He was part-hidden by the steam rising up from the pots on the hob, in a grey and yellow T-shirt with jeans. His dark hair needed a cut, she thought – it was almost resting on his eyelashes, but she kind of liked it that way. Those eyes – round and brown, like Minstrels. She smiled at the memory of when she'd first had that thought.

He'd asked her for her number in the street outside the courtroom, this man she'd only known a week, but who, with just a glance, a coffee from the vending machine, a shared joke, had dominated her every waking thought. The possibilities of them, of her with this man who seemed to take all of life in his stride, had already started to change her. Her flat had new depths to it – clothes at the back of the wardrobe she hadn't worn since her break up, the red lipstick at the bottom of her make-up bag, the northern soul CD that sounded so good with breakfast. He'd asked for her number and she'd made herself wait.

One – breathe. Two – breathe. Three – breathe. She'd looked at the ground for a moment. She felt his proximity and it made her chest constrict, the breaths hard to find. She heard Isabel's voice in her head: *Don't rush into this.* And her own: *You're still bruised. It hasn't been long.*

She could see his hands and forearms, strong, sure. *You don't need this.*

She looked up again, her gaze a trail from his arms to his mouth, his eyes. And there he still was, looking, as if he couldn't look away.

She might not need this.

But maybe wanting it is enough. Better.

She'd said the digits out loud, a string of numbers that he put into his phone. Then when she walked away she felt him holding on to them like a kite string.

She made her way over to him now, in the home they co-owned, and wrapped her arms around his waist. 'That smells great.'

She blurred out the table that was still messy from Riley's dinner, the toys strewn across the kitchen floor that Riley hadn't cleared up. It could wait until later.

Theo turned his back on the cooking and brought her in close, kissing her. It sent a pleasurable shiver over her skin. She kissed him again, more deeply this time.

'Careful,' he said, laughing. 'Or you'll end up with a seriously burned dinner here.'

'I don't think I care.' She smiled.

He pulled away reluctantly and went back to cooking, and she pulled up a stool so she could sit opposite him at the counter.

'So, Riley asked me what brains looked like this afternoon,' Sally said.

Theo laughed. 'Really?'

'Yep. They've been learning about the body at school,' she said. 'Put my drawing skills to the test, but I think it turned out OK.' She pulled her drawing off a pile of papers and showed him.

'Not bad,' he said. 'One for the new clothes range?'

She laughed. 'Or not. I think probably not.'

'How's the web design going?'

'It's going well, I think. I'm meeting with Isabel tomorrow to get her thoughts on it. She's the expert, really.'

This far, Sally's business had been operating on a small-scale level, orders generated by word-of-mouth and social networks – but now the production side of things was running smoothly, she was ready to put more energy and money into the marketing.

'You two and your lunches,' he said, playfully shaking his head.

'What?' She laughed. 'They're working lunches.'

'Yeah, right.'

'They are,' she protested. 'You're just jealous.'

'Probably,' he admitted. 'Things have been so busy at the

café lately, I can't remember the last time I took a lunch break.'

'Devising the summer menu?'

'You'd think, right? But actually that's been the easy part. Half our time's been spent on getting the food ready for Mum and Dad's anniversary party.'

'How's it all going?'

'We're nearly there – Gabi's sorting the cake, and she said she'd help out on the day too.'

'That's kind of her. We should take her out, say thank you.'

Gabi, Theo's friend and business partner, always went the extra mile.

'In fact,' Sally said, 'when things are quieter with work – for both of us – *we* should go out.'

'Revolutionary concept,' Theo said.

She laughed. It had been months since they went out the two of them. 'Seriously, your mum's always saying she'd be happy to babysit. And Riley loves it when she comes over. We should take her up on it. Do something together.'

'Let's do that.'

'Do you ever miss the days when it was just us?' Sally asked. 'Those long lie-ins with the papers, boozy Sunday lunches with friends, last-minute city breaks.'

'Come on, I can't answer that.'

'Go on. Honestly.'

'Yes, I do,' Theo said. 'I do – and I don't. And everything in between.'

The following morning, Sally marshalled her family into order – getting breakfast ready and Riley's school bag packed while Theo was still rubbing the sleep from his eyes. Sally was a morning person and her husband a night owl. Riley had taken after her dad, drowsy at the breakfast table and reluctant to settle in the evenings when there was still fun to be had.

Theo helped Riley choose her clothes. Sally spotted them out of the corner of her eye, stealthily removing Riley's favourite Pokémon T-shirt from the laundry basket.

'Hey,' she called out. 'Something vaguely clean at least, guys.'

'But I like that one,' Riley protested.

Sally was about to insist when a text buzzed through on her phone. *You still on for lunch? Iz x*

Sally texted back to confirm, one-handed, while stuffing Riley's PE kit into her schoolbag. Sally pictured her friend, probably drinking a coffee at the kitchen counter, in her calm, tidy flat. No Lego bricks underfoot, no Weetabix dried like cement on the table, no Haribo sticking to the inside of her handbag. No noise. Sally imagined it for one fleeting, blissful second – no noise.

Isabel had challenges and pressures in her life, Sally knew that, but she managed them calmly and capably. There was only one thing, one person, that had ever shaken her foundations, and still could. Freddie.

'When's your brother arriving?' Sally asked Theo.

'Saturday morning – he's just bought his flight.'

'He cut that pretty fine. The party's this weekend.'

'You're surprised?' Theo said, laughing.

Freddie was thirty, but hadn't changed much in the decade or so Sally had known him. He had been a music and culture journalist in London and, through Sally, he and Isabel had become close friends, going to gigs and exhibitions together. Occasionally, they were more than that. Freddie would always hold back from committing to anything more. Then, a year ago, he took a job in Berlin. Before he went, he and Isabel had gone out drinking and he'd opened up to her and told her he was serious about her. Only Sally knew that he'd broken through a wall in her she'd had up for years. But when he left, he didn't contact her for weeks, then started to text again. Sally found it hard to watch as Freddie kept her best friend hanging, never giving enough, and never quite letting her go.

'If he messes with Iz's head again, I swear I'll . . . '

'We could tell him she's left the country?' Theo suggested.

'Tempting, very tempting,' Sally said.

'You know he doesn't mean to . . . ' Theo said. 'He's . . . you know, he does care about her. I don't think that's the issue. He's just—'

'Don't say it,' Sally said, fixing him with a glare.

'He's just Freddie.'

Outside, after kissing Sally goodbye on the front step, Theo put Riley in the trailer on the back of his bike and put their helmets on. The sky stretched pale blue overhead and the early morning sun glinted off the cars in the surrounding driveways.

'Ride fast today, Dad,' she said.

He laughed.

'Faster than normal. Faster than Mum likes.'

He didn't make any promises. But as they rode down and out of Addison Road, Theo started pedalling hard and Riley's laughter came in wild waves from behind him. They left the cul-de-sac and turned on to the main road that led to Elmtree Primary.

'That was pretty fast,' Riley said, as he helped her down. 'Almost as fast as I can go.'

At the school gates, Theo said goodbye. 'You have a good day today.'

She hugged him and then sprinted away. She was nearly at the door when she turned and called, 'Bring some cake back from the café.'

Theo smiled to himself as he got on his bike. He liked Fridays, when his café, The Hideaway, opened late and he got to drop his daughter off, starting the day with just the two of them. He took the route towards east London, where his café was located. He could do it on autopilot now. After all the upheaval and excitement of moving house, they were settling into their new routines, and The Hideaway was starting to bring some regular money in.

When Sally had offered to put all her inheritance into the business, Theo had wavered. He knew how important it was to her, the money her mother had left her, which she'd kept in a savings account since she was a teenager, but in the end they'd decided to go ahead, and it had given them solid foundations to build the café on. It had been a risk, but so far it had all been worth it – creating the intimate coffee shop they'd envisioned in a cobbled courtyard just behind Columbia Road.

He locked his bike in the side alley. This place – this dream – was one that he and Sally had made real together a year earlier. He ran it now with his childhood friend Gabi, who cooked most of the fresh food there. He knew the regulars by name and the coffee they drank, and at quieter times he and Gabi would chat with them and get to know a little of their lives.

Theo brought the till to life, and Gabi came in, carrying boxes of cakes and fresh flowers, a few of her dark curls of hair visible on either side of the bouquet.

'Hey, Theo,' she called out.

He came over, taking the fresh flowers and putting them by the vases in the window. 'Could barely see you behind all that.'

She put the cake boxes down on the counter and opened them to show him. 'Right, check these out. Lemon drizzle with lavender here, banana and walnut and – you'll like this one – chocolate with praline frosting.'

Her face was bright as she described them. With her dark hair and wide-set brown eyes, customers often assumed she and Theo were family, which was how she felt to Theo. Her mother had followed her best friend Elena, Theo's mother, from Crete to England in the seventies with her boyfriend in tow, and Gabi and Theo had grown up together, sharing the same food, the same second language and jokes about the things their mothers missed about home.

'You must have been up all night making these.'

'Who needs sleep?' she said. 'Anyway, this is nothing compared to the cake I'm making for your parents' party. My mum keeps reminding me – as if I didn't know – "Elena and Stephen's party – this is an important one",' she mimicked her mother's sing-song Greek accent, and Theo smiled in recognition. '"Forty years of marriage. When you get there, you'll understand."' Gabi laughed. 'Has there ever been anything more nerve-wracking than making the cake for your parents' wedding anniversary? I don't think so.'

'Pressure. But I know you'll do us proud. Thanks for doing all this for it. It means a lot to us.'

His parents had always treated Gabi as something like a niece, and at family events she was as much a part of things as he and his brother were. He was looking forward to having the family together at the weekend, and catching up with Freddie again. The years of competing with one another had mellowed into a friendship that he now valued.

'It'll be fine, right?' she said. 'We've done the canapés, the main courses, the puddings . . . '

Theo ran through his mental list. 'That's it. Beyond that, it'll just be a few things on the day that need organising. You're sure you don't mind being in the kitchen for most of the party? My parents are going to want to see you.'

'It's my gift to them,' she said. 'And my friend's coming in to help out.'

'That's kind of her. We'll pay her, obviously.'

'And me?' Gabi smiled, and it carried to her eyes.

'I could do you a cappuccino, extra sprinkles?'

'Go on, then.'

He made them coffees, and they sat together at the counter, drinking in companionable silence, knowing that it was a matter of moments before the quiet was broken by their first customers.

Theo thought of Sally – knew that other women, different wives, might not have liked that he and Gabi were so close. But that wasn't Sally. She didn't do jealous; she never had. Plus she had grown to love Gabi just as he did.

'What would we do without you?' Theo said, at last.

She smiled. 'You'd cope. You'd probably still fit in your old jeans.'

That afternoon, Sally went to Covent Garden before meeting Isabel. It felt good to be in the heart of London again – the liveliness and anonymity of it all, the tourist buzz, the city workers' brisk stride, no one giving her a second look. She went into Zara and looked through the racks of clothes. She chose a silver-grey dress and a shrug for the party. She already had one for Riley – a red dress she'd made herself, with a satin skirt. Riley would look beautiful in it, and her grandma Elena would love seeing her in it. Sally bought her own outfit, then walked around the corner to the café opposite Isabel's offices.

She spotted Isabel right away – crisp white shirt, her dark hair up in a ponytail with a short fringe.

'Sal,' she said, taking her best friend into a hug. 'Good to see you. I thought suburbia might have swallowed you up.'

'No chance,' Sally said, laughing. 'I think it's more likely to spit me out right now.'

'You can take the girl out of the city . . . '

'Yep. It's pretty different out there. Adapting isn't quite as easy as I thought.' She'd thought that after eight months, she'd have a circle of friends, but building up a social life in Penville was proving to be slow process. 'I'll get there.'

'I felt like that when me and Dad left Dublin behind. Takes

time. And then I had the fine luck to meet you at work, of course.' Isabel smiled. 'By the way, I took the liberty of ordering your usual,' she said, nodding in the direction of the kitchen.

'Thanks.' Sally sat down and got out her notebook. 'You're sure you don't mind helping with this marketing stuff?'

'Of course not, Sal. You honestly think I could not be involved this?' Isabel smiled again. 'It's far too exciting.'

They talked through Sally's logo designs and her draft layouts for the website, Isabel feeding in ideas and giving advice on what they could do on Sally's budget.

'Let's take a break to eat,' Isabel said. 'But I'll put this all into a marketing plan and send it over to you. We can do this. And it's going to be brilliant.'

'I really appreciate this,' Sally said, glowing with the excitement of her little business growing wings.

'The clothes are gorgeous,' Isabel said. 'All we need to do is make sure that the right people see them. Then they'll sell themselves.'

'Thanks – and I hope so. Anyway, enough about me. How are things?' Sally said.

'Had a great weekend. I went down to Cornwall, surfing, with Jules and Ryan,' she said. 'I needed to get in the sea, catch some waves. It was good to chill out with a beer looking out at the horizon. A bit of perspective. I needed that.'

'Work?'

'No, work's fine. Work's what I do well, Sal. You know that.'

Isabel had the corner office. She was the woman everyone wanted – her phone used to buzz hot with headhunters calling her – but she'd stayed loyal to their magazine, and worked her way up steadily to Marketing Director. Sally had no doubt she'd soon be promoted again.

She glanced down. 'It's Dad.'

'How is he?'

'Oh, he's all right, muddling along. Happy enough in his own little world.' She shrugged. 'Right now he's got it in his head he's a roadie.'

Sally laughed, in spite of herself. 'A roadie?' She struggled to picture Isabel's dad, who she'd met a couple of times, in the role.

'Yep. Led Zeppelin this week. Last week it was the Stones. They're heading to San Francisco, I'm told.'

'So he's living out his dreams?'

'Yep. There he is in his flat in Holloway, milk going off on the kitchen counter, and he's on about getting the speakers on stage and enough beers in the trailer.'

'Did he even work in the music business?' Sally asked.

Isabel laughed. 'Dad? Nope. He was a dry rot specialist. I guess life gave him a second chance. Dementia's kind in that way, if no other.'

Sally reached across the table to hold her friend's hand.

Isabel had a way of turning everything into an anecdote. When life struck her a blow, she'd wring some lightness out of it, make it easy to hear. But it didn't work on Sally, who could see the hurt that lay underneath.

'I know he needs more care than he's getting,' Isabel said.

They fell silent for a minute.

'But I don't want to give up my job, Sal. I've worked so hard for this. Does that make me a bad person?'

'No,' Sally said. 'Definitely not.'

Isabel met her gaze, and the rims of her eyelids turned pink.

'Could anyone else help?' Sally said.

'I can't call on Mum – she's on the other side of the world, as you know, and she checked out of her marriage years ago.'

'What about your brother?'

'Rob's in denial about it all – he's not visited Dad in months. He thinks Dad's been misdiagnosed, that this is something that will get better. He sends me articles about mindfulness and the link between stress and poor memory.' She rolled her eyes. 'As if some deep breathing and focusing on leaves in a tree is going to stop him forgetting he doesn't smoke and restarting, shouting at the neighbours – who are lovely people, thankfully – or existing off crackers.'

'Would you consider other options?' Sally said.

Neither of them could bring themselves to say it: *a home*.

Isabel didn't answer. 'He's still Dad, down there, somewhere. We have a laugh together. I don't want to give up on him.'

'It wouldn't have to be like that.'

Isabel bit her lip. 'Sometimes all this reality can feel . . . a bit heavy. Do you know what I mean?'

Sally nodded. 'Yes.' She'd felt that way once. At eighteen, when it seemed like everyone else was leaving home and was full of excitement, her mum had died and life, for her, lost its colour. She'd had a place at art college but she found she couldn't draw. Some days she couldn't even summon up the energy to put the kettle on, and while her dad did what he could, she knew he was suffering too. She'd retreated into her mind, taking every paperback off the shelf in her mum's study and reading it, to be closer to the person she missed, and also to be somewhere else for a while.

'I'll work this one out,' Isabel said, straightening up and tidying her fringe. 'I guess I have to.'

Sally took a deep breath. 'You will. And I'm here. Listen, Isabel. I wasn't sure whether to mention this, but Freddie's back in town this weekend. For the party.'

A glimmer of interest came into Isabel's eyes.

'Not an endorsement. He may be family, but I take no responsibility for him,' Sally said.

Isabel sat up a little straighter. 'Well, I'm not going to call him. If he wants to see me, he knows where I am.'

*

Sally got the tube home. The Piccadilly line station was a few streets away from their house – the end of the line. She passed by their road, walked on through another almost the same – well-kept gardens, clean windows. At the weekend came the buzz of hedge-trimmers and the slosh of car-washing, their suburban soundtrack. It was nice. It really was. It was just different. Neighbours would smile and wave, but so far she hadn't managed to get further than that. Some days she felt as if she had forgotten how to start a conversation.

She would get used to it soon, she told herself. The past few months had been madly busy, decorating the house, starting her own business and ensuring Riley was settling in, so she hadn't had much time to linger at the school gates. Everyone talked about how great the community was here in Penville; it wouldn't be long until they were a part of things. The suburb was the perfect place for Riley to grow up: five minutes' walk to the park, a swimming pool nearby, and not too much traffic. There was a small high street with shops and a café that would fill up with school mums after drop-off.

Sally arrived at Elmtree – a new-build school next to playing fields. It was a stark contrast to St Michael's, where Riley had spent her first two school years, where the playground had been in the shadow of high rises. Sally recalled Riley's first day, when she'd wanted to hold on to her child's small hand and not let go. She'd forced herself to be bright, forced a smile, and ushered Riley off through the school gates with a kiss. 'Good luck, peanut,' she'd said.

She'd rushed the farewell, and when she turned around to go, the tears came hot and fast, too quickly for her to brush them away. Her vision had blurred and her cheeks flushed, but what she felt, more than anything else, was an immense pride. They'd done it. They'd got her there. She made friends easily, and loved learning. Then the previous September, they'd handed their daughter over again, to Elmtree Primary. Sally and Theo had worried about uprooting her, but she'd found her feet quickly and now, eight months in, Riley loved her new school as much as her old one.

Today parents were huddled around the school gates chatting to each other, clutching scooters and snack boxes. She smiled at a couple of familiar faces – Beth, Evie's mum, and Leonie, who also had a daughter in Riley's class.

Working in the magazine offices, Sally had felt full of confidence. She had always been asked along for lunch – if she hadn't been the one organising it. But here in Penville, she still felt like an outsider. They all seemed to know each other.

Maybe she'd have to change, just a little bit, if she wanted to fit in around here. She made her way over to the classroom and saw Riley's smiling face behind the glass. She thought of Theo and the home they all had – and the rest didn't seem to matter so much any more.

Chapter 2

Sally cooked for Theo that night, and they sat in the dining room together to eat. She caught sight of the date on the wall calendar behind him, the next day marked with a crayon heart, drawn by Riley. She'd been so excited about the party.

'Forty years,' Sally said. 'What do you think is your parents' secret?'

Theo shrugged. 'I don't know – maybe they know that no one else would put up with them?'

Sally smiled. 'Bit like us, then.'

He laughed. 'Maybe. We're sorted for the long-haul, then.'

Elena, Theo's mother, had grown up in Crete, but come to England in her late teens, met Stephen, and decided to stay and start a family. When Sally and Theo got engaged, Elena had been pleased, and treated Sally as if she was the daughter she'd never had. Then Riley had arrived and knocked Sally firmly into second place, not that Sally minded. Elena – or Grandma Elephant, as Riley called her – doted on Riley, and her grandparents would spend every moment they could with her.

Stephen's love for his granddaughter expressed itself more quietly. When he visited, he'd sit in the armchair by the window, letting the action happen around him, without needing to be at the centre of it. Elena had often commented that retirement after a career in the military was too slow for him, but to Sally, the opposite seemed true. His pace was slower, and he often didn't keep up with their conversations, as if another, different scene was taking place in his mind. Elena would help him keep up, filling in the gaps, maintaining his social links for him. The party had been her idea. But it was Riley who made her way most easily into his world. She'd choose a book and take it over to him, and they'd read together.

'That reminds me, I've been wanting to show you something,' Sally said. She went up to her study and found the red dress she'd made for Riley.

Downstairs, she held it up against her body. 'What do you think?'

Theo wrinkled his nose. 'Bit small.'

'Very funny,' Sally said, rolling her eyes.

He moved closer and touched it. 'Seriously, this is beautiful. Well done, Sal.'

'I got her this hairband to go with it,' she said, holding up the butterfly band.

'Doesn't she normally pull those out?'

He was right. But this time would be different. Sally thought of the way her mum had always taken the time to brush and style her hair before they went out to parties, choosing a special clip to put in it. Now she would do the same with Riley.

'It's a special occasion,' Sally said. 'I'm sure she won't mind this once.'

When Saturday came around, Sally got dressed for the anniversary party and laid out Riley's dress on her bed for her. Riley touched it tentatively.

'You get dressed, love. I'll be downstairs.'

Five minutes later, Riley still hadn't emerged. 'Riley, are you ready?' Sally called out.

'Coming!' Riley called back from behind her bedroom door.

Sally pictured her in the dress, and looked forward to seeing it on. As she waited, her gaze fell on the photos on their hallway wall: holidays with Riley's grandparents, birthdays. In the centre was Sally and Theo's wedding day in Cornwall.

Theo came through from the living room, wearing his suit. He paused beside her, and together they looked at the wedding photo. 'Good day, wasn't it?' he said.

'The best.' She turned and kissed him.

'I like what you're wearing, by the way,' he said. 'A lot.'

'Ready!' came a cry from the stairs.

They turned to see Riley descending the stairs in yellow welly boots, shorts, a Mickey Mouse T-shirt and a straw hat.

Sally couldn't help but laugh. 'Riley! What happened to your dress? You can't wear that.'

'Whoa. That's quite a look,' Theo said.

'I know,' Riley said, proudly. 'Grandma loves yellow. And hats.'

'That's as may be,' Sally said, picturing the social car crash if they arrived with Riley dressed that way. 'But we've got a dress for you already, love. The one I made for you. It's Grandma and Granddad's big party; you need to wear something a bit special,' Sally said.

'This *is* special.'

'Come on, sweetheart, let's go back up and put on the dress.'

Riley wrinkled her nose. 'Not the red dress. I don't like it. I tried it on and I don't like it. It's scratchy.'

'Riley . . . ' Sally said quietly, her heart sinking. She took a deep breath and tried to compose herself. This wasn't personal. She knew the more stressed she got, the less likely Riley would do what she wanted. 'Please, love.'

Her daughter pouted and stood firm. 'I won't wear it.'

'Let me have a go,' Theo whispered to Sally, heading up the stairs.

Sally waited anxiously at the bottom step. She could hear

some muffled sounds from upstairs – Theo's voice, and then what sounded like a giggle from Riley. A message from the cab driver beeped through on Sally's mobile.

'Two minutes, guys,' she called out.

Riley came down, and this time she was wearing the dress. She was tugging at it, admittedly, and wriggling her shoulder blades – but she was wearing it.

'OK,' Sally said, breathing a sigh of relief. She turned to Theo and whispered, 'How did you *do* that?'

He shrugged and smiled in reply.

'You look great, Riley.' She took Theo's hand and squeezed it as they headed out the front door.

Riley put on her jacket and pulled it tight around her as they walked down the path.

Sally reached into her bag and got out the matching hair-band. She reached over to put it in Riley's hair, which was a little wild.

'No,' Riley said, standing her ground this time. 'No way. Not that. I've got the dress on but I'm not wearing that.'

'Go on, Riley,' Theo said.

Riley shook her head firmly.

Sally's eyes met Theo's over their daughter's head, and as he smiled, she did too. Their daughter. Their tiny firecracker. Would they really want her any other way? Sally put the hair-band back in her bag, and they got into the taxi.

Twenty minutes later, they arrived at Theo's parents' home – a large detached house in Hertfordshire, with a rose garden out the front. Today the doorway was decorated with silver balloons.

Sally saw Freddie waiting for them by the gate, wearing jeans, a black shirt and sunglasses.

'Jeans?' Sally whispered to Theo. 'Maybe Riley's wellies wouldn't have been so bad.'

Theo laughed, then went over and gave his brother a hug. 'Hey, you made it.'

'Sis,' Freddie said, opening his arms to Sally.

'Hey, Freddie,' Sally said, kissing him on the cheek.

'Good to see you, Sal.'

'You too.'

'Uncle Freddie,' Riley shouted.

'Riley!' Freddie bent down to greet her. 'Kid, I got you this.' He passed her a pen with four colours you could click down. It was branded with the logo of the magazine he worked for – a freebie. Riley inspected it like a rare diamond. 'I meant to get her something proper,' he whispered to Sally. 'It's just—'

'Don't worry,' Sally said. 'You're here, that's the main thing.'

Theo and Riley went over to the open front door to greet his parents.

Freddie tilted his head in his parents' direction. 'Mum and Dad are already doing my head in.' He laughed.

'Stay with us?' Sally offered.

'Thanks,' he said. 'But . . . ' He looked sheepish.

'Freddie,' Sally said. 'You didn't ask Isabel?'

'Come on, Sal. We're grown-ups.'

She raised her eyebrows. 'One of you is.'

'She didn't have to say yes.'

'Don't mess her about, Freddie.' She looked him squarely in the eye. 'Or I *will* destroy you.'

She went over to the front door with Freddie and said hello to her parents-in-law. Elena wore a dress dotted with blue sequins, her dark brown bob curled under, and had one arm around Riley's shoulders. Stephen was dressed in an evening suit, tall like his sons, his grey hair neat.

'Happy anniversary,' Sally said, kissing them both. 'Congratulations.'

'Thank you, my dear,' Elena said, kissing her back. 'It's lovely to have you all here today. Such a special day.' She ran a hand over Riley's wayward curls and looked up at Sally. 'But what happened here? Couldn't find a hairbrush?'

Sally smiled. Elena didn't mean it to sound the way it did, Sally told herself. She just couldn't help herself. 'She wouldn't let me.'

'You parents these days – you're too easy on them. My boys would never have had a choice.'

Sally stayed quiet. Deep breaths. She'd managed all these years with Elena. She could get through today.

Riley seemed restless, and headed off down the hallway. She could never wait to start enjoying a party.

Sally went through into the living room and joined Theo by the mantelpiece. Together, they looked out at the room. Elena and Stephen were mingling with their friends and neighbours, and Freddie was with a crowd of older women, who seemed captivated by his conversation.

'Look at him. Back five minutes and he's already charming your mum's friends from church,' Sally said.

'Typical. Ever felt like you picked the wrong brother?' Theo asked.

'Well . . . '

He glared at her, and she laughed. She'd never been tempted to swap Theo for anyone.

'Nope. Not for a second. And you know it. Is your speech ready?'

'Yes.' He took a piece of paper from his jacket pocket and unfolded it. 'All set. Freddie's saying something first, then I'm up.'

Sally caught sight of Riley across the room. She was on her own, leaning against the wall, tugging at the skirt of her dress.

'Do you think she's OK?' Sally said.

As they looked on, Gabi appeared by Riley's side and gave her a hug. She took her by the hand and led her towards the kitchen.

'She's fine,' Theo said. 'It's hardly the first time we've had a row about what she wears. And I doubt it'll be the last.'

'I know. I just wonder if maybe I should have chosen something with her, rather than making her wear that dress.'

Theo picked up a glass of prosecco from a nearby table. 'Here,' he said. 'Take this and I bet you'll find you miraculously stop worrying about it.'

'Thanks.'

'I'm going to go and drag my brother away from those women before anyone writes him into their will. I'll see you in a bit.'

She laughed. 'Sure.'

Sally mingled, making small talk with Theo's relatives and family friends, answering their questions about the new house and how Riley was doing at school.

Half an hour later, Riley appeared at her side, with traces of chocolate around her mouth.

'What have you been eating?' she asked.

'Just some cake from the kitchen.' Riley pointed. 'Gabi said it was OK.'

Sally tried to wipe away the smears from her daughter's face, but Riley ducked out of the way and ran over to where some other kids were standing near the speakers.

Sally went through to the kitchen, where Gabi and her friend were. 'Hey, Gabi,' she said. 'Just wanted to check Riley hasn't been ploughing into the celebration cake.'

'No, no,' Gabi said, laughing. 'Still intact.' She pointed to a three-tiered chocolate cake with silver decorations on it. 'I let her have one of our cupcakes, that's all. She seemed like she needed cheering up.'

'Right,' Sally said. The comment unsettled her. 'Thanks.'

Theo and Freddie were standing together in the corner of the living room.

'How's Berlin treating you?' Theo asked.

'Amazing. Great city. Nice people. Good vibe. Everything London used to be before it got bought up by overseas investors and filled up with overpriced coffee shops.'

'Overpriced coffee shops?'

'Allow me a little dig. Sibling rivalry and all that. I kind of liked it when you fell out of favour with Mum for those five whole minutes after leaving your job. But you seem to have pulled it out of the bag. The Hideaway doing well still?'

'Yes, thanks,' Theo said. 'We had a nice write-up the other day. Here.' He found the article on his phone and showed it to his brother.

Freddie scanned it. 'Wow. This is great.'

'Word seems to be getting around.'

'That's good. Do Mum and Dad come by much?'

'Occasionally. Mum likes it there. But Dad . . . ' Theo aped his father's serious expression. '"Just a coffee, son. Not a macchiato or a cappuccino or a soya skinny whatsit. Just a coffee. Honestly."'

'You've got to love him.' Freddie laughed.

They both looked across the room. Riley was dragging a reluctant Stephen up into the centre of the living room – a makeshift dance floor – to dance to Justin Bieber. He moved awkwardly, holding her hands.

'Riley works a bit of magic on him, though,' Freddie said.

'She does, doesn't she?' Theo said, feeling proud.

'Turns him to mush,' Freddie said. 'Your daughter's the one in the driving seat in this family, these days.'

Sally and Riley went together to the toilet, before the speeches. Sally took a moment to retouch her make-up and her daughter appeared in the mirror beside her. Sally smiled. Riley had Theo's brown hair but her face shape, with a slightly pointed chin. People told her Riley had her eyes. And Sally would thank them, because to her it felt like the biggest compliment in the world. Her daughter's hazel eyes were large and clear and perfect. Sally's own eyes were nice enough, but they no longer held the brightness that Riley's did. They'd been weathered by time, by loss.

'I'm sorry about the wellies, Mum,' Riley said. 'And for being grumpy about the dress.'

Sally smoothed her daughter's hair. 'It doesn't matter. Not really. And thanks for wearing it in the end.'

Riley shrugged. 'It's OK. I get it. Grandma really likes it, so I don't mind.'

'That's kind of you.' Sally brought her daughter closer and kissed her forehead. She felt so intensely proud sometimes of the slightly wayward child they'd raised. 'I love you, you know.'

'Me too.' She took her mother's hand. 'Let's go. Let's listen to Dad's talk.'

'Sure. Let's go.'

'I'll get married one day,' Riley said. 'I'll be happy like they are.'

'I'm sure you will,' Sally said. 'If it's what you want. You can do anything and be anything you want.'

'Anything?' Riley said, eyes wide.

'Anything,' Sally said, giving her a hug.

Theo walked to the front of the living room, a buzz of nerves in the pit of his stomach. It had been a while since he'd spoken in front of so many people, so he was glad that the champagne, and Freddie's speech – full of funny anecdotes – had warmed the crowd up. The last time he'd spoken in public had been at the café launch night two years ago. But today wasn't about him. His eyes searched the crowd for his mum and dad. Today was about his parents, who'd seen him and Freddie through so much. It was about finally giving something back.

Two faces beamed out at him from the crowd. Sally and Riley. Their support radiated, lifting him up. He cleared his throat.

'If you're here today,' he started, 'you'll know that my parents aren't your average couple. They go days without speaking, yet know everything about each other – they know what each other wants to eat or watch on TV. Mum loves a chat, as most of you are probably aware.' There was laughter from the audience. 'And Dad is happiest in the shed. And yet I don't think they've ever had a cross word about that. And when it comes to being a mum and dad – they don't come better. They have done so much for us.

'They got married when they were both twenty – which these days is kind of hard to get your head around. Freddie and I certainly never understood. Right, Fred?'

Freddie nodded and called out, 'Why would you do that to yourself?'

Their dad shook his head and drew Elena closer to him.

'Freddie still thinks they're mad. But, with time, I think I've started to understand it. They've grown up together. They've got to know each other more with each year they've spent. It wasn't just me and Freddie growing up back then, but the two of them, supporting each other through our tantrums, our first days at school, the teenage nights when we didn't come home when we said we would. And they're stronger for everything they've shared.

'To steal a line from my wife's favourite film, *When Harry Met Sally*: "When you realise you want to spend the rest of your life with somebody, you want the rest of your life to start as soon as possible."

'I get that now,' Theo said. He caught Sally's eye. 'When Mum and Dad met, they didn't want to wait to start living.'

*

In the taxi on the way home that evening, Sally rested her head on Theo's shoulder.

Later, when Riley was in her pyjamas, Sally brushed her daughter's hair. Running a brush through the cotton-soft strands was as familiar an action as breathing, a dance they'd danced over and over through the years. Riley's curls, like Sally's own, weren't always easy to tame, but there was reward in the labour – they shone.

As Riley grew from baby to toddler and toddler to schoolgirl, the changes were so gradual and subtle that Sally rarely noticed them. But one day she'd seen that the curve of Riley's tummy had grown flat, and her face had slimmed out and lost its toddler chubbiness. The words that had been slow to come now came in torrents – big ideas, questions, demands – linked together into sentences and stories. The physical changes kept coming. Riley's pyjama bottoms would come up short on her legs and pull tight around the waist, and she'd outgrow her underwear and socks.

Toys once adored and played with lay discarded and untouched, their joys exhausted. Favourite books were put aside, as new favourites came in. But one thing remained the same: Riley's hair, and the ritual of gently brushing it, never changed, and in those moments, long-limbed Riley, with her expressive dark eyebrows and bold outbursts, was still Sally's baby.

Tonight, though, Riley wriggled in her arms, pulling away from the brush. She must be tired, Sally thought. She put down the hairbrush and Riley laid her head in her mum's lap.

Theo opened the door a crack, then let himself in. He crouched to join Sally and Riley where they were sitting on her bedroom floor.

'She's fallen asleep,' Theo said, touching his daughter's cheek.

'I was so proud of her today,' Sally said. She remembered how Riley had looked, dancing with her grandfather in her red dress, her smile lighting up the room.

Theo put his arm around her. 'Me too.'

'Will you help me lift her into bed?'

Theo picked his daughter up and lowered her down gently, and Sally tucked the duvet in around her. In the doorway, they stood for a moment, looking at their sleeping child, neither of them wanting to pull away. The moments slipped by so fast, and Sally wanted them to be there to watch every one.

Chapter 3

On Monday, Sally walked Riley down Addison Road and towards her school. Riley skipped along, still buzzing with the excitement of Saturday night.

'And then we danced, and then there was the amazing three-layer cake, and then it was pretty late when I went to bed, wasn't it?'

'Ten o'clock,' Sally said.

'Can we do it again?' Riley asked, as they arrived at the school gates.

Sally remembered Riley's face, dancing with the other children in the family on a sugar high, spinning and spinning around. 'When me and your dad have been married forty years, maybe,' Sally said.

'But that's *ages* away.'

Sally smiled. 'It'll be worth it, I promise. Here's your book bag.' She passed it over to her. 'You can give *Matilda* back now and get a new one.'

'Cool. See you at home time,' Riley said.

Her hand slipped from Sally's and she disappeared into the classroom. Everything felt quiet, so suddenly, when Riley was gone.

Sally turned around, ready to go back home, and saw Beth, Evie's mum, coming towards her. Act cool, Sally told herself. You have friends. Good friends. It was just that she was all too aware that she had none, really, around here.

'Hi. Sally, right?' Beth said. 'Riley's mum?'

Sally nodded. Beth didn't introduce herself; she knew she didn't need to.

'I was just hearing about the clothes you make. One of the mums mentioned them, said they're beautiful.'

'How kind,' Sally said. She dug around in her handbag and found one of her old business cards. She brushed crumbs off it, wishing she'd had the new ones printed. 'This is me. The web site's still under construction but you can see some of my designs on Etsy. They would look lovely on Evie.'

'Thanks. Anything to get her out of her sequins and unicorns right now.' Beth laughed. 'I've got something for you too.' She handed her a flyer. 'We're running a PTA fundraiser, to get more playground equipment.'

'Cool,' Sally said, taking it from her. 'Thanks.'

'It's on Saturday. Everyone will be there. It would be great to have your support.'

Sally read it. *Bake sale.* Her heart sank. Why was it always cakes?

Her mind flashed back through every flat, tasteless cake she'd made. Only one had ever turned out right, the one she'd made for Riley's third birthday. She'd never been able to replicate it. Cakes. Her Achilles heel.

Beth looked at her hopefully. 'We can count on you, can't we?'

On the way home, Sally stopped by the supermarket to get some cake ingredients. She'd do a trial run before Saturday.

That evening, once Riley was in bed, Sally went to the kitchen and started making a Victoria sponge. She could do this. Positive thinking.

Theo came in from work and through to the kitchen. 'Hey. Who's nicked my wife?'

'Ha ha. There's a PTA bake sale,' Sally said, adding more flour and hoping the consistency would improve. 'I'm giving it my best shot.'

'Why don't I bring you one from the café?' Theo said. 'We always have some left over.'

'No!' Sally said. 'I'm going to do this myself if it kills me.'

He came up to her and put his arms around her waist. 'And I'm sure you will. But does it really matter that much? Surely you don't need a personality transplant to make friends around here?'

'I'm still working that out. I don't seem to have made much headway so far.'

'Are you still fixated on that café?'

'Everyone goes there after drop-off, Theo. Everyone.' Sally lifted the spoon from the mixture – there hadn't been much improvement.

He turned her around to face him. 'Don't change too much, Sal. Because I really do like you as you are.'

The following night, Sally left Theo reading to Riley and went out to meet Isabel in Islington. It was a relief to be re-entering familiar territory. The city – she knew what to do there. On the walk from the station she looked up at the sky, seeking out a familiar constellation, but the streetlights masked the stars. She told herself that the clear night skies were one thing, at least, that was better about Penville.

She found the bar, and Isabel. 'Hey, you,' she said, giving her friend a hug.

'Hi, Sal. I got you a Manhattan. Because you know I don't like to drink alone.'

Sally looked at her friend's empty glass. 'I was only five minutes late.' She laughed.

'Drinking time is drinking time,' Isabel said. 'Sit down. Tell me about your weekend. Party went well?'

'I expect you've already heard about it, haven't you?' she said, raising an eyebrow. 'It was great, yes. But, more to the point, tell me what happened with Freddie.'

'No judging, right?' Isabel said.

Sally knew she might have to bite her tongue. 'No judging.'

'It was good to see him. We had fun, we said goodbye, he's gone back to Germany, I've got my flat to myself again. No talk of the future. No promises. It is what it is.'

'OK,' Sally said, trying to read her friend's expression. 'And you're fine with that?'

'Yes, Mum,' Isabel mocked. 'And I know you think I'm crazy, but yes, I am OK with it. He cheered me up. He makes me laugh. It gives me something else to think about that isn't Dad. Sal, being with Freddie makes me feel young, and free, and all the things I don't feel when I'm organising Dad's care. And I need that. I want that.'

Isabel isn't fragile, Sally told herself. She's strong. 'Well, in that case, good.'

'It *is* good.'

He's hurt you before, though, Sally thought. I haven't forgotten that.

'I know him, Sally. I know what he's like. I have no expectations.'

'In that case, I'm sorry for prying.'

'It's OK. I get it.'

'It's because I love you.' Sally smiled. Maybe she didn't need any new friends. Perhaps Isabel was enough.

'And because you think I should find someone else and settle down.'

'I never said that!' Sally said. 'You're projecting all over the place, missus.'

'I can see it in your eyes,' Isabel said. 'Your family is a wondrous thing. But not for me, Sal.'

'I know that,' Sally said. 'I can't see you in suburbia – not now, not ever. And I don't want you there either. You're my lifeline right now.'

'Things going well then?' Isabel teased.

'I baked a cake yesterday, for a PTA fundraiser.'

'Christ.'

'I know.'

'Your cakes are crap.'

Sally laughed. 'OK, don't rub it in. God, you and Theo both.'

The next day, Sally and Riley went up to school, and Sally carried her Victoria sponge over to where the bake sale was being set up. Riley dashed over to join some friends by the slide.

'Hi!' Beth called over. 'Glad you could make it, Sally.' Beth had said that the bake sale was 'just a little fundraiser', but it looked like everyone had gone to a fair amount of trouble. Sally tried to feel proud of her humble creation. It had taken her hours to make, but compared to the others, it was the stunted ugly sister.

A couple of the other mums of children in the class, Leonie and Grace, smiled hello. For the first time since Riley had started at the school, Sally felt as if the door was open. She just had to step through.

Faye, Euan's mum, a curvy redhead in dungarees, laid down a plate of carrot cupcakes.

'Thank God for late closing,' Faye whispered to her. 'Last night I nabbed the last ones M&S had on the shelf.'

Sally smiled, reassured. Euan called out to his mum.

'Duty calls,' she said, and she went over to disentangle his leg from the football net. Another boy was with him – Ben. Sally thought that was his name. He was laughing at Euan, not kindly.

Leonie, mum to Riley's classmate Ava, walked over to Sally.

'It's nice to see you here,' she said. 'I've been hoping we might have a chance to chat.'

'Same here. It's always such a rush at drop-off, isn't it?'

'Exactly. Beth showed me your clothes designs – they're great. Can I order that dinosaur hoodie? My son will love it. He's four.'

'Sure,' Sally said. 'I've a few in stock made up already, and I think I have one in his size. I could bring it along next week.' She remembered the half-term holiday – she and Riley would be going up to visit her dad and step-mum in Norfolk. She was really looking forward to it. 'After the break, I mean.'

'Great,' Leonie said. She shifted a little uneasily on the spot. 'Listen, I know the school mums, we might seem a bit, you know . . . '

Cliquey. Sally wondered if she'd actually say it.

'It's just that our girls went to nursery together, so we've known each other a long time.'

Sally was touched that she'd said something. 'Don't worry about it.'

'Ava hasn't talked much about Riley, but she seems a lovely kid.'

'Thank you. We are never bored, that's for sure.'

'Ava could do with a few different friends.'

'Different?' Sally said.

'Friends who aren't Evie, I mean. With Ava and Evie, it's love or hate,' Leonie went on. 'They're frenemies. One minute they're dressing identically, next they're adamant they never liked each other.'

Sally smiled. 'Primary school politics – I remember it well.'

'Mum, look,' Riley called out.

Sally turned towards her. She was standing next to Ava and Evie, waving something in the air. 'We found a frog!' Riley jiggled it up and down.

'Oh God,' Sally shouted back. 'Put it down.'

Beth and the other mothers turned to look.

'I think it's dead,' Riley said. 'Evie, do you want to hold it?'

'No!' Evie said. 'No way. It's horrible.'

'You sure?'

'Riley, put it down, right now,' Sally insisted.

'What, here?' Riley said, holding it above the cake table.

Beth's face paled.

Sally gave her daughter a look. 'You know what I mean, Riley.'

'All right, all right.' She tossed it back on to the grass.

'And go and wash your hands now, please,' Sally said, wishing she could disappear.

Leonie smiled. 'She's quite spirited, your daughter, isn't she?'

That night, Sally was in the bath, with Theo sitting in a chair and talking with her.

'So there she was, dangling this dead amphibian over the bloody cake table, everyone looking at us.' Sally laughed, in spite of herself.

'Oh man, that's a tough one to come back from.'

'Exactly. Leonie saw the funny side, I think – but I'm not sure Beth did.'

'This school social thing sounds like a minefield.'

'It feels like it's two steps forward, one back. I think I'm more relieved than Riley that it's half-term next week.'

She pictured the cottage where she'd grown up, a short walk from the sea. Going home – and it still felt like home to Sally – recharged her. The house itself had changed, was always changing – Catherine had updated the décor of almost all of the house when she'd moved in – but Sally still felt her mum's presence there. Her dad was retired from teaching now, so had time to do carpentry, fixing things and building shelves. The one constant was Wilson, their dog, an elderly mongrel with one ear that pointed up and another down. He roamed the garden and slept on the rug by the fire, and Riley adored him.

'I'm sorry I can't join you, but you know how it is with the café. I'm going to miss you guys.'

'We'll miss you too. I can't wait, though. Dad and Catherine are really looking forward to seeing Riley again, and I'm looking forward to getting out to the beach, the wind in our hair . . . God, I love it there this time of year.'

'Ah, now I really wish I was coming.'

'A week to yourself? No noise, no chaos? I think you'll survive,' Sally said, flicking bubbles in his direction.

Chapter 4

Sally and Riley drove up the motorway to Norfolk, listening to a Beatles CD. Each mile took them closer to Sally's childhood home. Sally sang along to the songs, and Riley hummed along in the back. Sally had lived in London for so many years that it had seeped into her, the city shaping her so firmly that now she was struggling to re-form out in Penville. But as she drove back towards the wild nature and beaches, she remembered that, deep down, she was made up of something else entirely. When she'd been Riley's age, the weekend would take her out into the leaves and mulch, or on to the wet sand. She could almost feel the texture of nature in her hands and under her feet – that, truly, was the person she was.

'Here Comes the Sun' came on and the sky outside lit up. Riley gave a cry of delight.

'Look at that, Mum,' Riley called out. 'The sun came out just like in the song!'

Sally smiled. 'Hopefully it'll stay out. Maybe we could take Wilson down to the beach this afternoon. Let him off the lead.'

'Yes,' Riley said. 'I'd love that.'

In Norfolk there was room for Riley's energy – she raced around the garden, up the staircases, down the country lanes.

Bringing her here felt, sometimes, like setting her free, and with her granddad by her side there was nothing she wouldn't try. Sally pictured her dad, and her spirits lifted at the prospect of spending some time with him. She got on well enough with Catherine, who was kind and well-meaning, if a little blunt, but their connection was more practical than emotional. Sally didn't let it show, but she liked it when she could talk to her dad on his own. It had been painful, at first, when Sally graduated from art college and returned to the house to find Catherine was living there, and had brought in her things, moving into the room where her mum had once slept. But Sally had accepted it, and, in time, Catherine. The loss had been hard for all of them, and her father needed someone in his life. Catherine's presence had no impact on her mum's absence, which was permanent, no matter what.

'I can see the sea!' Riley called out. And there it was, a band of blue on the horizon. 'We're nearly there.'

'Riley!' Jules called out. He was standing in the doorway of the whitewashed cottage, holding his arms out. He was dressed in green wellies and had a flat cap on, his thick white hair showing underneath. The garden was in full bloom, vibrant with cornflowers, poppies and peonies.

Riley rushed up the path towards him and gave him a hug, and Sally followed behind, kissing her dad and Catherine hello. Catherine was dressed in jeans and a blouse with colourful birds on it, which Riley was fascinated by.

Wilson ran between Sally's legs, then circled around and around her, nearly tripping her up. Riley came over and hugged him. He smothered her in dog kisses and the two of them rolled around the lawn, Riley's laughter filling the air.

'Kettle's already on,' Catherine said. 'I just had a feeling. Come on in.'

Jules got the bags from the car while Riley and Sally went through to the kitchen. It was filled with pretty crockery, 1920s plates and jugs that Catherine picked up from local auctions. When her mother had been alive, the kitchen had been where they ate and cooked and talked, but it hadn't been decorated – save for the bunch of wildflowers her mum would pick from the garden. It was a good thing, Catherine's care, Sally told herself – but part of her missed the peeling paint, the rough edges, the visual reminders that her mum had been so busy caring for her and working as a vet that she'd contentedly let the small domestic things go.

Now they sat around the large table, and Catherine brought over some biscuits. 'Good to have you here. We've been really excited about it.'

'Us too,' Riley said. 'I could hardly sleep thinking about it.'

'Well, you'll sleep well here, I hope,' Catherine said. 'All the sea air.'

'How have things been?' Sally asked.

'Good, thanks. Just pottering about, having friends over. I get out to a car boot sale or an auction now and then, and your dad's been going into the primary school to do volunteer reading with the kids.'

'I had a feeling he wouldn't stay retired for long,' Sally said. She poured out tea for all of them and passed Riley a biscuit.

'I don't think it's in him to rest.'

Jules appeared in the doorway. 'Don't get too comfortable,' he called out. 'We'll be taking Wilson down to the beach in a minute. Make the most of this lovely day.'

'Great!' Riley said, her face lighting up.

'Give us a minute, Dad, we've only just sat down.'

'Let's go!' said Riley, grabbing her granddad's hand. 'Let's go right now.'

'I'll stay here and get the lunch on,' Catherine said, laughing. 'You're welcome to stay too, Sally?'

'Thanks, but no – some fresh air will do us all good.'

The three of them walked down a pathway to the beach, with Wilson leading the way and the wind blowing in their hair. The weather seemed to whip up a new spirit in Riley, and she ran with Wilson, dipping in and out of the waves. His fur got wet and he stopped for a minute to shake himself off, dousing Riley in the process. Riley laughed so hard she bent double.

'Times like this,' Sally said to her dad, 'I wish Mum could've had the chance to meet her.'

'I know,' Jules said. 'She has something of your mum in her, I've always thought. That restless energy, her love of animals, her sense of adventure.'

'You think, don't you, when they're tiny, that you have some idea of how they are going to turn out. But Riley's ten times more of everything than I ever thought a human being could be.'

Jules put his arm around his daughter and they walked together like that for a while. Sally's father's pace had become a little slower this past year, after his heart operation. She had to remind herself of that and fell into step with him.

'In a slightly calmer way, Sally, that's exactly how it was with you.'

'Really?'

'Yes. You'd sit still for longer than Riley, granted, but you'd come out with these ideas and questions that were so grown-up, me and your mum felt like we had to educate ourselves just to keep up. Then there was the birthday where we gave you paints and an easel – and that was it, we saw what you'd needed. There was no stopping you. You'd paint the moment you woke up, and as soon as you got back from school, and you never stopped. Then the college course, your graphic design – and now clothes designing. You make something from nothing, Sal, and there's a kind of magic in that. Your mum would be really proud of you.'

'I hope so,' Sally said. Her emotions felt close to the surface. 'Being here feels like a link with her, somehow.'

He watched Riley, captivated by her. 'A schoolgirl, now. I remember when that was you. It's the beginning of letting go.'

Sally felt a tug at her heart. 'Yes,' she said firmly, ignoring the tears threatening to come. Riley was their only child – she and Theo had decided that when she was born. Conceiving her had been a tough journey, and neither of them wanted to go through that again. She was enough. More than enough. But one day there would be no small hand in Sally's; Riley wouldn't always need her the way she did now. 'I mean, it's great, building the business. Theo's been able to focus on the café. We're starting to get our lives back a bit.'

'Yes,' he said. He put an arm around her shoulder again and brought her in closer to him. 'You sound almost convincing, you know.'

At the café, coffee orders came in quick succession in the first hour as commuters stopped by for their caffeine fix on their way to the office. Theo and Gabi worked alongside each other, fluidly and naturally, not needing to say more than the occasional word.

Waking up at home had felt different that morning. No Riley, calling out demands and dropping Shreddies on the floor, no kiss from Sally as he left the house. Theo wondered what they were doing that day, picturing them on a windswept beach, with Jules, maybe also Catherine and Wilson. That's where they'd be.

When the morning rush subsided, there was a moment of quiet. Theo loaded the dishwasher and chatted to Gabi as she prepared food on the counter.

'How's the flat?' he asked. 'Are your neighbours still partying a lot?'

Gabi smiled. 'You know what, it's been so many nights now, I figured if you can't beat them, join them. I went round there last night with a bottle of tequila, and only left at three. The easiest journey home I've had in a while.'

'How was it?'

'It was fun. Though they're students, so I felt about a hundred, and this morning, with a hangover, I think I'm at a hundred and twenty.'

'Longevity. That'll be the Cretan in you. Mum's always saying we'll live for ever – genes, diet, whichever it is.'

'Not sure tequila's a key component in that diet. How are your parents, by the way?'

'They're good. Planning a trip over to the island at the end of the summer. We won't be joining them this time, we're skipping a year – you know I said we're going away with Sally's dad and Catherine? Next time, though. I want to take Riley out to that beach we went to as kids – the one with the rock pools?'

Gabi nodded. 'Riley would love that. I have golden memories of that place. She would be able to run free there.'

'Her energy – she never stops. She and Sally are in Norfolk right now. It's so weird when the two of them are away. Quiet. There's suddenly all this time to think,' he said. 'I'm not sure if I like it.'

'I would like that. A lot.'

'I've had a few ideas, actually – about the business. Maybe we could sit and talk through some menu concepts for autumn and winter. I know it's a while away, but I think they could be really exciting . . . '

Gabi glanced out of the window, then shrugged. 'If you want.'

Theo laughed. 'Wow, how's that for enthusiasm. I guess you've always known how to keep my ego in check.'

'Sorry, Theo. Yes. Let's do that.'

'What's up?'

'Nothing,' she said, forcing a smile. 'I'm just tired. I'm not built for late nights these days.'

That evening, with Riley asleep in bed, Sally left her dad and Catherine sitting in the living room and went upstairs.

She walked down the narrow corridor, the carpet soft under her sock-clad feet. Her dad and Catherine had changed a lot in the house, but the bones of the place remained the same: the dark timber beams, the walls that had stood for over two centuries. She went into her mother's study, which had been kept more or less as it was. Her dad had never said so, but she wondered if that had been done, perhaps, with her in mind. There were times, and now was one, when she missed her mum so viscerally. The warmth of her arms, her hugs. The softness of her skin. If Sally closed her eyes she could still hear her voice, the calming, soft way she spoke.

Sally looked up at the top shelf, where they kept the biscuit tin that her mum had made into a memory box. She reached up and got it, then sat in the wooden chair just holding it in her lap for a moment. She could already picture everything inside. Gently, she placed it on the table and lifted the lid.

The contents were both simple and imbued with magic: apple shampoo, to remember how she smelled; a postcard from their first holiday together, in Cornwall; a picture drawn in biro, of the three of them holding hands, with the words *Mummy, Daddy, Me* scrawled above it; a photo of the two of them together, when Sally was a toddler, Sally dressed in dungarees and holding her mum's hand in the garden.

Then, underneath the objects, was the letter, in its envelope. Her dad had passed it to her the day after her mum died, when they arrived back from hospital. Sally had taken it up to her bedroom, alone, and opened it. The envelope was still wrinkled with her tears. She had been eighteen, but after what happened, she'd felt both older and very much younger.

Sally took it out now, unfolded it and read it again. Every word was imprinted on her mind, but seeing them in her mother's handwriting brought her voice back.

To Sally. My sunshine. My heart.

How hard it is to leave you.

I wish I didn't have to go now, but someone, somewhere, tapped their watch and decided that it was time for me to go.

I'm so proud of the girl you are, and the woman you're becoming. I try and tell myself I've already been luckier than most, to have spent the time with you that I've already had – to have all the golden memories that I do. But each day you become more confident, more creative, more beautiful, and I want to see more. I want to be there for you always. I know that your life will be filled with good things, because, Sal, that's everything you deserve.

Talking to you, reading with you, walking with you on the beach – these have been the happiest moments of my life. You brought colour and laughter into our lives every single day. The deepest joy I've felt was just holding you in my arms – on the day you were born, on the day you started school, even on the day we celebrated your exam results.

Lately, you have had to be so brave. Braver than I wanted you to have to be. I hope you know that you have made these difficult days so much easier for me.

You have so much love in you, Sally. My Sally. My daughter. I know you will make a good life and share it with the right people.

When you open this letter, I'll already be gone. I won't be able to give you a hug – as much as I want to. But as you read, know that wherever I am, in a way, I am holding you now.

I want to leave you with this:

Love as deeply as you can, every day. Know that all the love you give away will come back to you, two-fold. The people you love most won't always get everything right. Carry on loving them anyway.

And always, always, be who you are.

Mum x

Sally held the letter close to her chest and felt her mum was with her for a moment. Then she folded it up, put it back in the tin and was alone again.

The next morning, Sally was woken by Riley at her bedside, telling her to come down for breakfast. Her child pulled her back into the present, and she was grateful for that. Reading her mum's letter again had reminded her of that empty place deep inside her that would always be there; the closest she came to filling it was when she focused on being a mum herself.

Sally, Jules, Catherine and Riley breakfasted on blueberry pancakes, juice and coffee in the conservatory, rain hammering on the windows around them.

'I'd hoped for another beach walk, or some football,' Jules said, looking up at the grey clouds. 'But perhaps we'll leave that for tomorrow. I think we'd be better off getting the board games out, don't you?'

'Definitely,' Sally said. 'It doesn't look like it's going to stop anytime soon.'

'I'm already daydreaming of Italy,' Catherine said. 'Especially if this is what summer looks like here. It's not long now.'

'Italy!' Riley said brightly. 'Ice cream, pizza, pasta . . . '

'And did we mention the swimming pool, Riley?' Jules said.

'Yes,' Riley said. 'It's going to be amazing.'

Catherine smiled at Sally.

'Riley's a real mermaid these days,' Sally said. 'Theo takes her to the pool at the weekend, but she's not been in an outside pool since she was a toddler.'

'I'm not a mermaid, Mum. More like a dolphin. A *shark*,' Riley said, baring her teeth.

'A shark, then,' Sally said, laughing.

'How do sharks wee?'

Catherine stifled a laugh. 'Excellent question, Riley.'

'Hmm. I honestly don't know,' Sally said. 'Do you, Dad?'

'Haven't the foggiest.'

'Not standing up, though?' Riley said.

'I can't imagine so,' Sally said, laughing again.

'And you, Granddad?'

'Sorry?' Jules said.

'You wee standing up, like my dad, don't you?'

'Erm, I do, yes.'

Riley paused, then returned to her pancakes. She ate them quietly. When she'd finished, Jules asked her if she could come and find Jenga and Guess Who? with him, and she hopped up from the table.

Catherine turned towards Sally. 'I love the way that kids think,' she said.

There was a genuine warmth in everything Catherine said, and yet Sally found she couldn't return it. Not here in her house, her mum's house. Perhaps not anywhere. It still felt like a betrayal to get any closer.

'I never know what she's going to come out with next,' Sally said.

'She's a smart one, isn't she? You can see her brain is sparking all the time. You must be very proud of her.'

'Thank you,' Sally said. 'And yes, we are.'

She glanced over at Riley, opening cupboard doors with her granddad in the adjoining room. That had been her and her mum and dad once – choosing games in the same place, to play in the same room. The past lived alongside the present in these four walls; there were memories in every piece of furniture, and she only wished that, somehow, Riley would be able to feel her own mother's energy the way she still did. Because nothing and no one would ever be able to replace that.

They passed the day playing board games and baking scones, and in the late afternoon the rain ceased for long enough that Riley and Jules could get out into the garden for a trudge through the mud in their wellies.

That evening, Sally and Riley FaceTimed Theo to say good night, and Riley told him what they had been doing, and their plans for the remaining days – a trip to a nature reserve, football in the park, and, if the rain held off, a picnic on the beach.

Afterwards, they went up to the bathroom. The avocado bathtub Sally had bathed in as a child was long gone, replaced with an elegant clawfooted tub, and the textured lino had made way for tasteful, white-painted floorboards. Sally could recall every detail of how it had been, though. The old bath had had a little mirror above it, and she remembered writing out her name in the steam as her mum sat beside her. She used to stay in there as long as she could, until her fingers wrinkled like sultanas and all the bubbles had gone.

'Right, time for your bath,' Sally said, helping Riley out of her top.

Riley pulled back and wriggled away from her. 'Tomorrow,' she said.

'Come on,' Sally said, gently.

'No,' Riley repeated, pulling her hand back more forcefully. 'I don't want a bath tonight. I'm clean already.'

'No, you're not.' Sally laughed. 'You and Granddad were digging up worms a couple of hours ago. Come on. Everyone needs baths.'

'I'm tired,' Riley said.

Sally took a deep breath. Riley had been running around outside for a while that afternoon, and Sally had got her up to the bathroom a bit later than usual. Some battles you fought, some you didn't. A bit of mud wouldn't hurt her.

'OK,' she said, getting a flannel to clean the mud off Riley's face and hands. 'But we'll have a proper bathtime tomorrow.'

Sally walked with Riley down the corridor, to the small bedroom where she would be sleeping. Riley climbed into the metal-framed bed, then she and Sally read together.

'Time to sleep, now,' Sally said, giving her a kiss on the forehead.

Sally turned off the light and made it as far as the stairs, when she heard the sound of carpet-cushioned footsteps behind her. She turned and saw Riley, her brown hair falling loose past the collar of her pyjamas.

'Hey, back to bed, you,' Sally said.

'I can't sleep,' Riley said, her voice husky. 'It's all different here.'

Sally sighed, then took her daughter's soft, warm hand in hers and walked with her back towards the bedroom. Riley wouldn't be young for ever, she told herself. The tiny frustrations of today she'd look back on with nostalgia tomorrow. That's what her mum had always said.

A picture of Sally's mum flashed into her mind – smiling and opening her arms for a hug. You'll look back tomorrow. If you get that tomorrow.

'Let's try again,' Sally said.

Riley climbed into bed and Sally tucked the duvet around her.

'Can you tell me a story this time?' Riley said.

Sally sat down on her daughter's bed and rested beside her, leaning on a cushion. 'OK,' she said. 'Right, remember when I told you about Laika, the Russian space dog?'

'The first dog in space,' Riley said. 'I liked that one.'

'She was up there exploring before any humans had even been there.' Sally had kept true to what she knew of the mission, but edited it, leaving out the part where Laika never came home – it felt like too much cruel reality for Riley, attached as she was to Wilson.

'Let's go to space again,' Sally said, mulling over an idea. 'This time, I'm going to tell you about some of the stars and constellations Laika went out towards. It's also a story about bears.'

'Space bears?'

'Yes. Space bears. A big one and a little one, who live way up in the sky. Ursa Major and Ursa Minor. Not the catchiest names, I know. These two bears were made up of stars.'

Riley smiled and turned on her side.

'The big bear promised she would do everything she could to protect her little bear, and for a long time, life for the two of them was easy. Because all they really had to do was shine a little, and that was only *really* necessary during night-time on earth, when the humans had their telescopes out.'

'But then . . . ?'

'One day a comet came, blazing a trail between them, and Little Bear was blinded by the light. He couldn't see Big Bear, and he thought she was gone. "You promised me," he said, "and now you've gone, and I'm all on my own."'

Riley clutched the duvet a little tighter.

'He was sad, but slowly he learned to do things by himself. To cope.'

'But she promised,' Riley said.

'I know. And she kept her promise. When the bright light faded from Little Bear's eyes, he saw that Big Bear was right there. She hadn't gone anywhere. But he was stronger, and he could help her now. In time her light would fade, but she would always be there for him.'

Riley reached out a hand and touched Sally's. She traced

a finger over the soft skin, and slowly Riley's eyelids lowered until they were almost closed. She stayed with Riley until her breathing deepened, her chest rising and falling gently, then kissed her daughter softly on the forehead and left the room.

Mum thinks I'm asleep, but I'm not. I can see a little bit of light coming through from the window. It makes a line across the rug.

I lift the duvet and get up. Quiet, quiet mouse steps, so that they won't hear me. At the window, I pull the curtain and look out. The sky looks different here in the countryside – all the stars are so bright. I can't see the shapes Mum was talking about, the bears, but I can see one big enough to wish on.

Star light, star bright, first star I see tonight . . .

I press my eyes shut, tight.

Chapter 5

Theo was sitting at the kitchen table at home, going through the café accounts. It was Saturday, and Sally and Riley were due back from Norfolk any moment. It had been a long week. As he updated the spreadsheet on his computer, he thought about Gabi and how distracted she'd seemed. Each time he'd tried to talk to her about his plans for the business, she had gone quiet, or asked if they could talk another time. She'd baked as usual, worked long hours, but Theo couldn't shift the feeling that something was up. He needed for her to be as committed as he was, and had always felt that up until recently, but now he sensed that she was wavering.

Theo heard a key turn in the front door, and it brought a smile to his face. His family were home.

'Dad!' Riley called out. He heard the thump of bags landing on the hallway floor and turned to see his daughter running towards him.

He picked her up and she wrapped her legs around him. Her hair was bouncing loose around her face and her eyes burned bright.

'I missed you, Dad,' Riley said, hugging him.

Sally came over to join them. 'Hello, you,' she said, kissing him. 'How's it been? Were you lost without us?'

'Completely,' Theo said. 'How was it with Granddad and Catherine?'

'We had the best time,' Riley said. 'Granddad and I played football, went and saw animals, and took Wilson to the beach a lot. It rained a bit, but we had hot chocolate, and played Connect Four, and Granddad and I played Moneypoly.'

'Monopoly,' Sally corrected, gently.

'Yes, Monopoly, and then we had popcorn and watched *Mary Poppins*.'

'They've still got a video recorder. It's the very same tape I used to watch. Can you believe it?' Sally said.

'Sounds like it was fun,' Theo said. 'I'm sorry I missed it.'

'You must have been *bored*,' Riley said.

Theo laughed. 'Not the whole time. It was pretty busy at the café. But it is nice to have you back.'

'We talked a lot with Catherine about Italy,' Riley said. 'We'll all be together then.'

'Yes,' Theo said. 'I can't wait.'

Theo and Sally's eyes met. It felt like a long time since they'd had a break, all three of them, and with the demands of both their businesses, they needed it.

'Right, I have news,' Theo said. 'Grandma Elephant and Stephen are on the way over.'

'They are?' Sally said.

He knew what she was thinking, and he couldn't blame her. There goes my quiet afternoon, getting on top of stuff before term starts up again.

'Great!' Riley said.

'Sorry,' he said to Sally, when Riley had left the room. 'I know you've just got back but they're desperate to see Riley again.'

'It's fine,' Sally said. 'The laundry can wait. Might as well cram as much grandparent time into half-term as we can. We can show them the photos of the party.'

*

Elena and Stephen came around in the afternoon, and Theo got his laptop out and located the photos of the party to show them. Riley went to sit between her grandparents, curled up under Elena's arm and snuggled into her. 'I love you, Grandma Elephant.'

Theo looked on. There was something very special about seeing his mum and Riley together.

'Here we go,' he said.

The slide show on the computer started up: Elena and Stephen feeding each other big slabs of cake and laughing, talking with friends and relatives. Then a photo of Sally and Theo dancing together at the end of the night came up, his arms around her waist.

'It was so fun,' Riley said. 'Can you be married forty years every year?'

Elena laughed. 'That's not quite how it works, sweetheart. But you're right. It was a wonderful day.'

'Yes,' Stephen agreed. 'Unforgettable.'

'And all the more special as Cora and Andreas were there.' Elena's eyes filled with tears. She dabbed them with a handkerchief.

'Good tears, I hope,' Theo said. He knew how much his mother's friendship with Gabi's parents meant to her – they'd known each other since they were children.

'Well, a little of both.'

Sally glanced over at him, confused. He knew no more than she did.

'Gabi didn't tell you they were going?' Elena said.

Theo shook his head.

'Cora and Andreas are moving back to Greece,' Elena went on. 'I always thought we'd spend this part of our lives together. But they want to retire over there. They feel it's time to go home.' Elena's voice cracked with emotion. Sally handed her a tissue, and she wiped her eyes.

'I had no idea,' Theo said. He thought back on the week he'd just spent with Gabi. No wonder she'd seemed distracted. Her parents were leaving.

'And Gabi?' Sally asked, tentatively.

It hit Theo then: Gabi hadn't committed to anything at the café beyond the summer. She had been keeping something from him, he was sure of it.

'But Gabi . . . Gabi's staying, right?'

'You'll have to ask her that,' Elena said.

The next day, Sally worked on her business Facebook page, taking Isabel's advice on how to broaden her reach. Her thoughts were with Theo, though. He'd been shocked to hear the news about Gabi's parents, and while he'd shrugged off her concern, she knew he must have been wondering whether Gabi had plans of her own. Sally told herself to stop worrying. Theo and Gabi had built the business up together, and it was doing really well – it wouldn't make any sense for her to leave now.

After lunch Sally packaged up her orders, adding her customised tags, and put Leonie's to one side, ready to give to her at the school gates. At three, she walked to school and spotted Leonie right away.

'Hi, Sally,' Leonie said, smiling. 'Survived half-term, then?'

'Yes. Actually, it was lovely. We were up in Norfolk with my dad. How was yours?'

'The usual chaos. You were wise to stop at one child. My three were at each other's throats half the time.'

'I don't know how you do it. I love kids, but Riley's always been more than enough for us to handle.' Sally reached into her bag. 'I brought this, for your son,' she said, bringing out the wrapped-up dinosaur hoodie. 'The invoice is in there – it's thirty per cent off for school parents.'

'That's kind of you,' Leonie said. 'Thanks. I'll spread the word.'

'Cool.'

'Oh, and I've been meaning to tell you, about the cake sale . . . '

Sally felt her cheeks flush as she remembered the frog Riley had held over the table. She'd hoped everyone might have forgotten.

'A hundred and sixty pounds, we raised,' she said. 'Pretty good going, isn't it?'

Sally smiled in relief.

'We're got a quiz night coming up soon. I'll send you the flyer.'

'Thanks.'

'Mum!'

Sally turned and saw Riley crossing the playground. She welcomed her with a warm hug. 'Hey, peanut. It's good to see you.'

'Did you bring a biscuit for me?' Riley asked.

'Now there's love,' Leonie said.

'Always conditional.' Sally laughed and handed her daughter a digestive.

Ms Sanderson, Riley's teacher, made her way over. 'Hi,' she said. Her eyes were bright green against dark skin, her hair in neat cornrows. She touched Sally lightly on the arm. 'Could I have a quick word?'

'Sure,' Sally said.

She took Riley's hand and said a swift goodbye to Leonie.

They stepped into the classroom and took a seat at the teacher's desk. Around them the walls were bright with a Roald Dahl collage and strings of handmade paper dolls.

'Those are mine,' Riley whispered to Sally, pointing to a string of dolls that were robots holding metal-claw hands. Sally noticed that she was wearing different trousers.

'Why don't you go and find a book in the story corner?' Ms Sanderson encouraged Riley. 'I just want to have a quick word with your mum about something.'

Sally felt a little anxious, but told herself it was probably nothing. They watched Riley walk over to the bookshelves and the teacher turned her focus to Sally.

'Riley had a toilet accident today.'

'She did?' Sally said, surprised. That explained the trousers. But Riley wetting herself? It had been years since she'd done that.

Ms Sanderson continued: 'I'm not sure that Riley is always going to the toilet when she needs to. There are times when she seems uncomfortable, fidgeting. But when I ask her if she wants to go, she says no.'

Sally felt concerned. 'I didn't realise that. This hasn't happened for ages. She must have been embarrassed.'

Sally looked over at Riley, who had picked up a book and was reading it on the carpet. She was cross-legged and hunched over, immersed in the story.

'It was fine. She dashed over to me right away and we sorted it out discreetly. Does it happen at home too?'

'No, it doesn't.' She looked over again at her daughter on the other side of the room. She looked content, calm. But this shouldn't be happening – not at her age.

It seemed that the move had affected all of them. There was never a good age to take a child out of primary school, and Riley had been settled with close friends at St Michael's. Sally thought things had gone smoothly, but maybe she'd been complacent.

'I wondered if perhaps it was something you might chat to her about at home?'

Sally nodded. 'Of course. Yes. I'll talk to her about it.'

*

As they walked home from school, Riley bent to touch the green moss that had formed on garden walls. She stopped and pressed it down, smiling to herself as it sprung back gently.

'Look, Mum,' she said. 'It's tickly.'

Sally bent down and touched it too. 'And better than that – check this out,' she said, spotting a baby snail on a nearby brick. She lifted it up on the tip of her finger and showed it to Riley.

'So cute,' Riley said, reaching up her hand for the transfer. The snail made its leisurely way on to her waiting finger. She admired it against the light. 'Its antennae are all see-through.'

They paused for a moment, watching the snail's lazy movements.

'Can we take it home?' she asked.

'I don't see why not.' She thought of the plastic sweet jar she'd kept in the garage, thinking it might make a home for some mini beast or other. 'We could make a little home from that raspberry laces jar.'

Riley seemed pleased with that, and they continued their journey with her finger outstretched, the tiny creature carried on the end.

Sally thought back on her conversation at the school and chose her moment carefully. 'Peanut. You know how I was talking with your teacher just now?'

'Mmm-hmm.' She was peering in closely, admiring the snail's patterned shell.

'She mentioned what happened today, with the toilet accident, and you needing new trousers. She wondered if sometimes you don't want to go to the toilet at school?'

Riley looked at her, eyes wide, as if to check whether she was in trouble.

'She wasn't cross, just concerned that you might be uncomfortable,' Sally assured her. 'When you need to go, you should go, you know that, right?'

Riley nodded.

'Is there a reason you don't want to?'

Riley paused. When she spoke, her voice was soft and quiet. 'I don't like them.'

Sally could still remember the primary-school toilets she'd gone to as a child. They'd always been cold, with a lingering smell of bleach.

Tentatively, Sally pushed her on it. 'Why's that?'

Riley shrugged. 'I just don't.'

'Is this to do with you moving school?'

'I don't want to talk about it any more, Mum,' Riley said, turning away. 'Let's just go home and make a snail house.'

At home, Sally and Riley made the snail house, putting in sticks, moss and leaves for their snail to climb on. Riley put in a bottle-top filled with water.

Riley tilted her head to the side, thinking. 'Saturn,' she said. 'Let's call him Saturn.'

She seemed younger than seven, sometimes, Sally thought. Other children in her class were caught up in computer games, or YouTube music videos, but Riley still seemed happiest doing the things she'd always done, out in nature.

They ate dinner together, chatting, and then that evening, Sally sat beside her daughter at the kitchen table as she did her homework. Sally watched her, that little frown of concentration – similar to how Theo looked when he was doing his tax return. Was there something up with her? Was she missing St Michael's more than either of them had realised? She'd ask Theo to talk to Riley. He had a way of getting through to her.

Theo and Gabi sat down in a booth at the end of the day, after the last customer had left the café, sharing a couple of muffins that had gone unsold. It had been on his mind all day, what his mum had said, but he'd wanted to wait for the right moment to ask her.

'Mum and Dad came over yesterday. They told me about your parents going back to Greece.'

Panic flickered across her face.

'Why didn't you say something? You must have known I'd hear soon enough. We've been working together every day and you didn't even mention it.'

'I was waiting until it was certain,' she said.

He had to ask her. He had to know.

'Are you going too?'

'It hasn't been an easy decision,' she said.

So that was it. She was going. Theo felt crushed.

'I've got so much here, this café, my friends . . . '

'So why can I sense a "but" coming?'

Gabi glanced away, then met his eyes. 'Listen. You know the business matters to me. Of course it does. I don't want to leave it, or let you down. But my personal life matters too. I'm thirty-three, but I'm still living like a teenager here. London's so fast. You work, go out, then it's on to the next thing. Another bar, another club. I want to slow down. I don't have a family like you do. I have my parents – and they're going. Maybe a new start, somewhere else, would be a good thing for me.'

He didn't want to lose her – his oldest friend, his business partner – but he was starting to see that he had to.

'OK,' he said, realising how ungenerous he had been. If the move was right for Gabi, then it was the right thing. 'I'm sorry. I mean, I do get it.'

She looked relieved. 'Thank you.'

'Your parents must be happy.'

'That's an understatement.'

Theo looked at the inside of the shop front, the OPEN

sign showing towards them. Reality slowly seeped in – Gabi was going.

'When are you leaving?' he asked.

'I'll be here for the summer – hopefully long enough for you to find an investor, and a replacement.'

'I can't really imagine doing this with anyone else,' he said. How would he find anyone who could compare to Gabi? It was an intimate thing, working together day in, day out, and with Gabi it had been natural and easy. But he couldn't see himself running the business with a stranger.

'I guess you could buy me out,' she suggested, tentatively.

'With what?' he said, with a wry laugh. He and Sally had enough money to keep ticking over, but hardly anything to spare. Even the holiday they were going on that summer Sally's parents had helped out with. The financial gap in the business would be far bigger than he could ever fill alone.

'I don't know,' Gabi said. 'But I know you'll be fine. I know that one way or another you'll figure it out. Because you always do, Theo.'

'I'm sure you're right. But anyway, let's forget about the business for a minute. This is about you. New beginnings. I hate you a bit for doing this to me, but if you're happy, I'm happy.' He gave her a hug.

She pulled back to look at him. 'No more of my control freakery. You could even get to like it.'

Back at home, Sally and Theo sat down to dinner. He told her how the conversation with Gabi had gone.

'I'm gutted, Sal. I mean, I'm happy for her, don't get me wrong, but . . . ' He could still barely get his head around it. It didn't seem real.

'It feels so out of the blue,' Sally said. 'Did you know she'd been thinking about it?'

'I had no idea. None at all. She's my best friend – you know that. But also this is going to be tough on the business. How am I supposed to replace her? She's going in two months.'

Sally came around to where he was sitting and gave him a hug. It felt so good to be close to her. 'You will. We will. We can do this.'

'Thank you,' he said.

'You've got me. You've always got me.' They stayed like that for a moment, holding each other. 'I love you,' she said.

'Me too,' he said. 'But anyway, distract me. Tell me about your day. What's been happening on Planet Riley?'

Sally smiled. 'We've got a new addition to the household.'

'Really? Another mouth to feed?'

'He's just outside the back door, in a sweet jar. Saturn. He's a snail.'

'Just what we need,' Theo said. He laughed, and it felt good to do that, in spite of everything.

'He's cheap to keep. Seemed happy enough with the leaves Riley tossed in there.'

'I suppose, as pets go, we should be thankful.'

'Exactly. Riley's delighted with him.'

'So she had a good day?'

'Kind of.' Sally paused. She didn't look at ease. 'Ms Sanderson called me in at pick-up. Riley wet herself today. She came home in a pair of trousers from lost property.'

'Really?' Theo said. He couldn't remember the last time that had happened. 'That's strange.'

'I know. The teacher's concerned that Riley's not going to the toilet when she needs to.'

'Weird. Any idea why?'

'That's what I've been trying to figure out. All I can think is this was never a thing at St Michael's.'

Theo recalled the old school, and the friendly teachers there. 'Maybe the move has affected her more than we thought.'

'That's what I'm wondering. She settled so well at the start of the school year, but maybe it hasn't all been straightforward for her.' Sally recalled the conversation with the teacher. 'Perhaps this is how it's coming out.'

'Have you had a chance to talk to her about it?'

'Yes, I asked her, but . . . nothing.'

'I'll try,' Theo said. He'd ask her when they were playing. She was sometimes more comfortable talking that way.

'Thanks. Well, there's nothing else we can do about it tonight.' She reached a hand up and touched his cheek, the rough stubble there, then kissed him gently. 'Let's try and forget about today. I have wine,' she said.

He smiled. 'You know me.'

'Too well.'

Chapter 6

Theo took Riley to her swimming lesson on Saturday morning. He sat with the other parents, watching her in the pool. She'd glance up at him every once in a while, in her green swimsuit and swimming cap. He tried to focus on her, and put aside thoughts of the business, but it wasn't easy. The night had been restless; the solutions he'd hoped might come to him by morning hadn't arrived. He couldn't imagine finding an investor who he could work with as well as Gabi. But Sally had been there beside him, sleeping in her silk camisole, not even stirring when he did, and he took some comfort from her presence. They would make it through this, just like they'd made it through the café's challenging early days, and the long wait for Riley.

Riley pulled herself out of the pool and shouted up to him. 'Dad! Dad! It's finished. Come down.'

He went downstairs, waited outside while she got showered and changed, and then they went to the café opposite the leisure centre. He ordered Riley a smoothie and they took the sofa by the window. Riley sat beside him and got a sticker book out of her Lego Ninjago rucksack.

'Can I do stickers?' she asked.

'Sure,' Theo said.

He took a sip of his tea as Riley worked through the first page. She sang to herself quietly as she unpeeled the stickers.

Sally had seemed so concerned. Theo looked at Riley now, though, and saw the same child he'd always seen – happy in herself, independent, brave.

'Can we go to the park after?' Riley asked, looking up.

'Sure. We can go to the park afterwards.'

Riley carried on for a while, as Theo drank his tea.

'How are things at school?' he asked.

'Fine,' Riley said with a shrug.

'Everything's OK?'

'Yep.'

They sat in silence for moment.

Theo asked the question as calmly as he could. 'Your teacher mentioned something to Mum. About you going to the toilet. She says that sometimes you forget. Is that right?'

Riley stared down at her sticker book and tried to unpeel one that was stuck to the inside cover. She spoke softly.

'What was that, Riley?'

She glanced up. 'Gotta catch 'em *allll*.'

'Sorry?'

She hummed a tune again. 'Gotta catch 'em *allll*.'

'Pokémon?' Theo said.

'Gotta catch 'em *allll*,' Riley said, finishing the theme tune loudly. A woman at the table next to them turned to look. Theo muttered an apology.

He took a breath. 'Riley. I was saying. When you're at school, do you—'

Riley's hazel eyes met his and didn't waver. 'I don't forget, Dad. I just don't go.'

'But why not?'

Riley shrugged. 'Just because.'

*

Isabel and Sally met for coffee that afternoon. Sally immediately detected a glow in her friend's cheeks.

'What's going on with you? You look different. It's Freddie, isn't it?'

'Might be.'

'So, it's a thing, then?'

'It's a some-thing,' Isabel said. 'He's told his parents about me.'

'Wow. So we share our in-laws now?'

'Hold up. I mean, we still live in different countries, which is a biggie. One step at a time. But I think there's progress. Actually, he wants me to go to Berlin to visit him.'

'That's great. When are you going?'

'I don't know if I am.' Isabel's expression changed, the light going out of her eyes.

'Come on. You're always at work. You can't have run out of holiday already.'

'No – the opposite, actually. HR are always on at me to use all my days.'

'So, what?'

'It's Dad.'

'How is he?'

'Terrorising his extremely patient neighbours. He accused them of stealing Badger yesterday.'

'Your old cat?'

'Who shuffled off this mortal coil ten years ago, yes.'

'Your poor dad.'

'I took him out in the garden to where Badger's gravestone is – well, if you can call it that. The cross we made when we buried him.'

'Did that help it sink in?'

Isabel nodded, then bit her lip. 'He started crying.'

'Upset about the cat dying?'

'No, not that. He's never been that sentimental about pets.

No. He just turned to me and said. "I'm losing it, aren't I, Iz?" And he looked right at me, and there was this moment of clarity. I could see him again. Dad – my real dad.'

Sally reached out and put an arm around her friend.

'Perhaps I should have been glad. But it was agonising, seeing that glimpse of him, and then watching it pass as quickly as it had arrived. I gave him a hug. Then he said he had to go.'

'Where?'

'Back to the tour bus,' Isabel said, laughing. 'Work to do.'

'Who was it this time?'

'Black Sabbath.'

Sally smiled.

'God, I love him, Sal. It would all be easier if I didn't love him so much.'

'You should go to Berlin,' Sally said. 'See Freddie. Let me keep an eye on your dad.'

'Would you?' Isabel said, the colour coming back to her cheeks. 'It would only be a couple of days. I could ask Rob to do the weekend.'

'It's fine. I'd like to.'

That evening, back at the house, Theo put on a DVD of *Moana* and he and Riley sat down on the sofa together under a grey fluffy blanket.

Sally brought in some bowls of popcorn for them and joined them on the sofa. When Riley was distracted by the film, Sally turned to him and whispered, 'Did you get anything out of her today?'

He shook his head. 'Nothing. She says she's fine. We had a good day.'

'OK,' Sally said. But she couldn't shake off the concern completely. 'That's good.'

Riley was singing along to one of the songs. She turned to

them and smiled, her hazel eyes bright, then returned her gaze to the TV.

'In other news, your brother . . . ' Sally said with a smile.

'Oh God, what now?' He laughed.

'He's cast a spell over Isabel. She's going out to stay with him next week.'

'Really?'

'Yes, four days in Berlin. I'm going to pop over and check on her dad on some of the days while she's out there.'

'So you're behind it, Isabel and Freddie getting back together? Or getting together? Whatever it is that's going on?'

'Yes. Whatever it is. Yes, I am. I think I am.' She smiled. 'He'd better not mess this one up, though. Because I haven't seen her happy like this for a long time.'

At school, we're all sitting on the bug rug. It's a big carpet with pictures on. I'm on a ladybird. Ms Sanderson is telling us a story. She has a nice, soft voice.

Ava is next to me. She's playing with Lucy's hair. She's always doing that, with Lucy and with me. Making plaits. She makes a long one in Lucy's hair and puts a band in it. Ms Sanderson doesn't see.

I know that she's going to want to do me a plait too. She always wants to. Even when I say I don't like it. It makes me feel sick in my stomach.

'I'm going to plait your hair now, Riley,' Ava says. I don't say yes. She reaches out and she touches it.

'No!' I say. It comes out like a shout.

Ms Sanderson stops reading and opens her eyes wide so you can see all the whites around. 'Riley, is there a problem?'

'No,' I say. I don't like being in trouble. Then I turn to Ava and I whisper. 'No, thank you.'

Chapter 7

Riley seemed quiet on the way home. There were days like this, Sally thought, when she was tired out. It was a long day for her. They stopped at the newsagents and Sally bought her a magazine, and Riley cheered up a bit after that. She sat at the kitchen table putting the stickers in place while Sally cooked.

At bedtime, Sally brushed her daughter's hair, and Riley pulled away a little.

'I'm just getting the tangle out,' Sally said, using her fingers to separate the small knot of hairs.

'It hurts,' Riley said.

'Sorry. Nearly done.' With two final strokes she finished and put the brush back on the bathroom shelf.

'Let's go to your room,' Sally said.

'OK.'

Sally waited for it – the words that always followed. That had come next since Riley was a toddler: 'Storytime!'

This was the part where Riley climbed into bed and Sally brought the duvet up around her, then sat beside her and either read, or ran through her mental jukebox for a story to tell – wizards, superheroes, bullies, magic – her mind flicking through her internal picture books and choosing a beginning, a Once Upon a Time.

Usually by the time she got to the end, Riley would be breathing more deeply, and her eyelids would lower. Sally would feel Riley's small hand grow weightier in hers. She'd absent-mindedly trace a pattern on the palm, enjoying the calm and quiet. Then she'd get to her feet, feeling a certain satisfaction at a bedtime well done.

Today Riley didn't get under the duvet. Sally sat beside her, but something was different. There was a hiccup in their script.

'So ...' Sally laughed. 'You're not going to ask me for a story? Is this it? I guess I always knew the day would come ...'

Her daughter was growing up. Of course she was. Sally bit her lip, a bittersweet sadness catching her. Of course this little tradition was going to seem silly at some point. And it seemed tonight was that night. You never know the last times – the last toothless smile, the last lullaby, the last unembarrassed hand-hold – until they've passed.

'It's not that,' Riley said.

'Then what's up, peanut?' she asked calmly. Her hand was resting gently on her daughter's leg.

'Can you help me do something, Mum?' Riley said.

Sally smiled. 'Sure. What is it?'

Riley touched her hair, pressing it flat against her skull. 'Cut it.'

'Your hair?'

'Yes.' Riley pressed the hair flatter still, until it looked as if it were barely there. 'I want it off.'

'Really?' Sally's heart constricted. She reached out and touched the soft locks. 'But you have such beautiful hair.'

'*Don't*,' Riley said, pushing her hand away. In the glow of the nightlight Sally could make out the sheen of tears in her eyes. She began to yank at the brown curls Sally had always adored. 'This hair – I don't like it. I hate it.'

Sally recoiled at the words.

'I want it off,' Riley said, resolute.

'But why?'

'I don't like it.'

'Why don't you have a sleep and see how you feel in the morning?'

Riley frowned. 'I'll feel the same.'

Images flashed into Sally's mind – the hairclips refused, the flinching at hair brushing, the way Riley had started to dislike having her hair washed. Before now she'd seen them as just signs of Riley's general stubbornness, but now they seemed cast in a different light.

'You really mean that?'

Riley nodded.

'You're sure?'

Sally was clinging on to the hope she might not be serious.

'Yes,' Riley said, without a moment's hesitation. 'I'm sure.'

Sally took a deep breath. This wasn't worth a fight, not really. 'I'll talk to your dad about it. How's that?'

A smile came to the corners of Riley's mouth. 'Thanks, Mum,' she said.

'Happier?' Sally said.

'Yes,' Riley replied.

Sally kissed the top of her daughter's head.

That night Sally lay in bed on her own, waiting for sleep to come. A sliver of streetlamp light came in through the window, and she told herself it was that that was keeping her awake.

She found herself once again in her childhood bathroom, her eyes on the wooden-framed mirror, quietly content as her mum brushed her hair with a Mason and Pearson bristled hairbrush, smoothing it with her left hand as she went. In those moments she felt complete, having all of her mum's attention simply for being her child. In the mirror she'd see her mother's tanned arms, and slender piano-player's hands, and get a flash of the denim of her dungarees. Then, when she was finished, her mum would duck her head down and appear in the mirror, their faces next to each other, and she would smile. That wide smile that spread irresistibly to Sally's face. She'd touch her daughter's cheek gently. 'All done,' she'd say.

Sally got up and pulled the curtain shut. As she did, she heard a key turn in the door. Theo was back.

She crept back into bed and pulled the duvet around her. A few minutes later he came into the room.

'Hey,' he said softly. 'I wasn't expecting you to still be up.'

He bent to kiss her and she looped both arms around him, bringing him closer. She kissed him and lost herself in the sensual connection, the way she ceased to be just her and became part of him instead. The way his mouth moved against hers, sending a tingle through her body, a shiver over her skin. There was deep comfort in the familiarity of his touch, but each time there was something new in it.

'I should go out more often,' Theo said.

She laughed. 'It's good to see you, that's all.'

'You OK?' he asked, hand still in her hair, but moving back a fraction so he could see her face.

After the pleasing drunkenness she felt at his touch, sobriety crept back. She remembered how the evening had upset her and why she'd needed to lose herself in that kiss so badly.

'Weird night,' she admitted.

'Weird how?'

'I was chatting to Riley at bedtime,' Sally said. She stalled. It pained her a little to think about it.

'And?' Theo prompted her.

'It's nothing, really.'

Theo seemed unconvinced. 'It doesn't seem like nothing.'

'She wants to get her hair cut.' Sally tried to say it evenly, as if it didn't hurt her to let that idea of her long-haired daughter go. 'She said she wants it all off. Short.'

'OK,' Theo said, hesitantly. 'I kind of like it long.'

'Me too,' Sally said. The picture she'd had, of her and Riley, an echo of her and her own mother together – she couldn't help feeling that she risked losing that now. But she knew deep down that this was her problem, not Riley's.

He paused. 'But if that's what she wants, I guess she's old enough to make up her own mind. At seven, she's starting to think more about clothes, about her own style. That's normal, right?'

'Yes. Totally normal,' Sally said.

'And it's only hair,' Theo said.

'Of course,' Sally said. 'It's only hair.'

I'm looking at my face in the mirror. I pull my hair back. It's better. All gone. I want it all gone. No ponytails. No bunches. No hairbands. Nothing for Ava to play with. Mum called the hairdresser and made an appointment. Now, it's going to be all gone.

Chapter 8

On Saturday morning, Riley ran down the local high street, ahead of Sally and Isabel, her brunette curls bouncing.

'Thanks for coming along,' Sally said to Isabel.

Theo had to be at the café, and it helped, having a friend there. Perhaps it shouldn't be a big deal, but it felt like one to her.

'Least I could do,' Isabel said. 'After your promise to dad-sit for me next weekend.'

Sally smiled.

Riley spun around, pointing at one of the shop fronts a few yards away. 'That's the hairdresser, isn't it?' she said.

'That's it,' Sally called back.

'Yes,' Riley said, running a bit further and then coming to a halt outside the shop.

'You excited, Riley?' Isabel said.

'Really excited.'

Isabel gave her a hug. 'It's going to be great.'

Sentiment, Sally told herself. That's all it was. Nothing more. There was no point getting upset about it. But inside she felt empty.

'Hi,' said the hairdresser. 'I'm Lauren. And you must be Riley. Am I right?'

'Yes!' Riley said. 'Can I sit in your big chair?'

'Go right ahead.'

Riley sat down in the chair, and the hairdresser looked at her in the mirror. Riley tugged at her hair in the way she had the other night. As if she wanted to pull the hair out by the root, as if she were shrugging off a wig. 'I want it all gone. Off,' she said.

'OK . . . sure,' Lauren said, suppressing a smile. 'Listen, why don't we look at a few styles together. See what might suit you?' She passed Riley a magazine. 'You've got a heart-shaped face, so perhaps something like this?' She pointed to a short, pixie cut and glanced at Sally for confirmation that it was along the right lines. Sally's heart sank as Riley's face lit up. 'Yes, like that,' she said, looking up at Lauren. 'Exactly like that.'

'OK,' said Lauren. 'If you're sure.'

Sally nodded, reluctantly. She touched her daughter's hair and remembered the moment she and Theo had first heard that she was having a girl. Before that moment, she hadn't really minded what sex their child was, but with that word came a warm feeling that spread through her body, from her heart outwards. A girl. She'd smiled and wondered if she would ever be able to stop. Her daughter. Mother to a daughter. She'd thought of that tiny pink hand in hers. But what she imagined most of all was this. The soft hair in her hands, running a brush through it, placing a butterfly clip or a hairband in there. Silly, really. But it was what she'd pictured, and now the picture was changing.

Riley's hair was washed, and Sally felt distant from it, disconnected. Then the hairdresser brought out her scissors. Damp locks of Riley's hair fell on to the salon floor, and it pained her to watch.

Isabel, sensing her discomfort, put an arm around her friend. They both looked on in the mirror as a lightness came to Riley's face and she smiled.

*

Theo got back at just after eight that evening and came through to find Sally in the living room, reading a book.

'I just had a peek in at Riley,' he said. 'She was fast asleep.'

'You saw her hair?'

'Yes.' His tone was measured – it didn't convey enthusiasm or dismay.

'Big change, isn't it?'

He nodded. 'Yes. But Riley's happy with it, right?'

'She loves it.'

'What about you?'

'I'm trying to like it. But I already miss her curls.'

'It'll grow, you know,' Theo said, gently.

'If she wants to let it.' She stopped herself, shook her head. 'It doesn't matter. We'll get used to it. We will. It's just . . . '

Theo could see through her. 'You're concerned what other people will think, aren't you?'

'A bit. Kids can be cruel about this kind of stuff. And your parents – they're going to see it when they visit tomorrow.'

'Don't worry about that, they'll be fine. Riley's made of tough stuff, you know,' Theo reassured her. 'She can handle it.'

'You're right,' Sally said. 'I know you're right. I'm overthinking this.'

'A bit,' Theo said.

Sally got closer to him, slipping her arms around his middle. 'Riley's growing up; it's about time I did the same. It's only a haircut.'

'You're worried because you care, and that's a good thing,' Theo said. He pulled her into a hug. 'But she's getting older now, and I guess we need to start letting go.'

The next morning, Riley bounced into her parents' bedroom while Sally was in the shower.

'Do you like it, Dad?' she asked, coming up to his side of the bed and shaking her head around, her short hair shining under the main light.

'It's cute, yes,' he said. She leaped up on the bed and climbed in beside him, pulling the duvet up over them both. He drew her in close for a cuddle. When he held her like this, she felt so tiny in his arms, so much smaller than when she was running around. He tickled her under her chin, and her laughter filled the room. That sound, and the warmth of her skin – there was nothing in the world that could make him feel more content.

He glanced at the clock – eight. His parents would arrive in an hour and a half. Something told him that his mum was not going to get this. She'd longed for a granddaughter, and for her that had always meant princess dresses and nail varnish, not mud and cropped hair. Not Riley, not the Riley his daughter was becoming more unquestionably each day. He would manage the situation; he knew how to handle his mum.

After they'd all breakfasted and showered, Elena and Stephen arrived. Riley greeted them both with excitable hugs, and they moved into the living room.

'I did you a painting, Grandma and Granddad. Let me show you.'

Riley dashed off to fetch the picture from the kitchen and the adults were left alone for a moment.

'Her hair,' Elena mouthed at them. She shook her head, as if a great tragedy had unfolded before her.

'Mum,' Theo said firmly. 'Don't. She's happy.'

Riley came back into the room with her painting. 'Look,' she said. 'It's a mermaid, and a crab, and some fish sandwiches.'

'That's lovely,' Elena said, beckoning Riley over. 'Do you think they'll eat those sandwiches? I'm not sure I ever saw a mermaid eat sandwiches.'

'They do. They have to eat, just like humans.'

Elena touched the nape of Riley's neck, newly exposed. 'So, my dear. You're really happy with your hair like this?'

'Yes,' Riley said. 'It's better.'

'You did it yourself, did you?' Elena said, teasing.

'No,' Riley laughed, a deep laugh that came from her belly. 'Mum took me to the hairdressers.'

'OK,' said Elena. Her eyes met Theo's, silently questioning.

'It's what Riley wanted to do,' Theo said, sitting back in the sofa. 'And we reckoned at seven, she's old enough to make up her own mind.'

'I've seen worse,' Stephen said gruffly.

Riley shifted awkwardly beside her grandmother.

'Well, now you've seen what it looks like, you can let it grow again, can't you?' She glanced in Sally's direction. 'So that it's nice and long like the mermaid's, can't you?'

'No,' Riley said.

Elena laughed, a different laugh to Riley's – brittle, forced. 'You'll change your mind about that. You'll see.'

'Leave it, Mum,' Theo said. 'Come on.' He could see the tension in Sally's face.

Silence hung over the room. A ding came from the oven timer, relieving them all.

'That'll be the pastries,' Theo said. 'I'll bring them through.'

Grandma and Granddad were here today. They've gone home now.

Tonight I don't want to talk in the bath – I just want it over. I want to put on my pyjamas and have cocoa and bed and a story. I just don't want to be here, with my own self like this. My body – I don't want to see it. I don't want to touch it. I ask Mum for more bubbles. Bubbles and bubbles and bubbles I can build a mountain with. Bubbles and bubbles and bubbles so I can't see any of me.

Chapter 9

Sally went over to Isabel's dad's house the following Thursday. She'd brought with her a bag with biscuits and fruit, which she carried down the street of terraced houses. She'd only been to Isabel's dad's flat twice before, both times with her friend and once with Riley in tow, and she wasn't sure if – even without the dementia – Noah would remember her. She could only hope that the visit didn't startle him.

He opened the door on the second ring. His eyes searched Sally's face. His hair was grey, his skin deeply lined, and he was wearing a Pink Floyd T-shirt – The Dark Side of the Moon tour – it was charmingly incongruous.

'Hi, Noah,' she said gently. 'I'm Isabel's friend . . . '

'Sally!' he said. 'Come on in.' He waved her through, past a stack of newspapers and some empty glass bottles in the hallway. 'Excuse the mess. Isabel's always telling me we need to have a tidy up.'

'Oh, don't worry about it. I brought some biscuits. Shall I get the kettle on?'

'I'd love one, yes,' Noah said. 'Mugs are up in that cupboard.'

He sat in an armchair and she brought the drinks through.

'Has everything been OK with you?'

'Yes, I'm fine. The meals on wheels lady has already been. And Joanna from next door came by. I know Isabel thinks I'm going to do something terrible to myself, or to them. I'd better get on, really; don't want to disappoint her.' He laughed.

'She just wanted to be sure, you were OK, that's all,' Sally said.

'She's a great girl.'

Sally had a glance around the room, to check if there was anything that needed doing. The living room was cluttered, but clean.

'Isabel said Rob would be visiting this weekend?'

'Yes. It'll be good to see him. Maybe we'll go out for a walk together. Take Joanna's dog out.'

'That's nice.'

'He's a good egg. Doesn't get down much. He's a bit of a loner, Rob. I always tell him he should find a nice woman, settle down. But he likes his hobbies. I don't think I'll end up with any grandchildren at this rate, do you?'

Sally laughed. 'You never know.'

'You've a son, haven't you?'

'A daughter.'

'Right, yes. A girl. Of course. I remember her being here. Bright spark.'

'She keeps us on our toes.'

'They're a gift, children,' Noah said. 'You take good care of yours.'

An hour later, Sally said goodbye, and left Noah to watch *Bargain Hunt*. On the way back to the car, she got a picture message through on her phone. A selfie of Freddie and Isabel posing in front of the Brandenburg Gate, smiles on their faces.

Thanks for helping me get here. Iz xx

*

Sally picked Riley up from school later that afternoon.

'I thought we could go to the park today, as the weather's nice. Would you like that?'

Riley shook her head. 'Not today.'

On the way home, Sally asked about her day and she gave one-word answers. Sally tried to lift the mood, talking about what she'd been doing, and what they might have for dinner, but Riley remained subdued. When they got home, she put her book bag down in the hallway and looked up at Sally for the first time.

'I want to go up to my room,' she said.

'Are you OK?' Sally said.

'Yes. I just want to be on my own.'

'I'll bring you some juice. A biscuit.'

Riley shook her head. 'No,' she said. 'I don't want anything.'

'Right,' Sally said, feeling concerned. 'Up you go, then.'

Riley went upstairs and disappeared behind her bedroom door. Sally recalled the times Riley had burst through the same door in high spirits, dressed as an astronaut or a space creature, proud and laughing. The memories caused Sally's chest to constrict. That child seemed so different from the one she had today.

Sally tried to distract herself by making tea, but couldn't stop thinking about Riley. After fifteen minutes, she crept upstairs and knocked on the door.

No reply came from Riley. Sally pushed the door open and saw her daughter in the corner of her room, cramming something into her wastepaper basket. When she looked up, Sally saw her eyes flash with determination.

'What are you doing?' Sally said.

Riley's face flushed deeply. 'Nothing.'

Sally got closer and saw that she was cramming shreds of material into the bin.

'Nothing? It looks like you're definitely doing something.'

'He's wrong.'

'Who's wrong?' Sally asked, as gently as she could. A feeling of unease was creeping over her.

'They're all stupid. They're all wrong.'

'Who?'

'No one.' Riley tugged at her hair, roughly.

'Don't do that, love,' Sally said, taking her hand. 'You'll hurt yourself.'

She carried on tugging at the short strands.

'Is this about your hair? Did someone say something?' Sally crouched down to her daughter's level. 'What have people been saying?'

'Nothing.'

Sally caught sight of the fabric again, a pale blue. It looked familiar. She refocused on Riley and the conversation.

Riley continued to push the fabric further into the bin, out of sight. Sally caught sight of a large pair of scissors on the carpet. She looked from them to the waste bin.

'No,' Sally said, reaching for the wastepaper basket. Her mind whirred. She pulled out a piece of fabric and then another. Delicate satin and net, cut to shreds.

The shock made Sally's voice catch in her throat. 'Riley! I made this for you.'

'Well, I don't want it,' Riley shouted. 'I'm glad it's all cut up.'

There were other pieces of fabric in there too, Sally saw now – a rainbow of ribbons, including the red dress from the anniversary party. Sally felt her heart break. She had made those dresses, with love. There were memories bound up in each one of them, and Riley had wilfully cut them up.

'I don't want them,' Riley shouted again, her stance solid and fixed. 'I don't want any of them.'

'Riley!' Sally said, her hurt turning to fury at her daughter's disobedience. The emotion caused her voice to rise even louder than Riley's. 'I don't know what's got into you, but it is *not OK* to ruin your things.'

Riley turned her back on Sally and kicked the wall, hard. 'You don't get it. *You're never going to get it!*' Riley shouted.

Sally felt as if she'd been physically struck. This behaviour – this wasn't the daughter she knew. She forced herself to keep her own feelings in check and get Riley back onside.

'Help me to understand,' Sally said at last.

After their distressing argument, it had taken Sally a long time to calm Riley down. Riley hadn't told Sally anything else, had refused dinner, but had gone to bed in the end. Her sobs had come so fast and deep that her face had become blotchy. She'd told Sally again and again that she didn't want her there, but Sally stayed, beside her bed, one hand on her chest until she fell asleep.

Can you call me? she texted Theo.

She felt raw, the emotion of the encounter with Riley still fresh. Of course it was normal that Riley would have her ups and downs, she told herself. School wasn't an easy ride for any child. Her own friendships at Riley's age had been a rollercoaster of inclusion and exclusion – she'd often gone into school not knowing if her best friend would still be her best friend that day. But she'd never lashed out at her parents like Riley had just now.

Sally looked out of the window, at the perfect lawns, the shiny cars, the glimmer of lights from security alarms. There wasn't a single neighbour here she knew. Did any of the children she'd seen walking to school behave like Riley just had – being defiant, cutting up their things?

She couldn't picture it. What was it she was getting wrong?

Theo got home close to ten. He slipped into bed beside Sally and curled up close to her.

Sally turned towards him. 'You're back late,' she said.

'I had to do the accounts. I texted.'

'I know, I got it,' she said. 'It's just . . . ' She didn't know if she could face going over what had happened with Riley again.

'What's up?'

She recalled Riley's face, pinched and flushed with anger, and the shreds of precious dress fabric than had littered her bedroom floor.

'Something's going on with Riley.'

'What do you mean?'

'Something at school. She wasn't clear. But her behaviour was terrible. She was angry, kicking the wall, cutting her clothes up—'

'What?' Theo said, shocked. 'Cutting her clothes up? That's not like her. Why would she do that?'

'I don't know.' Sally's head throbbed. She couldn't see any of this as clearly as she needed to. 'But I think something's really wrong.'

'Try to get some sleep tonight,' Theo said softly. 'I'll talk to her tomorrow. We'll get to the bottom of this, Sally. I promise.'

I heard the door open, the keys. But I couldn't get up – it's late and Dad would be cross. And then maybe Mum would tell him what happened – what I did.

I squeeze my eyes shut tight but I can still see his stupid face. Ben. There with the football by his feet, standing by me. I don't even really know him that well. I only talk to him because he's Euan's friend.

I only wanted to play football. They usually let me.

But Ben stopped right in the middle of the game, to tell me to go and play with the girls. He started to touch my hair. It wasn't like when Ava used to do it. It was worse. He was kind of pulling it.

'You look weird, Riley,' he said. 'Are you trying to copy us? Be like us?'

I pushed his hand away. Then I went for the football. Started to run with it. I could still hear him, calling out across the playground. I didn't look back.

'Go and play with the girls, Riley.'

My heart started to go really fast. I could see the goal ahead of me. I was ready to shoot when Jack tackled me. Ben was still shouting.

'You're one of them, Riley, not one of us.'

I don't want to see it, his face.

I'm going to rub it all out with a rubber. Make his face go away.

Chapter 10

The next morning, Sally woke up to the sound of Riley calling for breakfast. Theo was stirring beside her. She got up and pulled her dressing gown on, then remembered the previous day – Riley's hurt expression. The rage.

'I'm not sure what to do,' Sally said to Theo. 'I'm not sure it's right to punish her ... not when we don't know what's behind this.'

'Maybe just talk to her?' Theo said, only half-awake.

She expected more anger. Instead, outside on the landing, there was her daughter, standing in her rainbow-print pyjamas. Hair fluffed up around her head like a halo, smiling apologetically.

'Hi, Mum,' she said.

Sally belted her dressing gown and went over to Riley.

'I'm sorry about yesterday,' Riley said.

'What was going on? It didn't seem like you at all.' Sally tried to read her expression.

'I was angry. But not with you.'

They walked together down the stairs.

'I know you made those dresses,' Riley said. 'But I don't like them. I never have.'

'Right.' Sally paused. 'Well, I'm not happy that you cut them up – not at all. But I'm glad you were honest with me. I don't want to see you do anything like that again. What could we do to stop that happening?'

'I'd like some new clothes. Different ones. Some shorts for sports day.'

'Is it that time already?'

Riley nodded. 'Next week.'

'OK,' Sally said. 'We can do that. Would you like to go shopping together this weekend? Get some more clothes, ones that you like?'

Riley lit up. 'Yes,' she said. 'I'd like that.'

Theo came downstairs and found Sally making coffee while Riley was sitting at the kitchen table building something with Lego. He passed Sally some mugs and asked her quietly how Riley had seemed that morning.

'She seems much happier,' Sally said.

Theo looked over at his daughter – she had built a tower on one side of the Lego board, and a wall on the other.

'I told her we could go shopping for some new clothes,' Sally said, watching with Theo as their daughter moved a figure through the Lego city she'd built. 'I'll speak to Ms Sanderson about the other kids, make sure there's nothing going on at school that Riley's not telling us about.'

'Sure,' Theo said. Riley looked fine. Content. Hopefully her behaviour had been a one-off.

'I'm going to have a shower,' Sally said. 'I've got a meeting in town with the website designer after drop-off.'

'Cool. Go ahead.'

She passed him a coffee and kissed him before going upstairs.

Theo took a seat at the kitchen table opposite his daughter.

'Nice city you've got there,' he said.

'It's a tall, tall building and a prison. And she's escaping.' She moved one of her figures again. 'The prison guard is coming with handcuffs. I built it all myself. There's a horse stable too.'

'Pretty good,' he said. 'Can I make a building too?'

'Sure,' Riley said, passing him the box.

'So. You OK this morning?' Theo said, pretending to look intently at his Lego pieces, then glancing up at her.

'Fine.' Riley shrugged.

'And last night?' Theo asked. 'Mum said—'

'We're getting new clothes,' Riley said briskly. 'It's OK now. I said sorry.'

'Right. Sure. Your mum seemed quite upset . . .'

'I shouted at her. And I cut up the dresses.'

'You know that's not acceptable, don't you?'

Riley looked down. 'I know. I won't do it again.'

'Why did you do it?' Theo asked.

Riley shrugged. 'I don't know.' She tilted her head. 'Can I ask you a question, Dad?'

'Sure,' he said.

'Will I have tadpoles?'

Theo laughed. 'What – in the garden?'

'No, I mean, in my body.'

'Sorry?'

'Euan says his dad has tadpoles. That's how he got made. And that his mum said he'll have them too, one day.'

'Right,' Theo said. Oh Christ, he thought. I didn't see this one coming. 'I see. Yes.'

'So I'll have them too, when I grow up?'

'No, love,' Theo said. 'You won't. You'll be like Mum.'

'No.' She shook her head. 'I won't.'

'It's a long time away,' Theo said. 'You'll get used to the idea.'

'I won't,' Riley said quietly. 'I won't ever.'

*

Theo was at the breakfast table, Riley's words still running through his mind. Sally came into the room, a towel wrapped around her head, and glanced at the kitchen clock.

'You should get going, Theo. It's eight already.'

'Yes,' Theo said, getting to his feet. He felt slightly dazed.

'Have a great day at the café,' Sally said, kissing him goodbye.

'Thanks. You guys have a good day too. I'll be home late tonight, but I'll see you in the morning.'

'Sure. I was thinking Riley and I might swing by the café tomorrow. See you at work before we go shopping. Do you fancy that, Riley?'

'Yes!' she said.

'Great.' Theo put on his jacket and left the house, unlocking his bike and taking the familiar route to work. Riley's words were still ringing in his ears. 'I won't,' she'd said. 'I won't ever.' She kicked back. That was what she did. She said things she didn't understand, couldn't understand. It was what being a kid was all about. But there was something about the way she'd said it – the determination in her voice – that wouldn't shift from his mind.

Chapter 11

Sally brought Riley into the café on Saturday morning, before they went on their shopping trip in town. Riley skipped inside, full of excitement, and her dad greeted her with open arms. The previous day had reassured her. When she'd expressed her concerns to Riley's school teacher, Ms Sanderson had told her she'd keep an eye on how things were in the playground, but that the children seemed to be taking it in turns to leave each other out of things, rather than anyone picking on Riley. She and Theo hadn't had much of a chance to talk since the previous day, as he'd been working late. But they could catch up over the weekend.

'A macaron for you and a coffee for your mum,' Gabi said, putting them on the table.

'Thanks, Gabi,' Sally said, giving her a warm smile. 'Has Theo managed to convince you to stay yet?'

'Oh, Sally,' Gabi said, her conflicted feelings showing in her expression. 'It's not been an easy decision.'

'We won't hold it against you, too much,' Sally said. 'You need to do what's right for you.'

'We'll come and visit you, Auntie Gabi,' Riley said. 'At the seaside.'

'That's a given,' Gabi said, squeezing her cheek gently. Riley wrinkled her nose, but kept smiling.

Theo passed their table on the way back from serving a customer. 'It's crazy in here today. Wish I could come and sit with you for a while, but . . . ' He motioned to the full tables and the queue out of the door.

'Don't worry,' Sally said. 'We're only stopping by. We've got some shopping to do. Haven't we?'

'Yes,' Riley said proudly.

'Have fun, you two,' Theo said. 'Don't give our credit card too much of a hammering.'

Sally and Riley made their way to H&M in Oxford Circus. After just ten minutes, Sally had an armful of clothes on hangers, flip-flops and caps. Riley rushed from rail to rail, picking out the T-shirts she liked and passing them to her mum.

'Shall we try on what we've got?' Sally said. 'Because I'm not sure I can carry any more than this.'

They went into the changing room, taking a tag, and crammed into a small cubicle, mirrors creating the illusion of further company.

Sally passed her daughter a T-shirt from the top of the pile. 'OK, let's try this one on.'

Riley pulled it over her head – it had with a picture of a rocket on it. She looked in the mirror and seemed to scrutinise herself. 'I like it,' she said.

'Good,' Sally said. 'Let's get that one then.'

'But I'm still not right.' She tugged at the T-shirt.

'You're still not right?' Sally said, with a laugh. 'You look just right to me.' She brought Riley in close and kissed the smooth coolness of her cheek.

'I don't *feel* right.' Riley's hazel eyes were fixed on their reflection in the mirror. Telling Sally but also telling herself.

Sally paused. 'How?'

'I'm not sick. It's not that.' Riley tucked her hair behind her ears, making it appear even shorter. 'I'm different from the girls at school.'

Sally took a moment. She'd been waiting for this conversation, had known it would come. 'You know, Riley, there are all sorts of girls and all sorts of boys.'

The pink aisles in shops – the dolls, the dresses. If you didn't fit a sparkly princess-shaped mould these days, you could easily feel out of things.

'Girls can be whoever they want: astronauts, bus drivers—'

'I know that,' Riley said, impatient. 'I *know* all that, Mum.'

'So you know it's OK to be you, then.' Sally put her arm around Riley again and brought her closer. Riley's body felt awkward, her frame rigid.

'Can we get me some boy pants?' Riley said. 'Spiderman ones?'

Boy pants? What were they – Y-fronts, boxers? Instinctively, the thought troubled her. It didn't seem right. And Theo would hate it.

If she said yes – what then? Would the rest of Riley's underwear go in the bin? The nighties were long gone, of course, Riley had insisted on that, but the underwear and vests had stayed, and they were one of the few visual reminders that Riley was her little girl.

Sally took a deep breath. 'Why? You don't need them.'

'I need them. I really do.'

'Come on, Riley, you don't.'

'You're not *listening*,' Riley said, a fierceness in her voice. The same fury Sally had heard in Riley's room as she cut up the dresses.

'I am,' Sally said, defensive in spite of herself.

'You're *not*.'

They were only pants, right? It was only underwear. And

some were so similar you would barely be able to notice the difference. Surely all that mattered was that Riley felt comfortable and happy. She'd tell Theo and help him see that it was no big deal.

'Try me again, then.'

'I want to only wear boys' clothes,' Riley said.

Sally stopped still, wondering if she'd misheard. 'Sorry?'

'I want to dress like a boy,' Riley repeated. 'Because I *am* a boy.'

Sally took in the cupid's bow of Riley's mouth, the scattering of freckles on her nose. The same child she'd known as a baby, a toddler. There had been no transformation.

I am *a boy.*

The words whirled in Sally's head, making her dizzy.

I am *a boy.*

Riley was watching TV, her face completely still, her mouth a little open, that full bottom lip, similar to Theo's, jutting out slightly. Sally stood in the doorway, a mug of tea in her hands, and found she couldn't stop looking at her daughter.

What was it that had happened?

Reality, yesterday so neat and tightly stitched, was now being tugged at, the seams pulling looser, threads showing.

Riley was imaginative, Riley talked, Riley said stuff, and some of it made the most perfect, magnificent sense to Sally – her heart swelling with the pride of how her child could learn – while some of it was just as delightfully nonsensical. She loved those bits even more.

She shouldn't be too quick to jump on what her daughter had said, she knew that. She'd listened to her child – but that didn't mean she had to act. She told herself this, but all the same the back of her neck prickled and the words ran through her mind again, Riley's insistence. *I* am *a boy.*

Sally sat down beside Riley. Riley acknowledged her with a brief glance, the hint of a smile, before returning her eyes to the screen. Sally didn't need to talk or be listened to. She just wanted to be close to Riley. To see if by inhabiting the same physical space, feeling her warmth, she might start to understand.

Sally recalled the sound of her embryonic heartbeat at the ultrasound scan – and the announcement – her hand held tight in Theo's.

Perhaps it would blow over. Un-happen. It might.

But her doubts lingered. She hoped Riley knew she didn't have to change gender to be what she wanted in life. She and Theo had always told Riley she could be anything she wanted to be – prime minister, a doctor, an Olympic athlete. They wanted her to know that whatever future she dreamed of was there for the taking. But theirs wasn't the only message in society that Riley was exposed to. Maybe Riley felt limited by what she thought being a girl meant – what she thought it might hold her back from. Perhaps that was at the root of all of this.

How was it that Riley could feel like this about being a girl? Try as she might, Sally couldn't make sense of it.

If she pretended she'd never heard, would her daughter move on to another phase, another fad? Or was this here to stay?

'Hi,' Theo said, as he took off his coat in the hallway that evening.

'Hi, love.' They kissed, but Sally felt as if she was operating on autopilot.

'Riley go down OK?'

She nodded. 'I read to her for a while. *The Twits.* We're on chapter three.'

Theo smiled, kissing the top of her head. He held her close, but her thoughts were stuck in the previous hour. She'd tried to make up a bedtime story for Riley, but her mind had flickered over thoughts, unable to settle. *There was a robot dog, and he . . .* A beat, as she quickly pieced together the plot, the motivation, the climax, the denouement . . . There wasn't time. If she left even the smallest of silences, those words, Riley's words, might find space to return.

I want to dress like a boy.

Because I am *a boy.*

She'd picked up a book instead. Easier to read the words straight off the page. She read until she saw Riley's eyelids gently lower.

She looked at her sleeping child and thought again of what now existed that had not been there before, at least in her consciousness.

Had they really got it wrong, these past years when they'd been watching Riley so closely they could feel her breath, register every new word she learned? Had they told her a lie about who she was?

'You OK?' Theo asked.

No, she thought. No, *no.* I don't think I am. She should say it – she should tell him.

But she didn't want to. She couldn't bring herself to repeat what Riley had said. Theo would think she was overreacting.

Or maybe he wouldn't. Maybe this would strike him, as it did her, as something significant. If she said it out loud it would be real.

So she kept it inside, and nodded. Riley was wilful, that was all. This phase would pass, just like others had.

'Yes. Of course. I'm fine.'

Chapter 12

Riley darted over to join Euan by the fish tank that housed the class goldfish, and they peered in, tapping on the glass.

Why Euan? Sally thought. Why not Evie, or Ava, or any of the other girls?

Riley's words drifted back to her.

Euan nudged Riley in the ribs and Riley pushed him back. They both laughed.

Beth, Evie's mum, came up to Sally. She was dressed in blue skinny jeans with a loose white blouse and gold jewellery.

'Hi, there,' she said brightly.

Sally smiled, made an effort to push aside the numbness she'd been feeling.

'So, not long till sports day,' Beth said. 'I expect Riley's excited about it.'

Sally nodded. They'd chosen shorts for Riley to wear.

'Evie's always saying how good at running Riley is. As fast as the boys, she says.'

'That's what she says?' Sally said, telling herself to stay calm. She was being paranoid. Beth couldn't possibly know what Riley had said, even if it felt as if somehow she did.

'Yes. She was impressed.'

'That's nice. How is Evie?'

'Good, mostly.'

'Oh right,' Sally said, distracted. She glanced back at Riley and Euan. Maybe Sally should have done more to guide things, to encourage her to play with other girls. She'd never gravitated towards them, but perhaps Sally could have done more to give her the opportunity.

'The thing is, Sally, I worry a bit.'

The words came as a surprise to Sally. Beth always seemed so serene, as if she had no concerns at all.

'About what?'

'Evie's friendships. It all being about her and Ava. Being just the two of them all the time. There's a lot of drama. Last week was an off-week. I think it would do Evie good to have some more friends.'

'Right,' Sally said. 'Yes, of course. Those intense friendships can get a bit claustrophobic. I remember that from school.'

'Exactly. I think some fresh energy would do her good,' Beth said.

'Yes, I'm sure it would.'

'You should come around,' Beth said. 'For a play date. Next week sometime. What do you say?'

Sally's spirits lifted. This was it. Their chance. What both she and Riley had needed – a chance to be part of the school, of the community. Once Riley had formed close friendships she'd have no need to act out in the way she had been.

'Absolutely,' she said. 'We'd love that.'

The next morning, Sally brought Theo tea in bed and sat beside him. Time – that was all they needed. Days to pass, and for what Riley had said to fade, to be replaced with some other thing.

Thud.

'I don't want to know what that was,' she said.

Thud thud.

'Something heavy going down the stairs.'

A louder thud now, followed by successive bumps.

'Let's ignore it. Just for a minute,' Sally said.

Thud thud thud.

She picked up her tea and took a sip.

'Soft toys,' Theo said.

'Really? That loud?'

'It could be. Let's not think too much about it. It's keeping her busy.'

Sally smiled. 'So, get this: Riley and I have a play date.'

'Oh yeah? Who with?'

'Evie, the girl in her class that I told you about.'

'The mum you told me about,' Theo said wryly.

'Yep. Her,' Sally said, laughing at herself. He was right. 'The queen bee.'

'Do we have to call them play dates?' Theo asked. 'Can't we just say hanging out at your friends' houses, like we used to?'

'They have to be play dates,' Sally said. 'It's a thing, believe me. Round here even more so than at St Michael's. And you know what, if today goes well, it could make a real difference.'

'Sounds a bit serious. Isn't it supposed to be fun?'

'It *is* fun,' Sally said. 'It will be, I mean.'

'Sure.'

'It's just, you know ... If Riley has more girl friends, I think school would be easier for her.'

'Does it really matter who she's friends with, so long as she's got friends?'

'I think it would help her feel more settled if she had more close friendships. And girls, well, it's different. I used to tell my best friend at primary school – Hannah, she was called – I used to tell her everything, and she'd tell me. It was bonding.'

'Really? We just used to play with whoever was around, whoever had brought a football. Boys. Girls. Whatever. It wasn't complicated.'

'I know what you mean. But—'

Thud.

'That one was definitely louder,' she said, glancing over at the door.

Theo got up and went out into the hallway. 'Riley?'

Sally pulled the duvet up around her. Riley had been uprooted, and it was down to them to help her feel more secure again. It wouldn't take much, just some more time together, a few more friends for her at school. She hadn't told Theo about what Riley had said, because soon it wouldn't matter, she'd be in a calmer place. Less insistent. Less defiant.

'Riley!' Theo called out. 'Shampoo bottles? What a mess! Well, you're helping me to clear this all up.'

Theo went for a run in the park later that morning, after he and Riley had cleared the hallway. He'd told her off, but hadn't gone overboard. She was pushing for a bit of extra attention, and that was natural enough. It hadn't been her decision to move here.

He sped up and the trees and hedgerows became a blur. Leaving London hadn't been an easy decision, especially for Sally, who'd decided to leave her job at the same time, but they hadn't looked back. This was a better place for Riley to spend her childhood: fresh air, a smaller community – more similar to what he and Sally had experienced growing up.

He thought about what Sally had said that morning. She'd always been like that, inclined to worry about something. It was one of the things he loved about her, the way she cared about things so deeply, the way she always wanted things to be perfect – in her life, in his life, and now in their life with Riley. Getting it right mattered a lot to her.

He couldn't get worked up about Riley's friendships, though. Riley had always made friends easily. He wasn't concerned about who those friends were; Elmtree was a decent school and all the kids were nice enough. But if it mattered to Sally, she'd make it happen, whatever it was. She'd been successful as a designer, and would be now with her own business, he knew that, and she gave Riley everything. He was determined, yes, but less inclined to sweat the small stuff.

They might not always agree, but it didn't matter – he loved the very bones of Sally. They hadn't fallen in love through being the same.

Grown-ups always say: listen.

Listen to me, Riley. You're not listening to me. Your shoes, Riley – put your shoes on. Brush your hair. Urgh, brush your hair. Brush your teeth. Listen to me, Riley. Stop running, Riley, and listen. Stop climbing, Riley, and listen to me. Down from that wall, Riley. Look at me. Listen to me.

That's what Mum says. Dad not so much. Sometimes, if I'm doing something dangerous, or touching something I shouldn't be touching, then he'll grab me by the arm and say it. Listen.

But they *don't listen. I can say it, even shout it, and they still don't seem to really listen. I don't fit. That's why I shout sometimes. Because I don't fit in me.*

Chapter 13

After school, Sally and Riley climbed into the back of Beth's Range Rover with Evie, and Beth drove them around to her house, a three-storey new-build on an estate of other houses just the same.

It wasn't that different from theirs inside, just bigger and tidier, with shinier things – a breakfast bar in marble, a Nespresso machine that looked brand new.

Beth made coffee and Evie went into the open-plan living room. She got out her pony-grooming parlour on the floor, but Riley remained firmly by Sally's side.

'Why don't you go and play with Evie?' Sally said softly, trying to loosen Riley's grip on her arm.

Riley shrugged and whispered back, 'I don't want to.'

'She'd love to play with you,' Beth encouraged Riley.

'Go on, Riley,' Sally said, more gently.

'They can be so shy at this age,' Beth said quietly to Sally, over Riley's head. 'Evie can be just the same.'

'Evie's got some lovely horses,' Sally said.

'I'm not shy,' Riley said firmly. 'I just don't want to play with those things. They're dumb.'

'Riley,' Sally reprimanded her, embarrassed. She turned back to Beth. 'Sorry about this. She just takes a little while to settle in sometimes.'

'Don't worry,' Beth said, laughing. 'It's fine. Evie – why don't you show Riley some of your other toys upstairs?' she called over.

'Does she have any Lego?' Riley asked Sally.

'I've got Lego Friends,' Evie said. 'Come and see.'

Evie went upstairs and Riley followed, leaving Sally and Beth to drink their coffees.

'Lovely house,' Sally said, looking around. 'So light.'

'Thanks,' Beth replied. 'We're lucky we bought when we did. It meant we could afford to do this conservatory, and the loft conversion. We'll need that now.' She pointed to her stomach. 'Fourteen weeks. I've finally stopped throwing up, thank God. We're expecting another little girl.'

'Wow,' said Sally. 'That's wonderful news. Congratulations.'

'I'm relieved, really. I think Mark would have liked a boy, but to be honest with you, I'm thrilled. There's something special about sisters, isn't there?'

'Yes,' Sally said. 'I mean, I wouldn't know, I'm an only child, but I can imagine.'

'Oh, I see. I'm one of three. Our poor dad.' She laughed. 'It's a wonderful thing, having other girls to share things with. Clothes. Secrets.'

'It must be.' She'd never been unhappy, as a child, she'd had her parents, friends and the wilds of her imagination to dwell in. But as an adult, she had, at times, wondered how it might be to have the comfort and company of a sibling.

'Anyway, it means we have all the things already. The clothes, the toys. Plus the nursery's pink from when Evie was in it. I didn't fancy painting that again.' She laughed.

Riley came back into the room. 'Can I go outside?' she asked, looking out at the rope swing in the garden. 'I don't want to play up there with Evie any more.'

Beth smiled, but this time her lips formed a thinner line.

'Come on, Riley,' Sally whispered, bending to her daughter's level. 'Be polite, please. We came here to play with your friend.'

'I never wanted to come,' Riley said forcefully. 'It was you who wanted us to come here.'

Sally and Riley had driven home in near silence. Sally knew she should rise above it, but the shame of what Riley had said in Beth's house burned through her. She'd made their excuses and left as quickly as they could. The worst thing about it was that Riley had been right. Sally knew it, even if she couldn't face admitting it to Riley. She had been the one who wanted Evie and Riley to be friends. Because that was supposed to fix it. Because having more girl friends was supposed to make all of this – whatever it was – go away.

She went through the motions of bedtime and bathtime, but both of them were subdued. She read some of *Peter Pan* to Riley, and when she was asleep, went downstairs and poured herself a gin and tonic.

She had to tell Theo about the other day – what Riley had said. She should have told him from the start. He deserved to know. He would know what to do.

When he came home, he looked tired. She hugged him, noticed that the lines between his brows had deepened.

'How was your day?'

'It's over,' he said. 'Yours?'

Sally felt a lump rise in her throat. 'Come and sit down.' They went into the living room and sat on the sofa.

'What's up? Are you OK, Sal?'

'I don't know,' she said. 'I don't know what to think at the moment.'

'What is it?'

'The play date wasn't great. Riley hated being there.'

'Ah, well. You win some, you lose some, I guess. She didn't break anything, did she?'

'No,' Sally said. 'It's not like that.' She took a breath, trying to find the right way to say it.

'Go ahead,' Theo said, urging her on gently.

'Riley said something the other day, when we went shopping.' She shook her head. 'Theo – she told me she's a boy.'

Theo furrowed his brow. 'She did?'

They were silent for a moment.

'And you're taking it seriously?' he said.

'Don't you think we should?'

'As much as anything else, I suppose,' Theo said. 'I mean, she said she wanted to be Spiderman last week.'

'That's not the same.' He wasn't getting this. 'You know it's not.'

'Why not? They're just words.' He was saying it lightly, but she could see the strain in his expression. He wasn't certain.

'There have been other things, haven't there?' Sally said gently, putting a hand on his leg. 'It's not like she's said this in isolation. We've known for a long time that Riley is different.'

'Yes – she's not a stereotype,' Theo said. 'And thank God for that. Aren't you always saying that we should encourage her to feel she could be whatever kind of a girl she wants to be?'

'Yes, of course. I don't want her to be anyone different. You know I couldn't care less about Riley liking football, and not being obsessed with Barbie and French skipping.'

'She's always been a bit of a tomboy. You've never had an issue with it before. So why are we looking to fix something that isn't broken?'

'Because I think what we're dealing with here is something more serious. She didn't say she felt like a different kind of girl. She said: "I'm a boy." That she doesn't feel right in her body.'

Theo looked down.

'It was disturbing, Theo. I didn't tell you, right away because, well, I wanted to make sense of it myself first.'

Theo looked at her, seeming to register her concern now. 'If she's unhappy, then we need to help her. But this boy thing? They are still just words, a way of making sense of feeling like she's not like other girls, maybe. And we can help her understand that. But I don't think we should take it literally. I mean, she said she wanted to die because I took my iPad away from her last week.'

'Really?' Sally said, shocked.

'Yes,' he said. 'But that, your reaction, that's exactly it – it sounds alarming to us, right? But it's nothing to her. She's just repeating what she's heard somewhere – on the TV, from one of her friends' older siblings.'

'What did you do when she said that?'

'I ignored it. And the next second she was completely fine.'

Sally gave a sigh of relief. She hated to think of those words coming from Riley's mouth.

'Do you think they're related?' Sally said. 'What she said to you and what's going on now?'

Theo rubbed his forehead. 'Do I think Riley's suicidal because she's actually a boy? No, Sally.'

'Don't dismiss me like that,' she said, angrily. 'That's not fair at all.'

'I'm not dismissing you,' he said.

They sat in silence for a moment.

Theo's expression softened. 'I'm sorry. That was a crappy, insensitive thing to say. It's been a hard day. I'm tired. I just think you're over-thinking this. Kids say stuff.'

She strung the events together in her mind. The toilets. The baths. The anger. The shredded clothes. She couldn't ignore it. She wouldn't ignore it.

‘And some of what they say is true.’ Sally tried to pin it down, the sensation she had that this wasn’t something to gloss over – it required them to listen to their child and act. ‘I just have a gut feeling about this,’ she said. ‘That we should take it seriously.’

‘I can see that,’ Theo said. ‘But my gut is telling me something else entirely.’

‘What do you think we should do, then?’

‘The way I see it, if we take her seriously, and give this a lot of attention, then we are saying – definitively – that what she’s saying is real,’ Theo said. ‘That there is a serious issue.’

‘And you don’t think there is.’

‘I think she’s seven,’ Theo said.

‘I know. I know she’s young,’ Sally said. ‘But she seems so sure.’

‘She’s always been like that, Sal. Determined. Set on things.’

‘That’s true.’

‘I know it must be hard to see her upset. But try to remember she’s just a kid.’

Sally paused, took a moment to take stock of where they were. Maybe she was getting ahead of herself.

‘Try and relax about it,’ Theo said gently. ‘Hopefully it will blow over all by itself. She’s only said it once, right?’

Sally nodded. She felt like she’d lost perspective on all of it. All she had been able to think about was stopping the outbursts, making Riley happy again. Perhaps Theo was right.

‘We’ll keep a closer eye on her. Speak to her teachers again,’ he said.

‘OK,’ Sally said.

‘We’ll support her, together,’ Theo said. ‘But please – let’s keep this in perspective.’

The next day, Theo poured two cups of coffee for the waiting customers and tried to keep focused on the business at the café.

But his mind kept drifting back to Riley. Yes, kids said all kinds of things. And yes, he was sure about everything he'd said to Sally the previous night.

But at the same time, questions had started to raise themselves, nudging at his consciousness. There *had* always been something different about Riley.

He remembered Riley's third birthday. The dinosaur cake.

A memory of Sally cutting it. Three – it had seemed so big at the time. An important birthday, for their girl who had grown so quickly from their baby. The first time Riley had asked for a party, lost sleep in anticipation. A stegosaurus cake. Had the dinosaur been his idea or Sally's? He couldn't remember.

He remembered the day – there were Riley's grandparents, a few friends Riley had made at nursery school. Riley opened her presents. A painting set. A teddy bear. A Spurs football strip. Sally had got most of the presents online – but he'd insisted on that one. 'Get her onside early,' Theo had said. 'I don't want anyone steering her towards Arsenal.'

He pictured her in it now, three years old, smiling, so proud. She'd loved football ever since. He changed position in his seat, shifting his weight on to his right side. It wasn't like a present could have made this happen, though. Was it?

Had they missed something?

Were they missing something now?

As she got ready to go out, Sally looked at the photo of Riley's third birthday party and recalled the day.

Sally pressed the third purple candleholder into Riley's dinosaur cake. Theo's hand found hers. They looked over at Riley, in the corner of the room surrounded by a pile of presents. They smiled at one another.

'I think we're doing OK,' he whispered to her. 'Don't you?'

'Yes,' Sally said. 'I think we are.'

Riley's grandparents on both sides and a couple of kids from nursery had come over, and balloons filled the bay window area of the living room, bouncing gently on the mid-century furniture.

Sally and Theo went to sit a little closer.

Riley yelped with joy as she unwrapped a Play-Doh set, with a plastic turtle that spewed out the dough in different shapes.

Elena handed over her gift. Riley got hold of the Sellotape and started to tug it, ripping the paper slightly. Sally helped her to get it open. Inside was a fairy costume, with a satin skirt and glittery pink wings. Elena smiled proudly.

The corners of Riley's lips turned down and the lightness went from her face.

'You don't like it?' Elena said.

Riley shrugged. Sally gave her a subtle nod and mouthed the words: 'Thank you'.

'Thank you, Grandma Elephant,' Riley said.

Theo turned to Sally, silently acknowledging the awkwardness of the situation.

Sally could imagine how Elena must be feeling. That morning Sally had given Riley the dolls' house she'd had as a child. Weeks earlier she'd got it down from her father's attic and had spent the past few evenings tidying the wallpaper her mum had pasted up, and fixing the miniature furniture. She'd played with it for hours with her mum at Riley's age – the two of them sitting on the carpet, moving the little figures around the bedroom and sitting them around the dining table. She recalled the look on her mother's face, her eyes sparkling as she played with Sally, the two of them talking as if they were the little figures in their home.

Riley had opened it and looked at it. Then just walked away and played with something else.

Riley picked up another gift and ripped the paper off. 'Duplo!' she shouted. 'A Duplo garage!'

'Lovely,' Sally said. Her daughter's face was aglow again. Her brown hair was up in a ponytail, her jeans already dirty from mud in the garden.

Sally sat on the edge of her bed, thinking of that birthday in their living room downstairs, the memory still fresh.

Toys were just toys. Weren't they?

Part Two

SUMMER

Chapter 14

Two long weeks had passed. Riley's words still echoed in Sally's mind, and lingered, unmentioned, between her and Theo. *I am a boy.* Riley didn't repeat them, but she didn't return to normal either; she was restless, her fuse short.

That Monday, after drop-off, Sally got the tube in to meet Isabel. She found her friend on Highbury Fields, a stone's throw from Isabel's flat, on the bench under a weeping willow that had, long ago, during summer picnics and Pimm's-drinking sunsets, become their bench. They hugged hello.

Sally smiled. 'It's good to see you. Are you off the whole week?'

'Yes. Actually, I don't know if Theo told you but Freddie's coming over,' Isabel said. 'He's got a feature he can research over here. He's staying at mine for a while.'

'Are you official, then?'

'Yes. I think we might be.' Isabel paused for a moment and seemed to scrutinise her friend's face. 'Listen, Sal. I can tell something's up, so you might as well tell me now.'

'It's nothing,' Sally said.

'Try me with your nothing.'

Sally took a deep breath. 'Riley's been ... destructive. A

fortnight ago I caught her cutting up her dresses. Even that one I made her for her fourth birthday. Do you remember?'

'God. Yes, I do,' Isabel said, biting her lip. 'Ouch. That's not like her.'

'I know – not at all. Anyway, it turns out that the dresses were just the start. Now she's saying stuff,' Sally said.

'What kind of stuff?'

Sally found herself in that shop changing room again. Saw the pain in her young child's face. 'She thinks she's a boy. She says she is a boy.'

She'd wondered if Isabel would be shocked, but no shock registered on her face.

'What prompted it?'

'We were in H&M, trying on clothes. After she'd told me about hating the dresses, I agreed we could buy some different stuff – shorts, that kind of thing. I don't know. I don't really mind what she wears, as long as she feels comfortable. Then she turned to me and said . . . that she doesn't feel right in herself.'

'That must have been hard to hear.'

'It was. It is. I know she's never been typically girly. Whatever that is.'

'Just typically Riley.'

'Exactly.'

'Poor kid,' Isabel said. 'I feel for her. These pink and blue boxes society insists on putting kids in these days – it must be tough when you don't fit. I know I never did. I used to race around with my brother, get grazed knees, skateboard. You couldn't have paid me to brush a Barbie's hair.'

Sally smiled. 'That's how Riley's always been. A tomboy, I guess.'

'That's what I used to get called. But honestly, most people didn't even pay it much attention. No one really cared that I only wanted to wear my brother's hand-me-down corduroys and play in mud pits.'

'I always thought we supported her, embraced Riley being Riley. We've always told her that just because the other girls are into princesses, she doesn't have to be.'

Isabel nodded. 'Maybe you just need to keep doing it.'

'But now . . . now I'm starting to wonder. She seems . . . I don't know. I feel like that's not enough.'

'What does Theo think?'

'He thinks kids say things, and this is what she's saying. That we shouldn't take it too seriously.'

'Well, maybe he's right. Maybe you don't need to do anything about it,' Isabel said. 'Not yet, at least.'

Sally nodded.

'Maybe just wait and see if she says it again?'

The next day, in the early morning sun, Sally finished her coffee on the back step and watched Riley running to the fence and back in the garden. It was a long enough garden that she could build up some speed, and she moved her slim legs and arms with determination and grace. When she returned from the fence this time, she bent down, out of breath, and put her hands on her knees.

'Can you get me an egg, Mum?' Riley shouted. 'I'm going to need an egg.'

Sally went inside and boiled some water while Riley continued up and down in the garden.

Theo came in and put on the kettle. 'Coffee?' he asked her.

'Yes, please.'

He looked over at what she was doing. 'I didn't think you liked eggs hard-boiled.'

'Egg-and-spoon race. Riley's practising for sports day this afternoon.'

He looked out in the garden. 'Of course. Will you send me some photos? I wish I could be there, but there's just no way today.'

'Sure, will do.' Sally lifted the egg out of the pan with a spoon and put it on to a tea towel. 'At least you get to see the trial out there.'

He looked over at her from the doorway and cheered her on.

'I'm running so fast, Dad,' she said. 'I'm like a hurricane.'

'Fast enough that I'll never catch you?' he called back.

'Yes,' she said, picking up pace.

Theo put down his mug and went out to the garden, picking Riley up and spinning her around until she was laughing so hard her breath caught.

Perhaps they didn't need to fix anything, Sally thought. To look at Riley and think she was damaged – that, definitely, wasn't right at all.

Sally worked in the morning, checking over the designs for the website and supplying more content about herself and the brand. It was taking shape.

She got to the sports field behind the school just after lunch. It was a generous green space that the kids used for PE lessons. The sun beat down and she thought with relief of the sunhat she'd sent Riley in with that morning.

She searched for a familiar face. Leonie spotted her and waved her over. Beth was sitting on her other side, and Sally acknowledged her with a polite smile, hoping they could put the awkwardness of the play date behind them.

Riley waved from the start line, where the group were starting to take their places.

'I'm ready, Mum,' she called over. 'I'm ready to run really fast.'

Riley seemed happy. All that they wanted.

Sally watched as Riley changed her position on the line – moving away from Evie, Ava and the other girls, and towards the boys at the further side of the field.

'Three-two-one, *go*!'

Riley ran, picking up pace rapidly and getting ahead of the other girls. She was one of five nearing the finish line already. Sally squinted against the sun and saw her come in second. She turned and gave her mother a huge grin. Evie was walking over to where they were sitting, pouting a little after coming in last.

'It's funny,' Beth said. 'For a moment when Riley was running, with her hair short like that, I thought she was one of the boys.'

'How funny,' Sally said vaguely. There had been an edge to Beth's comment. She was sure of it.

Who cares, Sally told herself. Who cares what she looks like? My kid is doing the thing she loves.

Leonie smiled at Sally. 'Wow, Riley did really well.'

'Thank you.'

Her daughter was rushing over to her now, a medal glinting in the sunlight. Sally got to her feet.

Perhaps this was all Riley needed – more opportunity to do what she was best at, without being pigeonholed and labelled. More confidence and self-esteem. Because up there, with the teacher putting a medal around her neck, she looked calm and at ease.

'How did sports day go?' Theo asked, when they were both back home that evening and sitting with Riley in the living room. 'It looked good from the photos.'

'I came second in the first race and fifth in the egg-and-spoon,' Riley said proudly.

'She did really well,' Sally said. 'She made a lot of effort today.'

'That's great,' Theo said.

'Look, my medal!' Riley said, showing her dad.

'Well done, peanut.' He gave her a hug.

'I'm going to hang it up in my room.' She rushed past him and went up the stairs.

Theo looked over at Sally and she could see relief in his face. The same relief she'd been feeling that day.

'She seems happy,' he said.

'She does, doesn't she?'

Theo moved towards Sally and his arms circled her waist. She let herself relax.

That weekend, Theo and Elena took Riley to the local park. It was only midway through the morning, but it was already warm. They found a bench in the shade and sat down. Riley played with the other children in the sandpit, quickly making a friend, and helping the toddlers build castles.

'How are things with you, Mum?' Theo asked.

'Ticking along,' Elena said. 'Fundraising for the church hall. Bridge club. My book group. I fill the time.'

'And Dad?'

She laughed. 'Doing whatever he does in that shed of his.'

Riley passed a bucket to the little boy she was playing with and helped him fill it.

'Your brother seems keen on that friend of Sally's,' Elena said.

'Isabel. You know her name's Isabel, Mum.'

'I know,' she said. 'But I haven't been properly introduced to her yet, you see.'

'I'm sure you will be. She's great. You can take our word for that.'

'It's about time he found someone special. He's been acting like a teenager for too long.' Elena carried on looking at Riley, her gaze fixed there. 'It's growing back a little, her hair,' she said. 'It looks nicer.'

'We just thought we'd try it out for a while. She still likes it like that.'

'How is she doing at school?'

'Great,' Theo said. 'She really enjoyed sports day, and she's been learning a lot more this year.'

'Such a lovely age,' Elena said. 'Precious. It goes fast.'

Theo waited for the next question. It always came.

'You sure you won't have another one?' Elena asked, hopeful.

'Yes, I'm sure,' Theo said, trying not to let his irritation show. 'We're sure.' He must have had the same conversation with his parents fifty times. 'Riley's enough for us. We're complete. A family.' He thought of the mostly unspoken strain he and Sally had been under over the past fortnight, and felt sure again that it was the right decision. He felt relieved that they could now start to put it behind them, one less thing for them to worry about.

'But two – you and your brother, you were the best of friends, always playing together . . . '

'Or fighting. Most of the time fighting, Mum. Don't rose-tint it. Look, I know you want Riley to have what you had, what we had, I get that. But—'

'She's a wonderful girl. I just don't want her to be lonely.'

Theo laughed. 'Riley isn't lonely. She's got us, you, Dad, her other grandparents. If anything, she's spoiled for company.'

'I mean little friends. Does she have friends?'

'Yes, of course.' Theo wanted to give names, but none came immediately to mind. Riley always ran over to a group, though, in the playground. She never seemed alone.

'Does she? Such a sociable child, but she doesn't mention anyone. I asked her, but she only talked about football. The boys. She kept talking about that.'

'Yes, well, Riley loves football, you know that.'

'No girls?'

'She has friends,' Theo said, his patience fraying. 'She's seven. Does it really matter?'

'It's important. The influence,' Elena said. 'You may not have realised it, but your dad and I were always careful about who you were friends with.'

'Right, Mum. OK, I'll keep it in mind.'

Theo opted to change the subject. 'Shall we go to the café,

get some lunch? Riley's been running around for hours – she must be starving.'

'Yes,' Elena said. 'I'll go and get her.'

Elena walked over to the sandpit. Theo watched her retreating figure, in slacks, pumps and an emerald green cardigan. She perched on the wall of the sandpit and bent to talk to Riley, persuading her to come out, and helping her to collect up the buckets and plastic moulds and put them in a bag. She ruffled her granddaughter's hair gently, smiling at her. Then, with arms that were strong and loving, she helped Riley up out of the sandpit, and hugged her. Hugged her so tightly that Riley erupted into giggles. The years fell away from his mother's face. As a mother she had been firm and fair – she still was – but as a grandmother, she had blossomed into something softer. As a grandmother, he thought, she'd become beautiful.

Sally spent the day sketching out some new designs, taking advantage of the quiet and calm in the house. There was one design she kept coming back to – a pair of toddler dungarees with apples on the front pocket, one whole, one cut open. The idea had come from her own childhood – she and her mum and dad would take out a wheelbarrow late summer for the harvest, and bag up the best fruit to eat and make into crumble. She chose a bright green for the dungarees and a rich dark red for the apple skin.

The front door banged shut and Theo called out, 'Hi, Sal, we're home.'

Sally tacked up her sketches and then went downstairs, picked up Riley and gave her a hug.

'We had a good time in the park,' Elena said. 'It's a lovely day out there.'

'Great. Will you stay for some tea?' Sally said.

'I won't this time. Bridge club.'

'Of course. Another day soon,' Sally said.

Riley nodded. 'I was mostly in the sandpit. Playing with the little kids.'

'Yep,' Theo said. 'Actually, she brought most of the sandpit home with her.'

'OK. Come on,' Sally said, taking her hand. 'Let's shake you out in the bathroom and I'll put you in some clean things.'

Riley came after her.

Sally picked out some pants, tracksuit bottoms and a T-shirt from Riley's room, and they went to the bathroom together. She peeled off Riley's T-shirt and shook it out over the bath.

'Take off your trousers and pants,' Sally said.

Riley wriggled out of her trousers, but left her underwear on. 'I don't want to take off my pants,' she said.

'Come on,' Sally insisted. 'They're all sandy too.' She reached to help Riley.

'No,' Riley said, forceful now.

Sally recoiled. 'What's the matter?'

Riley shook her head.

'What is it?' Sally asked gently. 'You can tell me.'

'Grandma says I have to be friends with girls.'

'Does she?' Sally pushed her feelings of irritation to one side, but made a mental note to speak to Elena.

'Yes. But I told her. I told her I wouldn't. I told her I didn't want to. I told her I was a boy. That I'm *really* a boy,' Riley said, her voice louder and eyes red-rimmed now. 'But she wouldn't *listen*, Mum.'

She held her daughter close to her, her body wracked with sobs.

'Why is no one listening?'

'We are listening,' Sally said, into her hair. 'We are listening.'

Riley sobbed and sobbed into her shoulders, and Sally pulled her closer still to comfort her.

Theo appeared in the doorway, then, seeing them both, bent to their level, a concerned expression on his face. 'What's happened?'

'Grandma didn't listen,' Riley said to her dad through her sobs.

'To what?'

'I'm a boy, Dad,' Riley said. 'I'm a boy.'

Eventually Riley stopped crying. They'd sat there on the bathroom floor for around twenty minutes. Theo went and got a small packet of Smarties from the snack cupboard and gave them to Riley, which pulled her out of the mood.

'Do you want to come and watch *The Jungle Book* with me?' he asked her gently. 'We've got time before bedtime.'

Riley nodded and moved to take his hand, and slowly Sally let her daughter go. She felt emotionally raw. This wasn't the right way to handle things. She was sure of that. They couldn't just leave those words in the air, hanging, and do nothing, could they?

Theo looked at Sally. 'I'll put her to bed tonight,' he said. As if everything was normal. 'You go out and see Isabel, like you planned.'

'I can't . . .' Sally said, shaking her head. 'I can't go out now—'

'You can,' he said.

And she realised then that she had to.

That evening, Sally went to Isabel's flat, her mind flitting from one thought to another. She needed to talk, needed to share what was going on with someone who would understand. Someone who wasn't Theo.

'She's been saying it again,' Sally said. She felt butterfly wings tap at the walls of her stomach.

'The same thing? That she wants to be a boy?' Isabel said.

'That she *is* a boy,' Sally said, rubbing her brow. 'Today she even said it to Elena.'

'Oh God,' Isabel said. 'How did she react?'

'I get the sense she ignored it. Perhaps it didn't even register, I'm not sure. But Riley said it to Theo too. And she's desperately unhappy. She cried and cried tonight. It's heart-wrenching.'

'Come and sit down,' Isabel said, leading her to the sofa and pouring her a glass of wine. 'I guess this is more serious than I thought it was.'

'It's not going away. I can see now that it's not going away. This isn't about being a bit of a tomboy. She's distressed, Isabel. Really distressed. What's happening to her?' Sally said. 'What have we done wrong?'

'Nothing,' Isabel said. 'Of that I'm absolutely sure. You guys are great parents.'

'Then why? Why us?' Sally said, the emotion rising in her voice. 'We've always been so normal. We are normal. And now this? I don't understand it.'

Isabel put a hand on her arm. 'Riley is the child you've always loved. The same child. Let's keep that part clear.'

'I know that. I *do* know that.'

'And Theo?'

'Today, when Riley told him, he just sort of glossed over it. Brought her some sweets to cheer her up.'

'So maybe it hasn't sunk in for him yet.'

'It's more than that. It's almost like he's deaf to it – when it's all I can hear.'

'You'll find a way forward,' Isabel said calmly. 'We will.'

'Thank you,' Sally said. 'I needed to hear that. Because she's everything to me. I just want her to feel good about herself. I want her to be well.'

'It's early days, still,' Isabel said. 'Before this spring, she'd never said anything, right?'

Sally nodded.

'So let's take a breath. Give this a little space. But at the same time, perhaps you could start to research what might be going on.'

Sally knew what Isabel was implying. It was a concept that was both familiar and alien to her.

'You think she's . . . ?'

The word jarred on Sally's lips. A word she knew well, had read in the papers, heard on the radio, seen on TV. But it wasn't something she'd ever had reason to linger on, talk about. It wasn't a word in any way connected to her life.

'I don't have the answers, Sal,' Isabel said gently. 'I'm not a doctor, or any kind of expert. Just someone who cares about Riley like you do.'

Sally's lip quivered and she bit it at the side, hard, to stop herself from crying. 'Sorry. I know that. I do know that. I just . . . I just want to know what's right.'

'It could be any number of things. Riley could feel alienated because she's a different kind of girl from those in her class. That's absolutely still a possibility. Who knows, she could be doing all this for attention – for whatever reason.'

'I wonder if that's what Theo thinks,' Sally said. 'That she's playing up, being dramatic.'

'You'll work it out,' Isabel said. 'But understanding more about children who have experienced the kind of feelings you describe Riley as having, might help you to feel more in control.'

Sally tried to warm to the idea. 'I mean, I'm aware of it, obviously. I've heard of it,' she said. Her own voice sounded distant, detached.

'Have you seen any of the documentaries, looked online?'

Sally shook her head. 'No.' She felt ashamed at how little she'd done, other than hope Riley would cheer up and stop saying it. Like the way her and Theo's hearts had lifted when sports day had seemed to boost her mood. 'I think I've been burying my head in the sand, really.'

'Well, maybe it's time to bring it out. Have a look, with Theo, at some of the information that's out there.'

'Things have changed, haven't they?'

'Yes. Most young people don't bat an eyelid at this stuff. Only us. Bunch of dinosaurs that we are.' Isabel smiled kindly.

'Theo thinks listening to her could be a mistake.'

'And he might be right. But we're not talking about making a decision here, just starting to ask questions, to be informed.'

Sally put her head in her hands. 'It's all so confusing. I thought we were good parents. I thought I knew Riley.'

'You are. And you do know Riley. What you don't know – yet – is how to help her. Take a look online, with Theo if he will. Knowledge is power, right?'

Sally nodded. But deep down she wished she could go back to the time before. She wished she'd never opened this box.

When Sally got back home, Theo was still awake, sitting on the sofa, working on his laptop.

'Hi,' he said. There was weariness in his eyes. 'Just going through the accounts.'

She sat beside him. She would normally have reached for his hand, held it, but tonight his body seemed more rigid, tense, and she resisted.

'Was Riley OK tonight at bedtime?' she asked.

He put his laptop on the coffee table. 'She was fine,' he said. 'She calmed down when we watched the film. We skipped bath-time because she seemed so tired.'

'It was hard tonight, wasn't it?' Sally said.

'Yes,' Theo said. He paused, the words not coming easily. 'It was.'

'You heard her, what she said. You saw how upset she was.'

He nodded. 'I haven't seen her like that before.'

'Do you think we should talk to your mum about it?'

'I'll see if she mentions anything. If not, let's leave it for now.'

'I thought we could move past this, hoped it would disappear as quickly as it arrived. But it's not happening like that. It doesn't seem to be going away.'

'It hasn't been long, Sal. At the start of the school year she was fine. The teacher even made a point of saying how happy she was. Let's keep things in perspective.'

'I know. And I don't want to be over-anxious about this – she'd only pick up on that. But I do think we should find out a bit more about how she's feeling. Could we look online?'

Theo took a deep breath. 'I don't really see how that's going to help.'

'I don't know,' Sally said. 'But something's going on, and I want to at least feel we've looked into what it might be.'

He picked up his laptop again and opened a fresh window on Google. 'OK, if it will put your mind at rest.' They stared for a moment at the empty search bar.

'Daughter says she's a boy,' she said. She looked to Theo and he typed the words in, then pressed return.

A number of YouTube links came up. Her eyes scanned over the youthful faces, each beautiful in its own gender-blurred way. Children, teenagers. She found herself searching for clues in their features. Were they like Riley? Were they happy? Were they really who they thought they were?

Theo looked as if he would rather be anywhere else. Doing anything else.

Sally saw one video. From the title it seemed to be about parents with a child just a little older than Riley. It opened to a child in a ballet dress, twirling and twirling in their bedroom. She stopped and blew a kiss at the camera. The child's parents came on to the screen, a man and woman in their late-twenties.

‘Skye was never our little boy,’ the woman said easily. ‘As soon as she learned to walk and talk, she was letting us know who she really was.’

The dad began to talk. ‘She didn’t stop saying it. And she was starting to act out, getting frustrated at being called “he” or referred to as a boy. She made it clear we were all getting it wrong.’

‘After a while we realised it was us that had to change.’

‘Skye is who she is – and her brothers adore their sister. It was challenging at first, for all of us.’

‘All of us apart from Skye,’ the mum said.

Her partner nodded. ‘The day we told her she could be a girl, she had this huge smile on her face. And I don’t think she’s stopped smiling since.’

The clip ended with a scene of Skye playing with her two brothers in the back garden, dressed in a princess dress.

Theo clicked to close the window. ‘Maybe I’m just not ready for this. Maybe it’s too late at night. But this is a lot to take in.’

‘Sure,’ Sally said. ‘Of course. We can look another time.’

Theo put the computer away. He turned towards Sally. ‘That family isn’t us,’ he said. ‘We’re nothing like that. Their kid had been saying things since she was a toddler. That never happened with Riley. This is . . . This just feels like a blip. Something Riley probably won’t even remember in a few years’ time.’

‘But in the meantime?’ Sally asked. There was no saying how long the phase might last. ‘I feel like we have to listen to her, Theo. We owe it to her to believe her.’

‘No,’ Theo said, without hesitation. ‘We owe it to her not to confuse her. We owe it to her to get this right.’

Chapter 15

The heat had crept into their house. Riley had taken off her top in the night and thrown off the covers. Sally watched her daughter for a moment. Riley was sleeping later than usual, but Sally couldn't bring herself to wake her. She must have been tired after all the emotions of the previous night. With a new heaviness in her bones, Sally knew how that might be. Eventually, she leaned into Riley's bed and gently shook her shoulder.

'Riley,' she said. 'We need to get up and ready for school.'

On the walk to school Riley seemed subdued, and Sally needed distraction, so they played I Spy. At the classroom they were met by Riley's teacher. As Riley said goodbye and slipped inside, Sally asked if they could talk.

'I know you're already keeping an eye on Riley,' Sally said, 'but could you let me know if she's upset or feeling left out – anything like that?'

'Yes. Of course,' Ms Sanderson said. 'I'll keep a close eye on her. Don't you worry.'

'OK. Thank you.'

Sally walked back across the playground, crossing paths with Leonie.

'Sally – I was hoping I'd see you,' she said.

'Oh yes?'

'I've got an invite for Riley. Ava's birthday party.' She passed Sally a purple envelope. 'A pamper party at ours, God help me.' She smiled and wrinkled her nose. 'It's what she wanted. Insisted on. They'll be getting their hair and nails done, all of that.'

Sally's heart sank. She could just imagine that conversation with Riley.

'Ava wanted all of the girls there. I hope Riley can make it.'

'Thank you,' she said. 'When is it?'

'The second of August.'

'Oh, I'm sorry,' Sally said, relief flooding through her. 'We'll be on holiday. We're going away with my dad and stepmum, to Italy.'

'Ooh, you lucky thing. Don't worry for a minute. I understand. Always the issue when your kid has a birthday in the summer holidays.'

'Thanks for the invite, though. I hope she has a wonderful time.'

It's break time and I'm sitting on the mat. Ms Sanderson said I could. I've got a Harry Potter book. I wanted to be out in the playground, but Evie's there.

Evie talked about growing up to be like her mum and how I will look like mine. She says it's good as my mum's pretty and wears nice clothes. But when she said that I wanted to shout. I love my mum but I hate what Evie said.

But I didn't shout. I didn't want to get in trouble. I just walked away, like Dad told me to do if I don't like what someone's saying.

When Dad hugs me and his beard is prickly a bit on my face, I think maybe one day my face will be like that. With hair on it. Dark. On my arms and legs too. And my eyebrows will go all big.

I think it could happen like that, and the more I say it out loud – I'm a boy – the more real it gets. I will keep saying it until someone hears me properly, even if it hurts me in my chest. Then they'll hear me and I'll get bigger and taller, and I'll be like Dad.

Chapter 16

When Sally got home, she FaceTimed her dad.

'Hello, love,' he said, his face filling the screen. 'Nice surprise to hear from you. How are things?'

A lump came to her throat. 'Fine,' she managed at last.

'Everything OK, love?'

She nodded, not wanting to speak again in case the tears came. 'Looking forward to the holiday with you, that's all.'

'Well, so are we. Very much so. Catherine's just bought her sunhat—'

'Dad. Was there ever a point, when you were raising me, when you didn't know what to do?'

'Sal,' her dad said.

'Was there?'

He smiled. 'All the time. And after your mother died – well, you can double that amount.'

'How did you decide?'

'I listened to your mum, when she was still here. Listened to my gut. But most of all I listened to you.'

Sally nodded, welling up.

'Do you want to tell me what's going on?'

'I do. I really do. But I think we need to work it out for ourselves first.'

Theo was at the café all day, and he put thoughts of the previous night from his mind. They nudged their way back in on the journey home, though, and sat with him during his and Sally's dinner, a take-out Thai meal. They mainly made small talk about their days. Everything felt strangely hollow.

In the evening, Sally went upstairs to her study, and Theo got his iPad out and went to sit on the sofa. They'd only seen one story – one possibility of what this might be and how things could turn out. There must be hundreds of stories out there.

He flicked over some search results, settling on one of a family in North America.

> Eliot was five when he started to say things. He told us for six months that he was a girl.
>
> He'd chosen a name he wanted, Jasmine, after the Disney princess. He came to me every day and said it. The moment he woke up, there he'd be, holding up one of his sister's dressing-up princess outfits that he'd want to wear that day to school. He pleaded with us. We couldn't ignore him. We were both upset by it.
>
> We let Jasmine wear what she wanted at home, and with family. But we didn't want to rush into anything. We chose to draw the line at her attending the school as Jasmine, or wearing girls' clothes outside the house, or at school. We were worried about setting it all in stone, and also concerned that Jasmine might get picked on.
>
> The following year, on his sixth birthday, he announced he was Eliot again.

Theo felt a wave of hope sweep over him. Maybe if they gave Riley some space to explore it, she would grow out of it. The novelty would wear off.

> There are still a lot of unknowns, but so far he seems happy and content. Eliot might start saying the same thing again. He might not. He might grow up to be gay. We're open to all of those things. Whatever happens, we love him, and we're here for him.

Theo's heart told him that the same was true for Riley – this was a phase that would pass. At seven, what did she really know about gender, aside from the stereotypes? In time she'd see she could be everything she was, as a girl, and as a woman. He and Sally could help her to see that.

Upstairs, in her study, Sally got her phone out and scrolled through her emails. After a mealtime of sitting with Theo, skirting around what was happening to Riley, she needed to talk to someone. She found Isabel's message, with a link attached.

> Hey, Sal.
>
> I found this online. There's a forum for parents of kids with gender-identity issues. Might be worth a look?
>
> P.S. I am also here for you. And I have gin.

Sally clicked on the link to the parenting forum.

Teenage daughter says she's transgender.

Eight-year-old son dressing as a girl.

She clicked and read through the posts. Concerned mums and dads just like her and Theo. People seeking advice. Perhaps someone would have been where they were now. Perhaps someone out there could offer her some advice.

Her hands trembling, she set up a profile and posted her own message.

Hi. I'm new to all this.

I'm in shock, she thought. She typed again:

My 7-year-old says she's a boy. I don't even know where to start. I love her and I want to support her.

I feel heartbroken, she thought. I feel lost. I feel terrified – for her, for me, for us.

She couldn't say that, though, could she?

Any advice welcome.

She pressed 'post' and put her phone down on the desk. She got up from her chair and looked out of the study window. Outside, in the fading light, a fat wood pigeon balanced on the fence post. She watched as another flew down to join it. Her husband, her partner in everything, was sitting downstairs, and here she was reaching out to total strangers on the internet. It had come to this.

She sat back down, picked up her phone again and refreshed the page. A reply had come through.

Marianne. Her profile picture was a silhouette, like Sally's.

I've been there, she wrote. Still there. My seven-year-old is now at school as a boy. It's not easy – but he's happy. And that's what matters. That's what we keep focused on.

Another post came on the thread.

Daddancing76. A profile picture this time, of a man with dark hair.

Hi there. You've come to the right place. I joined this forum four years ago, when my daughter – then Sean, now Siobhan – came out to me. She's fourteen now. Two years ago she was diagnosed with gender dysphoria, and began taking puberty blockers. Pressing pause on it all for now.

Sally breathed in. What a thing to have to deal with, to support your child through. She read on.

It's terrifying, isn't it? At first. Those days when your world is turned upside down.

Yes, Sally thought. Tears sprung to her eyes. That was the word. The one it had seemed disloyal to even think.

Who am I kidding? Daddancing76 wrote. I still feel scared every single day. But things get better. It gets easier. Don't get me wrong, the worry doesn't go – it just changes. You worry about different things. Because you want to get it right.

Maybe this isn't helping.

It is, Sally thought.

You don't know how much.

It wasn't just her.

Chapter 17

Theo wrote Gabi a list of the things that would need doing while they were away on holiday.

She looked over his shoulder. 'You know I know all of this already, right?' she said.

'Not everything,' Theo said.

'I'll be fine. I can run this place for a week by myself. No problem. You guys go, enjoy your holiday. Relax.'

Relax. It was hard to imagine. Would it all go away, out in Italy? Would everything be better? Would Riley calm right down?

'This place will be in safe hands.'

'OK, OK,' Theo said. 'I'll be on email out there, you can FaceTime me—'

'Stop, Theo,' Gabi said, laughing. 'Let me do this. Let me give you a proper holiday. It's the least I can do.'

Next week is our holiday. That's only seven days left to wait. It's on the calendar. I've got my suitcase ready – it's hard and plastic and has wheels. I put my lion in there already, so I don't forget it, and the Harry Potter book I'm reading.

Dad says I can swim whenever I want to out there. At school, whenever I feel angry, or sad, I think of that.

Chapter 18

It was Riley's last week at school before the summer holidays. During the day, Sally got some clothes out of her wardrobe and started to pack for Italy. Summer dresses, sandals, cardigans, a swimsuit. She pictured herself by the pool, sitting with Theo and watching Riley in there, swimming. Riley would love the swimming.

She went through to Riley's room and started to pack T-shirts and shorts. She took out a blue one-piece swimsuit and held it up. She knew Riley wouldn't want to wear it. Knew it would make her feel upset.

A thought crossed Sally's mind. The holiday. A bubble of their own. A safe place.

Away from judgement. A place Riley could be more free.

Her heart rate picked up. This could work, she thought. She went through to the kitchen and got out her iPad. She typed a short post on the parenting forum.

Looking for advice. Has anyone let their child experiment with gender on holiday? How did it go?

After an hour, a reply came back, from the poster she'd spoken with the day before – Daddancing76.

> Yes. We did this. Caravan trip to Devon. Quiet little place by the beach, one we've gone to every year since Siobhan was small. It had been months of her saying she wanted to be a girl, and we didn't know what to do about it. That year, we just said, let's see what happens. I bought her some of the clothes she said she wanted and she dressed how she liked.
>
> I remember we went out to the corner shop, and the owner there said to me – I remember this so clearly – 'I didn't know you had a daughter.' And I couldn't believe it. I wanted to laugh. I wanted to say, 'Neither did I.' But then I saw Siobhan's face, and how proud she was – being seen that way for the first time. And I couldn't take that from her. I just smiled, bought the ice lollies, and that was that. From that point onwards I started to see things the way the man in the newsagent did.

Sally smiled to herself. He'd made the impossible seem possible.

That evening, Sally and Theo had dinner together. The holiday had been on Sally's mind all day – the chance to see how it might be to give Riley the freedom she was asking for, for a short while.

'Gabi's told me I can't check in on the café while we're away,' Theo said, with a trace of frustration. 'She's practically banned me.'

Sally smiled, silently thankful for Gabi's actions. 'She knows what's right for you, that's why. You haven't let go of that place for a day since you started it up. It'll do you good to have a break.'

'But what if—' he began.

'You're getting separation anxiety already?' Sally said.

'Maybe . . . a bit.'

'All the more reason to take a proper holiday.'

'I think she's doing it because she feels guilty about leaving.'

'Well, let her,' Sally said. 'It's her choice. And if it allows you to switch off properly and recharge, then that's all to the good.'

'I won't call her. But I'm not switching my phone off,' Theo said.

'OK, OK,' Sally said, smiling. 'Let's see how you feel when you're out there.'

She should mention it now, she told herself. She felt certain he would resist the idea, but she had to at least try.

'Listen, I'm glad you raised the holiday . . . because I've had an idea about it.'

He raised an eyebrow, curious. 'You have? What kind of an idea?'

'You know how Riley's been lately?'

'Ye-ess.' He lingered on the syllable, as if one wasn't enough.

'Maybe we could give her some more freedom on holiday. Let her feel in control.'

'What kind of freedom?'

'I thought maybe we could let her try it out – be a boy for a week. If that's what she wants, obviously.'

'Be a boy?' Theo said, looking confused.

'Wear what she likes. It wouldn't be such a big change. And she'd just be with us and her grandparents, people who love her.'

She could see Theo thinking it over. He hadn't said no.

'OK,' he said.

'OK?' Sally said. 'That was easier than I thought.'

Theo shrugged. 'I still think we need to be firm, in the long-term. But we're only talking about a week. Just us, right?'

Sally nodded. 'Just us. And my dad and Catherine – so we'll need to check they're on board.'

'If Riley wants this, let's do it.'

'Great,' Sally said. They had a plan. Hope. This holiday might be the start of something – the start of Riley feeling stronger again.

Theo went upstairs to the bathroom. It felt weird, what he'd just agreed to, and he wavered for a minute. Was it a mistake?

He didn't feel comfortable with the thought of seeing Riley that way, dressed as something she wasn't. Would she act differently too?

But it had to be worth a shot. If they gave Riley a chance to experiment, in private, the novelty would soon wear off. He was sure of that. And it would happen without anyone having to know about what was going on. They'd be helping her move through this phase, supporting her to be the girl she really was. It might feel awkward to him now, but it would be worth it, in the long run. If they did this, they would all be able to get back to normal more quickly.

The next day, Sally called up her dad and Catherine on Skype so that they could all speak to each other at the same time.

'Hello, love,' Jules said. His warm smile made her feel as if they were really in the same room together, and she realised how much she was looking forward to spending some proper time with him. So much had gone unsaid when they last talked.

'Was there something you wanted to talk about?' Catherine said. 'Because we've got a lot of packing to do.' Catherine brought a pair of sparkly flip-flops and a huge straw hat into the screen and plonked the hat on top of her head.

'There is something, actually,' Sally said. She had rehearsed this conversation in her mind but now the words she needed were threatening to desert her.

'Riley's been saying a few things lately. About wanting to . . . ' It was difficult to say it. *Be a boy.*

'You know she's always been a bit of a tomboy,' Sally continued. 'Well, recently she's been upset about certain things. Not fitting in with the other kids at school.'

'Sorry to hear that,' Catherine said.

'Obviously we want her to feel more confident again. And she's been talking about being more comfortable in boys' clothes.' Sally paused, feeling a bit nervous about how her dad and Catherine might react. 'So we thought it might help to let her have some freedom to do that on holiday. Wear trunks in the pool, that kind of thing.'

'Makes sense,' Jules said.

'She might say things,' Sally said. 'About . . . ' There was no way of skirting around it. 'Being a boy.'

'Playing pretend?' said Catherine.

'Yes,' Sally said, hesitantly. 'Something like that.' It didn't fit. But it would do for now.

'We know how Riley is,' Jules said. 'Never boring. Anyway, as long as you're all still coming, that's all we care about. Right, Cath?'

Catherine nodded. 'It'll take more than that to faze us, you know. Can I get back to my packing, now? I've got an awful lot of shoes to cram in.'

Sally went to collect Riley from school that afternoon, feeling relieved about how the conversation with her dad and Catherine had gone. It felt good to know that they were onside. She'd texted Theo at work to let him know that they were fine with the decision.

Sally made her way over to the classroom. It was Riley's last day of Year Two, her last day with Ms Sanderson. More change.

'Have a great holiday,' Leonie's mum called out, as she and Ava left. Beth waved goodbye.

Sally noticed Faye, Euan's mum, beside her. She wiped a tear from her cheek. 'Is it just me feeling emotional?' Faye said. 'I can't believe this year's gone so fast. Euan went in there a little boy still, and now look. He's enormous.'

'It's not just you,' Sally said, passing Faye a tissue. 'You want them to grow up, but not this fast.'

If only it were just that, Sally thought to herself. If only it were just Riley moving up to Year Three that she was thinking about. She'd give anything to go back to only having those concerns.

Riley dashed out of the classroom, carrying a sugar-paper folder of artwork. 'It's the holidays!' She turned to Euan and hugged him goodbye. 'Have a good summer.'

Faye smiled at Sally. 'See you in September,' she said.

Sally left school carrying the folder, Riley's hand in hers. Now was the time.

'Riley, there's something me and your dad wanted to ask you. About the holiday.'

Up in my room, I rip open the plastic wrapping and take out the swimming trunks. Mum and I went shopping after school, to get things for the holiday. They didn't have Spiderman pants in the shop, so we got these, with Minions on. I drop the packet and get to my feet, pull my shorts right down and off over my bare feet. I take off the stupid knickers, white and purple, and throw them on the floor.

I try not to look past my T-shirt at where I'm not right, and pull on my new green swimming trunks. They fit just right. I run into the bathroom, where there's a mirror that goes right to the floor. I look at me in my green trunks – boy trunks – and here I am.

This is me.

Chapter 19

Sally, Theo and Riley flew into Pisa airport, Italy greeting them with an engulfing heat and a buzz of activity. Sally relished the feeling of the sun on her shoulders and the lively noise all around them. They picked up their rental car and drove out past Siena and into the Italian countryside, the city giving way to rolling Tuscan hills. She would usually, at this point in a holiday, be starting to relax – the packing and most of the travel behind them, nothing but long, peaceful days ahead. But even as she looked out at the scenery, as visually intoxicating as nature could get, her chest felt tight. She had no way of knowing how the next week would go.

In the back seat, Riley was watching programmes on her iPad, the tinny soundtrack sounding out inside the car. Sally glanced at Theo, his gaze trained on the road ahead, strong hands on the wheel, his olive-toned forearms bare. Was he feeling like she was, anticipating the week ahead with hope, but also with a knot in his stomach that wouldn't shift? He caught her looking and turned for a second, giving her a warm smile. If he was nervous too, it didn't show.

When Sally and Theo had told Riley that she could be who she wanted on holiday, her eyes had brightened and her skin had glowed.

'I can be a boy?' she'd said.

Sally had nodded. 'You can wear whatever you want.'

The past week, Riley's excitement had built up. It had gone far beyond her usual pre-holiday buzz of chatter about the plane and the swimming pool. This time it was almost all about the suitcase of clothes she was taking. Riley had packed it full of shorts, caps, T-shirts and swimming trunks from the boys' sections of the high-street shops. Sally had felt uncomfortable when the shop assistants looked a bit longer than usual at Riley as they bagged up the clothes. But she told herself not to care.

The winding roads lulled Sally to sleep, and when she awoke it was to the sound of gravel crunching under the tyres. She saw that they had arrived at the villa.

'We're here!' Riley called out. 'Unlock the door! I want to get out.'

Theo opened the door and she darted out of the car towards the villa. Sally got to her feet and stretched out her limbs, cramped from the journey. Out of the car's artificial coolness, the air was warm and humid, and the sound of cicadas filled the air. Sally smiled as she took in her surroundings.

'Wow,' she said, looking at the villa with its grand front door and elegant shuttered windows. It was stunning.

'This is impressive,' Theo said. 'Your dad and Catherine didn't mention it would be like this.'

'They take their holidays seriously, I guess we knew that much,' Sally said.

A message buzzed through on Sally's phone, and she checked it. Catherine.

Just arrived at Pisa. See you in a couple of hours! Owner said she'd leave the keys under the flowerpot by the door. Cx

'They've just arrived at the airport,' Sally told Theo, as he unloaded their luggage from the back of the car.

'I want to see the pool,' Riley called out.

Sally located the keys and let them all in. They walked into the cool, airy hallway and through to the bright kitchen. She opened up the back doors so that Riley could see the garden.

'The pool is . . . *amazing*,' she exclaimed. Her enthusiasm came through in every syllable. She turned around, her cheeks flushed with excitement. 'I can't wait to go swimming.'

Sally and Riley went upstairs to look in all the bedrooms, and Riley tested out the beds by bouncing on them. Sally kept the master for Jules and Catherine, took a double for her and Theo, and then they found Riley's room, a single with a view of the swimming pool. Riley put down her suitcase and rifled through it quickly to find her swimming things and towel. She ran downstairs.

'Slowly!' Sally called out. The tiles looked so slippery and hard.

Riley paid her no attention. Downstairs she got changed swiftly and went out.

Theo was looking out through the open kitchen door, watching as Riley steadied herself on the side at the deep end, preparing to take a dive. Sally stood beside him, her arm loose around his waist, his skin warm through his T-shirt.

'You think she's safe out there on her own?' Sally said.

'She's a strong swimmer,' Theo said.

Unaware of her parents watching, Riley curved her slim arms over her head. Sally felt a swell of pride at the precision of her daughter's movements. Riley's heels lifted and she rose up, then dived beneath the surface, her body slipping into the water and disappearing entirely for a moment. She re-emerged and began to swim.

'She *is* good,' Sally said.

'She's great,' Theo said.

His attention seemed to be on more than just her movement though, his gaze fixed on the swimming trunks she was wearing. Riley and Sally had chosen them together, a simple green pair.

'Is it the trunks?' Sally said.

'Yes, I guess so,' Theo said. He seemed awkward, uncomfortable. 'It just looks strange to me.'

'I get that. For what it's worth, it does to me too. But this is the deal, Theo. This is the promise we made to her. She wears exactly what she likes – and that includes in the pool.'

Theo nodded. 'I suppose it's me who has to get used to it.'

Riley's voice interrupted their conversation. 'They're here!' she called out from the pool. 'Granddad and Catherine are here!'

Sally turned to see her dad and stepmother coming up to the villa with their bags. Theo helped Riley out of the pool and dried her off with a towel she wrapped around herself.

'Riley!' Jules said, putting their things down and going to hug his granddaughter. Catherine joined them and hugged Riley too.

'Your mum said we were going to love this short hair,' Catherine said, smiling. 'And she was right.'

Jules ruffled it. 'Dries quicker after a swim too, I bet.'

'Welcome,' Theo said, hugging them both. 'Can I get you guys a drink? Water, tea?'

Catherine looked at her watch. 'Something stronger, I reckon. Don't you?'

The sun set and dusk settled over the villa. Sally, Theo, Riley, Jules and Catherine sat at a table by the pool, eating ciabatta, cured meats and cheeses, the adults drinking wine. After dinner, Riley and Jules played Uno at the other end of the table, Riley in her pyjamas.

Drinking wine with Catherine, Sally felt herself begin to relax. It all felt easier than she'd expected. Nothing much had changed – not really. Other than Riley's smile, which was irrepressible.

Theo checked his phone and caught Sally's eye. 'I don't like to break up the party, but it's nearly ten,' he said.

'Riley, it's late,' Sally said firmly. 'It's bedtime.'

'Can Granddad do my story tonight?'

Sally looked at her dad. 'That OK with you?'

'Of course,' he said. 'That would be a pleasure.'

The two of them went upstairs together.

Catherine poured Sally and Theo more wine. 'As if you had to ask him,' she said, smiling. 'He adores doing bedtime.'

'Riley loves it when he puts her to bed,' Sally said. 'He always was a good storyteller.'

'I'll have to get him to tell me more in future,' Catherine said.

Sally looked at her stepmother and felt grateful for the way she'd made everything with Riley feel so easy.

'Thank you, Cath,' Sally said, 'for being so supportive about all of this.'

'Oh, it's nothing really, is it?' Catherine said. 'Riley's still the same Riley.'

Sally glanced over at Theo. He seemed distant tonight, distracted.

'Yep. Riley is definitely still Riley,' she said.

They'd decided to spend the next day at the villa. Sally sat with her dad and Catherine in the shade of a parasol, half-reading a paperback. Theo got in the pool with Riley and they darted down into the morning-cool water and back up again, skin slick. Riley was laughing.

Theo was starting to see it too, she thought to herself, how happy Riley could be. He had to understand it now.

The following morning, Sally and Theo were lying in bed. Sun filtered in through the blinds, landing softly across the sheets. Sally lay there, appreciating the moment of quiet. There was something in the quality of light, in the peace of the morning, which reminded her of her honeymoon with Theo in Santorini. At times she'd felt nostalgic about the romance, other times – when Riley was making them both laugh – she thought how much happier they were now. They'd thought their lives were full then, knowing nothing yet of how full they would one day be. But as they filled, it squeezed the time to nurture what they had, just the two of them. She looked at him now, fast asleep, and readied herself to curl in towards him.

There was a knock at the door.

'Mum? Dad?'

Sally brought her dressing gown around her and got up to open their door. Riley was standing in shorts, barefoot, in the hallway.

'Hey, love,' Sally said.

Riley's hair, ruffled with sleep, looked softer this morning. Sally was starting to warm to the cut, see how it worked with Riley's features, enhancing her eyes.

'Catherine says you should go out today. She and Granddad want to teach me to play tennis.'

'You're sure about that?' Sally said.

'Yep,' Riley said.

She turned to walk away and Sally called out, 'Not so fast.' She took another look at her daughter, standing there in just shorts, her chest bare, shoulders slight. She looked so vulnerable. Sally ducked back into the room and returned with a bottle of factor 50. 'If you're going out like that, let me put some of this on you.'

'Yeugh,' Riley squealed as Sally squirted the suncream on to her hands and warmed it slightly before applying it. 'It's slimy.'

Sally laughed. 'You need it. Your skin is light, like mine. We only have to look at the sun and we'll burn.'

Riley jutted out her chin and closed her eyes, reluctantly readying herself for the suncream. Sally applied the lotion to Riley's face, smoothing it over her freckled skin and nose. She paused. So sweet, this little nose, she thought.

'Tell Granddad to put some more on your shoulders and face later.'

'All right,' Riley said, then skipped away.

Sally watched her go. Her girl, like a boy. You could barely tell which she was from behind. Here, in their holiday bubble, it didn't matter to her as much as she'd thought it would. Riley was their child. She hadn't changed.

Her daughter was already halfway down the stone stairs when Sally remembered something. 'Your sunhat, Riley,' she said. 'Don't forget your cap.'

'OK, Mum,' she called back.

The same things mattered now as last year, before she'd had any inkling that her daughter wasn't at ease in her body. Riley's skin was the same skin – vulnerable to UVA and UVB. Their responsibility to protect. To keep safe. To keep healthy. It was the same with Riley's mind – she wanted to keep it every bit as safe and healthy as the skin on that nose. That was her and Theo's job, every single day.

Sally roused Theo gently from sleep with hot buttered toast and tea, and the news that they would have the day to themselves. He propped himself up on pillows and they sat there for a while together, drinking tea and talking about what they might do. Sally got out her guidebook and they looked at the pictures and read through restaurant reviews together.

Theo drove, taking the slip road out on to the motorway in the direction of Siena, and Sally flicked through her phone for the holiday playlist she'd compiled. 'Valerie' came on, and Theo smiled.

'You remember?'

She nodded. 'Of course I do. One of the best nights of my life.'

He'd waited two days after taking her number before calling. Sally had started to wonder if she'd made a mistake in dropping her defences, whether she had been reckless with her heart for the second time in a year. But then he'd called and invited her out. They'd gone for dinner on the South Bank, at a restaurant overlooking the Thames. After a couple of drinks, Sally told him about her break up, two months earlier, and then apologised, sure that she'd said too much. He told her she'd have to do far more than that to put him off.

They'd gone out for drinks afterwards, at a Mexican bar a short walk down the river. They were on him, he said. Sally had protested. He'd insisted. Then after a couple of shots, they forgot completely whose card was behind the bar. She and Theo had laughed until she was crying, and she'd wondered, in the glow of the moment, whether they might carry on making each other laugh, on other days, and other nights like this one. And then the song – 'Valerie' – had come on and she'd dragged him from his bar stool on to the dance floor, and he'd swung her around and then they'd kissed.

'I remember dancing back along the South Bank with you that night,' she said.

'You were brilliant. I got all caught up in you then.'

'Ha,' said Sally. 'Your memory is kind. I was all over the place.'

'You were crazily beautiful,' he said. 'And you made me laugh. I thought you were the full package, and I only knew the half of you then.'

She looked at him and he glanced away from the road to meet her eyes and smiled. His hair was greying at the temples now. She recalled how his strong arms had caught her that night, bringing her in towards him. This is where I'm meant to be, she'd thought. She thought it again now. It didn't matter where they were – Theo was her home.

An hour later, the two of them arrived in Siena, parked and walked into the town, taking in the new sights and sounds together.

Sally's hand found her husband's and held it. 'Today, just for the day,' she said, 'let's just be us.'

'No parent stuff?' he said.

'None.'

They both knew what it meant. No trying to work out if they were doing the right thing, no analysis of what was happening with Riley.

The sun warmed Sally's shoulders. Around them, the Italian streets were alive with locals chatting in doorways and calling out to one another from cars and mopeds.

'Do you remember that Vespa you had when we met?' Theo said. 'That was pretty cool.'

'I loved that thing. Right up until the day it gave up on me on the road down to Brighton.'

'You ever tempted to get one again?' Theo asked, tilting his head towards a Vespa that was careering around a sharp corner. 'Maybe you should.'

'When they make them with add-on child seats, perhaps.'

'Hey, bit close, that one. No parenting chat, remember?'

'You're right,' she said, putting her hand over her mouth. 'We're young and free today. Yes, of course I'll get another Vespa again, one day.'

'Fancy a coffee?' he said, pointing at a pavement café.

They sat there for a while in silence, people-watching. Sally couldn't remember the last time they'd been still, not distracted by Riley, house renovations, or their endless to-do list.

'It's good to slow down,' Theo said. 'Being here, with you. Drinking coffee someone else has made.'

'You're managing not to think about the café too much?' she asked.

He smiled. 'I'm trying. But it's kind of tricky when there's so much hanging in the balance right now.'

Sally sensed that he was trying to fix things himself, come back to her when he had a solution.

'You know you can always talk to me about it, don't you? You don't have to be alone in the decisions about the business.'

'I know,' he said. He paused, glancing down at his coffee. 'Actually, there is one thing I wanted to get your opinion on.'

'Yes?' It felt good, being let in.

'I've spoken to a few people about investing in the café, but no one so far seems even close to being right.'

'So we keep looking?' Sally asked.

'Actually – and this might be a mad idea – I was thinking of asking my parents to invest. I mean, I feel kind of bad about it – they've saved for so long for their retirement.'

'I don't think it sounds mad at all,' she said. 'You never know until you ask.'

'OK. Maybe I will. When we get back.'

'You seem hesitant.'

'A bit of pride getting in the way, I guess.'

'There's no weakness in it,' Sally said. 'You'd be giving them a chance to be part of a family business. See it that way.'

He smiled.

'And if they don't go for it, we'll work it out, one way or another,' Sally said. She reached out and took his hand.

'Thanks, Sal.'

'I've missed this,' she said. 'Just being with you.'

'Me too,' he said. 'Because whatever happens – with the café, with our family – we're in this together. We'll make it work.'

Sunshine. Tennis balls. Pizza. Granddad. Catherine. Hugs.

Italy is a good place. Italy is where I want to stay for ever and ever.

Chapter 20

That afternoon, Sally and Theo walked the cobbled streets of Siena eating gelato – hazelnut and chocolate – and talking about the first years they'd spent together, before becoming parents was an idea in their minds. They went to an art museum, had lunch in a restaurant in a small square, and let their spirits be lifted. Sally relished the feeling that the school gates and the café were a world away.

When they got back to the villa in the late afternoon, they found Riley and Jules sitting at the table, playing a game of dominos. Catherine was asleep in a sun lounger, a Maeve Binchy paperback by her side. Riley leaped up to greet them with a hug.

'Good day out?' Jules asked.

Sally glanced at Theo and a look passed between them. Sally felt content, happy, put back together. 'Pretty good, yes,' she said.

'It's a beautiful place,' Theo said. 'There's so much to see. Maybe you and Catherine could go tomorrow?'

'Perhaps we will,' Jules said. 'Though today will be hard to top.'

'How was it?' Sally asked Riley.

'Brilliant,' Riley said. 'We're playing dominoes, look. We

played tennis too. Granddad's taught me all of this stuff.' Her cheeks were pink with enthusiasm.

'Riley's been wonderful company, as always.' Jules smiled. 'He's taken to playing tennis quite naturally.'

Sally's breath caught. The earth shifted on its axis. Their child blurred.

'Is that right?' Theo said. His voice was strained. He had heard it too.

'You really should see about some tennis lessons,' Jules said, relaxed and appearing not to notice the impact of what he'd said. 'You've got quite a talent on your hands.'

Sally walked upstairs to find Theo. He'd gone up to their bedroom just after the conversation with her dad. She neared the room with a feeling of trepidation. If the 'he' her father had said out loud had made her feel uneasy, she knew that the impact on Theo would be even more intense.

She opened the door to find Theo sitting on their bed, reading something on his iPad. He kept his eyes on it even as she came into the room.

She went to sit beside him. 'Put that down for a minute.'

Silently, he put the tablet on the bedside table.

'You heard it too, right?'

He nodded. 'It felt weird. Really weird.'

'I don't think Dad even realised he'd said it,' Sally said.

'I don't know if that's better or worse,' Theo said. 'Him actively trying to talk about Riley as a boy, or him just starting to see her in that way. Either way, it doesn't sit right with me.'

Sally took Theo's hand in hers. She understood how he felt. Hearing the pronoun had thrown both of them.

'Dad's just trying to support Riley. He's trying to support us. I'm sure he wouldn't have said it if he thought it would upset you.'

Theo rubbed his brow. 'We didn't set the rules clearly here, did we? We didn't spell out what was OK, what we were allowing, and what not. I guess for your dad, referring to Riley as "he" is a natural progression. But it isn't for me.'

'OK,' she said.

'I'm confused by all this, Sal. I mean, once it's been said in front of Riley, when does this stop? How can it be unsaid?'

He was right. Each step they took now seemed more like a vow that would become harder to break. 'I'll tell him not to say it.'

'It's not just that,' Theo said. 'It's not just the words. Maybe it's this whole thing.'

Sally saw then what he'd been keeping in.

'This isn't playing pretend any more. Not now. When people start talking to her as if she is a boy, then maybe that will start to reinforce the thoughts she's having.'

'But if it makes her more comfortable, is that such a bad thing?'

'It is if we're creating it. Making it more real. Who's to say what's her and what's us?'

She saw the fear in his eyes and wanted to reassure him. 'I don't think this is something we can create,' Sally said. 'I really don't think that's how it works. Are you saying you want us to stop this?'

'I don't know,' Theo said.

'I think we have to give this week a chance. See how things go. I don't see that we can back out now.'

Sally went to read in bed, while Theo went outside, sitting on a chair by the swimming pool under the star-filled night sky. He and Sally had done their best to smooth things over, but the conversation had left him feeling raw. He had gone along with one plan, and now that seemed to be evolving into something that was much more.

He took out his mobile and called Gabi. She picked up after a couple of rings.

'Theo,' she said. 'I told you not to call me.'

'I know, I know . . . '

'Everything's under control,' Gabi said. 'The café's fine. Life is carrying on without you.'

'Good. That's good.' He wished then that the business was the only thing on his mind.

'There's nothing for you to worry about, I promise.'

'Actually, Gabi,' he said, 'that's not why I'm calling.'

'It isn't?'

He didn't want to talk about Riley. The way reality was blurring. But at the same time, he knew he had to. She would understand how he felt – she would get it.

'I just wanted to talk.'

The next morning, Jules and Riley made breakfast together and laid the table on the terrace for all of the family, putting out plates of freshly cut melon and raspberries, and trays of pastries from the local shop.

'Looks delicious,' Sally said.

She and Theo sat down. There was a new tension in the atmosphere, and she wondered if the others could sense it. She and Theo had slept restlessly in the heat, and thoughts had whirred in her mind. He. Him. Riley. Her son. Her boy.

She had done her best to make Theo feel better about what they were doing, but the truth was the words jarred for her too. Riley was still her daughter. Maybe this was all happening too fast. She'd speak to her dad later, when it was quiet, and tell him how Theo felt.

She was relieved when Catherine spoke and interrupted her thoughts.

'Did you know there's a horse ranch nearby? They do riding lessons. I saw a sign on the drive up. How about we go there today, Riley, see if they can fit us in?'

'Cool,' Riley said.

'Do you think Riley's old enough?' Sally asked.

'Sure she is,' Theo said. 'I was horse riding at her age. She'll be fine.'

'I'll be fine, Mum,' Riley echoed back.

Sally had a flashback of the rides she and her mum had gone on when she was a teenager, and her mum had just been diagnosed. Along the beach, just the two of them, their favourite horses from the local stable, the sand, the sea, the wind. Her mum had sworn to use every moment that she had to enjoy life with Sally.

'OK, why don't we all go?' Sally said. 'I haven't been horse riding for years.'

'Let's do it,' Jules said.

They drove down to the stables and booked in for the day. Riley chose a small white horse that the owner assured them would be gentle. Sally chose a chestnut mare. They got their helmets and saddled up.

'We could gallop through those hills.' Theo pointed out at the Tuscan landscape, lush and green. 'Wild and fast and free. What do you think, Riley?'

'Yes!' she said.

Sally's heart caught. 'Theo!'

Theo smiled. 'I'm just winding your mum up. We'll do that one day. But today, I think let's go for a few circuits of this farm, don't you?'

'Yes,' Sally said, relieved. 'That sounds better. Much better.'

They spent the morning riding. Sally and her dad watched on as Riley did one last walk around the farm on her horse.

'Your mum would have enjoyed watching this,' Jules said.

Sally nodded, and took her father's hand. She wished that her mother could see Riley, could know her. Could see Sally herself, as a mother. Could support her. There were moments, those long, lonely nights rocking her newborn, those days when toddler Riley would tantrum in the supermarket, and – well, there had been more recently – when she longed to be able to call her mum, sit with her, hug her, cry. Have her mum give her some words of advice about how to navigate this territory that all felt so new.

'I miss her so much sometimes, Dad,' Sally said.

'I know, love. Me too.' His eyes were fixed on Riley. 'But she isn't gone,' Jules said. 'She's still here.'

The last days of the holiday passed in a haze of sunshine and heat. After she'd spoken to her dad about calling Riley 'he', the topic hadn't come up again. Sally and Theo had both actively tried to stay in the moment, not talking about Riley's gender, but instead making the most of the time they had out there together. Sally felt it still, a certain tension around what was unsaid, but that was to be expected, she thought. She'd never expected this to be entirely easy.

On their last evening at the villa, Riley and Jules swam together, racing across the width of the pool, until they were both breathless. Riley came out, shivering and laughing, and Catherine bundled her up in a towel and rubbed her dry.

'Will you read me my stories tonight, Catherine?' Riley asked.

Sally watched Catherine with Riley. She was so caring, so natural – you'd never sense that there wasn't a blood bond between them.

'That would be my pleasure,' Catherine said. 'Jules – are you OK to get dinner ready?'

'Yes, it's nearly all done,' Jules said. 'I'll get the rest sorted now.'

'Anything we can do?' Theo asked.

'Relax. Look after my daughter. Oh' – he went inside and got a bottle of wine from the fridge – 'and open this.'

Theo took the bottle and poured out two glasses. 'Here's

to our last night,' he said, raising his glass and chinking it with Sally's.

They looked out together over the Tuscan hills.

'It's been a good holiday, hasn't it?' Sally said.

'Yes,' Theo said. His reply came out flat.

It was there again, impossible to ignore now – the tension.

'You're looking forward to getting back, aren't you?'

'In a way,' he admitted. 'I mean, it's been lovely out here. But I also want things to be back to normal again.'

'Of course,' Sally said.

She thought of Riley. How happy she'd been all holiday. A happiness they would now have to undo.

Chapter 21

Back at home, Riley cast down her bag in the hallway and skipped up the stairs to her bedroom. 'I want to see if everything's still the same,' she called back.

Sally and Theo went through to the kitchen and made some tea.

'I remember that feeling,' Sally said. 'Coming back from holidays. Wanting to see all my cuddly toys again. Everything in my room seeming new, just from being away from it for a week.'

'I remember that too,' Theo said. 'We'd go away to Crete – it was always Crete, as you know, with all the family we have there. And we'd come home, and after all the beaches and the sea, all I'd want was to pick up my Nintendo Gameboy and lie on my bed and play Super Mario Brothers.' He smiled. 'That makes me sound old, right?'

'Only as old as me,' Sally said. 'Though I was more of a Tetris fan.'

They drank their tea in companionable silence for a moment. Looking at Theo, with his tanned skin and white T-shirt, it was easy for Sally to imagine that the two of them were still in Italy. But, she reminded herself, they weren't – the holiday was over, and so was this chapter of their lives.

'Do you think we need to remind Riley?' Theo said. 'About how things are now?'

Sally didn't want to rush. She wanted to hold on to how things were – even if it was just a bubble they'd been living in – for a few moments longer.

'I'll go up and have a word in a minute.'

Theo's relaxed expression had gone. 'We were clear, right?' he asked, as if convincing himself. 'We told her this was just for the holiday.'

'Yes, that's what we told her,' Sally said. But that had been a week ago – before they'd seen what the change could do for their child, before the light came back into Riley's eyes. She couldn't face the thought of undoing it all.

'We have to let her know that things are different now,' Theo said, his voice taking on a more assertive tone. 'We're home. She's a girl.'

'Yes,' Sally said hesitantly.

Her promise to Theo had been real – as real as the one she'd made to Riley before the holiday. She couldn't break it. But something inside her had shifted, and keeping that promise to him was far harder than she'd imagined it would be.

'You don't seem sure,' Theo said, strain showing in his eyes.

'I am . . . it's just . . . ' Sally searched for the words to attach to her doubt, but none would fit.

'This is important, Sally. We don't want her getting confused. Possibly even being bullied,' Theo said. 'And that's what could happen if we drag this out.'

Sally pushed down her doubts. She owed it to Theo to stick to their agreement. 'You're right. I'll talk to her.'

Half an hour later, Sally went upstairs. She found Riley lying on her bed, cuddling her toy lion. She was staring up at the ceiling with a smile on her face.

Sally sat beside her. She looked at her child, hair short,

wearing a boyish T-shirt, a new glow in her cheeks. 'Happy?' she said.

'Italy was *the best*,' Riley said.

Sally felt a tug at her heart.

'I was me,' she said, squeezing her lion tighter. 'All week, I was really me.'

Sally smiled at Riley, touching her cheek gently.

'Before I wasn't right,' she continued. 'Now I am.'

A wave of guilt hit Sally. They'd let her down, all these years, she thought. They hadn't realised what their child needed. And now they had seen it – or at least she had – they were going to take it away from her again.

'Can I still be a boy?'

Sally saw Riley's excited expression. She couldn't break her child's heart. She couldn't.

'Just until school starts?' Riley said.

No.

Now was the time to say it. Be firm; be clear.

But as she went to say it, the word wouldn't come.

Sally walked down the stairs slowly. The hope in Riley's expression ... Sally hadn't had it in her to say the words that she'd intended to. Instead she told Riley she'd talk to Theo. Inside her, something had already shifted slightly; her loyalties were in conflict. She could hear Theo in the kitchen, a few steps away. In a moment she'd have to tell him that she hadn't been firm with Riley in the way they'd planned, and why. She had to phrase it in just the right way. Looking into Riley's wide, hopeful eyes, she'd felt sure about the right thing to do, but now, as she neared the conversation with Theo, it was all getting blurry again. She had to keep it clear in her mind.

She went into the kitchen, and Theo looked over at her, a concerned expression on his face. 'How did it go?'

'You know,' Sally said.

Theo laughed, but in an awkward, tense way that reminded her how much this all mattered. 'Not really, Sal. That's why I'm asking. Did she take it OK? Agree to go back to being a girl again?'

The decision seemed so stark, so black and white in Theo's eyes – but things looked different to Sally. Right now they were living in a grey area. She felt uneasy, as if Theo was an adversary, and the sensation was entirely unfamiliar. Theo, this man facing her, was her very best friend, her confidant, her life partner. Supporting Riley now was simply another challenge that they would get through together.

She took a deep breath, then spoke. 'I know what we agreed, about Riley returning to being a girl when we got home.'

'Yes . . . ' Theo said uncertainly.

'I know that we said that the end of the holiday would be the end of this.'

'Sal.' Theo's face clouded over, sensing what she was about to say. 'C'mon . . . Don't.'

Sally bit the inside of her mouth. She couldn't just forget what Riley had said. She couldn't ignore her wishes.

'Would it really do any harm to let her carry on?' she asked. 'Keep this going in private, indoors, until term starts again? She really wants to.'

Theo shook his head, his eyes closed. For a moment there was silence, then he looked at Sally and she saw the pain in his eyes. 'Sally – this isn't fair. We made a decision together.'

'I know . . . ' She thought again of Riley's face – the way she had beamed at the prospect of being able to be a boy for a while longer. Sally owed Riley her support and she would give it, even if that meant pushing Theo a bit, helping him to understand. 'If you'd seen her just now, you'd feel the same.'

'No,' Theo said, shaking his head again. 'I wouldn't, Sally. That's just it.'

A fissure had opened up. Sally could almost see it, a crack that she wanted desperately to fix. They hadn't ever disagreed about anything as important as this. But Riley's face came back into her mind, and she couldn't back down. She told herself to go more gently.

'It would be time-limited; it wouldn't be for ever,' she said softly.

'I don't think it would help any of us,' Theo said. 'We'd just be prolonging the inevitable, making it even harder on Riley when this all ends.'

Sally felt the urgency of the situation – this moment, Riley's hopes in her hands. 'But the way Riley was on holiday – so relaxed and happy . . . Didn't you see that too, the change in her?'

'I saw she was happy on holiday, yes. We tried this thing out and, for a short while, in that particular place, it seemed to make her feel comfortable. But now we're home, Sally.'

'So her happiness on holiday doesn't mean anything?'

'It means something – but it's not enough to base our decisions on. She's only seven, she's so young still – and we're her parents. We have a responsibility to know better than she does. Would you give her chocolate cake and new toys every day just because they made her happy?'

'No, of course not,' Sally said. Frustration built up in her. 'It's hardly the same.'

He was making out that she was a walkover, as if she were bending to Riley's wishes without properly considering what was best. That couldn't have been further from the truth.

'I think we're pretty relaxed parents, on the whole, don't you?' Theo said. 'But there are limits. Children need boundaries. I know that, you know that, the hundred parenting books on our shelves tell us that.'

Sally used to read relevant paragraphs out loud to him, on the sofa. She'd once had the hope that in an Amazon delivery she'd find the skills to navigate parenthood. The early issues – the disrupted sleep, the tantrums over dinner, the refusal to tidy up toys – had been tough, but they'd worked through things together. They seemed so simple now.

She was starting to see Theo's point about boundaries. It had all seemed so much clearer when she was upstairs talking to Riley, but now the waters were growing muddy, and she felt less sure of herself. Perhaps she was rushing things.

'I know this is hard, Sal. I know you feel like you'd be letting her down not allowing this,' Theo said, 'but maybe it's the opposite that's true. Giving Riley that kind of freedom could be letting her down too.'

Sally paused. Perhaps there was something in what he was saying. She resolved to try harder to see things from his point of view.

'But what would we say to her?' Sally asked. '"Riley, this is how it is. You had a chance to be who you feel you are – but now you have to be a girl again"?'

'Even the way you're saying it makes no sense. Riley has always been a girl,' Theo said. A crease appeared in the space between his eyebrows, his strain showing. 'She *is* a girl.'

Sally could see how stressed Theo was, but she couldn't let the point go. 'Maybe it's not that simple.'

Theo shook his head, a weary look in his eyes. 'We should never have started messing about with this, Sal. It's confused her.'

Sally felt annoyance build up in her. They'd discussed the trial together and they'd made the decision jointly.

'We had to do something,' she said. 'Riley was upset, and we couldn't just ignore what she was telling us.'

'We should have been stronger,' Theo said.

'No,' Sally said firmly. 'We had to try.' Why did she suddenly feel so isolated in all this? She saw now that the feelings the two of them had repressed, to keep the peace on holiday, hadn't gone away – they were all coming to the surface again. 'Why did you agree to her experimenting on holiday, if you were so dead against it?'

'I thought maybe if we let her do it, the phase would pass more quickly.'

'That was what you thought?' Sally said. She'd assumed that he felt the same as her – that they would continue to make choices based on the response they saw in Riley. Now she was faced with the fact that his mindset was clearly more fixed. 'You agreed to this because you thought the novelty would wear off?'

'Yes. I guess I did.'

'Well, that hasn't happened,' Sally said. 'Not yet, at least.'

There was an empty silence between them.

'A few weeks,' Sally said. 'What difference would it make, really, apart from to how she feels?'

'Don't you think it could make it more real to her?' Theo said. 'Each step we take is one where we're showing her we feel this is the right thing.'

Sally shook her head. 'I don't think so. All we'd be doing is giving Riley the space to decide that for herself.'

Theo looked at her. 'Are you giving me a choice here?'

'Yes,' she said defensively. But she knew, deep down, that she had to defend her child's right to be herself – or himself. She wasn't sure if she was prepared to compromise on that.

'Except it seems as if you've already made your mind up.'

At the café the next day, Theo tried to put thoughts of Riley to the back of his mind, but by lunchtime the strain was getting to him, and when Gabi asked him a simple question, he was short with her.

'Don't be like that with me, Theo,' Gabi said. 'I was only asking you when the delivery was arriving. There's no need to snap at me. What's going on with you?'

'Sorry,' he said. It hadn't been anything to do with Gabi. The argument with Sally the previous night had left him shaken up.

'Are you OK?' Gabi said. 'If this is about the café, about me leaving, then let's talk about it—'

'It's not,' he said. It had been on his mind – the need to talk to his parents to see if they'd invest. But the conversation with Sally, and the way they'd spoken to each other, was dominating all of that now. 'Not today. That's not it.'

'Is this about Riley?'

When he'd called her from Italy, he'd told her about what they were doing, the trial, with Riley being a boy. How his ideas about what to do, and Sally's, were starting to diverge. Gabi hadn't taken sides – she wouldn't ever do that – but he'd sensed, as he'd expected to, that she understood him. Talking to her had been a release.

'Yes. It's Riley. She's still saying stuff about feeling like a boy.'

'Right,' Gabi said. 'So this wasn't just a holiday thing.'

'I guess not.'

'So what now?' Gabi asked.

'That's the question. Sally thinks we should carry it on – have Riley be a boy, however crazy that sounds – for the next few weeks, until school starts.'

'Does Riley seem happier that way?' Gabi asked tentatively.

Theo thought back on the holiday. 'Yes. And it was good to see her happy. I'm not disputing that.'

'But you don't want it to continue?'

'I think we're going to confuse her. We need to start being clear. Whatever we do now we'd only have to undo once term starts up again.'

'What did you decide?'

'That we'd let it happen, in private,' Theo said. The decision had been a reluctant one, made to keep the peace.

'You don't seem comfortable with that.'

He wasn't. Everything felt out of kilter. He felt distant from Riley. Distant from Sally. He wanted it all to end, for them to go back to how things had been before.

'It's hard to watch, Gabi. I don't know if any of this is right – and I feel as if I have no control over it at all.'

'I'm wearing the robot pants,' Riley said excitedly. 'And these shorts.' She held them up for Sally to see.

Today was their first day of letting Riley dress how she wanted to at home. Sally looked at what she'd picked out – were those even really boy clothes, beyond the department they'd been bought in? Clothes were just clothes, surely.

'Sure, love. You wear those.'

Sally thought of Theo. It pained her, how they'd argued the previous night. They hadn't said goodbye that morning in their usual warm, loving way. Instead there had been a distance between them, a coolness in their farewell over breakfast. She hadn't wanted him to feel forced into a decision, but in the end that was how it had felt for him.

'I feel good, Mum,' Riley said.

And there it was. In a short sentence. In the smile on her child's face. She'd wanted so much for Theo to feel OK with the decision, for them to be able to agree. But in the end, it had come down to this. Those words were the reason Sally hadn't been prepared to back down.

That morning, Riley played in the garden, digging a hole and filling it with water from the hose, turning the heatwave's dust to slippery mud again. After lunch, Sally took Riley to the corner shop to get Cornettos. She'd felt anxious on the way there, wondering who they'd see, and what people might think of the way Riley looked. As it turned out, no one stared. No one asked questions. She walked back feeling relaxed.

In the afternoon they put out food for Saturn the snail,

replenishing the stocks they'd left to keep him going during their holiday. Riley drew pictures and played in the garden while Sally worked on her laptop, answering emails and taking down details of orders.

The hours blurred, one into the next. The straight lines of the house, the fence, the walls, were made pliable by the heat. A jug of lemonade would empty and they would make another.

That evening, with Theo still at work and Riley in bed, Sally went online and logged into the parenting website. The day had felt like a quiet success and had bolstered her confidence in the decision to go with Riley's wishes.

A direct message had come through on the forum, from the user she'd spoken to before the holiday: Daddancing76. His message was concise.

> Hi, it's me. We spoke about holidays. How was yours? How did it all go?

She smiled, heartened by the support from afar.

> It went well, I think. Riley seemed to really enjoy it.

She wondered whether to leave it at that, or say more.

> We're going to carry it on – a few weeks, until school. I'm not entirely sure I know what we're doing.

She felt she could be honest with him.

> I'm glad to hear the holiday went well. And if you keep waiting for the point when you know what you're doing, you may be waiting a long time.

Ha. Yes. I'm starting to see that.

I found a photo the other day. Of us on that holiday. I thought you might want to see it.

He sent a photo of himself with Siobhan, on a beach. He was dark, attractive, tanned, in a T-shirt, and beside him was Siobhan's mum, her black hair blowing in the wind, a hand raised to move it from her face. It was Siobhan Sally looked at for the longest – her wide smile, her long hair up in a ponytail.

They'd got it right, Sally thought. Look at her – she's happy. She's a happy young woman.

Siobhan's beautiful, Sally wrote.

Isn't she? he typed back. I don't think I could be more proud.

Proud. The way she had always felt when she'd looked at Riley. This summer, she'd seen that pride come from within. Riley was more confident.

Later that evening, Sally went to another section on the site, with links to videos. She wanted to inform herself. Knowledge had to help. She chose a short film to watch at random, of a primary-age boy, perhaps nine. There was an endearing chubbiness to his cheeks, an unruly quality to his short hair. Other than that, he could have been any other boy.

'Hi. I'm Jack. Welcome to my channel.'

Jack described the day he told his parents he was trans. 'They were great,' Jack said. 'I thought they were going to be really upset, but they were really supportive.'

Sally imagined how the conversation must have felt from the parents' point of view. She wondered if they'd had any idea of what was going on with their child prior to that moment.

'My dad even helped me buy my first chest binder.'

Sally pressed pause. What was that?

She put in the search term and images came up of what looked like white crop tops. The binders were made to flatten girls' chests. Were they something Riley might want to wear one day? Puberty was still years away, and yet, in trying to understand what her child was facing, Sally felt compelled to press fast-forward and look into Riley's future.

She remembered the moment her own breasts had begun to bud and how she'd wanted to hide away. She'd sometimes opted out of playing basketball in PE, even though it was her favourite sport, because she hadn't wanted to get hit on those tender parts of her chest.

'You'll be glad of those one day,' her mum had said to her gently, on seeing Sally trying to hide her torso with a towel after a bath.

Her mother had helped her see that her body changing made her powerful and beautiful. In time she'd come to appreciate her adult body, especially when she'd breastfed Riley. Sally had tried to instil that same pride in being female in her own daughter. But clearly Riley didn't share it – and Sally couldn't help feeling that in some way she'd failed.

Riley was rejecting her femaleness completely. She might never reach that point of feeling proud of being a girl, a woman. Did Riley genuinely feel like a boy? Or was she scared of what being a girl, and turning into a woman, might mean?

Theo texted Sally to say that he would be late – he was going up to see his parents to ask if they would invest in the café. He felt conflicted: he didn't want to be asking them for money, especially not at this stage in his life, but losing the café, after everything he'd put into it, wasn't something he could risk.

He sat down for dinner with Elena and Stephen, and told

them about the holiday to Italy. He told them about Siena, about the villa, about everything apart from the issue that he thought about every single day. He didn't want to think about it. He knew that each day, at home, Riley was dressing as a boy, but he found it easier not to talk about it directly with Sally. He tried to think about it as little as possible. He was glad to be able to answer his parents' questions without talking about gender.

After dinner, Theo brought the conversation around to Gabi leaving for Crete, and the future of the café.

Elena and Stephen looked at one another. 'You want us to help you buy Gabi out?' Stephen asked.

Theo's chest felt tight. Asking them for help wasn't easy, but he felt now, more than ever, that it was the best way forward.

'Yes. I know it's a big decision, but we could make it a real family business.'

'Well, I'll admit to being sceptical at first, but I suppose it is more established now,' Stephen said.

'It's a lovely business,' Elena said. 'We wouldn't want you to lose it. Not after all the work you've put in.' She looked at Stephen. 'We could talk about it, couldn't we, Stephen?'

Theo's father nodded. His expression gave very little away.

'It's a big decision,' Theo said. 'Take some time to think about it.'

On the train home that evening, Theo looked out of the window at all the houses and flats, all the other lives out there. He'd come so far to build his own life, with his own family, and yet now he felt as reliant on, and as closely tethered to, his parents as he had been as a child.

Sally was in bed reading a book when Theo's text came through.

On the train. Home in 30 minutes x

She wondered how the conversation had gone with his

parents. Hoped that they'd been receptive to the idea of investing. Usually she would have looked forward to a hug and a late-night conversation with Theo, to his warm body meeting hers, the touch of his hands on her skin by turns comforting and electric.

Tonight, she didn't feel that way. She didn't want to have to tell him how things had been that day with Riley, or try to help him to understand the day that she had had. The day that, in its most seemingly insignificant moments, had told her Riley was happier.

Sally put down her book, switched off her bedside light and closed her eyes. She needed to rest; she needed time to process it all. She would make it right between them. She just needed to find the words, to put them in the right order, to show him, help him see what she had seen in Riley. And perhaps sleep would help her do that.

Chapter 22

The August days passed, humid and slow, and Sally and Riley stepped out further with each one: to the playground, to the shopping centre, to the swimming pool. Riley was living as a boy, from breakfast until bedtime. What had been unthinkable a month before now seemed, to Sally, like an integrated part of their life. Sally had been concerned that Riley would be bored, without seeing her school friends, without play dates – but those were the conditions they had to maintain, if they were to keep things private. As it was, Riley had barely questioned it, and seemed content with the one-to-one time with her mum, and the slower pace. Sally felt relieved, and hoped it would last. She didn't have an answer for Riley about why it had to be this way.

Sally felt, when she talked with him, that Theo was becoming distant. Theo didn't ask her many questions about her and Riley's days. She told him about the things she thought he'd like to hear – how many lengths Riley had done and what they'd got up to in the park. There was a lot going on for Theo, she told herself. With the café, and his parents' recent agreement to invest. It was natural that he would be distracted.

She tended not to tell Theo what Riley had been wearing. She didn't mention the other little things that happened in the course of their days, like when strangers who met Riley mistook her for a boy. When it had happened for the first time, Sally noted the way Riley's shoulders lifted, how her child walked straighter. She didn't correct anyone. She didn't want to diminish Riley's joy. And – she wondered sometimes – perhaps, after all, those strangers were the ones who had it right.

It felt to Sally that as Riley grew in confidence, so her little girl was disappearing more each day. She tried to put those feelings to one side, telling herself that this wasn't about her. But she felt the loss of her daughter all the same. It scratched at her heart.

After a week the heat subsided and the rain came, and they began to spend more time inside. Sally found it easier then – no one to meet, just long days of card games and Hungry Hippos, and Disney movies, and helping Riley with her homework.

One afternoon, while Riley took a rare nap on the sofa, Sally went back to the parenting site, and saw that Daddancing76 was online.

Hi, she typed.

Hello there. How are things?

Sally was about to type 'fine'. Perhaps even 'good'. But she paused instead, and wrote: The truth?

Always, he replied.

Confusing.

She thought of the way she and Theo had started to talk to each other lately – bluntly, minimally. There was an atmosphere there that was new to their household. And a feeling she'd never expected – loneliness. She'd wanted to do this on her own – purposely holding back from calling Isabel or her dad to talk about how things were going. She'd wanted to see for herself what was happening with Riley – to be able to judge clearly. But she hadn't anticipated how isolating that would be. There was also the sense of loss. The visceral, unwelcome sensation of losing something precious.

He wrote back:

It is confusing. Everything is about your child – and of course that's how it should be. No one talks about the parents, apart from to give their opinion (usually what you're getting wrong). I'll get on and deal with every day. But sometimes I feel like the heart has been ripped out of our home. You're supposed to be there, celebrating this new life – but the truth is you're mourning a death at the same time. Our child – the one in the baby photos (and yes, I still have a few, although Siobhan wanted us to throw them out) – that child is still real to me. Like your little girl is to you. That little boy or girl was your little boy or girl, and you had dreams for them. Some of those dreams won't fit any more. You've just got to focus on building new ones together with them.

That's it, Sally thought, the tears she'd been holding back forcing their way to the surface until they spilled down her cheeks. That's it.

She wrote back: School will be starting soon. We need to talk about what to do next. It's like my husband's shut down. I need help to work this out.

A minute later came his response:

Listen – I'm here. Whenever you need someone. But talking to someone face to face is probably better for you now. There's a good support group in north London. I used to go there, before we moved. They're nice people, helpful for discussing what was going on with Siobhan, with us. I'll send you the details. You should go.

Sally thought about it. It seemed like a leap. Messaging other parents was one thing – but going out to meet with other parents? Talking to them about things she could barely understand, much less articulate when the language itself still eluded her? But of the two things, the alternative – continuing to navigate her way on her own – seemed less preferable. Talking the little she had with people who understood her had already helped, and someone there might be able to give her advice that would make a difference to Riley's happiness. She hoped she might be able to talk Theo into it.

Thank you, she typed. I think I will.

An email came back with the details of where the meeting would be. Wish I could be there myself, but it's too far to travel to regularly now. We found another place locally. But you'll like them.

She'd go – just to this first meeting. She'd try it out, see what the other parents were like.

Thank you, she said. For everything. I'm Sally, by the way. Can I ask your name, if it's not breaking any rules?

After a pause, a reply came through.

Like I said, anytime. I've been where you are, or somewhere like it.

And your name? she asked again.

Matt.

The following morning, Sally spoke to Theo over breakfast while Riley was watching cartoons in the living room. She didn't want things to be how they had been since they got back from holiday – talking only about domestic tasks, or to arrange something. It was natural that things felt awkward at the moment, Sally told herself – they were still finding their way. They had to work that bit harder at their relationship, that was all; make time for themselves, like they'd promised on holiday they would, so that everything didn't revolve around what was happening with Riley.

'Shall we get Isabel and Freddie round for dinner soon?' Sally said. From what Isabel had been telling her, things had been going well. Sally had been biding her time before asking so as not to put pressure on their relationship, but she got the impression that the time was right.

'Sure. Let's do that. Freddie seems – dare I say it – pretty serious.' Theo smiled. It warmed Sally's heart to see him smile. It felt like too long since she'd seen it.

'I hear the same from Isabel. I guess I was hasty, assuming he'd mess her around again. I'm glad he seems to be proving me wrong.'

'A night with them would be great.'

'I'll check dates.'

'Sal,' Theo said. 'Listen, I'm sorry – about how it's been lately.'

'It's OK,' she said.

They could have left it there, and part of Sally hoped they would. Theo would leave for work, she'd take Riley to the park, they'd have the dinner party to look forward to. But Theo didn't leave it.

'But it's not really OK, is it?'

'No.' She looked at him, grateful that he could see through her. 'I've felt on my own, some days this summer, with this.'

With *this*. She didn't want to say with Riley. Because it was so much more than that.

'You're not,' he said. 'I know I've not been around as much as I could have been. But you're not on your own.'

Sally glanced over at the wall calendar. Her gaze rested there, on September. 'School's starting again soon,' she said.

Theo looked relieved. 'Exactly. Everything will be easier then.'

Sally felt her chest tighten. That wasn't how she'd been feeling. Not at all. 'I think we need to talk about what we do next.'

'We've already talked about it,' Theo said, his voice firm.

'I know . . . ' Sally said. But things had looked different back then.

Theo shook his head, exasperated. 'We talked about it when we got back from holiday. There was never any suggestion that this would continue once school started.'

Sally thought back over the past few weeks. Riley had seemed calm and at ease, enjoying wearing her new clothes.

'Theo, every single day this is what Riley's been happy doing. Being. She hasn't wavered – not for a minute. It doesn't seem to be going away.'

'I can see what you're saying, and I don't want to dismiss it, but at the same time the summer holidays are so long, so unstructured. Don't you remember that feeling of losing your way a bit, missing your friends, the routine?' Theo said.

Sally nodded. She'd loved the long summer days in her back garden, pressing flowers with her mum and splashing about in the paddling pool. But she remembered that feeling too, she hadn't known how to name it then, but it had been a certain kind of directionlessness. 'Yes. I felt like that.'

'So you see what I mean? Once the structure of the school day is back—' Theo said, gathering pace with the idea.

Sally shook her head. 'Yes, I remember it. And no – this is not that.' Theo looked at her, shocked at the interruption. 'What Riley is experiencing is not that.'

'How can you tell?' Theo said.

Sally knew, more with each day, that what Riley was feeling ran far, far deeper than being at a loss in a school holiday. It wasn't even mother's intuition. She hadn't had to use that – Riley had *told* her. All she'd had to do was listen.

'Because she said so,' Sally said.

Theo didn't answer right away. He just stood there, silently. It left Sally feeling even more alone.

'Isn't that enough?' Sally asked.

Theo shrugged. 'Is something Riley's said, at seven, enough for us to go ahead and help her turn her whole world upside-down? No, Sal. I'm sorry, but I don't think it is.'

Sally felt as if they were locked in a kind of stalemate. They couldn't afford to stop talking, not when Riley needed them to be unified. Sally knew she had to push through.

'I think we need to keep on talking about this.'

'About what, though? Because I can't keep track. I thought this was all coming to an end, and it turns out you're already planning for it to continue.'

'About our options.' Sally paused. She knew that raising the support group was a risk. 'There's a place where we could meet with other parents who are in the same situation we are. Maybe we could go along to it together?'

A flicker of distrust came across Theo's face. 'Some kind of support group?'

Sally nodded. If she could just get him there, he might start to open his mind a little.

He shook his head, and she saw instantly that he had shut down. 'No way. I don't want to share what's going on in our family with strangers.'

'But it might help,' Sally said. 'These are people like us. People who've been where we are now.'

Theo bristled. 'No one's been where we are now, Sally – because you, me and Riley are you, me and Riley. What do you mean, "people like us", anyway?'

She paused, then said it. 'Parents whose kids are trans.'

There it was – the word – in the air between them. It felt right to say it.

Theo looked at her sceptically. 'Or parents who *think* their kids are trans.'

'If that's how you see it.' Sally took a deep breath. He wasn't going to make this any easier. 'I thought it might be helpful. We could get a babysitter—'

Theo shook his head. 'I already said this isn't what I want. They're bound to have an agenda, and I don't want to be brainwashed—'

'It's a support group, Theo,' Sally snapped back, her patience running out. 'Not a bloody cult. I need someone I can talk to about this.'

'Then go!' he shouted.

The TV in the front room went quiet.

'Dad?' Riley said.

Sally's stomach twisted, and she wished they'd kept their voices down.

'Everything's OK, Riley,' he called back.

Theo looked back at Sally and spoke again, quietly now. 'If you want to go, go. But don't expect me to understand it. Because I don't see how involving strangers in our family life is going to help us – not at all.'

Theo went through to the living room and sat beside Riley on the sofa. After their argument, Sally had gone upstairs to shower. Their discussion had left a bitter taste. He rarely raised his voice, and had done so at home only a handful of times, when Riley had done something really naughty. He didn't recall ever shouting at Sally. He had become, for a fleeting moment, someone he didn't want to be. But a man pushed into agreeing to things, forced into decisions he didn't want to make, about something as important as his own child – that wasn't someone he wanted to be either. He'd reached his limit. He'd had to draw a line in the sand.

Riley curled in towards him.

'I wish you didn't have to go to the café today, Dad.'

He stroked her soft, sun-streaked hair. She was the same child she'd been before the summer. Before everything got messy. She hadn't changed.

'I know. I wish I could hang out with you too.'

Maybe if he'd had more time off over the summer, it would have been better. He would have been there to bring some more balance.

'It's busy at the moment, with Gabi about to leave, and Grandma and Granddad joining the business. It won't always be like this.'

Her eyes widened. 'But the summer's nearly over. Soon I'll be back at school.'

The days so quickly turned into weeks, and months into years. The wait for a quieter time that rarely came. He wished sometimes that he could pause time, slow everything down. Never more so than now. She needed him right now.

'I'll see you tonight,' he said. 'I'll put you to bed, do your stories.'

'OK,' she said.

He kissed her head, took in the sweet honey scent of her kids' shampoo. Riley was Riley. She was the same sweet girl he'd soothed to sleep as a baby. The toddler he'd once laid down next to as she tantrummed in a supermarket aisle, kicking his legs beside her and forcing her into reluctant laughter. She was just confused.

No kid was happy all the time. They had overreacted, read too much into her behaviour in the early summer, and he and Sally had moved too quickly in allowing her to act like a boy on holiday. Now was the time to admit that mistake and move back from it, not make it more concrete. Talking to other people who might want them to follow the decisions they'd made with their own children seemed like a dangerous game to be playing. Riley needed to get back to school and the usual routine. In her first term at Elmtree she'd been happy, and she would be again.

They'd keep talking to her, keep listening. But that didn't, and couldn't, mean going along with what she thought she wanted.

At the café, he found Gabi cleaning the tables and setting up. While he'd been sorry to leave Riley, he had to admit he was grateful for the change of scene. The conflict at home had unnerved him. It felt today as if work was his refuge, rather than home.

'Hey, there,' Gabi said. 'There's a scone on the counter for you. I just made a batch.'

'Thanks,' Theo said, finding the scone and eating it while he got things ready. Everything was behind the counter where he'd left it the day before. Tidy, controlled. He appreciated it today.

'So, I might have got the finances sorted now, but I've still got to find someone who can do everything you can here. It's a tall order, Gab.'

She laughed. 'Well, I hope I'm not *too* easy to replace,' she said.

'You're not, believe me,' he said. He'd interviewed over a dozen candidates, and no one even came close. They were either experienced baristas who couldn't bake, or the other way around – or, well, they just weren't right. They weren't Gabi. 'I need to get less picky, I guess, or I'm going to be running this place on my own. Anyway, the woman coming in at noon sounds great – on paper, anyway. She's just left a similar job in central London and seems to have a ton of experience.'

'Hopefully she'll be the one,' Gabi said, with a smile that didn't quite reach her eyes.

He registered Gabi's mixed feelings. 'Hey, what's with the sad eyes? With any luck this means you head off to your bright future, leave everything ticking over here, more or less as before . . . '

'I *am* glad,' she said.

'Really? You don't seem it.'

'It's just . . . everything's changing, isn't it?'

'Listen, I know I got Mum and Dad involved, but I made them promise – cast-iron guarantee – that they wouldn't try and convert this into some kind of taverna, with mates' rates for all their friends . . . '

She laughed.

'What's up, Gabi?' he said.

She shrugged. 'It's just strange, I guess. It's such a big change, and now, with you looking for a replacement, it all feels more final.' She wrinkled her nose. 'I want it all, right?'

'A bit,' he said. 'You won't look back, Gab. Not to this place. Not to London. You'll be lying on a sun-drenched beach, eating some delicious feta salad with sun-kissed tomatoes, wondering why you ever wasted your time here in this grey city.'

'You're right,' she said. 'Maybe I'm just starting to realise everything that I'm leaving behind.'

'But this is your dream, isn't it?' Theo said. 'Going back to where we grew up . . . ' He almost envied her – the simplicity of the life she had ahead of her. The lack of responsibilities that freed her up to do anything she chose.

'You're right,' she said, more resolutely. 'This *is* my dream. And I'm going to embrace it.'

*

That night Sally left Theo to put Riley to bed. She didn't remind him where she was going; she didn't have to. He didn't ask for any details. She still felt raw inside from the argument they'd had about the group, and the fact they hadn't properly made up after it.

The LGBTQ parents' support group was held in a hall about half an hour away. Sally didn't mind the journey into London, and the location made it less likely she'd meet somewhere there she knew. She entered the community centre and walked into the hall. There was a circle of chairs, some occupied, some empty.

Sally felt awkward, self-conscious. She was keenly aware that she was on her own, not with a partner, and Theo didn't even want her to be there.

'Welcome,' the leader said. 'I'm Carla. You must be Sally. I run the group. We've emailed, I think? You said you'd heard about the group from a friend online?'

'Yes,' she said. Carla was in her sixties, older than Sally had imagined from their brief communication. She wasn't quite sure what she'd imagined. 'That's right.'

'Take a seat,' Carla said.

There were about twelve parents in the group, and Sally found a space between two women.

She glanced around at the men and women, the youngest perhaps thirty, the oldest maybe double that. There was no one there you'd look twice at in the street.

'We're still waiting for one or two people, but I expect they're caught up in the traffic. Sally, would you like to tell us a little about yourself?' Carla said.

Sally felt thrown. She hadn't expected to have to speak first. 'I'm . . . '

I'm here because of Riley.

I'm here because she says she's a boy.

I'm here because I didn't know where else to go.

I'm here because I feel alone, even with Theo.

I'm here because I'm terrified of getting this all wrong.

I'm here because I love our child. So much it hurts sometimes.

'I'm here,' Sally said at last, feeling embarrassed that she couldn't articulate herself at all.

'Well,' Carla said with a smile, 'that's a damn good start. You *are* here. And for tonight, and as long as you want, just being here is fine.'

Sally looked around the room, seeing warmth and encouragement in the other parents' faces, and felt reassured.

'Who else would like to get us started today?' Carla asked.

'I will. I'm Dan, by the way.' He must have been about forty-five, and was dressed in jeans and a grey sweater, an earring in his left ear. 'I took Ariana to get her make-up done this week, in a department store. I've never felt quite so out of my comfort zone.' He smiled. 'But you know what? She looked incredible.' He paused for a moment. 'It wasn't the make-up – I think they put far too much on her; they always do, don't they? – but the way she looked, in that chair, being treated as a woman. Relaxed. Content. I don't think I've ever seen her look happier.'

During the break Sally went over to the coffee table and poured herself a cup. She got talking with Dan, about his teenage daughter and her recent transition at college. His wife was usually there too, he said, but she'd had to work a late shift that evening. A woman approached the table; she'd been sitting opposite Sally in the circle, with long black hair and an amber necklace, her eyes darkened with sweeping eyeliner. Like Sally, she had barely spoken in the first half of the session.

'Hi,' she said, reaching for a biscuit. 'I'm Robyn.'

'Sally,' she said, with a smile. The easy conversation with Dan had stoked her confidence.

'I know your name,' Robyn said coolly. 'You're the classic newbie.'

Sally felt her cheeks grow hot.

'It's no big deal. We all came here for the first time once.'

Sally told herself to relax.

'You feel like you need a dictionary, don't you?' Robyn said.

Sally nodded, feeling more comfortable. That was exactly how she'd felt – clueless, out of her depth. 'There's a lot to take in.'

'Everyone's talking about their kids, and whatever trans, non-binary, gender-fluid thing is going on for them. And you're just trying to work out what language they're speaking and how on earth you ended up here. Am I right?'

Sally smiled. 'That's it. I certainly didn't see this coming. We're just a normal family.'

Robyn visibly stiffened. 'And we're what? A bunch of weirdos?'

'No.' Sally regretted what she'd said immediately. 'I didn't mean it like that.'

'There are some words you might want to learn, and some others you might want to forget,' Robyn said. 'And "normal" – I'd say you're best forgetting about that one altogether.'

Dan offered Sally a plate of biscuits. 'Don't mind Robyn,' he said. 'She likes to test people. Her bark's worse than her bite.'

Robyn flashed him a look.

'None of us here have an easy ride,' Dan said. 'Whether you're getting looks from the neighbours or taking your teenager for hormone injections. When you're in this, you either soften up like me, or get some hard edges. Robyn got the latter.'

That evening Sally felt relieved to get home again. She was glad she had gone to the support group, and decided she would go back again – but it had been challenging. It hadn't felt right to tell them about Riley, and that was the whole point of her being there. It all felt too personal. Perhaps, in time, it would get easier.

In the living room, she found Theo and Riley asleep together on the sofa. Theo's arm was draped around Riley's shoulder and her soft body was curled into his.

It caught at her heart. Here was her family. She loved Theo so much. So very much. Nothing could undo that. They would find a way to work this out.

Nothing was easy, and perhaps the woman at the group had been right – they might never be normal. But she would do everything she could for Riley, and Theo would too. Their intentions were the same – to protect their child.

She sat beside them. In a moment she would rouse Theo gently, then carry Riley up to her bedroom. But first she wanted to sit with them, in the calm and quiet, and feel how it was to be together.

A message came through on her phone, and she checked it. Matt.

How did it go tonight?

She smiled. It was kind of him to remember.

It was good, thanks. They were welcoming.

She paused. Well, in their own ways, she thought, remembering Robyn.

I felt a bit out of my depth, though, she typed. I didn't say anything.

She thought for a moment about what had held her back. It was more than shyness. More than it all feeling personal.

I think maybe I feel like a bit of a fraud. I don't know if

this is real or not yet – if Riley really is trans, or if this is just a phase.

She waited. Matt replied.

Don't worry about that. You're not a fraud. And Riley's certainly not. You don't have to have all the answers. You're just being brave enough to ask the questions.

Chapter 23

The next morning at breakfast, Sally cooked scrambled eggs for all of them. She looked at Theo and Riley as they ate around the big wooden table, sun streaming in through the windows, and felt the same warmth she had the night before. This was her small world, and even when there were disagreements and upsets, she deeply loved the people in it. That was family.

The previous night she'd carried Riley to bed and tucked her in without waking her. For Sally, sleep had taken longer to come. The faces of the people she'd met at the support group ran through her mind. She'd appreciated the warm welcome, but the stories they'd told had stirred a lot up in her. They'd talked about prejudice, hormones, treatment plans. Even surgery. It pained Sally to think about what Riley might have to face just in order to be at ease. Those stories hinted at a potential future Sally didn't feel ready to think about yet.

In the morning, Theo hadn't asked about the support group, and contrary to what she'd expected, Sally found she was relieved. She hadn't figured out how she felt about what she'd heard herself yet. She didn't want to – and wasn't sure she even could – convince Theo that it would be a good idea for him to go.

Now, looking at Theo and Riley at the breakfast table, Sally felt sure that the best way forward was for them to spend good family time together. Enjoying each other, not arguing. Then when they talked, they'd be doing so knowing that their foundations were solid.

'Is it tonight Isabel and Freddie are coming round?' Theo asked.

'Yes. Sevenish,' Sally said. 'Do you think you can make it back for then?'

'Uncle Freddie's coming!' Riley said. 'Brilliant!'

Theo ruffled her hair. 'I should get back around then,' he said. 'I might be slightly later, but I'll bring a few things from the café to make it up to you all.'

'We could eat out in the garden,' Sally said. 'Make the most of the last few days of summer.'

Riley looked up at her. 'How long is it till school starts again?'

'After the weekend,' Theo said. 'Five days.'

Sally and Theo's eyes met. The mention of the new term had brought tension.

'Yes,' Sally said, keeping her tone light. 'Then you'll see your new classroom, meet your new teacher, and see all of your friends again.'

Later that day, Sally and Riley were in the garden. Riley was watering her small vegetable plot, and Sally was sketching out clothing designs. Sun warmed Sally's shoulders, and there was a distant hum of lawnmowers. Everything felt calm.

'Can I stay up a bit later tonight?' Riley asked.

'Perhaps,' Sally said, still focused on her drawing. 'Let's see how your behaviour is today.'

'Because it's still the holidays, and you get to stay up later in the holidays,' Riley said.

'We'll see,' Sally said.

Riley turned towards Sally. 'Mum, when school starts . . . '

The question Sally had known would come. The one that she and Theo had been skirting around ever since their argument. Her heart started to thud.

'Can I stay like this?'

Sally took a deep breath. She didn't know what she was going to say, but she had to say something. She couldn't leave Riley's question hanging. She went over and bent to her child's level.

'Almost the same, peanut.'

'Can I wear these clothes?' Riley asked, pointing at her shorts.

'Sure. Most of them. Though you'll need something warmer soon.'

Riley seemed unconvinced. She asked hesitantly, 'And can I use the boys' toilets now?'

Sally paused.

Riley's eyes filled with tears. 'It's going to be like it was before, isn't it? I'm going to have to go back to being a girl again, aren't I?'

Sally felt for Riley so deeply it gave her a pain in her stomach. Theo had made his feelings completely clear: Riley attending school as a girl was non-negotiable. Riley was Theo's child too. In that moment, which seemed to stretch out painfully, the man she loved was the one standing in their way.

'I'm sorry. Yes, it will be, love.' Sally kept her voice neutral, her tone measured.

'No!' Riley said, her eyes growing red. 'No, Mum. I can't! I won't.'

Her face flushed with stress, and Sally reached out a hand to take Riley's.

'Please, Mum. Please.'

Sally glanced back at their empty house. She and Theo should have talked more. They should have planned this together. The start of term had hung over each conversation they had, but even as the days before school dwindled to a handful, they'd been too cowardly to confront it.

A flat 'no' seemed too harsh. Riley's reaction proved it. The change was so abrupt it was almost cruel. Sally had to find a way to soften it.

'Maybe we can ...' She started the sentence, not knowing how she would finish it.

'We can talk to my new teacher about it?' Riley said hopefully.

'Hey, I didn't say that,' Sally said. What had she been saying? What could she say now to make things better?

'You'll talk to her, about me being a boy?' Riley begged.

Sally's heart went out to her child. A handful of words, a glimmer of hope, not even a promise, that was all Riley needed.

'I'll talk to your dad about it,' Sally said.

That evening, Freddie and Isabel arrived at the house, carrying a bunch of flowers and a bottle of wine. Sally hugged them both and welcomed them in. Theo had just texted to say he'd be back in a few minutes. She had hoped to have a chance to talk to him about the conversation with Riley – clearly now the time for avoiding the subject was long gone – but it would have to wait until the end of the evening, when they were on their own.

'Where's my favourite niece?' Freddie asked.

'Upstairs,' Sally said, nodding in the direction of Riley's room. 'She said she wanted to finish making something for you. She said to tell you that you have to wait.'

'OK, sure,' Freddie said, laughing. 'I'll expect something big, then.'

'I'd expect something made of Lego and glitter, from what I saw going on.'

Freddie had his arm around Isabel's waist, holding her tightly, as if they couldn't not be physically close. It made Sally smile to see it. She remembered when she and Theo had been like that, in the early days, permanently drawn to each other as if by magnets.

‘So,’ Isabel said playfully, ‘are you going to offer us a drink, or what?’

‘Sorry,’ Sally said. ‘Where are my manners?’ She went inside, then brought out a tray of Bellinis. ‘So you’re finally here for dinner,’ she said. ‘This is quite the occasion.’

‘Indeed,’ Freddie said, laughing. ‘I guess it’s a kind of initiation into the smug marrieds, right?’

Sally smiled. That must be how she and Theo looked, from the outside. But it was a world away from how she felt.

She heard the front door open and close, and Theo came through to join them in the garden.

Sally kissed him hello. ‘Let me make you one of these,’ she said, lifting her glass.

‘Thanks,’ he said. He gave Isabel and Freddie a hug.

In the kitchen, Sally fixed Theo’s drink and put the oven on to preheat. That kiss outside. Their kiss hello. It had felt different. Almost like it was for show. She tried to push the thought aside. Every couple had to pretend a little, at some point, to get through the rockier patches.

She took the drink outside and passed it to Theo. ‘Did today go OK?’ she asked.

‘Yes. I was just saying, the woman I interviewed for the café today was another no-go. But I’m sure I’ll find someone.’

Isabel nodded.

‘Maybe it’ll even be better,’ Theo said. ‘Trying to think positive.’

Freddie asked Theo a question about their parents, and they started to talk to each other.

Isabel turned to Sally and asked quietly, ‘So I don’t say the wrong thing, Riley’s still being a boy, right?’

‘Yep,’ Sally said. ‘Until school starts.’

‘Right, cool,’ Isabel said. She paused. ‘And then what?’

Sally glanced over at Theo, who was thankfully still engrossed in talking to his brother. ‘We don’t know.’

'Well, Pandora's box is kind of open now, isn't it?' Isabel said.

Riley came out into the garden and walked over towards them, a grin on her face.

Sally flashed a look at Isabel to signal that it was time to change the subject.

'Look, Uncle Freddie!' Riley said, holding out an aeroplane she'd made from Lego, with big white paper wings attached, sprinkled with glitter. 'I made you a plane.'

'Wow. Thanks, Riley,' he said, delighted. He took it from her and lifted it up towards the sky, whirling it around. 'I love it.'

'You have to give the Lego back, though,' Riley said.

'Smart thinking,' Isabel said. She gave Riley a hug hello.

'Are you staying longer this time?' Riley asked Freddie. 'Now that you love Isabel?'

Isabel's cheeks flushed, and Freddie choked out a laugh.

'Sorry,' Sally said.

'No, you know what, it's a fair question,' Freddie said, recovering his composure. 'And the answer's yes. I'm here for a while.'

'And . . . ?' Isabel prompted him.

'And I'm thinking – *thinking* – ' he said with a smile, 'about coming back to live over here again.'

'Really? That's wonderful news!' Sally said, embracing him.

'Yay!' shouted Riley. Riley and Theo joined Sally in the hug.

'Wow,' Theo said, stepping back. 'I think I'm in shock. What's brought this on?

'It's been on my mind for a while.'

'Not just Isabel that's swayed you, then?' Theo said.

'That's definitely part of it,' Freddie said, glancing at Isabel. 'But no. It's not just that. I want to see more of you guys. And Mum and Dad aren't getting any younger. When I saw them at the party . . . I don't know . . . Something clicked in me.

I guess that it's our turn now, after everything we put them through as teenagers, particularly me. It's our turn to be there for them.'

'Whoa,' Theo said, laughing. 'You've changed.'

Freddie smiled. 'I suppose maybe I'm chang*ing*.'

'I think this is worthy of a toast,' Sally said, raising her glass.

'To Freddie sticking around,' Isabel said.

They clinked their glasses together.

Sally caught Theo's eye, and he smiled. Her heart lifted.

Riley tapped her uncle on the arm. 'Uncle Freddie,' she said. 'Did you know I'm a boy now?'

Theo took it better than Sally had expected. 'The summer,' he said calmly. 'I told you about this, right? We said she could do what she wanted for the summer.'

'Cool,' Freddie said.

'Do you want to see my new pants?'

Sally silently hoped, for Theo's sake, that Riley wouldn't pull down her trousers, but she did, showing Isabel and Freddie the Transformers logo.

'Do you like them?'

'Pretty awesome,' Isabel said.

'And when I get back to school, I'll wear them in PE.'

Theo glanced at Sally. Her heart started to race. Not here. Not now.

'Mum's going to talk to the teacher about me staying as a boy,' Riley said.

'No, love,' Sally said, panic rising in her.

Theo looked at Sally, confused. 'You said what . . . ?'

Riley looked at her mum, then at her dad. Freddie and Isabel looked like they were desperately wishing to be anywhere else.

'Mum said—'

'I said I would talk to your dad about it.' Sally turned to Theo. 'That's honestly what I said.'

'Did I say something wrong?' Riley asked, her eyes wide.

'No,' Sally said, flustered. 'It's just a misunderstanding.'

Sally took Riley upstairs shortly afterwards, reassuring her that everything was OK, and reading a chapter of a Moomin book to help her settle. She'd clearly sensed the atmosphere change, and after they finished their dinner, she didn't push to stay up any later.

Downstairs Sally could hear Theo talking with Freddie and Isabel. She wished she could rerun the evening, do it all differently. She wished that she had called Theo, or taken him aside briefly to fill him in, so that everything hadn't come crashing out in a muddled mess like that. She could tell Theo had been upset, and she couldn't blame him – she would have been annoyed too. She would explain it all later. Make things right.

Once Riley was asleep, Sally went back downstairs and bumped into Freddie in the hallway.

'Listen, Sal. I get the sense you guys need to talk. We're going to head off.'

'Don't go,' Sally said, feeling a rush of disappointment. She'd been looking forward to the evening for a long time. 'I mean, really – you don't have to.'

'We'll do it again,' Freddie said with a smile. 'With any luck, lots of times.'

After Isabel and Freddie left, Sally and Theo were alone together. They cleared the plates and tidied the kitchen in silence. The air was thick with tension. Theo broke it.

'So, were you going to tell me anything?' he said.

'Yes. Of course I was,' she said. That defensive tone. She didn't mean for her words to come out that way, but they did – and it was happening more often these days. 'There was no time to talk before Isabel and Freddie got here, that was all. I'm sorry it all came out in the way it did.'

Theo frowned. 'What exactly happened today? What did Riley say?'

'Riley asked me if she could go back to school as a boy.' She paused. It should feel easier than this, talking to her husband, but each word seemed a struggle.

'And you didn't say no.'

Sally shook her head. 'I said I'd talk to you. And I was planning to.'

'But you obviously gave her some kind of hope.'

Sally thought back to Riley's tears. 'She was really upset about it. A flat no felt too harsh.'

'I should have known this would happen,' Theo said, fury rising in his voice. 'You backed me into a corner before – about Riley staying as a boy for the holidays – and now you're doing the same again.'

Theo's words felt like a slap. Was that really how he saw it?

'That's not how it is,' Sally said. 'That's not how it is at all. I'm just looking out for Riley.'

'And you think I'm not.'

Sally felt as if she was treading water, getting nowhere with the conversation. 'Come on, Theo, I definitely didn't say that.'

He looked at her, his eyes weary and strained. 'Is this because of the group last night?' he said. 'Is that why things have changed? Why Riley being a boy at school is now up for discussion? Because this is not where we were. This is a huge step.'

'No. No, it's not the group. This came from Riley. And while it might seem like a big step, it's not as if it's come out of nowhere. You saw how she was on holiday,' Sally said. 'She was so much calmer. None of the acting out that we'd started to see. She really doesn't want to go back to school like how it was before, having to dress as a girl again.'

Theo nodded, with a hint of reluctance. 'I saw that she was happier on holiday. Yes.'

They fell silent again.

'But, Sal, it's not that simple. It was never that simple. This isn't just about letting her keep on doing what she's been doing. We both know it's about far more than that. This is way beyond what we did on holiday, what we've been doing the past few weeks. This is about sending her out into the world as a . . . '

'As a boy,' Sally finished. 'And yes, I do know how serious that is.'

'So why do you want this? Why on earth would you want us to rush into it like this?'

'Because the alternative isn't easy either,' Sally said. She felt as if she was going to cry, remembering how upset Riley had been in the garden, but fought to keep her own emotion back. 'Riley being unhappy in her own body, every day. I can't watch that happen. I can't ignore it.'

Theo fell quiet. Sally thought perhaps something she'd said might finally have hit home for him.

'What would happen,' he asked tentatively, 'if we did speak to the school?'

'I don't know yet. Hopefully they would be willing to make changes that could help Riley feel more comfortable – like letting her use the boys' toilets.'

Theo shook his head. 'It's all so weird. I feel like we're heading down the rabbit hole here.'

Sally felt frustration well up inside her. 'Except this isn't fantasy, Theo. This is reality. And we need to make it a better reality for Riley.'

'It doesn't feel right.' Theo shook his head again. 'It really doesn't. Once we get the school involved, something gets set in motion. This is an issue we've dealt with in private up till now. I don't see why that should change.'

Sally took a deep breath. 'Because sometimes things move on, whether you want them to or not.'

'I get that. I really do. But, man … the teachers will be involved, the other children … Christ, the other parents will even be involved. It just all seems so complicated. Is this really what we want Riley to have to deal with, at her age?'

Sally had thought through the same scenarios. She understood his concerns – she'd had them all too. She'd woken in the night various times, imagining how things might be for Riley in the future, the hostility she might encounter. But, on her own, and in the support group, she'd worked through those fears and now felt differently.

'I know it's difficult, Theo, and that she could face other people's prejudice. Neither of us chose to sign up for this – it just happened. The reality is that Riley already feels different. She already feels out of things. What message are we giving her if we say her feelings should be a secret?'

'I'm not saying they have to be a secret … ' Theo said. 'I feel like you're putting words into my mouth.'

'I'm sorry. That's not what I intended. I don't want you to feel that way,' Sally said. 'We're in this together.' She wanted to reach out to him, to touch him, put a hand on his arm, show him that they *were* still in this together. But something in her held her back. She couldn't afford to let Riley's needs fall into second place.

'It doesn't feel that way right now,' Theo said.

'I just wish you could see that nothing's really changed. It's not as if it's something shameful … '

Theo's eyes flashed with anger. 'You're doing it again. I never said that. All I'm saying is isn't there some kind of middle ground, a way to take this all slower?'

'This is our child's life – right now,' Sally said. 'Every day that she lives as the person she believes she is – as a boy – is a day when she can be relaxed and happy. Maybe I'm there to see it more—'

'That isn't fair,' he said. 'I might not see her as much as you do, because of the business, but I know her.'

'I wasn't implying . . . ' But through being at home more she had seen Riley's sadness towards the end of the summer term every day. If Theo had witnessed that all first-hand, he'd get it. She was sure of that. She stopped herself. 'Look, this isn't about us. If Riley is transgender, we need to support her.'

'Sally, can you stop talking like that?' Theo said. 'She's a child who's having a hard time. But turning her into a boy isn't the answer.'

'We wouldn't be *turning her into a boy,*' Sally said, feeling exasperated. 'Riley feels that's who she truly is. Sometimes the doctors get it wrong. The child is assigned a sex at birth, on the basis of the outward signs, but that child, in their psyche, is actually another gender. It happens.'

Theo sighed. 'I don't get it. All these terms – these things you're saying . . . you sound like a different person.'

It felt that way to Sally too. She suddenly felt conscious that the new language she'd learned was one Theo didn't speak. 'It's my way of trying to understand, I guess,' she said.

'I just don't think that going into Riley's school is the right thing to do. This could all blow over in a few days or weeks. Then what would we be left with? A lot of confusion for everyone.'

Sally started to feel less sure. Maybe this was all happening more quickly than it needed to.

'I just want for us to slow down,' Theo said. For a moment, she saw him again – the man who understood her, the man she loved. 'I don't want to argue with you. And I don't want to fall out with you. But doing this – talking about Riley in that way – it's too soon, Sally.'

She fell silent. 'I just want to keep her safe,' she said eventually.

'So do I,' Theo said, taking her hand.

His touch reminded her that, even if she had felt it lately, she was not alone in all of this.

'I don't want to start something that we can't come back from,' Theo said softly. 'That's all. Not now. Not yet. Can't we have her start term as usual and then see where we are in a few weeks?'

Sally realised she had pushed as far as she could. Theo wasn't going to give in on this.

'But if Riley keeps on insisting?'

'Then we keep on talking,' Theo said.

'You're not ruling out talking to the school, further down the line?'

He shrugged. 'If it seems necessary.'

This time, Sally saw that she had to put her marriage first, to keep a strong family home for Riley. It was her turn to compromise.

'OK,' she said. 'Let's wait.' She thought of Riley's distress earlier that day. 'But how are we going to tell her?'

'We'll do it tomorrow morning. We'll do it together.'

Chapter 24

The next morning, the events of the previous evening came flooding back to Sally. The awkward scene in the garden, and the charged, hostile words that she and Theo had exchanged afterwards. She looked to see if he was still in bed beside her, but the bed was empty. She heard sounds from downstairs – he was having breakfast with Riley. It was Sunday, and tomorrow school would start. They'd said they'd talk to her together. Sally got up and put on her dressing gown.

She texted Isabel: *So sorry about last night. What a mess. Tell me we haven't put you off coming for dinner for ever?*

Moments later came the reply: *It'd take a lot more than that, Sal. I'm here for the rough and the smooth. You know that. x*

Downstairs, Theo and Sally were sitting on the sofa, while Riley played with dinosaurs on the carpet. Theo looked across at his daughter, still dressed in her pyjamas, her feet in furry claw slippers. Her head was bobbed down over a hard plastic stegosaurus, launching him into an unsuspecting diplodocus.

He glanced at Sally – an unspoken question. Was this the right time? She nodded.

'Riley,' he said. 'We wanted to talk to you about something.'

Riley looked up, dinosaurs in hand, with a pout and expression of indignation. 'I'm having a war.'

'Could we pause it?' Sally asked gently.

'Pause a dinosaur war?' she asked. 'Can you do that?'

'Sure you can,' Theo said, motioning for Riley to join them on the sofa. She put her toys down and went to sit between her parents.

'Is this about yesterday?' she said, hesitantly. 'When I said that thing in front of Uncle Freddie and Isabel and everything got weird?'

'No,' Theo said. 'Well, kind of. But you didn't do anything wrong.' He steeled himself. They had to be clear and firm. They had nothing to apologise for. 'Riley. We've all had a great summer together, haven't we?'

She nodded. 'The best. Especially Italy.'

'And you got to wear whatever you wanted,' he said.

'And Granddad Jules called me "he" and a boy,' Riley said proudly.

Theo hesitated. This felt like untying a knot that was becoming tighter with every action. 'And yes, that,' he said.

'But next week it'll be time for school to start again,' Sally said. 'You'll have a new teacher, Ms Bailey, and a new classroom. That's exciting, right?'

Riley nodded. 'They have a guinea pig in the new classroom. I saw that already.'

'When we're at school, some things are different, aren't they?' Theo said. 'There are different rules than at home, like having to put your hand up when you have a question. That kind of thing.'

'Yes,' Riley said. 'And having to hold the penguin when we want to talk in circle time.'

'Exactly,' Theo said. He took a breath. Just do it, he reprimanded himself. Rip the plaster off. You're doing this for her.

This is the best thing for Riley. She has to see the reality of the situation at some point, and the sooner the better.

'When you go back to school, we'd like you to go back as you were before the summer. As a girl.'

Riley drew her bottom lip in and breathed deeply. Her cheeks reddened and her eyes took on a sheen. 'I told Mum no,' she said quietly. 'I told her already.'

Theo tried to touch her hand but she pulled it away.

'This ... this trying out being a boy thing ...' Theo said. 'This was something we did on holiday and here at home. School is different.'

Riley looked down at her trousers and started to pick at a patch of Play-Doh that was stuck to them. She pulled it off and rolled it into a tiny ball, then dug a nail in, hard.

'We love you, Riley, and we want you to be happy,' he said. 'But school is starting again and we have to get things back to normal.'

Theo arrived at the café, and made a coffee for him and one for Gabi, who was at work in the kitchen. He felt an overwhelming sense of relief. He'd been dreading the conversation with Riley – breaking the news to her – and it hadn't been easy. But now it was done. They'd taken a difficult but necessary step so that she could start to invest again in being the girl she was. In the end, he and Sally had found a way to work together. He was optimistic that soon they'd be able to chalk this all up to experience. Look back on the summer that things got turned upside-down from a better place.

He heard a knock at the locked door – Freddie. Theo got up and let him in.

'I was passing on my way back from Isabel's. Thought I'd pop by.'

'Sure,' Theo said. 'Come on in.'

Freddie sat up at the counter on a stool. 'So it all got a bit intense last night, right?'

'Yeah. Sorry you had to be in the middle of all that. Kind of a weird time for us.'

'I get it,' Freddie said.

'It's sorted now, though. We spoke to her this morning and explained how things will be tomorrow.'

'And she was OK with that?' Freddie said.

Theo saw a softening in his expression. He had always cared for Riley, had an affinity with her, somehow. Sally would complain sometimes, good-naturedly, about how erratic his visits were, how his birthday gifts would arrive half a year after the day – but none of that really seemed to bother Riley. He would arrive, play Top Trumps with her on the rug, and that was all that really mattered in her world.

'I think so,' Theo said. He recalled the way she had been that morning, sitting on the sofa quietly, the nail on her little hand digging into the small bit of Play-Doh. 'She *will* be fine with it. It might just take her a day or two.'

'That's good, man. I'm glad for you. This is what you wanted, right? Back to normal, everything easier again, you and Sally on the same page.'

'Yes,' Theo said.

This should all feel better, he thought. But if this was what he'd really wanted, why didn't it feel better?

'Cool,' Freddie said. 'Isabel said Sally was pretty thrown by it all.'

'Sally worries a lot about Riley. She always has.'

'Well, I'm glad you guys worked it out. And I'm really looking forward to seeing more of all of you soon.'

'It'll be good to have you here,' Theo said, relieved to be changing the subject. 'You're serious about the move, right?'

'Yes. Very serious. In fact, there's something I want to talk to you about. Something that's kind of central to all of this,' Freddie said.

'Yes?'

'With Gabi leaving . . . Look, I'm just going to ask you straight out. How would you feel about me coming in to work here?'

Theo hesitated, searching in Freddie's face for some familiar shred of his younger brother.

'I know it's a big decision for you. And God help me I'm not about to tell you I'm an ace baker.' He smiled. 'I wish. Maybe some day. But I can make fantastic coffee, and word is I'm not bad with people. We could make this a real family business.'

Theo thought of the way his parents had helped him when he'd needed it. How it would feel for them to know that the café was now something that was run by both their children. He warmed to the idea.

'But what about your work?'

'I want a change,' Freddie said. 'I don't expect you to trust me. I know that I don't have the best track record on stuff like this. But, bro, I promise you – I will give you everything I've got.'

Theo sensed someone behind him, and turned to see Gabi had come out of the kitchen.

'Give him a chance,' she said to Theo. 'I think he might just be the one.'

On Sunday evening, Theo came home around seven. Sally had just put Riley to bed, earlier than usual. She'd refused to have a bath, and said she was tired from the day in the park. But Sally knew it had far more to do with school starting again the next week.

Theo had told Sally about the conversation with Freddie. He'd agreed to let him come and work at the café, and seemed really positive about it. Given the changes she'd seen in Freddie, Sally was happy for him, for all of them.

‘Listen, I’m sorry to run, but I’ve got to go out.’

‘Sure,’ he said. ‘You seeing Isabel?’

She wished she could say yes and avoid the conversation. But she wasn’t going to lie. ‘No,’ she said. ‘I’m going to the support group.’

Theo looked surprised. ‘You still think you need to go there?’

She nodded. ‘I don’t think it’s all been resolved, Theo. Did you see how Riley was this morning when we told her?’ Sally recalled Riley’s face. She’d been expecting an outburst. A protestation. A shout of ‘no’. But instead Riley’s response had been muted. It hadn’t reassured her. It had done the opposite.

‘She resisted. But that’s what we expected. I thought it went OK, considering. And I bet in a couple of weeks, she’ll be fine. Things will be back to normal.’

He seemed so sure about it all. So certain that this was all going to draw to a neat conclusion. The whole idea of getting back to normal – it jarred. Robyn’s advice came back to her: *There are some words you might want to forget.* Was getting back to normal doing what was best for Riley, or best for Theo?

‘I want to be able to help Riley through whatever it is she feels this week,’ Sally said. ‘And I’m going to keep on going to the group for as long as Riley expresses these same feelings.’

‘OK,’ Theo said. His voice was colder. The distance between them had crept back.

He didn’t say anything explicitly, but she got the sense he’d be happier working things out just the two of them. Sally realised it didn’t matter. They were different people, and they’d have to find their own ways of staying strong.

She left the house. Their kiss goodbye had felt empty. The pressure of what the next day might hold seemed to colour everything.

On the journey to the support group she listened to a playlist on her iPod that Isabel had made her – rare groove and northern soul. The music lifted her spirits. She would talk tonight at the group, she told herself. She wasn't sure exactly what she would say, but she was ready to talk.

She was one of the first to arrive, taking a seat and watching the other parents come into the room and take off their coats. She felt far less of a stranger than she had the previous time she'd come. She spotted Robyn, in a coat with a feathery collar, and she nodded hello.

Carla opened the session and asked who would like to talk first.

Sally took a deep breath. 'I would.'

'Great, Sally,' she said. 'Go ahead.'

'Riley – my seven year old – told me at the start of the summer that she's a boy.' Rather than freezing up, like she'd been worried she would, Sally felt more liberated with each word she spoke. 'We were in the changing rooms at H&M.' It seemed surreal, the ordinariness of the high street shop where ordinary had been cast out of their lives for ever. 'Riley told me that's who she is.'

She looked around the room at the faces: Carla, Robyn, Dan, the man who'd spoken last week, a handful of other parents whose faces were familiar. They were all listening.

'I didn't know what to do. Neither of us did. I was in shock. My husband Theo wanted to wait for it to pass. I wanted to do what I could to help Riley feel better.' It was difficult to return to that time, remember how pained Riley had seemed, and imagining how she might be feeling now.

'We decided to try it out on holiday, let Riley be who she wanted to be. My dad and stepmum were great about it, really understanding. Riley seemed happy. When we came home, we carried it on.'

She thought back on the long summer, snapshots in her mind of Riley's irrepressible smile.

'But now summer's over,' she said, 'and school starts tomorrow. Riley will be attending as she was before, as a girl.'

Carla nodded.

'She's really upset,' Sally said, a lump rising in her throat.

'It's not what you want?' Carla said.

Tears sprang to Sally's eyes. 'It's not. It's not at all.' Her voice caught, but she didn't want to stop. 'I know her attending school as a boy wouldn't be easy. But I'm scared I'm not going to see her smile the same way again.'

Sally made tea in the break and found she was beside Robyn again. She felt stronger for having spoken out loud, talking about Riley and some of the things she had been feeling.

'It's funny, isn't it,' Sally said, passing Robyn a mug, 'how it all comes spilling out? None of the usual stuff – what job you do, where you grew up. You kind of skip over all that, right?'

'Yes,' Robyn said. 'It suits me. But then I've never been a great one for small talk. And something like this throws everything into sharp relief, doesn't it? You see what matters. Who matters.'

'Yes. That's true.'

A thought came into Sally's head. She wondered if she should voice it.

'Did you – do you – ever think any of this might be down to something you've done?'

Robyn paused and Sally wondered if she'd gone too far.

'I mean . . . I'm not saying . . . I just ask myself that sometimes.'

'Don't worry. I get it.' Robyn nodded. 'Was it because I let her play with my make-up when she was young? That I gave in and let her wear that princess dress to her party? Or because when I was pregnant I hoped it was a girl?' Robyn said. She smiled wryly. 'None of that makes a blind bit of difference. Of course it doesn't.' She paused. 'Then I'd hear other people talking about me, or hear about it, asking the same question: was this my fault?

At the start I wasn't sure enough, or thick-skinned enough, to brush off that criticism. I am now.'

Sally smiled. So that was where Robyn's hard edges had come from.

'It's nothing you did or didn't do. I promise you that.'

'I hope not,' Sally said. 'Not because I mind. I don't. I just—'

'I know,' Robyn said. 'You just want your child's life to be easier. We all do.'

'That's right. And I know that's what my husband is thinking too.'

'He's the one pushing for your kid to be a girl, right?'

'Not pushing . . .' Sally tried to find the words. 'He doesn't see things quite the same way as me.'

'I understand.' Robyn nodded. 'Everyone loses someone along the way.'

Sally laughed awkwardly. 'No – it's not like that.'

'You sure?' Robyn said.

The directness of her response threw Sally for a moment.

'It's just easier for me to come to the group on my own.'

Robyn raised an eyebrow. 'That's what I used to say.'

Part Three

AUTUMN

Chapter 25

The next day, the first of the school year, Riley was standing by her chest of drawers, wearing just an oversized T-shirt, hands on hips, shaking her head.

'Please, love,' Sally said. 'We talked about this, didn't we? You can wear the trousers, but not the pants. You'll need to put on the usual pants.'

She glanced over at Theo in the doorway. They would show that they were a team, no matter what. She'd hoped the support group might help her feel strong enough to face today, but instead talking out loud had made her question why she was going along with it at all.

'Please, Riley. Put on your normal pants,' Theo said. It was PE later that day, and Theo had insisted she wear girl's underwear – he didn't want her to be picked on in the changing rooms.

'But they are *not normal*,' Riley said, distressed. 'They are *girl pants*.'

Sally held a pair in her hands – yellow with a blue trim, nothing fancy, but yes, feminine. She could see it in Riley's face – she knew what that underwear represented, and would be aware of it all day. A return to a self she felt she had never truly been. Sally's heart ached. She hated seeing Riley so upset. Did underwear really matter so much that they had to insist on it?

'Why do I have to do this?' Riley said. Her voice cracked with emotion. 'Why do I have to go back to being a girl?'

Theo got down to her level. 'I know this isn't easy for you now. I know this isn't what you want to do. But you'll get used to it. You have to trust us.'

'But on holiday—' Riley started.

'There are things we do on holiday,' Theo explained, 'like eating ice cream every day, taking naps in the afternoon, that we don't get to do every day. When we come home, things go back to how they were before.'

Riley bowed her head and looked at her bare toes, wriggling them.

Sally felt a fresh pang of guilt – for letting Riley think living as a boy was possible. She had promised something that they couldn't deliver.

'Put them on today,' Theo said gently. 'Please.'

Riley shook her head. 'I won't. I won't ever.'

Sally could see Theo trying to think of a better approach. He changed tack. 'How about, if you do it today, we can go swimming on Saturday and get muffins afterwards?'

Riley looked as if she might cry.

'Come on, love,' Theo said.

'I only have to do it today?'

Theo hesitated. 'Today – and tomorrow,' he said. 'And then we'll see.'

So bribery is where we are at with this, thought Sally. Everything about it felt wrong to her. Theo seemed so confident that Riley would have eased her strong opinions by the weekend. But she couldn't share that confidence.

Reluctantly, Riley took the yellow knickers from Sally and pulled them on. 'OK. I'll do it.'

With the underwear on, Riley's posture changed. Her back became more rigid, her legs stiff. Her face, animated almost constantly with laughter for weeks now, took on a serious expression. She pulled on her trousers as quickly as she could. Sally felt as if a sliver of her child had disappeared.

At drop-off Sally kissed Riley goodbye and sent her off into the playground, watching her say hello to some of the other children. Outwardly, nothing about Riley was different than it had been the previous term. But Sally felt deeply anxious.

Leonie caught her eye and came over. 'Good summer?' she asked.

Sally nodded. 'Yes, thanks. We had a great time in Italy.'

This is how it would be, Sally realised. Skimming over the truth, never mentioning what had really happened to their family that summer. Letting it become a secret. As if it were something shameful.

'How was Ava's party?' Sally asked.

'Chaos,' Leonie said, smiling. 'I feel like I've only just finished tidying up. But she loved being a princess for the day. All of them did. We all missed Riley there, of course. You'll have to come over another day.'

'Thank you,' Sally said, distracted. 'We'd like that.' She caught sight of Riley and saw that she was standing on her own, looking back at Sally. Looking lost.

A betrayal. That was what it felt like. Riley was a shadow of the child she had been during the holidays. The other children might not know that, the other parents might not know that, but she did.

'You OK?' Gabi asked Theo. 'Because, with respect, Theo, that is the third order today you've forgotten to pass on.'

'Sorry,' he said. God, had it really been three? His focus had deserted him that morning. 'I'm a bit distracted.'

'Thinking about Freddie starting?' Gabi asked.

It wasn't that. Not really. Freddie joining the café would ordinarily be at the forefront of his mind, but not today.

'No, it's not that.' He thought of how Riley had looked that morning in her bedroom. How she had stiffened. They owed it to her to be firm, consistent, clear, so that she didn't go on feeling as confused as she'd been that summer. But he had felt like he was forcing her – and that feeling had stayed with him. He told himself that in a few weeks, Riley would be past this, and he was making that progress out of this muddled time easier for her. In time she – and Sally – would understand.

All the same, a slight doubt lingered. Had he been too harsh with her? Too much like his own dad? Because nothing had felt good about that moment. Nothing at all.

Riley hadn't been far from Sally's thoughts all day. She'd been thinking over and over about how it had gone, so was relieved when pick-up time came around. Theo seemed to think it was only a matter of time until Riley got used to being a girl again, and even though she found it difficult to believe, Sally hoped he was right. When she caught sight of Riley coming out of the classroom, though, her eyes lowered to the ground, she knew instantly that it hadn't been a good day.

Sally gave her a hug, but Riley seemed unbending in her arms.

'How was it today?' Sally enquired gently.

Riley shrugged. 'It was OK, I guess.' Her voice was quieter than usual.

'What's Ms Bailey like?'

'She's cool,' Riley said flatly. 'A bit strict but not bad-strict.'

'And the classroom?'

'Bigger.'

As they walked home, Riley kicked up leaves on the pavement. Sally tried again to ask about school, but Riley's replies were monosyllabic.

'Can I watch a Pokémon when we get home?' Riley asked, as they neared their road.

'Sure,' Sally said. She ruffled Riley's hair.

'Stop,' Riley said, pulling away.

Sally shrank back. 'Sorry.'

In the house, Riley sat on the sofa and pulled her legs up towards her, watching the TV in silence.

Sally went into the kitchen to make dinner, wishing she could believe that food might fix everything.

She called Riley through and they sat together at the kitchen table. Riley looked down at the scrambled eggs on toast, with baked beans forming an amber oxbow lake around them. She looked down at them for a long time, eating nothing.

'Just a couple of mouthfuls,' Sally said.

'No,' Riley said. 'I'm not hungry.' She pushed the plate away, and then her cup of water.

'Just a bite?'

Riley shook her head, even more resolute.

Sally ran through her toolkit of mealtime emergency management. 'Cheesy pasta?'

'No, thank you,' Riley said.

One last try.

'Babybel? A banana?'

'I don't want anything.'

The last B in her arsenal. She hated to see Riley eat nothing at all.

'Biscuit?'

Riley shook her head and her eyes remained glazed.

Sally lay a hand on her daughter's arm. 'What's up, sweetheart?'

Riley frowned. 'Nothing.'

Anything – Sally would have taken anything. Any word that came. But there was nothing she could do with nothing.

'Is it to do with school?'

Riley nodded. Then shrugged. 'I don't know.'

Sally knew she needed to tread carefully. 'What might make you feel better, Riley?'

Riley looked out of the window, seemed to drift away to somewhere beyond the kitchen, somewhere beyond the roofs and treetops.

'Riley?'

'TV,' she said at last. 'Another Pokémon.'

Pika.

Pika.

Pikachu.

Pikachu.

Ben is not my best friend. He's absolutely not my best friend. Actually, I think I hate him.

I didn't know he was watching me. I went into the boys' toilets. I know I'm not supposed to, that Mum and Dad said I have to act like a girl again, but I thought no one saw me go in. I closed the metal door and locked it, then put the toilet seat down and sat on it. I didn't even need a wee. I just wanted to be in there. Then I looked up, and there he was, laughing. He called Euan in and Euan looked too. Just kind of stared at me sitting there. Euan didn't laugh and I was glad about that.

I got up quickly, but Ben was already shouting things.

'What are you doing in the boys' toilets, Riley?' he kept saying. 'You're a freak. A girl-boy. You sit down to wee.'

I went out the toilet and back to the classroom. Ms Bailey saw that my eyes were red and asked if I was OK. I said yes. They came back into the classroom after that. Euan didn't say anything but Ben whispered it when he went past me.

Girl-boy.

I hate Ben.

Chapter 26

Later that evening, the front door opening woke Sally. She'd fallen asleep on the sofa in front of the TV, and felt disorientated. She pieced together the living room, trying to remember why she was there and not in her bedroom. Riley had been difficult at bathtime, she remembered that much, and had resisted going to bed. When Sally had finally got her to sleep, she'd poured herself a large glass of wine, put on some TV to numb her mind, and fallen asleep before she'd finished the glass.

Theo came to sit beside her on the sofa. 'Hey there,' he said softly.

'Hi.' She sat upright and rubbed her eyes.

'How were things tonight?'

'OK, kind of. Riley was a bit upset. I had to read her a ton of stories before she'd fall asleep.'

'What was up?'

'She didn't say,' Sally said. But she hadn't really needed to. She and Theo had made her do something that day that had made her feel uncomfortable, and it was only natural that she was acting out. It pained Sally to think that they'd do the very same thing the next day too. 'But I think we can probably guess.'

Theo brushed off her concern. 'I guess it was always going to take a little while for her to settle back in.'

Sally tried to put her doubts aside. She had no real evidence to back her worry, beyond a quiet teatime and a reluctant bedtime, neither of which were unusual. Perhaps she was picking up on things that weren't even there.

'I don't know, something didn't seem right. I'm worried about how this is affecting her.'

'But she didn't actually say anything?'

Sally shook her head.

'We need to give it longer,' Theo said. 'It's too early to tell anything. She's probably just adjusting.'

Sally's gut told her not to give it another day, to act now, talk to Ms Bailey and ask her to keep an eye on Riley. But she couldn't draw on anything solid to back that feeling up. Only the things she'd heard, at the support group, online, about what could happen when children weren't listened to or accepted – the way children could turn their hurt inwards. She didn't like to think about it.

'At primary school, a day is a long time,' Theo said. 'By the end of the week the clouds might have cleared all by themselves.'

The end of the week came. Riley had continued to be irritable, but there had been no outbursts. Sally decided that talking to the new teacher could wait.

In the school playground, Sally gave Riley a hug. She held her close, breathing in the honey scent of her. Nothing major had happened. They'd made it.

'What are we doing this weekend, Mum?' Riley asked.

'Actually, I've been meaning to tell you – Grandma and Granddad are coming to pick you up this evening.'

'For a sleepover?'

'That's right,' Sally said. 'And they wanted to take you to the zoo.'

Riley looked brighter than she had all week.

They went home and packed an overnight bag. After tea, Elena arrived in her car, a black Saab.

'Grandma Elephant!' Riley said, running up to her. Sally was relieved to see the light come back into her eyes.

Elena bent to hug her. Riley seemed so very young and sweet when she was with her grandparents.

'You sure this is OK?' Sally asked.

'Of course it is. We've been so excited, Sally. Are you ready to go to the zoo tomorrow, Riley?'

'Yes,' she said. 'I can't wait.'

While Riley went upstairs to get her bag, Sally had a moment with her mother-in-law, to catch up on their investment in the business, and on the news about Freddie working there. Elena seemed positive about it all. Sally realised they hadn't talked properly in a while, handing over with a few pleasantries when she came to collect Riley. A lot had changed lately.

Sally gave Riley a hug and squeeze. 'Have fun, love.'

When Theo got home, they sat and ate together. Sally poured wine and put on music – the small things that they did when they had an evening to themselves. But it hovered there in the air: the tension that the past few days had brought about.

'Riley was OK today, then?' Theo said.

'Yes. She seemed excited about the sleepover.' Riley was happy when she wasn't going to school, Sally thought. When she wasn't being shoehorned into a mould that no longer fitted.

'She'll enjoy it at Mum and Dad's. She always does.'

Sally nodded. But then next week? She'd still be unhappy next week.

'We are doing the right thing,' Theo said, as if reading her thoughts. 'It may not be entirely easy, Sal, but we are doing the right thing.'

They ate in silence. Riley, in her absence, was more present than ever.

Later that evening, Sally was getting ready for bed when an instant message came through from Matt.

Hi there. Just wanted to check in. See how you are.

Sally smiled. But as she went to type a reply, she felt conflicted. Was it really right to be talking to someone else, a virtual stranger, when she and Theo were barely communicating? She paused. Matt was just a friend. She needed someone to talk to, and he'd been kind enough to ask.

We're fine, Sally wrote. Riley's restarted school. We decided it was best for now if she went as a girl, like before.

OK. And how's that going?

Well, I think.

I don't know, she thought.

Good, he replied.

She paused. Bit her lip, then typed again.

Matt – do you think it can all just go away? That this could all just be a phase? That everything could just pass?

Yes, he replied. Yes, of course it can be a phase. And seven is young, still. It might come and go, and that's it. Or it might go and come back again. Or, when they're older, the child might turn out to be gay, rather than transgender. Pretty much anything's possible.

OK, she thought. Anything's possible. It was possible they had passed through the phase.

You're Riley's parent, Matt typed. You know your child better than anyone. What is your gut feeling?

Sally let in the emotions she'd pushed out of the way, because they made things difficult. Complicated.

This isn't the end, she wrote. It's not over. It feels like the beginning.

Chapter 27

Riley came home from her grandparents on Sunday seeming happier. Sally went to bed that night pushing her worries to the back of her mind. She didn't want to dismiss a gut feeling, but if something were seriously wrong, surely it would have shown this weekend? Instead, Riley had talked about the trip to the zoo, and the film they had watched, giving no sign that she was anything but content.

On Monday morning, Riley was quiet again as she got dressed, but she didn't resist. Theo dropped her off at school, while Sally got to work sewing for her latest orders – they had really picked up since she'd implemented Isabel's marketing advice.

At pick-up, as Sally waited for the doors to open, she texted Isabel.

Orders going great, all down to you – thank you! How are you? Good news about Freddie and the café, right?

Hi. You're welcome. Yep, seems like you and I are getting closer to being family every day (!)

Sally smiled to herself. A year ago she would never have predicted the turn that Isabel's life was taking – bringing them even closer together.

When Sally looked up from her phone, she saw Riley coming out of the classroom. She was on her own, walking slowly.

Sally gave Riley a hug, and hoped she would smile, but she didn't. 'You OK?' she asked.

Riley shook her head.

Sally caught sight of something on Riley's forearm. A large plaster.

'What happened?'

Riley lifted up the edge and Sally saw a deep scratch – about an inch and a half long, raw and red.

Her breath caught. 'What happened?'

Riley shrugged and looked down at the floor. When she looked back up, Sally could see that her eyes were filled with tears. She took her daughter by the shoulders and held her gently.

Oh God, she thought. Someone's hurt her.

In trying to make Riley's life easier, maybe she and Theo had somehow made their child more of a target.

'How did this happen?' Sally asked, as calmly as she could, but her hands were shaking. 'Who did this?'

Riley shook her head. 'No one.'

'It can't be no one,' Sally said softly. She whispered to her, 'Whoever it is, you can tell me, sweetheart.'

Riley just carried on shaking her head.

Out of the corner of her eye, Sally saw Ms Bailey come striding quickly over towards her.

'Ms Pieterson. Have you got a minute? I need to talk to you.'

Sally waited for Theo to come home. Riley was upstairs playing and she took a moment to compose herself, trying to get a hold on her spiralling thoughts. She'd tried to talk to Riley all the way home, to get more information from her than her teacher had given, but her responses had been guarded and minimal.

'What's happened?' Theo asked. 'You look terrible.'

'It's Riley,' Sally said. 'Something happened today at school.'

'What? Is she OK?'

'Yes, she's fine, it's just a scratch – a bad one but just a scratch.'

'What happened?' Theo asked, concerned. 'Did she have an accident?'

'No.'

'So, what? Someone hurt her on purpose?' His protective instinct kicked in.

'Yes. A boy scratched her with a sharp stick.'

'Who?' Fury rose in him. She could see he felt the same protective instinct, the same drive to put the situation right.

'Theo – stop,' Sally said, tears coming to her eyes. 'It's not that simple.'

'What do you mean?' Theo asked, confused.

'It was Riley who started it. It was Riley who lashed out. She hurt the boy first.'

Theo went upstairs. He needed to talk to Riley – make some sense out of what Sally had told him. She didn't act like this – she'd never hurt anyone. There must be more to it than what the teacher had told Sally.

He found Riley in her room, playing with Lego on her carpet.

'Hey, Riley,' he said. He got down to her level. 'Can I help you build that?'

Riley shrugged. 'If you want.'

She passed him a few pieces and he joined in, putting in a window and a door.

'So, your mum told me something happened at school today.'

'Yes. It was bad.'

'Is it true that you hurt someone?'

Riley fixed him with a glare, narrowing her eyes. 'Ben deserved it.'

'Hey,' Theo said. 'No. You're wrong there. No one deserves to be hurt.'

'He did it back to me, anyway. Worse.' She pointed at her arm. Theo was used to seeing his daughter covered in cuts and bruises, but still he had to admit that the scratch looked pretty bad.

Riley went back to building.

'Look, Riley. Let's stop for a minute,' Theo said. 'Because this is important.'

Riley reluctantly put the bricks down. 'I know I'm not meant to hit,' she said.

'So what happened? This isn't like you.'

'He said things. Mean things,' Riley said.

'Like what?'

'I don't want to say.'

'You can tell me.'

'No,' Riley said. 'I can't tell you. I don't want to.'

'Please,' Theo said. 'It's important.'

'He called me a freak. A girl-boy. He said I'm not a boy and I never will be. But it's not true.' Riley's cheeks flushed red. 'What he said, it's not true.'

Sally hoped that when Theo came downstairs, they might know a little more. He had a way with Riley. She might open up to him.

Sally wondered how well she really knew her child now. Riley had never been violent. She'd never lashed out at other children. This was so unlike her.

Theo came and sat beside her. 'Ben,' he said. 'That's the boy Riley hurt.'

'Ben,' Sally said. She vaguely recalled a dark-haired boy, taller than the others. 'Riley's barely even mentioned him before.'

'He said something to her.'

'What? Did she tell you?'

'Yes, in the end.'

'What was it?' Her pulse raced.

'Just kids' stuff.'

'Tell me, Theo,' Sally said, feeling exasperated. 'I need to know.'

'Don't get annoyed with me,' Theo said. 'It's nothing major. He was mean to Riley, that's all.'

'What did he say?'

'He called her a freak. A girl-boy.'

Sally eyes widened. She could imagine how those words would have struck at Riley's core. She felt desperately for her. Now it made sense, or was starting to. The only thing that could make Riley behave in a way that was so out of character.

'Just playground stuff,' Theo said.

'Is it?' That wasn't how it felt to her. Riley had clearly been very affected by what had been said. Sally couldn't rest easy – wouldn't rest easy – knowing that something wasn't right.

'I think we should take Riley to the GP,' Sally said.

Theo paused. 'Because of this? Isn't that a bit extreme?'

'Not just because of this – because of everything that's going on. Because I think we both want her to feel better than she does right now.'

'You think a doctor will be able to help?' He seemed sceptical.

'They might,' Sally said. 'I'm hoping, Theo.'

Theo went upstairs to bed on his own that evening. He and Sally had called and managed to get an appointment for Riley at the local surgery for the end of the week. His feelings were mixed. He'd been resistant at first – it seemed wrong to be treating something as medical when it seemed so clearly to be down to how Riley was feeling. But if the doctor could put Sally's mind at rest – reassure her that they could wait, that they didn't need to do anything – then it would be worth it.

Chapter 28

On the morning of the doctor's appointment, Theo got Riley's school bag and books together, and Sally bent down to Riley's level to talk to her.

'So you understand why we're going today?'

'To talk about why I get angry. About why I hit Ben.'

'Yes,' Sally said. 'And about anything else you might be feeling.'

'OK,' she said. 'Like about being a boy.'

'That's right,' Sally said, feeling slightly nervous.

They all walked over to the local surgery together. Riley seemed relaxed. Sally was grateful for the fact she'd never been scared of the doctor's surgery like some children could be – she'd rarely been ill, so, aside from her pre-school jabs, associated doctors with stickers and kindnesses. Sally laid a hand on her child's shoulders and led her towards the reception desk.

The waiting room was full, mostly with elderly people, and there were mutterings about the waiting times. Sally found seats for them. For a moment she felt that perhaps they shouldn't have come – these people had real, quantifiable illnesses, some with symptoms you could see. The body and mind are one, Sally reminded herself. Many serious conditions aren't visible. What

Riley was going through was as real as these coughs, the shingles and heart conditions.

Riley began to fidget in her seat.

Theo got out his iPad and passed it to Riley, loading up a paintbox game. 'Here you go. Let's do this one together.' Theo gave Riley a gentle squeeze. 'Then a few questions and we'll be out of here.'

He was reassuring himself, not Riley, Sally thought.

'Riley Pieterson.'

The family gathered up their things and went through into the surgery.

'Hello, take a seat,' said the doctor. She was in her late twenties, with a short bob and dark-framed glasses. She was young. For some reason that gave Sally hope that she might understand.

'Now, you must be Riley,' the GP said warmly. 'I'm Dr Lewis. You can call me Danielle.'

Riley glanced around the surgery at the stethoscope and medical equipment, and the bed with its small green curtain.

'What can I help you with today?' Danielle asked.

Sally sat up straighter and prepared to speak, but Theo got in there first.

'Riley's fine, physically.'

Sally flashed him a look.

Riley looked from her father to her mother.

'She's healthy,' he said. 'That's what I mean.'

Sally spoke. 'At the start of the summer, Riley began to say she was a boy.'

'I *am* a boy,' Riley said, clearly and firmly.

'OK,' Danielle said. She glanced at the record on-screen. 'And you're seven years old, Riley, is that right?'

'Yes, I'm seven.'

'And what's happened since then?' Danielle asked.

'Well, you've said it pretty often, haven't you?' Sally said, as

Riley nodded. 'That she's a boy, I mean. She wanted to make certain changes. The haircut. Clothes. Then during the summer we took her on holiday and allowed her to dress as she wanted. Be who she wanted,' Sally explained.

'It was brilliant,' Riley said. 'But then school started, and they made me be a girl again.'

'It hasn't been long,' Theo said. 'We didn't want to rush into anything.'

'I understand,' Danielle said.

Sally bristled. She felt as if Theo was trying to win the doctor over, somehow. As if he wanted to be sure that she would come out on his side in all this.

'Since then . . . ' Sally paused. 'Well, there was an incident at school. Riley hurt another child. It was very out of character.'

Riley shuffled awkwardly in her seat.

The doctor turned to Riley. 'I'd like to ask you some questions. Would that be OK, Riley?'

Riley wriggled slightly in her seat, but didn't look away. 'Sure.'

'You say that you're a boy,' the doctor said. 'Can you tell me a bit more about that, how it feels?'

'My body . . . ' Riley wrinkled her nose. 'It's not right.'

Sally felt a pain in the middle of her chest. Those words. She would never be able to get used to hearing those words.

'What's not right about it?'

'I don't like it. I'm a boy and I want a boy's body. I want to wee standing up.'

Theo sat back in his seat, as if he couldn't deal with what she was saying. It was almost as if he wanted to physically distance himself from it, Sally thought.

'Anything else?'

'I want to be a man when I grow up. Like Dad. Because I'm a boy, and boys grow into men. I'm not a girl. I don't want to be like Mum.'

Sally looked over at Theo, to see his reaction, but he was looking straight at the doctor, emotionless. What was he thinking? What was going on in that head of his?

'What would be different if you were a boy?'

'I would be me.'

The words hit Sally in the chest again. Riley didn't feel like herself. Each day she woke up and didn't feel comfortable.

The doctor looked up at Sally and Theo. 'And prior to this year, Riley hadn't given indications that she was unhappy in her body?'

'No,' Theo said. 'And she's into a different thing each week. You know how it is—'

'Theo,' Sally said, stopping him. 'There have been things. Getting upset about the toys, the—'

'I've said it before, but they didn't listen,' Riley cut in. 'When I was five. At the swimming pool.'

Sally and Theo looked at each other for a moment. Did he remember? She couldn't. Sally's mind flicked back through the memories, searching. Maybe. It was possible. Perhaps they hadn't been listening carefully enough.

'She might have said it,' Theo said. 'But it wasn't like this.'

'How does it make you feel when people treat you as a girl, talk to you as a girl?' Danielle asked.

Riley looked at the floor, silent. When her answer eventually came, it was quiet but firm. 'Horrible.'

The word brought goosebumps to the surface of Sally's skin. Riley shouldn't be feeling that way. She wanted to take her into her arms and hold her close, tell her that everything was going to be all right. That nothing would ever make her feel that way again. That she wouldn't let it. But she couldn't.

'Really horrible,' Riley said. Her eyes were red-rimmed now. 'That's why I hurt Ben. Because he says things to me. Mean things.'

'Right,' the doctor said. 'People can be unkind sometimes, can't they?'

Riley nodded.

The doctor typed something else on the digital record, and Sally had a sudden urge to ask what it was she'd put down, what she thought, what the solution was. The solution to her child, who had never been a problem.

The GP turned to face them. 'I hesitate to say anything too concrete here, given Riley's age, and how new this all is, but there are some signs of gender dysphoria.'

Those two words Sally had never heard a few months ago, and were now all too familiar to her.

Theo looked lost.

'Do you have any understanding of what that is?'

Sally nodded. 'We've asked Doctor Google. And I've been to a support group.'

Theo didn't react.

'Right. Well, don't believe everything you read online, but it's good that you've done a little research. It's a condition where a person experiences discomfort or distress because there's a mismatch between their biological sex and gender identity. It's sometimes known as gender identity disorder or transgenderism.'

Sally glanced over at Theo. *Transgenderism. Transgender.* She was sure the word would have an impact on him, but he looked blank, numb.

The doctor continued. 'We look for a persistent, insistent and consistent cross-gender identification.'

Persistent. Insistent. Consistent.

'In other words, your child will keep telling you, again and again.'

Riley hadn't wavered. Not since she'd first said it, in that changing room. The definition seemed to fit, Sally thought. She felt strangely reassured. They had been right to bring Riley this far, at least.

'But Riley's still very young. Let's just follow this for a while and see how things go. I'd suggest we make an appointment for two months' time and see how things are then. Does that sound OK to you?'

Sally nodded. 'Sure. OK.'

She wanted to ask about school. The right thing for them to do at school. But she looked over at Theo, shifting in his seat now, and decided not to push things any further.

When they left the surgery, on the way down the path, Sally reflected it had been something. A step forward. Perhaps now Theo would see that she hadn't been exaggerating.

Riley turned to her parents. 'She used a lot of long words,' she said. 'Did she mean I have to wait to be a boy at school?' She looked at them hopefully.

Sally felt a pang of guilt. She should have raised it – asked at least, what the best thing was to do for now, at school. Instead, they were no closer to being able to give Riley what she so desperately wanted.

'No,' Theo said, taking her hand. 'She said we should come back and see her in a little while. That's all.'

On the way home in the car, Sally glanced out the window. They passed house after house, just like their own. Perhaps they all had their own secrets. Maybe all of those families that looked so normal were anything but. They'd been brave enough to talk openly with the doctor about what was going on in theirs.

She glanced behind her at Riley, sitting in the back seat, and smiled. Riley stuck her tongue out, and then smiled back.

That day might not have given them any solid answers, but it had cemented something in Sally. The doctor had said there was a chance that Riley was experiencing gender dysphoria. She'd confirmed that the way Riley had been feeling wasn't going to be 'fixed' by changing her hair or clothes, that this wasn't necessarily a phase that would pass. This was about how Riley saw herself.

Himself.

At some point, as the doctor spoke, Sally had realised this wasn't about trying to second-guess what Theo thought – to placate or please him. She was Riley's mum, and she would be by her child's side, trying her best to understand how Riley felt, whatever it took.

After Theo and Sally dropped Riley back at school, an awkward silence fell between them in the car, and Sally knew they couldn't afford to let it linger.

'Well, that wasn't easy – but we did it,' she said. 'What did you think about what the doctor said?'

Theo shrugged. 'I think she's right: we should wait, see how things go. Riley's young. It's what I've been saying all along.'

'But she also mentioned gender dysphoria. She said Riley might be showing signs of it. Did you take that part in?'

'Yes,' he said, distantly. 'I heard her mention it as a possibility. But she doesn't want to see Riley for another two months – which makes me think there's no hurry here. It's been a few weeks, Sal – not much in a lifetime, even her short one.'

Sally felt as if they'd gone to two different appointments. What she'd heard was a potential diagnosis, an acknowledgement that it was likely that something was genuinely the matter with Riley. 'It's long enough. For her to become unhappier, or for her to start acting out, and doing things she wouldn't otherwise be doing.' She thought of the scratch on Riley's arm and felt for the child that Riley had hurt first.

'Kids say things,' Theo said. 'Do things. Stupid things, sometimes. It happens.'

Something inside Sally snapped. 'That's your answer for everything, isn't it?'

'Sorry?' Theo seemed thrown.

'Kids say stupid things, do stupid things . . . but sometimes they act like that for a reason, to tell adults that something isn't right. And yes, hurting another kid might be a one-off. But it might not be – if we don't listen now, this might become Riley's way of being heard.'

'I doubt that,' Theo said. 'Riley's always been a good kid. She still is.'

'We can't afford to ignore this stuff, Theo.' Sally's voice began to crack with emotion. 'I don't want to force her into things she feels uncomfortable with. And the toilets, the underwear – they're things that upset her. I think we should go easy on her, let her do what she wants at school.'

'And it's what you think that matters,' Theo muttered.

'Come on – it's not like that.'

He fixed his eyes on hers. 'That's how it sounds.'

She snapped. 'But you're insisting on her doing things that make her feel worse.'

The words were out before she had a chance to stop them.

'Whoa.' Theo recoiled.

She'd gone too far. Theo would never do anything to hurt Riley – they both knew that. She'd been trying to put the blame on him. Because somehow it felt better that someone – even if it was the man she loved most in the world – was at fault.

What was happening to them? Things had changed so much over the past few months. There had been a time when they would never have dreamed of talking to each other like this – the edge in their voices, the vitriol. Kindness had once been at the centre of their relationship, and now something else – a fierce wish to protect Riley, or, perhaps, the drive to be right – had taken its place.

'I'm sorry, I didn't mean it to come out like that,' she said.

'That was pretty harsh, Sally. All I'm doing is exercising a little caution here. Everything I've suggested is for Riley. It's not about you and me. I'm trying to protect her.'

She reached out to him, but he moved away. The gulf between them widened.

'We have both been worried about her,' Sally said. 'Worried enough to go to the doctor this morning.'

Theo nodded, seeming weary of it all. 'I thought the GP would put everything straight. I thought we'd get some answers.'

'I hoped that too,' Sally said. 'I thought we'd get ... I don't know, a plan. A referral. Something.'

'Me too.' Theo paused. 'And it was hard hearing those things Riley said. The way that she feels.'

'Yes,' Sally said. Maybe Theo did get it. For the first time since this all started, she felt they were on the same page. 'I know. Imagine saying – shouting, sometimes – that you are not what everyone says you are. And then those shouts go unheard. When she said she felt horrible ... '

Theo shook his head. 'It was tough, finding that out.'

'She feels horrible. That's what she said. She's telling us that we all have it wrong,' Sally said. 'If we keep telling her something different, making her wear clothes to school that remind her how her mind and body don't fit, I don't want to think about how that makes her feel inside, believe me. But it's our duty to.'

Sally looked at Theo, waiting for him to reply. To see how that morning had helped it all sink in for him.

'It hurt me as much as it did you to hear how upset Riley's been feeling,' Theo said, looking at her directly. 'It's clear Riley needs our love and support right now, more than she ever has. That's hard – it really is. Because I thought we were getting it right. I thought we were good parents, and she was happy—'

'We *are* good parents,' Sally said, feeling for him. 'And Riley *has* been happy—'

'Well, now we have to deal with the fact that it's not that simple.'

Sally nodded. They could do this. Together, they could find their way through.

Theo's expression hardened. 'But do I think the best way to help her is to change her gender? To help Riley become a boy? Do I think that will make everything right? No. No, and no again.'

Sally felt his anger. It hurt, but she knew it wasn't meant for her. Just as hers wasn't really for him. This had become far bigger than the two of them.

'Sally, I don't. And I don't think I ever will.'

And there it was – he hadn't changed his thinking at all. They weren't side by side. Maybe they never would be.

'I need to get to work,' Theo said.

The door that Sally had thought was opening had shut.

That evening, with Riley in bed, Sally was alone with her thoughts. The appointment with the GP, and the discussion she'd had with Theo afterwards, were running through her mind again and again. She thought about calling Isabel – she knew she would be there for her – but she hesitated. Isabel was in a good place, she deserved that happiness, and Sally didn't want to drag her into this, and that's what it would feel like.

Perhaps there was someone who would understand. She needed more than anything to feel that somebody understood.

She picked up her phone and went to her messages. She started to type.

Hi – you free for a chat?

[Matt]: Hello there. Yep. Go ahead.

[Sally]: We went to the doctor today.

[Matt]: OK – big step.

Sally thought about it. It had felt like a big thing, at least to her. Their first step into formally acknowledging that something was wrong.

[Sally]: I'm glad we went. She thought there were signs of gender dysphoria. I'm not sure if it helped, or made things worse, but we both needed to hear it. It was clear, to me at least, that Riley needs our help. She needs to be listened to. But her dad doesn't want us to change how things are. How do I stay here? Not doing anything? While she's hurting?

[Matt]: I know it's not easy, but try to slow down. You are there for her, even if you're doing nothing right now. With Siobhan we didn't know what action to take at first. We had those earliest inklings, the first things she said, but it was years before we acted on any of it. It was even longer before we considered puberty blockers.

[Sally]: Thanks. You're right. I know you're right. I just hate seeing her so upset.
What was it with Siobhan? How did you know?

[Matt]: There came a day. She said something. We knew. It's really different – Siobhan was much older. She was twelve then, her male puberty starting, and that was very distressing for her. The pressure was very immediate. You're not in the same position. I'm sure it won't be like this for you.

[Sally]: What did she say?

And then, without another word, Sally knew.

The statistics. The proportion of trans young people who wished, at some point, that they weren't alive any more. The number that acted on it. A chill ran through her.

She thought, then, of the empty teenage bedrooms. Parents with empty arms – because of this, their children not being heard. The mums and dads with photos on the mantelpiece that were no longer the markers of a journey still being lived, but the sole reminders of a child gone too soon.

Perhaps those parents, like her, had sensed, deep down, something wasn't right.

[Matt]: There are some chances you aren't willing to take.

Later that night, while Sally was downstairs, Theo sat alone in their bedroom and turned on his laptop.

Normal. What a seductive word it had become.

Before the summer started, it was what they'd been. They had never been perfect. They'd had misunderstandings, there were tantrums and arguments. But they had been just like any other family. And now? Everything had changed.

He didn't want them to be a tabloid news story. An interview on *This Morning*, if things turned out well, or *Jeremy Kyle* if they didn't. What parent ever would?

He loved Sally – more than that, Sally was a part of him. The part of his life that had mattered most had her right in the centre of it. Her smiles, her laughter, her support. Having Riley had brought them closer in ways he'd never even imagined. But this situation was chipping away at all of that.

He wanted a good life for Riley. He'd always known there'd be bumps in the road – he'd envisioned that – but this would mean more than bumps. It would mean all of them dealing with other people's judgement.

The films he'd watched in the past came back to him now. *The*

Crying Game came instantly to mind. For children, for adults who were trans . . . the threats to their wellbeing, to their happiness, to their lives were immense.

Theo had always thought of himself as accepting. Tolerant. Yet here he was, sitting at his computer, alone, because he wanted to work out how to fix Riley.

He typed into the search bar: *Transgender child.* Then added: *Conversion.*

He was just thinking of the future, he told himself. If they continued to follow this path – if Riley started school as a boy – there might be no going back. That path to becoming an adult male would be set. What prejudice would Riley encounter – in school, in the streets, in the workplace . . . ? If Riley became male, would she ever fall in love, have a relationship? It would all be more difficult. More painful. He couldn't just sit back and watch that happen – the stakes were too high.

Shame nagged at him. He couldn't square the urge to change Riley with anything he'd thought he was: open-minded, liberal. But this situation called for him to look at everything in a different way. It called for him to be strong.

What drove him on was hope – hope that they could still undo what had been started. That there was still a chance they could help Riley to come through this without any damage.

Conversion therapies. He read through the forum posts from parents whose children had thought they were trans, but with guidance had passed through that phase and out the other side. They'd gone back to normal. It happened – it looked like it happened a lot. There were parents who'd chosen to take away certain toys, reminded their children that you could be a boy who loved *Frozen*, or a girl who wanted to be in the army, that there was no reason to assume you were in the wrong body just because the toys you liked and the friends you had didn't fit the stereotype. They just refused to let their children change gender, refused to go along with it all. They supported their children but enforced boundaries.

Theo heard the door open with a creak, and turned around to see Sally's face in the half-light.

'Are you still working? It's late.'

'Yes,' he lied. 'Nearly finished.'

She was wearing the silk camisole he'd bought her for her birthday. He loved the way it hung on her body, and the way her hair looked, loose like that. Another night, things would have ended differently. He missed that closeness so much it hurt.

She sat beside him. He closed his laptop.

He couldn't tell her what he'd been looking at. He couldn't admit to her that he'd been searching for ways he could make the problem – the problem with their child – go away.

Chapter 29

Sally lay back in the bubbles of the jacuzzi. The spa was a converted Victorian bathhouse, peaceful and calm. Opposite her, Isabel, her cheeks pink with the warmth of the bath, flicked bubbles in her direction.

'Stop it,' Sally said. She flicked some back and Isabel responded by kicking her under the water.

'Shame they don't let you bring wine in here,' Isabel said. 'I quite fancied starting early today.'

'Flaw in the otherwise perfect set-up. Mind you, if I started now, I'd be asleep by the time we got to Gabi's leaving party.'

'Oh yes, you definitely would be. Lightweight.'

'Anyway, this is enough,' Sally said, her whole body relaxing in the warm water. She couldn't remember the last time she'd felt this calm. 'This is the best. It was a good idea of yours.'

'It came to me yesterday at work. I realised how long it had been since we did anything like this.'

'Elena was happy to have another day with Riley. They've gone to the Science Museum. She loves it there.'

'Elena,' Isabel said. 'You know I'm meeting her for the first time tonight. As Freddie's girlfriend, I mean. How scared should I be?'

'Petrified,' Sally said, laughing. 'No, really, she's fine. And you're the woman bringing her son back to the UK, Isabel. She must love you already.'

'I thought I'd wear my dark red dress, with the cowl neck – do you remember that one?'

'Yep. Good mother-in-law-meeting dress.'

'I was looking through my wardrobe for something non-slutty. That was the only one that made the cut, really,' she laughed. 'Obviously Freddie thinks I should wear one of the others.'

Sally smiled. She let herself relax in the moment again. The pressures and upsets of the past week started to slowly slip to the back of her mind. Sally wondered whether to mention the GP appointment, the way things had been with Theo ever since. But she didn't want to – she wanted to stay in this moment longer.

'We're moving Dad to a home next week,' Isabel said.

'Oh, Isabel,' Sally said, realising she'd been caught up in her own thoughts. 'I'm sorry.'

'I'm not,' Isabel said, shrugging. 'How's that for a bad daughter?'

'You're been saying for a long time that he was struggling at home. I saw myself when I was there the kind of things that might go wrong. The heater. The hob.'

'It became impossible, Sal. It wasn't safe any more.'

'Where's the home?'

'Rosemount. It's around the corner. It's nice there. We'll have to sell his house to afford it, but it's a nice place. And it'll be as easy to get to as it was seeing him at home. I just have to try and forget that I promised him, when he was well, that I'd never let this happen.'

'You couldn't have predicted then how things were going to turn out.'

'That's what I've been telling myself.'

'Do you need a hand, next week, moving his stuff?'

She shook her head. 'My brother's coming down. He finally

seems to have woken up to the fact that this kind of memory loss isn't going to be cured with sugar pills or acupuncture.'

'That's good.'

'And Freddie's renting a van to help us move.'

Sally's eyebrows went up.

'He hasn't messed up yet,' Isabel said. 'You're surprised, aren't you?'

Sally held her hands up, laughing. 'I didn't say a thing.'

Isabel glanced over Sally's head at the clock behind her. 'Nearly lunchtime. Shall we have a swim and head up to the restaurant?'

'Sure,' Sally said.

'You can tell me about Riley. How things have been.'

Sally nodded. Emotion welled under the surface.

'Are you OK, Sal?'

Sally thought of the night before. How she and Theo had lain in bed in the dark together, their bodies barely touching. Silent, aside from the sounds of their breathing. In the knowledge that neither of them was really sleeping. She felt – and she hated to admit it – awkward and uncomfortable beside Theo. And lonely. Strangely lonely.

She knew deep down that she shouldn't be feeling that way. She and Theo were a team. They were the cornerstones of each other's lives. They *were* each other's lives. Yet right now she didn't want to talk to him; to have to think about the things that neither of them had answers for.

'Let's talk about something else,' Sally said. 'Just for today.'

At the café, Freddie was helping Theo and Gabi prepare food for her leaving party that night. Theo was grateful for their company, and the distraction.

'So, you looking forward to getting started here?' Gabi asked Freddie.

'Of course I am. I know yours are big shoes to fill, but I'm ready to try.'

'Well, I'm glad,' Gabi said. 'Really glad. It's a good feeling knowing that I'm leaving this place in safe hands, and that it'll be a family business for you guys now.'

'Don't feel too OK about it,' Theo said. 'I'd still rather you weren't going.'

'Thanks, mate,' Freddie said.

'Nothing personal, Freddie. But the two of us have history here, you know that.'

'You're still annoyed?' Gabi said.

'Not annoyed. Just – I don't know.' Theo struggled to pin it down in his own mind. He didn't want things to change. Everything had been fine, and now it was all changing. 'You're a good friend, Gabi. Happy as I am that we'll all be celebrating together tonight, I just wish it was for another reason.'

Gabi put down the bread she was cutting and gave him a hug. 'I know. Me too.'

'Just think of the cheap holidays, Theo, when she's got her own place,' Freddie said. 'That'll ease the pain.'

Theo laughed. 'Good point, actually. I hadn't thought of that.'

'So, Freddie. Your parents are going to meet Isabel tonight, right?' Gabi said. 'This must be serious.'

'Ha,' Freddie said. 'Yes, it is. Did the fact I'm moving home not give you that idea already?'

'You're nervous,' Gabi said. 'I can tell.'

'I am not.'

'You are,' Theo said.

'OK – maybe a bit. I haven't introduced anyone to them since . . . I don't know. Emma, when I was at college? That was years ago.'

'It'll be fine,' Theo said. 'Isabel's already got the Sally seal of approval. That will count for a lot with them.'

'If they can see a fraction of what I can see in her, they'll love her,' Freddie said.

Gabi glanced over at Theo, a smile forming.

'What?' Freddie said, defensively.

'Nothing,' Theo said. 'Nothing at all.'

That evening, as they walked down their front path, after settling Riley with the babysitter, Theo turned to Sally. She could see in his eyes that he felt the same as her – tonight, they would leave it all behind. Be there with each other, in the moment, without the heaviness that had been weighing on them lately. Have fun, if they could.

'You look beautiful tonight.'

'Thanks,' Sally said. For the first time in a while, she felt it. Having the whole day with Isabel had given her space to unwind, and talking about other things over lunch than Riley had helped her get back a bit of perspective.

'Is it bad that Riley's been with your mum all day and we've just handed her over to someone else? I mean, considering what this week has been like?'

'No,' Theo said. 'She's fine with the babysitter. You saw her. And Mum won't see Riley for weeks once she and Dad go to Crete next week to help Gabi and her parents get set up.'

'I suppose so.'

'And we need this, Sal, every so often. We say it and then somewhere along the way it gets forgotten again. We need to go out together once in a while, just the two of us.'

'You're right. I know you're right,' Sally said. 'Forget I even said that.' She took his hand. 'No more parent chat.'

Gabi's farewell drinks were at her flat, near the café in east London. The garden was strung with coloured bulbs and nightlights lit the way down the paved stairs. The outside area was filled with friends and family, many of them familiar faces, including Isabel and Freddie, who were standing with their arms around each other, talking. Theo went over to join them.

Sally went over to say hello to Gabi. She embraced her and gave her the present she'd bought: a linen-bound travel journal.

'It's lovely,' Gabi said. 'Thanks, Sally.'

'I thought you could use it to make notes for your blog. The one I'm going to insist you write over there, because we want to hear all about it.'

'Thank you. Maybe I'll do that.'

'We wish you weren't going,' Sally said. 'You know that.'

'I know,' Gabi said, tears in her eyes. The doorbell rang, and she nodded in the direction of it. 'I'd better get that. Sorry.'

'You go, answer it,' Sally said.

Elena came up to Sally, taking Gabi's place. 'Hello,' she said, kissing Sally's cheek. 'Lovely party, isn't it? Freddie just introduced me to your friend, Isabel.'

'What did you think?'

'A good woman,' she said. 'Freddie likes her, I can see that. You know, for a long time, I thought Gabi was the one for him.'

'Gabi? Really?' Sally said, surprised.

'I know, I got that one wrong. He must've told me a dozen times he wasn't interested in her.' She laughed. 'But I didn't give up, Sally.'

'And now?'

'Freddie knew what was right for him. He stood his ground. And look.' She pointed over to where Freddie and Isabel were sitting, a bottle of wine between them, talking as if the rest of the world didn't exist.

'They seem happy,' Sally said.

'I've never seen him like this before,' Elena said. 'This ... I don't know, energy. And what he wants to do with the business – I think she's done this to him, brought him down to earth a little bit.'

'Maybe it was happening anyway,' Sally said.

'Perhaps.' Elena looked at him again. 'You think you know what's best for your child, don't you? Even when they're grown-up. But sometimes you get it wrong.'

Sally smiled.

'You'll take care of everyone, won't you, when we're away in Crete?' Elena said.

'Of course I will,' Sally said.

'We'll miss you all,' Elena said. 'A few weeks without Riley is a long time.'

Later on that evening, a few wine glasses down, Sally and Theo found their way back together in the courtyard.

'Isabel seems to have made quite the impression on your mum,' Sally said.

'Yep, Mum can't stop talking about her.'

'Isabel's relieved. She was nervous about all this.'

'She didn't need to be,' Theo said. 'My mum's not that bad, is she?'

'No ... but you know what I mean. This stuff matters. Family matters.'

'You're right. It does.' Theo put his hands on her waist. It felt good – his touch. The lightness that had come back into their conversation, their connection.

'Now can we stop talking about my mum and go and have a dance together?'

'Yes,' she laughed. 'Let's do that.'

He took her to the middle of the courtyard, next to the speakers. Together they danced, and Sally felt herself lifted up by the music, by the closeness with Theo. Closeness that just that afternoon she'd been worried they were losing. She rested her head on his chest. He smelled good. He was all hers.

He whispered in her ear, 'Shall we get a taxi back now?'

The party was quietening, and a few guests had left already.

'Yes, let's do that.'

In the cab home, they giggled like teenagers. She ran a finger over his bottom lip and then replaced it with her mouth, kissing him hard. He pressed closer to her, kissing her more deeply each time, until the taxi drew to a stop outside their house. They left the taxi, still laughing together, and Theo paid the babysitter in a hurry.

The two of them went upstairs in the dark, shushing each other so that they wouldn't wake Riley, and then staggered into their bedroom. In the half-light, Theo brought Sally's dress up over her head, and she gave in to the pleasure of his touch. He kissed her neck, touched her over her bra, then, as it fell to the floor, took her bare breasts in his hands. She couldn't undo the buttons on his shirt fast enough. She felt breathless with it all – the desire, the adrenalin rush, the sheer blessed relief that they weren't broken.

When she had taken his shirt off, she ran her hand over the taut muscles of his stomach, kissed the tanned skin of his chest. He picked her up and she wrapped her legs around him, letting him carry her to the bed, where he laid her down, the two of them laughing, until their laughs gave way to deeper breaths, to a rhythm that took its own control of them. Their two bodies, so distant the night before, found one another again.

The next morning, Sunday, Sally woke to the smell of Theo cooking pancakes. They ate them with Riley, the happiness of the previous night seeping through to light their day as a family.

Then Sally read her book in the garden while Theo and Riley kicked a ball around. Later, they went inside to make biscuits. It was a day that had come from nowhere, only to become something so close to perfect.

At midday, Sally put down her book and went into the

kitchen, taking one of the freshly baked chocolate chip biscuits from the rack. It melted deliciously in her mouth.

'These are good.'

'I made them!' Riley said. Her hair was getting a little longer now, and it fell across her eyes just like Theo's did. 'Dad helped, but not that much.'

'Well, you guys did a great job.'

Sally stood behind Theo and put her arms around him, hugging him close. His jumper smelt faintly of laundry powder, the same scent that hung on all their clothes. When, from time to time, Riley would come home in a jumper that was borrowed from a friend, or taken from the school lost property box, she'd notice how strange it was, having someone else's laundry powder smell in their home. An alien element – invasive, cutting into the familiar smells that united the three of them, marked them out as a family, a team.

There were things they'd say, threads left over from Riley's toddler years: people never had measles, but weasels; the dogs weren't whippets, but flippets. Their family was made up of these fragments. They were the people their shared moments had shaped each one of them into.

Sally went to the fridge and got out some vegetables. 'Riley, seeing as you've done such a great job in the kitchen today, could you help me cut some veg for lunch?'

'Sure,' Riley said. She took the vegetables over to the kitchen table and sat on her chair, focused on lining them up in a row.

Sally turned to Theo. 'I thought we could have a roast chicken.'

'Yum,' Riley said.

'Sounds great,' Theo said. His eyes drifted over the garden and lingered there. 'I've had an idea,' he said. 'After lunch, how about we set up camp in the garden?'

'Camping,' Riley exclaimed. 'Yay!'

'Are you serious?' Sally said.

'Completely,' Theo said, smiling. 'It's been ages since we did that. I'll get the tent.' He went up the stairs and Sally heard him getting down the attic ladder.

'Could we have marshmallows?' Riley said.

Sally opened the kitchen cupboard and found an unopened packet. She waved them in Riley's direction. 'I think that could be arranged.'

'Brilliant.' Riley looked out the back door. 'I'm going to find a good spot to pitch it.'

'OK. Let me get some more camping snacks together.'

Riley turned back and looked at her. 'Mum,' she said.

'Yes, love?'

'I like it. When you and Dad are like this.'

'Like what?' she asked. But she already knew.

'Happy.' Then Riley turned and went out into the garden, picking up pace until she got to the apple tree.

They spent the whole afternoon out in the garden and in the tent, playing Uno and toasting marshmallows on the barbecue. Sally felt relaxed and close to carefree. There was nothing that had to be done, nowhere they had to be. Nothing, right then, that she and Theo had to discuss.

'Can we stay out here tonight?' Riley asked.

'Of course!' Theo said. 'That's the whole point, right, Sal?'

He looked over at Sally. She nodded, but she knew that she couldn't be there.

'Sleep under the stars, wake up with your feet in my face,' Theo said to Riley. 'That's the dream.'

Riley laughed. 'We'll need my torch. To do shadow animals.' She left the tent and ran back to the house.

'After dinner I'll need to head out,' Sally said apologetically. It was Sunday. The support group. She'd wavered about going. The weekend had been perfect and she didn't want to disrupt it.

'Do you really need to go tonight?' Theo said softly. 'I mean, I understand, it's just . . . '

She knew what he was thinking. The previous night and day had been a slice of everything she'd been missing – everything they'd both been missing. But the questions that had been in her mind on Friday hadn't gone away. She still needed to talk. This wasn't over.

She looked at Theo and felt the warmth of their intimacy. It had come back, that feeling that they were a team.

'I suppose I could miss this one session,' Sally said.

Theo took her hand and held it. 'Thank you.'

Chapter 30

After Riley went to sleep in the tent, Sally and Theo had stayed up drinking rum, sitting in camping chairs under the night sky. Then, when it got late, they'd slept together on mats in the tent, Riley sprawled out and taking up most of the space, Sally and Theo curled up close to one another for warmth. They'd woken up the next morning to birdsong.

On the walk to school, Sally felt the warmth of the sun on her face and felt a lightness inside. Spending the night with Theo, with their family, had been so much better, so much more valuable, than talking to people she barely knew. She and Theo should make time for their relationship, to keep that same feeling going. That, more than anything, would help Riley.

'Good weekend, wasn't it?' Sally said.

'Yes,' Riley said. She seemed distracted, though, swinging her book bag.

'You OK, love?'

'It's over now,' Riley said. 'School again.'

She whacked her schoolbag against the walls and fences. After the relaxed contentment of the weekend, it jarred. It was like watching a different child.

'Riley, don't do that,' Sally said.

Riley did it again, harder.

Sally reached out an arm and stopped her. 'Hey. I said stop.'

Riley looked up at her mum, her eyebrows brought together, her face pulled into a scowl. 'I'm not doing anything.'

Sally bent to her level, crouching down. 'You know you are. And please stop or your bag will get ruined.'

'I don't care if my things get ruined,' Riley said. Then, almost under her breath, 'Stupid PE day.'

'PE? You love PE.'

'Not any more,' Riley said.

'Why not?' Sally said, shocked.

'I just don't like it any more.'

'But why?'

Riley went quiet, and Sally realised she wouldn't get anything else out of her. The rest of the way they walked in silence, but Sally couldn't shift the feeling that something was wrong. Running, football, games – these were things Riley had always come home talking animatedly about, the activities that seemed to bring out the very best in her. She knew that couldn't have changed in such a short space of time. They neared the school gates.

'Is it about getting changed, Riley?' Sally asked.

Riley frowned. 'You know what it is. Why I don't like it.'

The other children filtered past them. Sally didn't want to let Riley go into the classroom that day. She wanted to understand better what was happening. She wanted to be sure that Riley was going to be OK. But one of teachers crossed the yard, ringing the bell, signalling the start of the school day, and Sally was forced to say goodbye.

She stood for a moment, watching Riley go, then noticed Beth beside her.

'Hi, Beth,' Sally said, finding a smile. 'It's been a while. How's the pregnancy?'

Beth put a hand on her stomach, which had rounded out over

the summer break. 'It's going OK, thanks, Sally. A bit tiring, but fine.' There was a tautness in her voice that Sally put down to the strain of managing the parenting balancing act while also pregnant.

'I'm glad to hear that,' Sally said. 'And is Evie—'

'Look, Sally,' Beth said, cutting her short. 'There's no easy way to have this conversation. So I may as well get straight to the point.'

Sally's heart rate quickened. 'Sorry?'

'I'm sure the teacher must have mentioned it to you. Riley. The problems she's creating in the classroom.'

Sally felt awkward, but pushed past it. 'We're aware of the incident last week, yes,' she said. 'It's out of character for Riley, and we're addressing it.'

'I'm afraid it's not just the one incident,' Beth said, slowly. 'I've held back before, Sally, because . . . I don't know, perhaps I felt sorry for you.'

Sally recoiled. 'Excuse me?'

'I mean coming here new. Still settling in. But the way she's been speaking to Evie is inexcusable. I'm going to have to talk to the teacher about it.'

Sally took a deep breath. She would have to swallow her pride and hear this.

'What is it that Riley's been saying?'

'She's been calling Evie stupid. A "stupid girl". I know they're just words, but it's been really hurtful to her. And Evie says sometimes she snatches her toys, only to throw them.'

'God,' Sally said. 'I'm so sorry. I didn't realise.'

'Evie says Riley is angry. That she hides it from the teachers but in the playground she's rough, and mean.'

Sally felt winded. Could this really be true? It didn't sound like Riley. But given how she'd been acting out recently, she had to take it seriously.

'We didn't know,' Sally said. 'I'm so sorry. I'll do something. Leave it with me, Beth.'

'I appreciate that, Sally. Because it's really affecting Evie. This isn't how children treat each other at Elmtree. And if you can't bring Riley into line, then perhaps this isn't the right school for her at all.'

Sally got back home, and took a biscuit from the tin. Before she could take a bite, tears started to fall, hot splashes on her cheeks, the emotion she'd held in all the way home from school came flooding out. Had things really changed so much, so quickly? Had her child turned from a loveable livewire into a cruel bully, without them even realising?

She picked up her phone and tried Theo's mobile. It rang through to answerphone.

She would talk to Ms Bailey after school. But the stretch of time from now to pick-up seemed interminable, and all she could think about was what Riley might be doing, how she might be acting, who she might be hurting. Or . . . how she might be hurting.

She ate the biscuit in a hurry and felt no better for it. She paced around the room, hoping it might clear her head. She ate another biscuit. Then she opened her laptop. She would work. She checked her emails, read through them, then sat there unable to decide what to do next.

A green spot blinked, indicating that Matt was online.

She hesitated for a moment, then opened a message screen. Have you got a minute? she typed.

Hey! Of course. What's up?

Everything, she thought. A big mess of things.

A big mess of things, she typed.

Ha. I know that feeling, he replied. Try me.

I don't know where to start.

In the middle, right where you are.

One of the school mums said something about Riley. Now I'm crying. I'm binge-eating Hobnobs. And I'm worried my child's become a monster.

First – I bet she's one of those mums. Am I right?

Sally smiled. She is. A bit.

Second – take a breath, Sally.

She did. A long inhalation that she kept inside for a couple of seconds, before letting it go.

And another one.

Her lungs opened and she drew in more air this time. When she exhaled, she let out some of the tension. Her body started to feel like her own again.

Now, let's talk about today.

'The woman who makes those cakes is gone?' the elderly man asked Theo.

'I'm afraid so,' he replied.

'You shouldn't have let her leave,' he said. He took his cup of tea, shaking his head and going to sit by the window.

Theo looked around the café. Soon he'd work out what to do

without Gabi. It would just take a bit of time. In truth he hadn't really, truly appreciated everything Gabi did until today, now that he was doing it all without her. It was tiring, and he was making mistakes – but what bothered him most was that even when the café was full of customers, it all felt so quiet. Far too quiet.

That afternoon at pick-up, Sally and Ms Bailey talked, while Riley collected her things.

'How has Riley been today?' Sally asked, tentatively.

'Not quite her usual self, actually. She had to sit out PE.'

Sally's fears were confirmed. 'What happened?'

'She wouldn't get changed with the others. Having her miss the class wasn't an ideal solution but we couldn't have her doing it in her normal clothes, and setting a precedent. Hopefully this will be a one-off.'

'Right. I'll talk to her about it. Other than that, how does she seem?' She wondered if Beth had spoken to her already.

Ms Bailey glanced away momentarily.

'It's tricky, because I'm new here, and I haven't known Riley long,' she said, 'but she does seem rather ... I don't know. Agitated.'

'Agitated, how?' Sally said, her concern rising.

'Restless. Even a bit aggressive, sometimes. I've kept Riley and the child she had an incident with last week apart today. So there's been no repeat of that behaviour. But there were a few unkind words today towards another child.'

Sally's heart sank. She must mean Evie. 'This isn't like her,' she said. 'I mean, I know you only have my word for it. But she's not usually like this.'

'Perhaps it's the new classroom and new teacher,' Ms Bailey said. 'It can unsettle children sometimes.'

Sally wished she could believe that was the reason. But knew deep down that it wasn't.

She had to ask. 'Was there any trigger when she was unkind to the other child?'

'I don't think so. I just told her to go and play nicely with the other girls on the carpet, and she seemed to … I don't know. To snap.'

That evening, when Sally heard Theo's key turn in the lock, she wished for a moment that they could talk about something other than the issues with Riley. Wished that they could preserve their newfound reconnection for an evening longer, stay in the peaceful, happy bubble they'd inhabited that weekend. But she couldn't bury her head in the sand and let Riley's behaviour deteriorate. It wasn't fair on anybody. And Theo wouldn't want to do that either. Sally had held back from asking Riley anything outright during the evening, wanting to talk to Theo about it first.

When Theo came into the living room, she filled him in what had happened that day – the information from Beth, the PE session, and what Riley's teacher had said.

His brow furrowed as he listened to the update. 'Are you sure Beth wasn't exaggerating? That doesn't sound like Riley at all.'

'I don't know,' Sally said. 'But what the teacher said would seem to back it up.'

'The PE thing is odd, too. Did you talk to Riley about it?'

'I wanted to talk to you first.'

The strain began to show on Theo's face.

'You think this is about her wanting to be a boy, don't you?' he said.

'About her feeling she is a boy. Yes. I think it has to be. She was OK in the summer.'

'So we're back here again.' He said it wearily.

'Would it really be such an issue to let her be who she wants to be at school?' Sally asked.

'Yes. Yes, it would be,' Theo said.

There it was – her proposal. His refusal. It might have been the end of the matter. But instead Theo's resistance had brought things sharply into focus for Sally. If Riley was going to have a chance to behave better, she needed a chance be herself.

'I think we need to do this. I think she needs to be free to attend school as a boy.'

'Sal, no,' Theo said, firmly. 'Come on – this isn't who we are.'

'What do you mean, who we are?'

'We're not . . . you know . . . We don't need this kind of attention. We don't even want attention. We're just a normal family.'

'Maybe we don't get to decide that. And this isn't about us. It's about Riley.'

Theo paused, seeming to consider it. 'And if we do let her attend school in the way you suggest, what are the other kids going to say? The bullies would have a field day. Would that really be any better for her self-esteem?'

'I don't have answers to those questions.'

Theo shook his head, but wouldn't meet her eye. She wished he'd look at her, remind her that they were in this together, no matter what. She needed that.

'We'd be making a huge mistake.'

She could see he wasn't going to shift. She wouldn't back down, though. She cared too much. 'I disagree,' she said. 'I think we need to give Riley space, to be what she feels she is, otherwise this could all get worse.'

'Not necessarily. It might pass, like all the other phases she's been through. And if it doesn't – there are options we haven't even looked at yet, ways of . . . ' He paused, as if he couldn't quite say it.

'What?' Sally said, hoping against hope her suspicions were wrong.

'Preventing this happening.'

She shook her head. He was really doing this. He was going there.

'People have done it, successfully. Helped their children to see that they're not really transgender, but are actually just—'

'So now we're on to trying to *convert* Riley?' Her voice rose with fury. 'Are you serious?'

'I'm just looking at our options,' Theo said. 'You make it sound awful.'

'That's because it is. Have you seriously been thinking about this?'

'Is it really any worse than what you've been doing?' He started to speak but his voice caught. 'This path – telling the world that Riley is transgender – it's a serious decision, Sally. I was scared. Christ, I still am scared.'

Sally told herself to keep listening. If they were to do this together she had to keep on listening and trying to understand. 'What is it about all this that scares you?'

'The speed of it. There are some steps we might not be able to backtrack from. Sending Riley to school as a boy still seems crazy to me. It's like our lives have been turned upside-down overnight – we've gone from being a normal family to this.'

What was Theo really saying? Sally thought. That their family wasn't right any more?

'From a normal family to what?' she said.

'I don't know,' Theo said. 'What are we?'

The words stung.

'Is normal really everything you want?' Sally said, her voice cracking with the emotion. 'We're still us. If Riley went to school as a boy, we'd still be us.'

Theo shook his head. 'I don't want this for our family. It doesn't feel right.'

'What about if it feels right for our child, Theo?' Sally said, her frustration turning into something new, a force that insisted her words be heard. 'What about that? Isn't that what matters here, most of all?'

I'm staring at a poster on my wall. It has a jaguar on it. If I look at the spots for a long time, my eyes go blurry. I don't mind it. It's sort of nice.

I was asleep but I woke up when I heard a noise. It wasn't shouting, just a sort of loud talking – Mum and Dad's voices. They sounded different, and it made my skin feel prickly, kind of, and I couldn't get back to sleep.

Tonight I pull the duvet up and press it against my ears. If I press it really quite hard on my ears, it is almost quiet. It doesn't hurt, because the duvet is soft, it just stops the noise. I pressed the duvet like that and then, if I stare very hard at the jaguar's spots on my ceiling, I can block the voices out.

Chapter 31

Sally was sleeping beside Theo. Her back was to him, her long hair draped across the pillow, the curve of her neck laid bare, inviting a touch, a kiss that he knew he couldn't give her – the argument was still too fresh.

It was his love for Sally that meant he'd eventually given in, ending what had felt like a very long evening of heated discussion. He'd backed down and said that they could talk to the school. He wasn't happy about the decision – but they couldn't stay locked in stalemate over it either. Nothing had changed in his mind – it still didn't feel right. But he held on to the hope that the school would see things the way that he did and refuse the parental request.

It wasn't that he wasn't aware of how sections of society were changing and becoming more inclusive and accepting of trans people – he saw the news, had read articles. OK, maybe it wasn't the easiest thing for him to understand, but he supported it, in principle. It was only right that adults who were trans should make their own choices and be able to be themselves. But children? That was where he stalled. How could a child really know enough about gender to be sure? And to make a change like this before you were certain, there was a risk in that, wasn't there? At

Riley's age, wasn't it more likely that she was simply confused? It made sense that she would be – she didn't fit into the same mould as some of the other girls, never had and quite possibly never would, and at her age that probably would be confusing. Into that mix, they'd thrown a new home and school, uprooting her from the friends she'd had back in London, girls who had been more similar to her. He and Sally needed to help guide her through all the mixed emotions.

The school must be used to dealing with children feeling out of sorts, as Riley was. He hoped that they would see sense – see that seven was no age to be making a change that Riley couldn't possibly understand the consequences of. One that could affect her whole future. It was in nobody's interest to run too fast with this.

The next day, Sally dropped Riley off at the classroom and went upstairs to the headteacher's office. Theo had said that morning that he had something urgent to deal with at the café, but it hadn't been hard to see through the excuse. She knew – from the way he'd reluctantly agreed to the course of action, from the conflicted look in his eyes – that his heart wasn't in this. She resolved to be strong for Riley, strong enough for both of them. As she came to the door, though, Sally started to doubt herself. Perhaps it was too soon. Perhaps Theo was right, after all. Elmtree seemed very old-fashioned, compared with Riley's previous school. Would they even understand what she was asking? But then she pictured the alternative – coming to pick Riley up that day, knowing she'd done nothing to make her child's life easier. She'd come this far; she owed it to Riley to keep on going.

Inside, Mrs Miller the headteacher motioned to a chair. 'Do come in and take a seat. You wanted to talk to me?'

'That's right,' Sally said. 'It's about Riley.'

'I'm glad you came. I must say, I was surprised to hear about some of Riley's recent behaviour. She got off to a flying start last year, and Ms Sanderson always said what a good contribution she made to class.'

'It came as a shock to us too, believe me. I've talked a little with Ms Bailey about Riley being agitated. But I haven't really told the full story to her, or in fact to anyone here.'

'Right,' Mrs Miller replied. 'And what is that?'

'I think there's an underlying cause. A reason for the way Riley's been acting out.'

'Yes?'

'Riley has told me and her dad that she is a boy.'

'I see,' the headteacher said, taking a breath.

'We've seen a GP about it, and they feel she might have gender dysphoria.'

Mrs Miller appeared to be taking it all in. 'How long has this been going on?'

'Riley first said it at the start of the summer, and since then she's said it frequently. She hasn't wavered in her conviction. I've seen a change in her ... We've all seen a real change in her since our holiday, since the first time we allowed her to be a boy.' The 'we' felt like the right thing to say, presenting a united front, but at the same time, given Theo's feelings, it rang hollow.

Mrs Miller nodded, but her face gave nothing away. Sally got the sense she was practised in not letting her emotions get in the way.

Sally made herself say it. 'We are hoping that there's a way to improve the situation, for everyone. We'd like Riley to be able to attend school as a boy.' She readied herself to fight her corner. 'The Equality Act states that—'

'I'm aware of it, Ms Pieterson. Don't worry. We might look like dinosaurs around here, but we're up to speed on these things. If this is what Riley would like, and what you feel is right, then we'll do what we can to accommodate Riley's needs.'

Sally, who'd prepared herself for a debate, felt a little thrown. 'Including Riley using the boys' toilets?'

'I should think so. Is there a new name you'd prefer us to use?'

Sally shook her head. 'No.' She tried to think of what else to ask. She hadn't expected it all to be so easy. Pronouns. That would make the biggest difference to Riley. 'But please could you use the male pronouns – call Riley he, use him and his.'

'Of course,' Mrs Miller said.

'We don't want any fuss,' Sally said. 'We just want Riley to have the space to be herself.' She paused, then corrected herself. 'Himself. I haven't quite got used to it myself, yet.'

'I understand,' Mrs Miller said. 'I'll make sure all the teachers are informed of that and know how important it is. Do you think you could give us a couple of weeks to speak to a specialist clinic so that we can make sure this all happens as smoothly as possible, and that we get things right?'

'Yes,' Sally said. 'Of course.'

A weight had been lifted from her shoulders. The resistance from the school that she'd expected hadn't come. Instead, they were actively helping. Which meant something Sally could barely comprehend. Something that left her feeling dizzy – Riley's new life was about to begin.

That evening, Theo sat in their bedroom, needing a moment to himself. He could hear Sally pottering in the kitchen, preparing Riley's packed lunch for the next day. As if nothing had changed, and everything was still the same.

But it wasn't. Everything had taken on a surreal air. Nothing seemed firm or solid any more.

He and Sally had talked about Riley over dinner. He recalled the words she'd spoken, but it still seemed like they'd come out of someone else's mouth. The conversation was functional, businesslike – as if Sally was a woman he barely knew. Not one he knew and loved bone-deep.

'I spoke with the headteacher. They're going to meet with someone from a specialist clinic about making changes that'll ensure Riley's comfortable attending as a boy.'

As a boy.

Attending as a boy.

So, that was it. The school had said yes. This was going to happen. Sally said that the headteacher had been really supportive and helpful. The resistance he'd been counting on hadn't come – it was already too late. He'd thought at the very least there would be a delay that might buy them all time, but no – in just two weeks the change would come.

The moment to push back, to resist, had come and gone, without him even realising. While he'd played along, expecting reason to return, the action had been set in motion. He'd hoped that the school would see things the way that he did, even if Sally couldn't. He'd stepped back, thinking this could never really happen – because how could it be happening, that Riley, at her age, was being supported to change gender?

He'd thought that he and Sally could work together, keep their love and relationship intact, and still ensure that Riley was safe. But instead things were moving fast. Riley was being led into something that could lead to her being singled out, bullied, even hurt – and it seemed unstoppable.

Sally walked into school with Riley the following day. They stopped to pick up pine cones, sycamore helicopters, conkers in their spiky shells. Riley handed them to her for safekeeping and she put them, damp, into her handbag, telling herself it didn't matter if they got everything else wet.

'Dad will like those,' Riley said. 'Let's keep them to show him.'

Their world was shifting. What had seemed inconceivable just a few weeks ago was becoming real now. She felt a surge of pride that she had been able to help Riley, to enable things to change. She'd hoped to tell Riley the news together with Theo, but he'd left the house in a rush that morning, seeming distracted. She'd have to do it alone.

'Riley,' Sally said. 'We've got a bit of time this morning. Shall we sit on that bench and have a snack?'

'Sure,' Riley said.

Sally passed her an apple and they sat together as she bit into it, looking out at the high street, most of the businesses still shuttered.

'I've got some news for you, actually,' Sally said.

'Yes?'

'It seems like things haven't been that good for you at school lately. Is that right?'

Riley looked down at the ground, her cheeks flushed. 'I was mean to Evie.'

'It has to change,' Sally said, firmly. 'I want to see the old Riley back. I want to see you behaving well.'

'I know it wasn't OK.'

'That's right. And you can be better than this. I want you to say a proper sorry to her, and anyone else you've been unkind to. Will you do that?'

Riley nodded.

'Listen,' Sally went on. 'Me and your dad have been talking – about what might make things easier for you. More comfortable. I spoke with your headteacher yesterday.'

'Am I in trouble?' Riley said, frowning.

'No, love. That's not it. I spoke with her about how you've been feeling. What we spoke with the doctor about.' Sally realised she had to say it. If they were to expect everyone else to accept it, she had to lead the way. 'About you being a boy.'

Riley's smile was a streak of light.

'And she says – if it's still what you want – that you can be yourself at school.'

Riley grabbed her mum and squeezed her hard. 'Really? Really, you're sure?'

'You're happy about that, I'm guessing,' Sally said, laughing.

'Yes!' Riley shrieked. 'It's the best news I've ever heard.'

Sally's heart lifted. As they walked the final stretch together, Riley's pace was swift, and she swung her mother's hand in hers. When she finally let go of her hand, Riley skipped up the ramp and into the classroom.

Her bold and brave child.

The parents started to disperse, some forming new pairings, as people chatted before heading off to work, or home. Sally fell into stride beside Beth.

'Hey,' she said.

This wasn't going to be easy, but she had to start somewhere.

'Listen, Beth. I wanted to say thank you for telling me about Evie.'

'Oh yes?' Beth said, visibly surprised.

'I'm sorry it happened – and Riley knows she has to make it right.'

'I'm glad to hear it,' Beth said, though her expression didn't reflect it.

'It helped me realise that something needed to change. Riley's been unhappy. And that affected Evie. So we're going to be making some changes in a couple of weeks. Ms Bailey will explain everything to the class. I hope you can all be understanding.'

'Of course,' Beth said, smiling. 'We'll be there for you. Of course we will. Elmtree School is a very supportive community.'

*

When she got home, Sally made a mug of tea and sat on the sofa looking out at the street. The street she and Riley would soon be walking out on to as mother and son, in a fortnight's time. What would it feel like? Would the neighbours stare? Would they even notice anything different?

She picked up her phone and pressed 2, speed-dialling her dad. She hadn't spoken to him in a while, and she'd missed it. Speaking to him always made her feel stronger, and now, with all that lay ahead of her, she needed that.

'Hello, love,' he said. 'Nice to hear from you.'

His voice, soft and low, comforted her. Instinctively she cradled the phone closer to her ear.

'How are you doing, Sal?' he asked.

She took stock, tried to place how she was feeling on the spectrum that ran from OK to not-OK.

'You know what, Dad, I'm not really sure.'

'Is it to do with Riley?'

'Isn't it always?' she said, smiling. 'Riley's kept saying it, about being a boy, since the holiday. Kept saying who she feels – who *he* feels – he is inside.'

'And you've listened to that.'

'I've done what I can.'

'And what about Theo?'

'He's still resistant. There's been a limit. And now we're reaching a new stage. Riley wants to attend school as a boy.' She paused. It was only just starting to feel real. 'And we've arranged for that to happen. Riley's going to be transitioning there.'

'Right,' Jules said. 'Wow. That's a big step.'

'I know. But it's one we need to take.' Even as Sally said it she realised she was trying to sound surer than she felt. 'We've spoken to the school and they've been really supportive. They've agreed to talk to the teachers and children about transgenderism, and Riley's transition, and they're making the relevant provisions.'

Sally paused. The words – transition, transgender – the words that were a central part of her vocabulary now, and yet belonged so much to this time, not her father's. 'This must seem slightly insane to you.'

'No, not at all, Sal. I've seen – Catherine and I have both seen – how much more comfortable Riley is as a boy.'

Sally breathed a sigh of relief. Felt grateful to have her dad and Catherine as allies in all this.

'It's a choice children never had when you were young – and Riley has it. I'm proud of you. You're being very brave.'

Brave. It wasn't a word she'd ever connected with herself. But this new situation, which she'd been cast into and would never have chosen, demanded new things of her. Courage, it turned out, was one.

I've told Riley that the school said yes. He's very happy. Sal x

As Theo read the text message, he felt numb. It wasn't just the news – it was the 'he'. The first time Sally had said it. The café still felt empty without Gabi there. He wished again that she was there to talk to.

After lunch, he called his brother, and they spoke for a while about the business, and what Freddie's role would be when he came to London. Then, after a while, Freddie asked about Riley.

'How's the little one?'

Theo paused. 'It's complicated.'

'The boy thing's still going on?'

'Yes. More than that. Sal's been concerned for a while that Riley's unhappy. She spoke with the school about it. I don't know why I agreed to it. It's taken everything to another level. They've agreed to let Riley attend school as a boy.'

Theo could hear his brother suck in his breath. 'Jeez. It's moving quickly.'

'That's how it feels.'

'You OK with it?'

'Nope,' Theo said. It felt good to say it out loud. 'I'm really not.'

'So, what, Sally pushed this through? That doesn't sound like her.'

'It's not like that. I said we could talk to the school. I agreed to it. Because I knew it was something Sally really wanted – and because I thought they'd say no.'

'But they didn't.'

'No. They're supporting it. And now I feel like it's running out of my control. If we're saying she's a boy at school . . . what if this is making it all permanent? I don't know, Fred. I only agreed to what happened in Italy – and God, I wish I could go back and undo it . . . I only agreed to that so that we could watch her pass back out of this phase again.'

'There's still a chance it could be a phase, right?'

'Yes. Definitely. It's only been a few months.'

He could hear his brother exhale. 'It must be pretty confusing being a kid these days,' Freddie said.

'Tell me about it.' It was a relief to talk to someone who understood. 'I'm lying awake at night thinking: where did this come from? Did someone give her this idea? Encourage it?'

He thought of the support group Sally went to, wondered whether that might be some part of the problem.

'Because this is a hard path, Freddie. One that – if she were to stay on it – could lead to her being medicalised for the rest of her life. I know I'm jumping ahead. But I don't want that for her, I really don't.' The emotion welled up in him.

'Couldn't you push back?'

'I've tried, and Sal thinks denying Riley this is hurting her. I'm starting to think if I say we can't do this, I could lose Sal. Lose everything.'

'This is tough, man,' Freddie said. 'I'm sorry.'

'At least Mum and Dad aren't here at the moment.'

'They're still in Crete?'

'Yes. Thankfully – because I can't see them understanding all this.'

Theo saw a customer approaching and drew the conversation to a close.

Riley – his vibrant, loving daughter, their wildfire. It felt like just weeks ago that he had walked her around in a sling to quieten her cries and get her to sleep. And now, all of a sudden, he and Sally and Riley were here. In uncharted territory.

That afternoon, after closing the café, Theo rode his bike through the streets of east London. Realised he was taking the long way, because he didn't want to go home. He'd tried to accept what was happening – was still trying. But he couldn't force it. He couldn't see Riley the way Sally could. The way that they, supposedly as a family, were now saying Riley needed to be seen. He couldn't do it. He just couldn't.

Theo walked his bike through into the hallway later that evening, and Sally came out to talk with him. 'Hey,' she said.

'Hi.'

He took a deep breath. He had to do this. Be honest.

'Is Riley around?' he asked.

'Watching TV.'

'Cool.' He stood there for a second, not knowing how to start. He leaned his bike against the radiator and took off his coat.

'I've got something for you, actually,' Sally said. She reached into her handbag. 'Here,' she said. She passed him a handful of conkers, sycamore helicopters and bark. She smiled. 'Riley wanted you to have them.'

'Thank you,' he said, holding them, cold and damp in his hand, but beautiful to him all the same. His chest felt tight.

He had to stay on track, say it before he had a chance to change his mind.

'Sal, there's something I need to talk to you about.'

'OK,' she said, looking confused.

'This thing, with Riley at school – this is big.'

'I know.' Sally reached out her hand towards his.

His stomach tightened. He couldn't take it. He loved her with a force as great as ever, but to take her hand would be to lie.

Her hand hung there in the air for a moment, then dropped back to her side. Her face paled; she knew what it meant.

'I can't get my head around this, Sal. I can't just press a switch in my brain and tomorrow start calling Riley "he", and referring to her as a boy. It's not going to happen. I can't do it.' He shook his head. There was a pain in his chest that wouldn't shift. 'Right now, right at this moment, I can't do this. I can't be here.'

'But you have to be here,' Sally said, tears coming to her eyes.

He could see that Sally was in distress – and yet, for the first time in their marriage, he felt no draw to comfort her. He felt distant, cold.

'I think it'd be best if I stay somewhere else for a while,' he said.

Sally stared at him, as if she couldn't quite believe it. 'Stay somewhere else? Where?'

'I don't know. Maybe a hotel,' Theo said.

'For how long?' Sally said. 'Why?'

'I think we need space. I can't be here when this happens at school.'

'But . . . ' He could hear the panic in her voice. 'We need you, Theo. I don't know if I can do this without you.'

He saw it in her eyes, then. The same realisation he'd had that day. That she couldn't do it with him, either.

'I can't pretend, Sally. I can't go into this and support you and Riley, and act as if I think this is the right thing. Because I don't.'

Sally was properly crying now, tears running down her cheeks, and still he felt nothing. Only that he needed to be somewhere else.

'Riley needs us. Needs us to be together. Now more than ever.'

'I know.' He didn't want to be apart from Riley – but if he was still there, Riley would see how he felt. 'I can't lie – to you, to Riley, to myself. I can't be here and go along with this. Because I don't think it's right.'

Danger Mouse *is ending and there's another programme starting, but Mum and Dad are talking in the hall and they haven't told me to stop watching. I'm going to watch it. They don't seem to mind so much about me watching a lot of TV lately.*

I have a bubbly feeling in my stomach. All the time. It's a happy feeling. Mum says soon we can start telling people about me really being a boy, since I'll be a boy at school tomorrow. I already talked to Granddad Jules and Catherine about it on the phone. I'm going to put those girl pants in the bin and never get them out again. This time I'm allowed.

Chapter 32

When he'd left the house, Theo called the only person he wanted to talk to: Gabi. He heard the foreign dial tone and willed her to pick up. She did. As he told her what was happening, she just listened. At the end of their conversation, she told him that her flat was empty, as the tenants she'd lined up had pulled out, and he could stay there – for the time being, at least.

An hour later, Theo let himself into the building with the keys he'd collected from Gabi's neighbour. He put down his bag and closed the front door in a daze.

The flat felt hollow and soulless. He missed Riley's laughter. In the morning, his only child's life would change completely, and here he was, choosing not to watch it happen. He'd stay here for a couple of weeks, no longer. Just until the teachers had seen sense, or Riley changed her mind. He would still be there for his child. He just needed time and space to think of how to support her, let her know that this wasn't the only way.

Theo went to sit on the sofa, looking around. His home, for a while. Gabi had left some of her furniture, the mid-century coffee table and her framed pictures of Greek beaches on the walls. She pictured her new life out there. Things must be easy for her – no ties, no responsibilities, no guilt. For the very first time, he envied her that.

Today the sun is big and yellow and the sky is bright blue. Today I can scoot really fast. My hair is shorter again, we got it cut yesterday, and I can feel the wind on my neck. This morning Mum said I could wear whatever I wanted to wear to school. I chose a Spiderman T-shirt and a pair of shorts, with my flashing trainers. I put a cap on too. I can wear that on the way to school. But not at school.

I kept saying it, and Mum and Dad did listen. And now I don't have to be a girl any more. Today everyone will see me as I really am.

Chapter 33

Sally watched Riley scoot ahead of her. If he was nervous about today, it didn't show. *He. Him. His.* She practised the pronouns in her head. It still didn't feel completely comfortable, but it would with time, she hoped. Soon the wrong word would stop slipping out. It mattered. She could tell from Riley's face that it mattered.

Riley was the same child, just more relaxed. Happier.

Theo came into her mind. Where their affection had been there was now just a hollowness in her bones. She missed him, and yet the anger and frustration she felt at his stubbornness was equally strong. He should be there with them today – he was Riley's father. They should be standing together on this.

Riley swung around and called out: 'It's OK for me to use the boys' toilets today? You're sure?'

'Absolutely.'

'Yes!' His face lit up.

They reached the school gates. 'Will Ms Bailey really tell them all I'm a boy?' Riley asked.

'Yes. She said she'd do that. Unless you'd like to do it yourself.'

Riley shrugged. 'It's OK. She can do it.'

'You know that people might not understand right away. They might get it wrong at first, make mistakes.'

'I know,' Riley said. 'Like Dad.'

Sally bit her lip. Had Theo even tried? She doubted it.

'But now when they get it wrong, I'll tell them.'

'Yes,' Sally said. She bent down to Riley's level. Nervous excitement caused a flutter in her stomach, but she didn't let it show. She stayed calm. She held him close to her for a moment, letting her love wrap around him in a blanket, feeling his chest against hers. He started to wriggle, and she let him go. It was time.

'You've got this, Riley.'

Riley dashed up the ramp and into the classroom, the lights on his trainers flashing with each step.

Sally thought back on Riley's very first day of school, starting reception at St Michael's, and remembered how tearful she'd felt. How little she'd known of the changes that would come after it, of what she would be letting go of so soon. The switch from nursery to school – and then from Riley's first school to Elmtree – seemed like nothing compared to today. Today she was saying goodbye to her daughter's past, present and the future she'd pictured all at once. Letting go of her child's hand, she silently prayed that the world would be kind, not cruel.

Theo left Gabi's flat and cycled down the streets towards work. Drivers around him tooted their horns, traffic lights turned from red to green, shops raised their shutters. The city carried on, exactly as usual, as the city always did. But inside, Theo's world was fracturing.

Today. Today was the day Riley was going into school as a boy; the day that everything would change.

Theo felt as if he was on the outside of an aquarium tank, tapping on the glass. Trying to get Riley's attention. Trying to get anyone to listen.

No one could hear him – or no one would. He had to keep trying. Had to stay involved.

When he got to the café, he got out his phone.

Tell Riley I love her, he texted Sally. *Let me know how it goes.*

On the way home from school, Sally saw that a message had come through from Theo. She replied: *Drop-off went well. Riley was happy. I'll update you later. S*

She lingered over the sign-off. A kiss didn't seem right. She left it off. A small cut to their love.

We're all sitting on the bug rug. I'm on the ladybird, like always. The other children are there too. Ms Bailey is talking. She tells them I'm a boy, and they should say 'he' when they talk about me. I feel that bubbly feeling. The good feeling. She asks if there are any questions. Euan puts up his hand.

'Will Riley still be my friend?'

'Obviously!' I say.

'Well, there's your answer,' the teacher says. She's laughing. Her face is nice when she's laughing.

'Any other questions?' she says.

I look around at Evie, at Ava, at Ben. No one puts their hand up.

Chapter 34

At pick-up, Sally looked anxiously over at the school doors, waiting for them to open. When they did, she saw Ms Bailey first of all, and she gave Sally a reassuring nod of acknowledgement.

Riley came out next and dashed over to her – confident, with a huge smile on his face.

'How was it?' Sally asked, hugging Riley.

'It was great, Mum,' he said. 'Ms Bailey spoke to the whole class and explained that I'm a boy now.'

'And your friends were fine about it?' Sally said, trying to sound relaxed, though inside she was wound tight.

'Yes. They didn't mind. In the playground Evie said it was a bit funny. But she wasn't mean. She just doesn't understand yet.'

Sally felt proud of the way Riley could see things for what they were. 'Exactly. She'll start to understand.'

Sally gave Riley a squeeze. And as she pulled away, she took in the smile on her son's face, and breathed out for what felt like the first time that day.

Theo was in the café when he got Sally's call.

'It went smoothly,' Sally said. 'The kids reacted well to the change, and Riley seemed really happy.'

He'd kept his phone on him all day, waiting to hear news. Now that news was here, and he felt numb.

It had happened. He couldn't undo it.

Riley was OK, he told himself. The most important thing. The knot in his stomach loosened, and he breathed out for what felt like the first time that day.

On Friday Sally went to see Isabel for lunch near her work, at their usual café. She was longing to talk to someone about everything that had happened – someone other than Theo.

'We've done it,' Sally said, a smile on her face. 'It's happened. Riley's a boy at school.'

'And it's gone OK?'

'It's been more than OK. It's been completely normal – as if nothing big has changed at all. And that's exactly how I'd hoped it would be.'

'Well done,' Isabel said. 'What an intense week it must've been.'

It had been hard, Sally thought – not because of Riley, but because Theo hadn't been there. His reaction on the first day had seemed so distant and flat. He didn't want it to be happening – it was there in everything that was unsaid.

'Now it's done. I'm expecting bumps in the road but I'm ready for them. And at least the first few days have gone better than I could have expected.'

She and Isabel lingered over lunch, as Isabel's boss was away, and there was so much to talk about. She and Freddie were talking most days, making plans for when he was back in London, and working out what furniture would fit in her flat once they were both in there. Sally loved seeing her so animated – Freddie seemed to give her the strength to make the arrangements she needed to as her dad's move to the retirement home neared.

Their lives were both shifting and changing in ways they

never could have planned for, or expected, but here, together, they could be anchors for each other.

A week later, Theo went into Riley's school. In Riley's classroom, Ms Bailey motioned for him to come and join her by her desk.

'Come in, come in,' she said. 'Take a seat, I'll be right with you.'

Theo sat down in the chair opposite her and glanced around the classroom. The walls reflected how the children had grown up: sums, grammar and Aztec projects taking the place of the Hungry Caterpillar collages in reception. The interactive white board, something that hadn't existed in his own school days, dominated the front of the class. The cosiness of the early years classroom had gone, and with that the atmosphere of softness and security.

Ms Bailey closed her register and focused her attention on Theo. 'You wanted to have a word with me about Riley?'

'Yes.' He cleared his throat. 'I know you've spoken to Sally a few times, but I wanted to talk to you myself too.' He didn't want to mention the separation. The fact he was living somewhere else, and didn't know when he'd go back.

'Of course.'

'How has it all been, with Riley's' – he made himself say the word – 'transition?'

'Riley seems to be doing well. He told me he's much happier using the boys' toilets, and he goes whenever he needs it now.'

The male pronouns leapt out of the teacher's sentence, hitting Theo in the gut like a stone. He wouldn't ever get used to it. He refused to.

It was all a mistake, a fiction. Made in good faith, but erroneously. His child wasn't the boy they all thought she was. She just wasn't. He tried to stay focused on the reasons he'd come there.

'Have there been any issues with the other children?'

'Not that I'm aware of, and I've been keeping a close eye on things. The transition doesn't seem to have had any negative impact on his friendships. He and Euan get on particularly well.'

'That's good,' Theo said, willing himself to concentrate on Riley's behaviour and happiness, not her gender. 'There hasn't been any repeat of Riley hurting anyone?'

'Not at all,' Ms Bailey said. 'I haven't seen anything like that since Riley started attending as a boy. It's only been a week, of course, but my general impression is that the change has been a positive one for him, that he's more confident.' She smiled warmly.

Theo's doubts lingered. 'Can I ask what you think about all this?'

'It's not really my place to say,' Ms Bailey said, looking surprised.

'Of course,' he said, embarrassed that he'd asked. 'It's just . . . ' He couldn't go into it. Not here – not anywhere. He couldn't admit that he and Sally were so far apart in their positions. 'It hasn't been an easy decision.'

'I can imagine,' Ms Bailey said.

'Thanks for being so understanding about this. We feel lucky.'

The lie came easily. It fitted there, in their conversation, more comfortably than the truth would have done.

'If Riley's happy, then we're all happy,' Ms Bailey said.

Theo nodded. The deep sadness he felt, the feelings of loss, betrayal and powerlessness, had no place on the surface. He had to keep them inside.

Sally watched as Riley played with the peas on his plate, making a smile from them, and singing to himself, a soft, contented hum. A week had passed since the transition. He had seemed steadier, Sally reflected. Each morning he'd been happy to go into school and would come out bubbling with stories about what he'd been doing.

For Sally, the only real issue with Riley's transition had been the silence at the school gates. She'd expected questions from the other parents, but instead there were only awkward glances. She didn't force any conversation. If she had to be on the outside again for a while, she could do that.

Sally glanced at the clock – an hour until Theo arrived. A scheduled visit, the way things happened now. It hurt Sally that things had to be this way. They'd told Riley Theo would be home soon, that he was at the flat to be closer to the café while he was running it alone. Riley missed his dad, though. Sally could see that.

Her gaze returned to the peas. 'Those things are edible, you know,' she said.

'You're not eating them either, Mum,' Riley said, laughing and pointing at his mother's plate.

'You have a point.' Sally scooped up a forkful and ate them, giving an exaggerated purr of pleasure, as if they were the most delicious thing she'd ever tasted. The truth was she'd lost her appetite lately, without Theo there to cook for her. It had gone the same way as her sleep, which was hard to find, and easily broken. Even with the lift of Riley's happiness, her days had taken on a new brittleness as she struggled to get any real rest at night without Theo beside her. But they were doing it – managing – moving forward.

After dinner she and Riley went through to the living room, Sally put on *The Lion King* and they sat together on the sofa. Riley was immersed in the film, but Sally's mind was elsewhere, thinking about when Theo would arrive. It was different when he came, now. A distant echo of what their life had been before.

Theo would come and put Riley to bed that night, but then

he would leave. It would seem almost normal to Riley, which was what mattered. But it would never be that for Sally. She and Theo wouldn't have dinner together. They wouldn't laugh. They wouldn't sit beside each other on the sofa. They would be physically close and yet barely touch.

'Is Dad nearly home?' Riley asked, as if reading her mind.

'Soon.'

'I'm going to hug him when he's back.'

When he's back. Sally smiled and hoped that her mixed emotions didn't show in her face. Knowing that what he was doing was visiting, not returning.

Sally glanced over at the bay window and saw Theo approaching. The surge of emotion she felt at seeing him took her aback, the deepest need to have him in her life again, to stitch back together what had been pulled apart.

As Riley dashed over to the glass, a smile came to Theo's face. He was trying. But it wasn't a smile like the one he used to have.

She opened the door and let him in. He swept Riley up into his arms. She longed to join their small circle, to kiss Theo. She desperately longed for his arms to move from Riley to her. To hold her again, the way he used to. But they didn't.

He caught her eye, and she saw he was stuck too, unable to find the next move in this broken dance. Her chest ached.

Theo set Riley back on the floor. 'Hey, love. I've missed you.'

Riley smiled. 'Can we build a den?'

'Sure,' he said. 'Let's make one in your room.'

'Yes!' Riley cried, turning and running upstairs. *Thud. Thud. Thud.*

They should get a stair runner, Sally thought. But, no – she stopped herself. It didn't matter. None of those little things really mattered any more.

Theo passed her, following Riley up the stairs, and within minutes the house was ringing with Riley's laughter. Sally went into the kitchen and tidied away Riley's dinner plate, swept underneath the chair and began the washing up. The things she usually put off until later. There was no reason to leave them that night.

As she cleaned, she thought back to when she and Theo first went away together. They'd been together less than a month and stayed in a rented cottage in Norfolk near where Sally had grown up. She'd wanted to show him the beaches she'd known all her life.

They'd sat on the sand dunes, drinking rum from Theo's hip flask. They'd laughed until they were crying. They'd kissed until Sally's lips felt raw.

Being there had brought her childhood memories flooding back. As the night went on, she told him about her mum – that place in her that would always feel empty. He'd listened, and asked what she had been like.

She said she'd always wanted a family of her own. She bared her soul to him – this man who just a few weeks before she hadn't even known.

She said she wanted to care for someone the way she'd been cared for.

He hadn't said anything. But he looked at her, and he didn't look away, and somewhere deep within her, she'd known. It would happen with him.

She looked around the kitchen now. Their house, the walls she and Theo had painted together and hung with their favourite artwork and photos, sticking up their child's scribbled drawings. It all still felt like home to Riley.

But, without Theo, it no longer felt like home to her.

'Tell us, Sally, how are you doing?' Carla looked directly at Sally.

It was Sunday night. While Theo minded Riley, Sally went out to the support group.

She looked around at the faces in the group. When she'd first seen them, she'd thought she was different from them. Now, she no longer felt that. There was Robyn, opposite her, in a polo neck and a lot of eye make-up. Watching her. Waiting for her to talk.

When she'd arrived, they'd been figures who she felt sorry for, who were going through unimaginable difficulties; who were part of a world she'd hoped she'd never have to be part of. Now, she realised, they were companions. They would be with her on this journey, however long it was. And she felt immensely grateful for that.

'I'm OK,' Sally said. 'Riley's transition at school is going well.'

She looked out at the faces, all eyes on her.

I feel so lost some days.

When she turned towards Theo's pillow in bed, looked across an empty dining table. When she doubted herself. When the other parents at the school gates fell quiet as she approached.

So lost.

She dug deep. So much had turned out well – better than she'd even expected. She needed to stay positive.

'I've helped my child to be himself. I have to feel proud of that, don't I?'

Part Four

WINTER

Chapter 35

They were heading into November, and Sally felt as if she had barely paused for breath.

That morning it was raining as Sally and Riley had their breakfast. A heavy rain that thudded against the glass panes and pooled on the windowsills. A rain that had kept coming for two days now, luring out snails and slugs, and filling the streets with umbrellas. Riley was smiling. A smile that lit up his face. These past days, Sally noted, Riley had been smiling a lot.

Once things had calmed down for Riley at school, Sally had found time to focus on her work. Isabel's marketing ideas and the launch of the new website had brought in a lot more clothing orders, so she'd stayed up into the nights sewing, fuelled by squares of marzipan Ritter Sport. It stopped the house feeling so quiet in the evenings.

In the early hours, though, when she didn't have to be strong for anyone else, doubts would creep in. The ache of solitude would make itself known to her, and sometimes she'd lie there quietly, wondering if Theo really would be back soon, or if this was how it would be now. Theo's absence had left a hole in her heart.

Sally rounded up Riley's things for school and passed him his wellies and a raincoat with storm clouds on it. Outside, he took Sally's hand, and together they walked, huddling under Sally's umbrella, Sally dodging the puddles and Riley splashing on in.

'When's Dad back?' Riley asked.

'He's coming on Saturday,' she said.

He's coming – but he's not coming back. Not yet. There was no lie in it.

Promising without promising too much. A delicate balancing act in managing Riley's expectations. She managed her own the same way. She longed to have Theo back in her life – her lover, her best friend, her partner – but she knew she couldn't make it happen. She wondered if he felt as torn as she did. They'd barely talked this past fortnight, beyond the practical arrangements.

'Can he take me to the big playground? The one with the zipline?' Riley's eyes were wide as he waited for the answer.

'I'm sure he'd like that.'

Riley moved on, weaving a path to school, picking at bark on a nearby plane tree. He pulled off a section to add to the collection.

Riley was unquestioning in his trust that soon his dad would be back. Sally was certain, though, that he, like her, missed the in-between times: bumping down the stairs together in the morning, the wrestle with sofa-cushions, the arguments about shoes that ended in a hug. Those moments didn't happen in pre-planned windows of time.

They arrived at school and Sally watched Riley walk away to join his friends. A group of kids were kicking a ball against the wall and they passed it to him.

Riley seemed to have settled well at school – not once, like most children, but twice. Her child. Her son. *He.* The pronouns were coming to her more readily these days.

Riley was resilient, had grit: that quality that gets you up no matter what life throws at you. Sally's real strength had only arrived in her teens – when life started to throw its punches. It had built slowly, in increments. Sometimes it felt less solid than others. But Riley had always had grit.

Sally glanced at the other parents. Plenty of curious looks, as usual, but no one approached her – there had been virtually no contact at all. Today, she told herself, she would make the first move. She took a deep breath and went to stand beside Leonie.

'Hi, there,' she said.

'Hi,' Leonie said, looking sheepish. 'How are you? I'm sorry, it's been a while, I just—'

'Don't worry,' Sally said, as if it were nothing. 'And I'm fine, thanks.'

'How's Riley doing?'

It felt so good to be asked. 'He's doing really well, thank you,' she said. 'It's been a big change for us all, but he seems much more comfortable.'

'I'm glad to hear that.' Leonie smiled.

Sally looked over at Riley, who was running and laughing. 'Actually, the hard part was seeing Riley unhappy. Seeing him act out of character. So, in a way, this is all easier.'

'I admire you, taking it all in your stride,' Leonie said. 'I mean, you hear about this kind of thing, but you don't think it'll ever happen to you, do you? I mean, to your child.'

'No,' said Sally. 'I certainly never saw this coming.'

'Listen,' Leonie said, glancing over at Beth and some of the other parents. 'A few of us are going for coffee after school on Friday. Would you like to come?'

There it was – a bridge.

'Yes,' Sally said, smiling. 'I'd like that.'

Today I'm with Euan and we're running and running in the playground. The sun is bright in my eyes and I see him ahead with his red T-shirt on, and I think he sees something, because he's pointing but I can't hear what he's saying. I'm just running and running, and there's no sound, just a free feeling.

Chapter 36

On Saturday, Theo cycled up familiar roads, heading towards Addison Road. His house. Their house. It was still that.

When he woke in the early hours his mind would play tricks, fool him that Sally was beside him, and he would reach out and touch the duvet. Then, under his hands, it would press flat, that imagined form disappearing, and he'd be forced to remember. Remember the choice he had made and was making again each day. The choice that kept him from the people he loved most.

He registered the door numbers, like a countdown to the moment he'd see Riley again. *49. 47. 45.* He walked his bike up the path and let himself into the house, his key turning easily in the lock, as if he'd never been away. But as he brought his bike into the hallway, it felt different, as if he were walking into a stranger's home.

'Hi,' Sally said. She was halfway down the stairs, dressed in her pyjamas, her hair pulled up into a rough top-knot and her glasses on. She touched her hair self-consciously. 'I'm a mess. It's been one of those mornings.'

He didn't say anything. But she didn't look that way to him.

Riley rushed towards him, a huge smile on her face. He

hugged her close. He'd missed this, her small body close to his, the way it made him feel complete. When he glanced up, his eyes met Sally's.

'I'll have her back at lunchtime,' Theo said.

'OK,' Sally said. 'Have a good time in the park.' Her tone was cooler. It would be. Of course it would be. Sally passed Riley her scooter and she took it out towards the front gate.

Theo stood there with Sally on the doorstep for a moment.

'Are your parents back from holiday yet?' Sally asked.

She said it with trepidation, and he knew what she was really saying, without her having to say it.

'They get back today. I'll talk to them,' he said.

I don't know how yet, but I'll tell them.

'Thank you,' Sally said.

This partnership that had once brimmed over with love now felt cold, transactional.

'Dad, Dad, come on,' Riley said, rushing back and tugging his sleeve.

'I'll call you later,' he said to Sally.

He caught up with Riley, then glanced back to see Sally close the door.

He thought about what she might do next: have a shower, make tea, read the papers. A domestic scene that he had once been a part of.

Riley ran ahead of him and through the playground gates, dumping her scooter and heading straight for the slide. He hadn't let himself have space to miss them. He'd focused on his work at the café, the endless rush keeping his mind occupied. Now, out in nature, that space had opened up, and with it came a dull ache. This life, with him and Sally as co-parents, not partners, with him as the weekend dad – it wasn't what he wanted, not at all. But he couldn't see another way, not with things as they were.

It was painful, the knowledge that he couldn't feel close to Sally, not when his gut told him that the way to support Riley was not to act, but to wait. The sacrifices in standing his ground cut deep, though; he missed the chats and laughter – in the hallway, making toast, loading the washing machine. He was already missing moments of her childhood that he'd never get back.

Riley waved from the top of the slide. He could see it, how others might mistake her for a boy now: the haircut and cap, jeans and trainers. But to Theo she was his girl, his daughter – he couldn't see her any other way.

Riley dashed from the foot of the slide to join a group of older kids by the zipline. She chatted easily with them and took her turn, swinging her legs out in front of her to go faster. The other kids gave her no more or less attention than anyone else – they didn't seem to think anything about her was different.

When she'd finished, she dashed over to him. 'Dad – were you watching?'

'I was. You were super-fast.'

She smiled. 'I was faster than all those big kids, wasn't I? OK, this time I'm going to do it even better. Will you watch?'

'Of course.'

Riley ran, then turned to see if his attention was still on her. She got to the zipline and looked behind her again, her gaze more searching. She'd never looked at him like that before.

Was Riley just checking that he was watching, or was she looking to see that he was still there?

Sally showered and dressed, then went to meet Isabel for coffee near the station, taking advantage of the time she had to herself while Theo was out with Riley. Isabel embraced her and Sally welcomed the hug. They ordered drinks and found a sofa by the window.

'Only a week now till Freddie gets here,' Sally said. 'You must be excited about it.'

'I can't really believe it.'

'Ready to share your flat?'

Isabel paused, considering it. 'I know you must think we're mad, leaping into it all like this. But being together now, properly, after so long messing about, we both feel we have to go for it.'

'I think it's good you're going for it,' Sally said with a smile. 'It seems like a lot has changed, and perhaps Freddie's changed too. It sounds like he was really there for you, with your dad.'

'He was. He helped me move all of Dad's things into the home, sorted the estate agents' valuations on the house, and did whatever he could to make it easier for me and my brother.'

'And how's your dad doing now?'

'OK, I think,' Isabel said. 'He doesn't seem to have registered that the move is permanent. I haven't mentioned that we're selling the house, and I won't until he asks. The home's a nice place. They do music sessions there every week, and he really responds to that. Even Rob is starting to come round to this being the right thing.'

'You must be relieved.'

'I am. I think I'm done with guilt, Sal. This isn't a perfect situation. Of course it's not. But what good would me feeling bad about it do anyone, really?'

'Exactly. Do you think it's time for you to focus on your own life for a while?'

Isabel smiled. 'Yes. I think it just might be.'

The next day, Theo got the train up to his parents' house. His heart was heavy – he was dreading this visit. He mentally rehearsed how he would tell them, as objectively as he could – just the facts – about Riley's transition and the changes at school. It had to be done. It was only right that his parents heard it directly from him. But it wasn't going to be easy for them to comprehend, he knew that.

His mum answered the door, her face lighting up. She gave him a hug. 'Son. It's so good to see you again.'

He hugged her. 'How was Crete?'

'Wonderful. The weather was perfect, we went to the beach, saw your cousins . . . ' She led Theo inside the house and called out to his dad. 'Stephen, Theo's here!'

'You should see the place that Gabi's found,' she continued. 'It's just beautiful. She has a sea view, and a lovely balcony.'

'That's great,' he said, trying to sound enthusiastic. His interest was genuine, but Crete felt like a world away. Theo was holding so much back. He was living in Gabi's London flat, and his parents didn't even know it.

'Has she found a job yet?'

'Oh, they're fighting over her, Theo – there are two restaurants in the square who both want to take her on. She's making her mind up.'

Theo smiled. Of course she was in demand.

'And there's already a man on the horizon,' Elena said. 'A friend of her cousin's is trying to win her over. Handsome, and well set up.'

'Good,' Theo said. Gabi hadn't mentioned that. But he'd been so self-involved. Maybe he hadn't even asked.

Theo's dad came in from the garden and took off his shoes. Theo saw he'd been mowing the lawn, now striped in alternating light and dark greens.

'Hello, son,' he said, greeting Theo with a handshake.

'I'll get us all some tea,' Elena said.

'How are you doing, Dad?'

'You know how it is with holidays.' He lowered his voice. 'Your mother enjoys them. That's the main thing. Me – I'm glad to get back home.'

Elena brought in a teapot and cake, and they sat down. 'Just a week until your brother arrives home.'

'I'm counting the days,' Theo said. 'It'll be good to have him at the café.'

'He'll soon see that it's good to be back home,' Elena said. 'He's always had this – what do you call it – wanderlust. But you can't keep that up for ever, can you?'

'No, no.'

He couldn't put this off any longer. He just had to say it.

'Mum, Dad, there's something I need to talk to you about.'

'Yes?' Elena said.

'I need to tell you something. It's about Riley.'

Elena leaned forward in her seat, concerned.

'Riley's fine,' he said. 'She's healthy, she's happy.'

'Oh, OK,' Elena said. 'Theo – you had me worried there. I thought something had happened.'

Theo wished he could stop, leave his parents in the blissful ignorance where they currently resided. He looked at their faces – positive, loving – and knew he risked shattering all of that. If he could choose to unknow it all himself, would he? Probably.

'Something has happened. But not in the way you think. We've made a decision that will affect certain things in Riley's life, and in all of our lives.'

We've made a decision. That was the only way to put it. He didn't want this to change the way his parents saw Sally.

'This has been going on a while. At the start of the summer we started to notice changes in Riley's behaviour . . .' He paused. 'She told us she wasn't happy.'

'Really?' Stephen said. 'I'm surprised. She's seemed happy enough to me.'

'We've had some lovely times together,' Elena said. 'The party—'

'Yes, she loved the party,' he said, though the memory, to him, wasn't golden in the way it should have been. Riley hadn't wanted to wear that dress, had she? She hadn't been comfortable. Something had been amiss even then.

'She told us . . . ' Theo stopped. He couldn't say it. *She feels like she's a boy.* He couldn't say that to his parents. 'She didn't feel like the other girls. We made a few changes: her hair—'

Elena shook her head. 'That terrible hair. You never should have let her do that.'

Theo frowned. 'Come on, Mum.'

His mum went quiet and looked down, as if ashamed at being admonished. She was toying with her bracelet, a gold chain. Then she spoke. 'It's no wonder she's been saying those odd things.'

'What odd things?' Stephen asked, looking at his wife.

She was going to do this for him, Theo realised, with a mixture of fear and relief.

'She's said she's a boy,' Elena said. 'She said that to me, the day you and I took her to the park, Theo. Nonsense, obviously. I just ignored it—'

Theo cut her off. He couldn't let his own views sway his parents'. They had the right to make up their own minds. 'It might be nonsense. Or it might not be, Mum. We took her to the doctor, and they think she might be experiencing something called gender dysphoria.'

'Gender what?' Stephen asked.

'It means Riley believes she's a boy,' Theo said. 'And she wants other people to see her that way.'

'Ridiculous,' Stephen said, shaking his head. 'She's only seven and they think she's gay?'

'No,' Theo said. 'This isn't about sexuality, Dad. That's a completely separate thing, and yes, it's too early to think about it. This is about identity. Who Riley feels she is.'

'Oh God help us,' Elena said. 'You think she's transgender, don't you? I've heard about this, on the TV. Riley's not like those children. What you need is to see another doctor.'

Theo made himself push on. He couldn't let his own resistance show, it wouldn't be fair. 'We've spoken with her school and Riley's now attending as a boy. The teachers and other children address her as a male, and she's using the boys' toilets.'

'No,' Elena cried out. It was a guttural sound Theo had never heard come from his mother before. A cry of deep distress. 'No!'

The sound went through him.

'She's been brainwashed,' Elena said, shaking her head in disbelief. 'You all must have been.'

'Listen, I know it's a lot to take in. But that's not how it is. She might pass out of this phase, who knows?' Theo said it as objectively as he could. 'For now, Riley seems happier attending school as a boy—'

'My granddaughter,' Elena said, her eyes shining with tears. 'You must have always wished for her to be a boy.'

'It's not like that,' Theo said. 'She's still the same child. And believe me, I don't wish for her to be—' He stopped himself, but not before his mother had registered his doubt.

'You don't want this to happen, do you?' Elena said.

'The decision's been made.'

'But it was Sally's decision, wasn't it?' Elena said.

He didn't want to cause a rift, but perhaps it was only right to be more honest. 'I would have preferred to wait a while.'

'Of course you would have,' Elena said. 'Because to race ahead like this is madness. She's going to be so confused.'

'Riley seems to be doing well at school now. Better than before. The other children have taken it well—'

'Poor child,' Elena said. 'That poor, poor child.'

*

How did it go today?

On the way home, Theo looked at Sally's text on his phone.

How could he sum up in just a few words what the news had done to his parents? He put his phone away without replying.

The broken look on their faces. As if they had lost their granddaughter for ever. The decision had hurt them – just like it had him.

Theo still hadn't replied to her text. Sally told herself to be patient. He might still be with his parents. She could wait.

'Mum, what are these big books?' Riley was on tiptoes, reaching up to a shelf in the living room. 'The really big ones?'

'They're photo albums,' she said, putting her phone down on the side. 'Shall we look at them?'

She picked a couple at random and took them over to the sofa. Riley sat himself down beside her. Sally opened the album. The first picture was of their first flat, her and Theo standing in the kitchen with Riley strapped to Sally in a sling, her tiny head resting against Sally's chest. *His* tiny head.

'We'd just brought you home from the hospital. You were so, so small.'

The sensations of that day came back to her – the exhilaration of having just given birth, combined with a brand new, completely overwhelming sense of responsibility.

'We couldn't believe we were actually allowed to take you home.' She smiled at the memory. 'We had all these visitors. Look – Isabel's there, your grandparents, Freddie.' In all of the photos, Theo was there: holding Riley in his arms, by Sally's side, or talking with friends. A younger version of him, slightly slimmer, and without the flecks of grey his hair had now, but mostly unchanged. Sally's heart caught.

'I was just a baby then,' Riley said. He turned over the pages quickly, then picked up the next album. 'And this one?'

The second album was older, one Sally had brought over from her family home in Norfolk. The navy cover was faded where the sun had reached it on the study shelf.

She opened it. The first page held a photo of her mother. She must have been about thirty, close to Sally's age now. She was in the long grass at the back of their garden, in a flowery dress with her long blonde hair loose. Sally was beside her, aged around six, wearing a crown of daisies in her own hair. They were both squinting against the sun, with wide smiles for the camera.

'That was my mum. She would've been your other grandma.'

Riley looked up at her, his eyes wide. He didn't say anything.

'She was a lovely woman.' Tears came to Sally's eyes.

'Are you sad because she's dead now?'

'Sometimes. Yes,' Sally said. She didn't mind Riley's directness. 'There we are, making lemonade.' Sally pointed at another image. 'Your granddad must have taken that.'

'And pressing flowers in the flower press,' Riley said, indicating a different shot. 'And there, she's brushing your hair. That's you in the yellow dress, right?'

'That's right,' Sally said, wondering if she could really remember the day like she felt she could, if it was only the photo she really remembered. 'That was my sixth birthday party.'

'You were a little girl,' Riley said.

Sally smiled. 'Yes, I was.'

'And I'm a boy.'

'Mmmm-hmm,' Sally said, a lump forming in her throat. 'Yes, that's right.'

Sally put Riley to bed that evening and ate dinner on her own in the kitchen, a meal for one, leaning against the counter. She'd told herself to have a night off work, that she needed a break, but without it there was too much silence. She didn't want to be alone with her thoughts. She washed up and put the TV on, anything to block those thoughts out.

She and Riley wouldn't have the same relationship that she and her own mother did. There was no replacing that, no replicating it. She could get used to that – she would have to. But the finality of realising it stirred things up, brought out keenly how very much she missed her mum. She longed for a hug from her – especially now. She longed for the gentle reassurances that might make all this easier. If she were here, her mother would remind her that Riley's happiness was the most important thing. She'd remind her to trust herself. Those memories – of her mother's warm embrace, her soft hair – were all she had, now.

She felt suddenly, deeply lonely. Sally reached for her phone – still no reply from Theo. She browsed Facebook and Instagram, saw an update from Isabel, out at an industry party, one she might have gone to if she'd still been working at the company. A couple of the photos of friends' children made her smile, and she pressed Like, but as she closed the apps the empty feeling remained.

Then she saw, blinking on her instant messages, one from Matt.

Hi. How are things with you?

The space inside her filled up a little.

Hi. I'm OK.

She paused. That was part of the story, but not all of it.

But?

Sally didn't want to admit it. The way the conversation with Riley that evening had affected her. Before she could write anything, another message from Matt came.

It's natural, you know. Missing the girl you had, or you'd dreamed of having.

His words opened something up in Sally, and she began to write.

I miss her so much it hurts, Matt. This girl who never even really existed. It hurts even more because I know I'm not supposed to think about it – that it's selfish, and I'm betraying Riley by feeling it.

His reply came.

But this is it – you're not betraying Riley. Any more than you'd be betraying your schoolboy by missing him as a newborn. I wouldn't go back to having Sean, just like I don't want to turn back the clock and toddle around all day helping him to walk again. That time's passed. That child is gone. And that's OK.

She felt a sense of release, hearing it said out loud like that. Maybe she wasn't such a bad person for thinking it.

Try to go easier on yourself, Sally. You're just a parent, doing the best that you can. This is just another thing to deal with that you didn't see coming.

Chapter 37

Theo went for a run in the park before work. With his iTunes on shuffle, he pounded the tarmac, keeping his eyes trained on the path ahead. He wanted to block it all out that morning, but the thoughts kept coming back, intruding.

He'd left his parents' house with a lot left up in the air. They hadn't said, explicitly, that they didn't want to see Riley, but he felt sure that was what would happen. If they pulled away, they'd be hurting themselves more than anyone else, Theo thought. It was a cruelty that would benefit no one. And yet he couldn't rule it out.

'Valerie' came through on his headphones. The music jolted him back to another time. He had a flash of Sally dancing, on the night they'd got together. Of her singing out the words as they'd driven towards Siena that summer, her hair windblown.

Sally.

It wouldn't fit into his mind, all this. These feelings. These contradictions. He flicked on to the next tune.

Stay focused, he told himself. You can't give in and go along with all this, call Riley a boy like everyone else. It matters too much. Wait it out, and Riley will have the space to change her mind when she's ready.

He finished his run, showered at the flat, and then went into work.

After drop-off, Sally got on the tube and went to The Hideaway. If Theo wasn't going to respond to her texts and calls, she'd just have to go and see him in person. As she made her way across the cobbled courtyard, she recalled their launch party. It had been on a warm summer's night two years before – though it felt now as if it had been in another life.

At the time it had felt like they'd arrived. Their café, their home from home. Decorated with prints of their favourite film posters and filled with their dreams. Now, as Sally arrived and pushed open the front door, she felt as if the café was Theo's. It didn't feel like hers any more.

Another day, she might have gone around behind the counter to stand with him, looped her arms around his waist from behind. He'd have turned around, kissed her. But not today. That wasn't where they were today.

Sally walked in and took a seat on one of the stools, looking directly at him.

'Sal.' He looked startled.

'What's up with not returning my calls?'

'I'm sorry. I should've got back to you.'

'Yes, you should have. You can't do this. You can't just go AWOL on me. Not now. We're parents, whatever else might be going on. We need to work together.'

'I meant to call you.'

'So why didn't you?'

He was searching for an excuse. She knew him well enough to see that.

'It's been busy. Freddie's due back at the end of the week. I'm getting things set up for him.'

'OK. And that affected you picking up the phone how?'

'It's been busy, that's all.'

'But Theo, you still could have called. I've been worried. How did things go with your parents?'

He stayed quiet, and she knew then why he hadn't called her.

'It didn't go well,' Sally said, her heart sinking. 'Oh no. Maybe I could talk with them—'

'No,' Theo said firmly. 'I really don't think it would help right now.'

'How bad was it?'

'On a scale of one to ten, somewhere around eleven.'

Her heart raced. She didn't want this to create a rift. Riley would be devastated if this came between him and his grandparents.

'Did you tell them everything, how happy Riley's been—'

'Sally, I did what I could. I tried.' Strain was etched on to his face. 'They are finding it difficult to understand. Right now they think we're ruining Riley's life.'

'They really think that?' She thought of Riley. He couldn't know how his grandparents had reacted – it would colour everything. 'But when they see Riley—'

'They didn't say anything about coming to see Riley.'

Later that morning, after Sally had left, a stream of customers came in. Theo didn't notice Freddie among them right away.

'Not going to say hi to your brother?' Freddie said.

'Hey!' Theo said, hugging him. 'I wasn't expecting you . . . I thought you weren't coming till later this week?'

Freddie shrugged. 'I got impatient. To see Isabel again. To start work here. And, well, I hadn't twigged that the lease on my flat would run out.'

Theo smiled. 'Organised as ever. I'm glad to see you, though.'

Theo needed this. New energy. A distraction.

'Can you start right away?' he asked.

'You sound pretty desperate,' Freddie said, laughing.

'Don't make me beg. But I will. I'm not built for running this place on my own.'

'I won't. I can start just as soon as I've moved my stuff into the flat. Hey – what's this Isabel says about you living somewhere else?'

Theo paused. 'Listen, what kind of coffee do you want? I'd better fill you in on what you're coming back to.'

Theo and Freddie closed the café together that afternoon, then went their separate ways – Freddie to Isabel's, and Theo back to the flat. Perhaps Freddie being back was just the glue that their family needed – the golden boy returning.

Theo let himself into Gabi's flat and saw that there was a light on in the living room. He felt a prickle of unease – he never left that light on. He shut the front door quietly behind him and walked down the hallway, his heart rate quickening. In his house, he knew every floorboard that creaked, but here he was on less familiar territory and he stepped with trepidation. If someone was in here, he didn't want to alert them to his presence.

The flat wasn't as he'd left it, he was certain of that now. One of Gabi's artworks from the hallway was missing, and a vase from the sideboard had been moved. Her photos in silver frames were missing. He approached the doorway to the living room with adrenalin flooding through him, unsure what he would find.

Gabi was standing in the middle of the room, beside two cardboard packing boxes. She was dressed in a white T-shirt and denim dungarees, her dark curls pulled up into a loose ponytail.

'Surprise!' she said, a smile lighting up her face.

Theo put a hand on his chest and then the relieved laughter came. 'Gabi, Christ! You nearly killed me just then. I thought someone had broken in.'

'Sorry,' she said. 'Nice to know you're looking after the place for me, though.'

She held out her arms for a hug and he climbed over a box to get to her. He wrapped his arms around her, squeezing her tight and lifting her off the floor. She laughed and he loosened his hold.

'It's good to see you,' he said. Hugging her, as he had since he was a child, was a comfort that was both intense and familiar. 'So good.' He pulled back to look at her, her olive skin darker, her brown eyes wide and bright. 'You've got a tan,' he said. But it wasn't just that. She looked lighter. Happier.

'Greek sunshine has a knack of doing that,' she said.

'Well, it suits you,' he said. 'How long are you back for?'

'Just two days. I need to ship back a few more things, and I thought I could help train Freddie up, give you a bit of time to focus on the business?'

'You're amazing – thank you,' he said. The gesture meant a lot to him. And her friendship, so warm, so accepting, so constant – he realised now how much he'd missed it.

She looked back at him. 'You, by the way, look terrible.'

He let out a burst of laughter. 'Thanks.'

He knew she was right. The bathroom mirror hadn't allowed him to harbour any illusions. He hadn't shaved for a couple of days, and there were dark shadows under his eyes – the strain of the past few weeks showed.

'Well, it's hardly surprising,' she said.

They stood for a moment in silence. It felt easier, that she already knew the details of what had been happening. He didn't have to explain – or pretend everything was OK.

Gabi spoke first. 'Right, I've got some moussaka in the oven that's just about ready – and I was hoping you might help me eat it.'

Theo smiled, recalling the flavours of his favourite dish. 'You don't need to ask me twice. You know that.'

*

Sally dropped Riley off at school. She watched her son race away from her, book bag swinging. *Her son.* It was starting to fit now.

She and Riley might never do some of the things she did with her own mother, or not in quite the same way, but she was starting to accept that now. She would never be able to replicate that connection, and it was OK. There would be new things, different things. She had a son, who was happy in himself. She was grateful for that.

She noticed Beth and Leonie standing with some of the other parents. She should go over. Today was Friday, and she'd be going to the café with all of them – at last.

They were looking at Riley as he played.

Sally heard a single word, carried on the wind: 'damaging'.

She told herself she'd heard it wrong, tried to imagine a different context it could have been said in. But she knew in her heart what they'd meant. And it hurt.

Leave, she told herself. Let it go.

Beth turned and their eyes met. Beth looked away quickly and it was all the confirmation that Sally needed.

She wouldn't walk away. Riley deserved better than that.

Sally walked over to the group. 'Beth, hi,' she said.

'Hi,' Beth said, straightening out an imaginary crease in her maternity dress.

'I thought I heard you say something. I'm hoping perhaps I was wrong,' Sally said. Her heart was beating hard in her chest.

Sally had half-expected an embarrassed denial, but instead Beth held her ground. 'You heard right. I don't agree with the school's decision to let Riley attend as a boy. I think this is a trend that's getting out of control – and it's damaging. That's what I was saying.'

'Right,' Sally said, feeling shaky, surprised at Beth's directness. 'OK.'

'I'm entitled to my opinion,' Beth said.

'You are,' Sally said. She felt as if she might fall over, or pass out. She took a deep breath and felt a little calmer. She looked to Leonie, seeking support. Leonie looked away, awkwardly.

Sally was on her own.

'It's Riley's wellbeing I'm thinking of,' Beth continued. 'Of course we all know that you love her, and I'm sure this is well intentioned. But this isn't the way to help her, Sally, I'm sure of that. Setting her path this young. She's not old enough to know what she wants.'

Sally felt her cheeks grow hot, a fury building up in her.

'He,' Sally said.

'Sorry?'

'*He*,' Sally said, the word coming from her with a force that took her aback. 'If you honestly care about my child – which I'm not convinced you do – you'll call Riley he.'

Beth's eyebrows went up.

'Listen, Beth, I'm sorry if this has upset you. But try for just a minute to put yourself in my position. Imagine if you had Evie tell you she wasn't happy, that she hated her body, that she wasn't who you all thought she was.'

'I'm sure it's not been easy,' Beth said.

'Damn right it hasn't been. We had to do what we felt was right, for Riley. We're his parents, and we know him better than anyone else does – which definitely includes you. I hope that in time you might be able to see that. In the meantime, I'd ask you to respect our decision, and the school's decision.'

Sally turned and walked away. Her tears came hot and fast. At least no one could see her now. It wasn't so much what Beth had said – she'd expected at least one parent to object – as Leonie, who had privately offered support, then stood by saying nothing. She'd thought Leonie was becoming a friend, but she saw now that she had been completely wrong.

*

Theo and Gabi were sitting in her small kitchen, eating dinner, the windows steamed up and the room filled with cooking smells. They'd spent the day together at the café with Freddie, Gabi training him up in the kitchen while Theo served the customers.

'Freddie told me about your parents. How they reacted.'

'He did?' He hadn't been able to face talking it through with her the previous night. He pictured his mum and dad. God, how easy it would all have been if he'd somehow hidden the truth from them. 'So I guess he told you it was bad. It was pretty bad.'

She nodded.

'They don't get it,' Theo said. 'I don't think it's even possible for them to get it. They're broken-hearted.'

'Perhaps with time . . . '

'I don't know, Gabi. In all honesty, I don't even know if I *want* them to get it. I want Riley to have her grandparents – don't get me wrong – but at the moment it feels like I'm the only one pushing back on this. I can't believe I'm the only person.'

'It must be really difficult.'

'And some. I thought me and Sally were rock-solid. I never thought anything could affect us like this has.'

'Nor did I.'

Theo thought of the house, and what it would mean now to go back. 'I'm not ready to go home.'

'So you're still here.'

'I'm still here.'

That night, Sally couldn't sleep. She kept rerunning the conversation with Beth in her mind, thinking of better ways she could have stuck up for herself and for Riley. She'd wanted to call Isabel – she would have shared in Sally's righteous anger, and allowed her to let off some steam – but Freddie had just arrived and she didn't want to intrude on the time they were sharing together.

She sat up in bed and got out her iPad, then started a new message to Matt.

[Sally]: Are you awake?

[Matt]: A fellow insomniac. It's good to hear from you.

[Sally]: You might regret saying that. I'm awake because I'm really angry about something. Can I tell you about it?

[Matt]: Go right ahead.

[Sally]: One of the school mums gave me a hard time about Riley today, I was expecting some kind of resistance, but still, I feel so shocked by it. I don't know who's on our side, who isn't. You think it's a personal decision – your child, your family. But it's not, is it?

[Matt]: Nope. Sadly not. Everyone has an opinion. It should be about you and your child, but it can't ever be about that.

[Sally]: Why not?

[Matt]: Because it's a huge thing telling people the rules they believe in might not be so fixed after all. A lot of people resist it. Some will never agree. And even when you do change people's minds, they don't always react well to that. Whether you want to or not, you change the way they see the world, themselves, the very nature of boundaries. It gets messy.

[Sally]: I don't want to do all that – upset people. I'm not an activist. I just want my child to be happy.

[Matt]: I'm afraid you'll upset people anyway. Some people will welcome you and your child with open arms, others – conservatives, certain feminists, anxious parents, you name it – they'll react. All you can do is decide how much you care.

Sally saw there were even more words in this new vocabulary that she would need to understand.

[Sally]: I can't unsee the change in Riley. I can't just not know that my child is happier this way. If I could – if I saw things the way my husband does – everything would be easier. I wouldn't have to tread this path I've never wanted to go down. But what I see in my child's face tells me what I have to do. It's as simple and as complicated as that.

Sally sent the message and felt lighter. Here, if nowhere else, she could tell the truth.

You know I get it, he wrote.

That was it – all she'd wanted.

When she spoke to Matt she felt as if maybe she was getting things right, not messing them up.

Theo poured out the last two glasses in the bottle of wine for himself and Gabi.

'So, I hear you've made quite an impression out in Crete,' Theo said.

'You know what it's like: I knocked on a couple of doors when I first arrived, said hello to a few old family friends, and before I knew it everyone had heard I was back. Two restaurants have offered me jobs.'

'Do you know which you'll go for?'

'The one in the square,' she said. 'It's got a good vibe to it.'

'You're living your dream.'

'Am I?' Gabi said.

'That's what you said, when you left. Going back to the place where we grew up . . . '

Gabi took a big sip of her wine. 'I bet it sounded good when I said it.' She chewed her lip. 'Good enough for you to believe it. Almost good enough for me to believe it.'

Theo looked at her, confused. 'What do you mean?'

'Going to Crete. What I'm doing now. It was never really about what I was going to, Theo. It was about what I had to leave behind.'

'Am I drunker than I thought, or is this making no sense?' Theo said.

'I couldn't stay here any longer,' Gabi said. 'Being in London, working at the café. I couldn't do it any more.'

Theo furrowed his brow. 'But I thought you liked it here – living here, working together—'

'I did. That was the problem.'

'OK, you've got me here,' he said, puzzled.

'Theo. Don't make me say it.'

'Say what?'

'I did like it. Too much.'

The words sank in slowly. 'Whoa.' Theo sat back in his seat. 'Are you saying what I think you're saying?'

'Yes,' she said. 'And I'm only saying it now because I'm gone. I'm out of this. I'm out of the picture now. I've never expected anything – of course not. Sally and Riley are like family to me.

I wished so many times that the feelings would go away, but they didn't.'

'Was this ... Was any of it me?' He thought back on how they'd chatted, the intimacy they'd shared for so many years.

'No,' she said. 'You didn't do anything wrong. You were just you. That was enough.'

He didn't know what to say. How to make this right. He didn't want to lose her.

'It hit me that I was getting too old to want something I couldn't ever have. I got tired of pretending to be OK. Because I never was. Not really.'

'I had no idea.'

'I'm glad,' Gabi said. 'I know how much you love Sally – and Riley. And I love them too. Which is why this feels even worse. But it wouldn't shift. I had to make a fresh start.'

He looked into Gabi's dark eyes and saw the way she wanted him. She felt like part of him. Home. A home where he could be understood.

Through all of this, she'd been on his side. She hadn't needed to say so – he'd felt it. She'd been there for him.

He reached out and touched her shoulder, her skin warm.

He felt alive. Talking with Gabi, being with Gabi, made him feel alive.

He was tired of being so confused – of trying to get things right only to end up getting them even more wrong. In Sally's view. In his own.

Theo moved his hand to her face, touched her cheek. If something felt right – and this felt right, *so right* – then why should he have to fight it?

They were close enough for him to hear her breath catch.

He could feel different. Right now, with Gabi, he felt different. Better.

His heart raced. For the first time in months he felt as if he was in the right place. He held her gaze, and touched her hair, drawing her towards him – just the tiniest fraction, but enough that she felt his intention.

This could happen for them.

This could happen.

She didn't move away, but he heard her whisper, 'Don't.'

Sobriety came over him in a wave, changing the colour of everything.

Tears shone in Gabi's eyes as she shook her head. 'Don't,' she repeated.

Damn.

He pulled back. Let out a breath.

Relief.

Nothing was simple.

He'd let Gabi down.

'Gab – I'm sorry.'

She shook her head. 'Don't be.'

He'd let himself down.

Sally. Riley. Damn.

'I'm a mess,' he said.

'I know,' she said. 'I can see that. I should've known better than to step into it.'

I'm in bed. I pick up my elephant soft toy. Grandma bought it for me in the zoo shop last time we went there together. She said I could get any one, and I chose this, because of her name. When I was a baby I called her Elephant and it stuck. That day we went to see the penguins at penguin beach – you can see them on the land but they look best in the water. They swim really fast and gracefully. They are free.

While we watched them Grandma put her arm around me and it felt warm. I haven't seen her and Granddad for a long time now. Dad says they're still on holiday and when they come back they'll come and see us. I hope that's soon. I want to tell them all about being a boy.

Chapter 38

'What are we doing today?' Riley asked Sally, as he poured cornflakes into a bowl. It was the weekend, and Riley liked to have a plan.

'Actually, I have a surprise for you – Granddad Jules and Catherine are coming. They're going to take you swimming.'

Riley's face brightened instantly. 'Awesome!'

Sally had made the call to her dad the previous night, and he'd told her he and Catherine would be happy to make the trip down to London. If Theo's parents were stepping back, then Riley's other grandparents would step in. He wouldn't miss out. She'd make sure of that.

'Are you coming too?'

'Yes. I'll be there too. '

Catherine and Jules arrived mid-morning, and they drove together to the leisure centre. Catherine went into the pool with Riley, leaving Sally and Jules to catch up in the café. They looked down through the internal window. Catherine was sitting on the edge of the pool, dangling her legs in the water, laughing, while Riley splashed nearby. Sally felt grateful to her – the easy, natural way that she had accepted Riley's transition, always making an effort with the new pronouns. She and Jules could have reacted very differently, she knew that now.

'You sure you wouldn't rather be swimming with Riley?' Sally asked.

'Catherine's enjoying herself. And anyway, I wanted to talk with you. Find out how you've been doing.'

Her dad's kindness brought her emotions to the surface, and the pressure of the previous couple of weeks caused the story to spill out. 'I knew it wouldn't be easy for Elena and Stephen to accept, but I thought they'd try. I'm angry with them, Dad. I know they find it difficult to accept, but not seeing Riley ... They've made him a pawn in all of this.'

'Does Riley know how they feel?'

'No. It would be really hurtful for him to feel they weren't on his side. I've told him they're still in Crete, because I didn't want him wondering why they haven't visited. But I hate lying – and I can't do that for much longer.'

'What about Theo? How is he dealing with all this?'

'He's upset too. Which is why he's not at home. He wants Riley to stay a girl, just like he always has – but he's had to accept that the transition has happened, and the last thing any of us want now is for Riley's own family to keep their distance. Theo's going to keep talking with them.'

'They won't be able to stay away for long. You know that, love. Riley has a special kind of pull over all of us.'

Catherine and Jules stayed over, and Sally sat up late with them talking. They didn't talk about Riley, they talked about *The Archers*, and *Masterchef*, and then Catherine got out the Scrabble board and they played until midnight, arguing good-naturedly and grabbing for the dictionary. Somewhere, in the course of that evening, the pain in Sally had started to ease. She saw what it was in Catherine that her dad had fallen so much in love with.

The next day they took Riley out to the Natural History Museum, and he came back full of stories. When they finally left, Sally hugged her dad and Catherine in silent gratitude – for knowing, as they always had, what Riley – and she – had really needed.

Theo looked out of the window of Gabi's flat on to the park. Gabi was on the plane home, and he was still here. Nothing fitted. For one fleeting moment, holding Gabi close, he had felt the possibility of another life – but as quickly as it had arrived, it was gone. He wished Gabi had never told him how she felt – or better still, never felt it. She was his closest friend – the one he'd been able to talk to through all of this – and now she was out of reach.

He couldn't go back to Addison Road, to Sally and Riley. Not now, not yet.

When – if – he did go back, he wanted to feel differently. He wanted to believe they could work together, not pull in two opposing directions.

He glanced down at the platinum wedding band on his left hand. Did it still mean anything? It had meant just enough for him to step back from finding comfort with Gabi, hurting her at the same time as himself, and his family. He had done a lot wrong in his life, but at least he hadn't done that.

'Sally? Sally?'

Sally looked up and around the community hall, realising she'd drifted off in the middle of the support group. She'd been thinking about Theo – how long it had been since they'd last spoken.

'How are things with you?' Carla asked.

'Riley's doing well at school still. We've had solid support from some friends and family. But we've encountered a bit of . . . resistance, I guess you'd call it.'

She pictured Beth's face, felt the sting of that encounter all over again. Then she thought of Elena and Stephen, who hadn't called or seen Riley since hearing the news.

'It's unfortunately fairly standard,' John, one of the older dads, said. 'People do love to judge.'

'I'm concerned that Riley's grandparents are struggling with this, and that their way of coping is to keep their distance from him.'

'That must be very hard on you all,' Carla said.

'Riley misses them so much. I haven't told him why they haven't visited, but I know I have to do that soon.'

'What about Riley's dad? You haven't talked much about him in the sessions,' Carla asked. 'Can I ask what he thinks about all of this?'

'He's upset by it too. But our views are different. He doesn't believe that he's transgender – or at least he can't understand it. He wants Riley to stay a girl and finds it hard to see him transition. He's chosen to move out for a while.'

Robyn spoke up. 'Probably for the best.'

'It's just a temporary thing,' Sally said. As much for herself as for anyone else in the room.

Robyn kept talking. 'If he's against the transition, then he's not on your child's side.'

The comment felt intrusive. 'He's had difficulty understanding it. But he didn't block it. He's supporting us in the ways that he feels he can.'

'You're right to put your child first,' Robyn said. 'If I'd stayed with my husband, let him talk me out of doing what I knew was right—'

'Robyn,' Carla said. 'I think you need to give Sally a bit more space for her own feelings here.'

Another man, Sam, spoke next. 'It's very early days for your family,' he said. 'People's minds change.'

Sally thought of Theo. Their history, the rich tapestry of it, myriad moments they had enjoyed in each other's company, before any of this happened. They couldn't let this break them. Theo might not be ready to move home yet – but he would be.

'We love each other,' Sally said.

'And you still think that's enough?' Robyn asked.

Chapter 39

Sally put Riley's packed lunch into his school bag. He was searching through the laundry pile for a pair of socks, throwing the rest of the clean clothes aside. Whenever they woke up, however much time they had, getting dressed for school always seemed to end up being a rush.

'Hey, don't mess up all the other washing, please,' Sally said.

'I'm sure I saw the other spotty one.'

'Does it have to be the spotty ones? There are plenty of socks in your drawer.' Sally's patience was running short.

He pulled the sock out triumphantly. 'Here!'

'Great. Now put them both on.'

Sally was on edge that morning. Last night the support group had left her feeling adrift. She hadn't been comfortable with all the questions. Perhaps it wasn't even the right place for her any more.

Riley was sitting on the sofa facing the TV, pulling on his socks.

'That lady looks like Evie's mum,' he said, pointing.

Sally turned to look at the screen. It was a breakfast TV show, one she often had on in the background while they were getting ready. There, on the couch, was a heavily pregnant Beth. Her hair was blow-dried into a bigger style and she was wearing more make-up than usual, but it was definitely her, with her husband Mark by her side. She was wearing a bright blue dress and had a hand on her bump.

'So it is,' Sally said. 'How funny.' She turned the volume up so they could both hear the programme.

'I'm sure it's been done with the best of intentions, but you can't help worrying, can you?'

No, Sally thought. No, Beth. You would *not* do this.

'It's our daughter we're worried about. It's our job to look out for her best interests, and she seems very confused and worried.'

She was. She was doing this. Sally's heart beat hard in her chest. Oh God. Make it stop.

'It's not appropriate,' Beth's husband said.

Sally grabbed for the remote again and pressed mute.

'That was Evie's mum and dad,' Riley said, excited. 'What are they talking about?'

'It's nothing, love,' Sally said calmly, though a chill was running through her. 'Nothing important. Get your shoes on, it's time to go to school.'

She picked up her phone and texted Theo: *Put on ITV now.*

Theo got Sally's text and switched on the TV.

He recognised the woman from school. It took him a moment to work out why they were on the breakfast TV show and what they were talking about.

'It's trendy now, isn't it?' the dad said. 'The school have rolled over and accepted this child attending as a different gender, without even questioning it. That can't be right. It could confuse others. Lead to other children wanting to do the same. An avalanche, potentially.'

Theo stopped still. The backlash was happening, and their child was right at the centre of it.

*

Sally took Riley to school, distracting them both with a game of I Spy. When they reached the school, she kept her eyes focused on the classroom door, crossing the playground, Riley's hand in hers. She could sense the other parents looking at them. Was sure she could hear them talking.

'Mum,' he said. 'You're squeezing my hand too tight.'

'Sorry, sweetheart,' she said, loosening her grip. Her hold on Riley had been vice-like. She hadn't even realised.

'Why is everyone looking at us?' he said.

Sally gave a quick glance around. The adults looked away. Beth and Mark weren't there, of course – the show went out live – and given the way that Sally was feeling right then, that was probably a good thing.

'I don't think they are, peanut. Don't worry about it.'

Sally gave her son a big hug. Please don't let anyone tell him, she thought. Please let the children be kind.

'If anyone says anything to you today,' she said, 'anything mean. You just hold your head up high. Ignore them. Who cares what other people think, right?'

Riley nodded, but seemed uneasy. 'Right.'

Sally watched him walk towards the classroom.

On the way home, she called Theo. She needed to talk to him. He must be as angry as she was about all of this.

'Did you see it?' she said.

'Yes,' Theo said. 'It was awful.'

'I think I'm still in shock,' Sally said. 'I know Beth and I aren't close, but I never imagined she'd do something like this. We need people to support us, and she's chosen now to stab us in the back—'

'Hold on a minute,' he said.

'Sorry.' She took a breath. 'I know I'm running away with myself a bit here, but it's just the gall of—'

'Sal, I'm as horrified as you about this, believe me. But this isn't personal. This isn't about you and Beth.'

'I know,' she said, irritated by the suggestion. 'I know this isn't about me and Beth.'

'OK, as long as you see this isn't some kind of a vendetta. She has strong opinions, but that doesn't mean she's trying to stab you in the back.'

'I'm angry, Theo – I'm angry with her, because I can't understand how any parent could do this to another, whatever their beliefs.'

'I am too, Sal. But not because of how one couple have acted. I'm upset that Riley has been dragged right into the middle of a political debate. This attention, this controversy – it's the last thing she needs right now.'

'I know,' she said, tears in her eyes. 'I know. What they did was wrong, really wrong.'

'It could have been avoided. It's us who put her in this position. I never wanted this for Riley. To be singled out, centre stage, treated as a freak. You've talked and talked about what damage not listening could do to her – but *this* is what's going to damage her, Sally. *This.*'

It hit Sally. Theo wasn't on the same side as her – even now. He couldn't even see her point of view.

'Theo, I never chose this, Riley being transgender. You know that, right?'

'You chose to act on it,' Theo said. 'You decided that the right thing to do was to talk to the school, make all this happen. Regardless of the long-term impact on Riley, on us, on the rest of our family.'

'No,' she said. His words had come as a blow. 'I didn't make anything happen – it was already happening.'

'You decided to make it public, to make all of this public, and you made that choice for all of us.'

Sally blinked away her tears. Theo – this Theo – was a stranger to her.

I give Saturn some fresh lettuce and a cherry. He climbs up on the cherry. Mum says not to think about Evie's parents on the TV and what the other children are saying about me being a boy. She said not to worry about it. But when she says not to worry about things, she gets this little line on her forehead, between her eyes, and I think sometimes she's worrying about it for me.

Chapter 40

That evening, Sally poured herself a large glass of wine. The argument she'd had with Theo earlier had left her feeling lost. They'd never spoken to each other like that before. Bringing up Riley – it hadn't always been easy, but they had always done it as one. The moments of joy – immense when they came – were shared, earned together. Now it seemed as if they were pulling in opposing directions – pulling each other apart. They saw what was happening in two completely different ways.

Maybe she'd been wrong to put all her hopes on Theo coming home, and them resuming family life as it had been. He seemed to have moved so far away from her, and from their love, that she was starting to doubt whether they could go back. The relationship that had once been so precious to her, a nurturing, loving place she could feel safe – now seemed like an altogether different thing. She didn't even want to think about it, because of where looking too closely might lead her. She didn't even want to talk about Riley – the worry and sense of responsibility she felt every day. She didn't want to talk about herself, or the mess that everything was becoming. She wanted to think about something else for a while. Be somewhere else. She glanced over at her phone. Picked it up.

It was as if Freddie had always been there, Theo thought the next day, as he taught his brother how to make a flat white. They worked well alongside each other, and while it was different from the days when Gabi had been there – and he still missed how that had been – his brother was uplifting company, and was proving to be a good fit.

'How's everything going, living with Isabel?' Theo asked him.

He wanted to hear about it – and also to be distracted. The argument with Sally had shaken him up, and he wanted to forget about both the way they'd talked to each other, and the TV interview itself.

'I'm enjoying it so far,' he said. A smile, calm and content, which Theo hadn't seen before. 'I think I'm finally getting what everyone's been going on about. It's nice, right, coming home to someone who makes you laugh, who makes you dinner sometimes, who you can sit on the sofa with and watch box sets with—' Freddie stopped himself. 'Sorry. I wasn't thinking. That was kind of tactless.'

'Don't worry about it,' Theo said. He didn't begrudge his brother the joy of that companionship. It didn't feel like a comment that even related to him and Sally, which was sad in itself.

Theo knew he'd been harsh with Sally when they'd last spoken, and he didn't feel good about it. He'd dug in, said things he'd known would hurt her. He wasn't even sure if he'd really meant them – it hadn't been conscious, but perhaps it had still been in there somewhere, that if he could make her angry, make her feel pain, he could at least still make her feel something. It wasn't right, but the truth was it had felt better than the numbness, the distance.

'You and Sal . . . ' Freddie started.

Theo saw his parents approaching the door. 'Later,' he said. 'Mum and Dad are here.'

Theo seated his parents at a table with drinks, then went into the kitchen. He didn't feel much like talking to them that morning. He could hear the chatter of their voices, but his thoughts were elsewhere. He'd been too hard on Sally. He'd blamed her.

He'd call her. Make it right again.

When the food was ready, Theo brought the plates over and sat down with his family.

'What a way for people to hear,' Elena said, shaking her head.

'Word's got around to Mum and Dad's neighbours. About Riley,' Freddie said quietly, meeting his brother's eyes.

'Jean Carey and her husband came round yesterday, after that show on the morning TV,' Elena said. 'She said how sorry she was to hear about our grandchild. That it was going around online that the couple were Elmtree parents, and having seen Riley, with her hair, and those clothes, they could only assume it was her they were talking about. Can you imagine, the shame of it? Them, pitying us?'

Theo sank into his seat. It was worse than he'd even imagined it would be. 'I'm sorry, Mum. We knew that some parents weren't happy with Riley's transition, but we had no idea they were going to do that.'

'We didn't even have a chance to tell people ourselves before they heard about it that way,' Elena said. 'We don't want our friends' pity. We just want this over, Theo.'

Freddie spoke up, in solidarity. 'Mum, don't give Theo a hard time. It's been difficult for all of them.'

'You need to stand up for yourself, son,' Stephen said brusquely. 'Clearly we're not the only people who think this is madness. Your job is to protect your family.'

Theo heard his father's words, and the accusation that they

carried – one that had reverberated through his life to that day. Theo was not being a man. Or, at the very least, he was not being man enough.

That morning, Sally walked to school with a new determination and purpose. She had no patience left for being polite. Beth had made her position clear. She'd gone out of her way to make life more difficult for Riley, and to clear the way for others to do the same. For Sally, staying silent didn't feel like a choice – not any more.

After dropping Riley off, she looked around the playground for Beth. She saw her standing by the gates. Sally took a deep breath and went over.

'Beth,' she said. 'Could I have a word?'

Beth stiffened. 'If you want.'

Beth's friends dispersed, until it was just the two of them standing there.

'I know what you're going to say,' Beth said, keeping her guard up. 'And I expect you're very angry. But it wasn't a decision we made lightly. It was something we felt we had to do.'

'You *had* to go on television, bringing our child into the spotlight?' Sally said. 'When there were a dozen other ways we could have resolved this in private?'

'I wasn't confident we could resolve anything that way.'

'You could at least have tried. We could've talked about Evie and how she was feeling. You said all of this has confused her.'

'This may have started with Evie – but to be honest, Sally, it's now become bigger than that.'

'Why?'

'Look, Sally. I'm sure making this choice wasn't easy for you. But these are worrying developments for all of us. Riley's transition – this insanity – it might give the other kids ideas. These talks and assemblies they have to do – sowing the seeds of doubt in our children's minds. This isn't normal – it's a fad, a trend. It's not just me who's worried.'

Sally forced herself to remain diplomatic; it was the only way she'd get anywhere with this. 'I can understand what you're saying. But I doubt very much that our decision about Riley will affect your lives or your children's lives.'

'You're sure about that?' Beth said, fighting back. 'Because a lot of people on Twitter—'

'God. Twitter. You'll find whatever answer you're looking for there,' Sally said. 'I can't be sure, no. But I'd be very surprised.'

'There have always been tomboys,' Beth said. 'Only now we're expected to accept that they are really transgender.'

'They are two different things,' Sally said, trying to stay calm. 'Believe me, I've thought about this.'

'It isn't right,' Beth said. 'And confusing them like this – it isn't fair on our kids.'

Sally saw what she would have to contend with from now on – judgement, whether spoken or unspoken. And if she was going to protect Riley, she had to stand up for herself – for both of them. Starting today.

She looked Beth directly in the eye. 'And forcing Riley to be a girl when that's not who he is? How is that fair on him?'

Beth looked at her blankly, shocked. She didn't try to carry on the conversation, and Sally realised she had no need to either. She'd made her point. It was unlikely she'd change Beth's mind, but she'd asserted herself and stood up for Riley. As she turned and walked away, she felt stronger.

Theo locked the door to the café, his work day over. Maybe his dad was right. He hadn't been man enough; he hadn't been strong enough.

Things needed to change. He needed to do something for himself.

He scrolled through his contacts and stopped on one. He hesitated for a moment. He'd thought about calling her so many times, but something had always held him back.

His heart beating faster, he pressed call.

In the evening, with Riley in bed, Sally picked up her phone. A few weeks ago she wouldn't even have considered meeting up with a man she barely knew. Even if he was just a friend. But she wasn't the person she used to be.

She messaged Matt.

I know this is a bit out of the blue. But can we meet? I really need to talk.

She made herself a cup of tea, trying not to stare at the phone. When she reached the bottom of the cup, she picked it up and checked her messages again.

Sure. Where?

She hesitated, unsure what to write next. Another message came through.

Tomorrow? The Prince Regent in Islington?

Sure. See you there at 8.

Her heart thudded against her ribcage. The boundaries blurred.

Another message came through.

Relax. Don't think it.

Curious, she replied: Don't think what?

That you shouldn't be doing this.

How was it that he knew her so well – almost better than she knew herself? One final reply.

It's only a drink.

Chapter 41

The following morning, Sally woke before Riley. The house was silent. She went downstairs, made some tea and sat out in the garden in her coat. Heard the birdsong. The mug of hot tea warmed her fingertips and hands.

Over the past few years, she'd forgotten how it could be – alone like this. She'd forgotten where she ended and where Theo and her child began, and now she was starting to feel her own edges again, see the shape of herself.

She looked past the apple tree, past the fences, to the blue sky beyond. There were other ways to be. Where the weight of responsibility didn't feel quite so heavy.

There was another way to live. And tonight she was going to try it.

Theo came by the house and picked Riley up on his bike. He and Sally exchanged a quick hello as she handed Riley over. She'd looked different. More confident. He'd wanted to stay longer, to talk to her, but he hadn't known what to say. Part of him still felt angry with her, for putting Riley in the spotlight. But another part of him was starting to long, physically and emotionally, to have her back.

'Faster,' Riley called out, from the seat on the back. 'Faster, faster.'

He dropped Riley at the door to the classroom and found Ms Bailey. 'Do you have a minute?' he asked.

'Of course.'

'After everything that's happened this week, I wanted to check with you, see how she's doing.' He corrected himself. 'He. Old habits. And how the school's been.'

It felt strange to say it, yes. He didn't like it. But it wasn't as hard as he'd expected. He glanced over at Riley, playing with some classmates. They – the teachers, the children – they had all adjusted to it.

'Well, obviously we weren't expecting all that publicity,' Ms Bailey said. 'We would have preferred for this to stay within the school. But these things happen, and if we can set a positive example, then we're committed to doing that. I'm glad to say none of it seems to have affected Riley too much. He's polite and helpful, as always, and he looks after the other children when they are upset. I'm really happy with how things have been going.'

Theo breathed a sigh of relief. 'I'm glad to hear that.'

'Listen,' Ms Bailey said. 'I'm not sure if I should say this or not . . . but one thing Riley does keep saying is that he misses you. That he hopes you're coming back to live with them soon.'

Theo felt a pang of guilt. 'Yes,' he said. 'Well, I hope that too.'

'I know it won't have been an easy week for you, as parents, after what happened.'

'It came as a shock, that's for sure.'

'I want to assure you that the school aren't going to bow to this kind of pressure. We won't let certain parents dictate what we do or don't do.'

'Thank you,' he said. He was surprised to feel grateful. The school reversing their decision would have solved certain problems, after all. But confusing Riley with rule changes wasn't going to help anyone at this point.

'Listen,' Theo said. 'If any of the parents approach you and have questions or issues with what we're doing, please tell them to come and talk to me about it. Sally's dealt with enough of this on her own. Let them know I'd like to talk to them about what we're doing and why.'

Riley's babysitter, Juno, a local teenager, arrived at seven. She sat with Riley on the living room sofa, reading stories with him. Juno hadn't batted an eyelid at Riley's appearance, his close cropped hair. Kids Juno's age didn't care about this stuff, Sally thought. The thing that was tearing her and Theo apart, and unsettling the community they lived in – almost no one under the age of twenty-five seemed to notice it, let alone worry about it.

Sally went upstairs, and put on black jeans and a pale gold top. She brushed her hair and clipped it back, then replaced the hairbrush on the bathroom shelf. Then, after a moment's hesitation, she placed her wedding ring beside it.

Downstairs, she bent and gave Riley a kiss. Riley's arms looped around her neck and he held his mum there for a moment longer than usual.

'See you later, Riley. Be good for Juno.'

'I will be,' Riley chimed. 'You look nice.'

'Thank you.' The guilt. What was she doing? What was she even thinking?

But at the same time she couldn't wait to get out of the house – to be away from responsibilities and worry and angst. Even if just for an evening.

She turned to Juno. 'There's macaroni cheese in the fridge, if you're hungry. And you're welcome to a small glass of the wine on the side. But don't tell your mum I said that.'

Juno smiled. Sally left before she could change her mind, closing the front door behind her and getting into the waiting taxi.

'The Prince Regent in Islington, please.'

They drove into town, and through the streets of north London towards Highbury. Sally watched the raindrops on the glass as they trickled their path to the bottom. She found, slightly uncomfortably, that she missed Riley. If Riley were here, they'd be choosing raindrops to race, and cheering on their watery jockeys, willing theirs to be the winner. But tonight she wasn't that mother. Tonight she wasn't doing anything for Riley, or for her family. She was on her own.

A message beeped through on her phone, from Matt. *I can't wait to see you.*

Sally's heart raced. The adrenalin told her she could be someone other than the woman she'd been. There was a way out. An escape. She felt alive. So alive.

She felt a connection with Matt, had done since the first moment they spoke. They were on the same journey – with all its twists and turns, and pains and joy, the immense, endless responsibility. They were part of their children's transition. It was not a path they chose, but one that had chosen them – and that had become a dominant and significant part of their life. He understood.

She remembered her first date with Theo. Over a decade ago, the last time she'd felt this rush of anticipation. She remembered searching the bar, running her gaze over every seat and booth, looking for him. Then their eyes meeting. Then they'd spent the evening in animated conversation, getting to know the details of one another's lives, familiarising themselves with the coloured threads that made up their personal tapestries. Theo who was now far from her. Theo who wanted to cut every thread that, over the years, had joined with hers, and made a woven picture that was shared. Theo was somewhere else, happier without her, and she didn't want to feel this alone for ever. And – she thought of the challenges that might lie ahead – she couldn't be.

Another text: *What are you drinking?*

She smiled. He was already there. She glanced up at the window again, looking out for a street sign – Holloway Road. She'd be there in the next few minutes.

The twitching curtains on their street, the school mums at the gate – what would they think of her, standing on this line? About to cross it. She was barely a wife any more.

She was coming undone, and she didn't want to stop it.

Vodka and tonic.

Theo cycled past the plane trees and houses, on this street, one he'd never been down before. He found the address he was looking for: 34A. All it had taken was a phone call.

A woman opened the door to him, with a smile that was warm and welcoming.

'Hi, Theo,' she said. 'Come on in.'

Sally approached the door to the pub. Her stomach was tight in a ball, and for a moment she thought her legs might stop of their own accord, holding her still and preventing her from pulling the door open. But they didn't. They kept on going, and she kept on going with them. Her hand found the bronze handle, and she felt the resistance of the heavy door. She pulled it open and a burst of Bruce Springsteen greeted her. She took a breath. You're here now.

She went inside and looked around the pub. It was busier than she'd anticipated – the booths by the window were populated with groups and cluttered with beer bottles and glasses, the smaller tables filled with couples and lone drinkers. Then she saw him, over by the bar – dark, handsome. He looked over and their eyes met. He smiled.

This was it. She was doing it. After all this time, here he was. Matt.

She took a step towards him, but he turned back to his friend and resumed his chat. Her fiction fell back into reality. His hair was too long; his eyes were too deep-set. It wasn't him.

She felt her cheeks flush at the error. She only had one picture of Matt to go on, and it wasn't even very clear. She felt foolish, inexperienced, out of her depth. She took a seat at the bar – he would have to come and find her. Her eyes travelled to the toilet door with a large M on it. Perhaps, in a moment, it would open, and he would be there.

Her phone buzzed with a message.

Theo. She put her phone away – she'd read it later.

God, what was she doing? Why was she even here?

Then the phone vibrated again.

Matt.

You look stunning.

Startled, she looked up, looked around. Her heart raced. Another message.

Over by the window. I'm here. So is your drink.

She saw the glass of clear liquid and ice first, on a table she'd missed on her first look around. Then, beside it, a hand, an arm.

Her chest felt tight. She couldn't breathe properly.

It didn't make sense. This didn't make sense.

Theo sat down by the window in the therapist's consultation room, and she poured him a glass of water.

'Would you like to talk about what's brought you here today, Theo?'

Her voice was gentle and lilting. Harriet, that was her name. He'd found her details online, and hadn't known quite what to expect. She was a little older than him, smartly dressed. There was nothing about the room, about her, that should be making him feel this uncomfortable. But he really wanted to get up and walk back out of the door.

No, he thought. I don't really want to talk. In fact, I'm kind of considering how I could exit before we even get started.

He felt exposed under her gaze. He was sure she could even see him considering leaving. He was here, he told himself, because he'd chosen to be. Because he'd realised that he wasn't the man – the husband, the dad – that he wanted to be.

'I want to be stronger.'

'Stronger, how?'

'I want to be able to . . . '

She nodded, leaving room for him to carry on.

'The thing is . . . '

His voice cracked. Damn it. Damn.

It had started with Riley, hadn't it? He'd tried to fix it himself. He saw now that it was too big for that. Had always been.

'I'll be fine,' he said. 'It's just . . . you know. There's been a lot going on. I'm not sleeping. I miss them. Both of them. I want us to be how we were – but things have changed and I can't change them back.'

She didn't prompt him, just waited. That same nod. The silence was harder because he knew he was the only one who was going to fill it.

'For a while I thought I didn't know who my child was.'

'Yes?'

He hadn't believed it was possible for Riley to know what was right for her. Even when he'd seen how happy she was as a boy – the holiday, school – even when he'd seen her gaining confidence, all the while he'd wanted the change to stop.

Nothing Sally had said to him had made any difference. He'd wanted to fix things. He'd wanted to get back to normal. A normal life – it was what he'd longed for all along, and what he had fought so hard to keep. It had mattered so much to him – perhaps too much.

'And now I'm not entirely sure I know who I am.'

Sally's head was spinning.

Robyn was sitting in front of her, offering her a drink.

Matt wasn't here. And instead, Robyn was.

Robyn – from the support group. Robyn – a woman she barely knew.

Sally felt a pain in her stomach, as if she'd been struck there.

'It was you,' Sally said.

Robyn nodded.

Matt's face vanished. Robyn's remained.

But the private messages, the username, the things that had been said ... Sally's mind raced. The assumptions that made her so sure she was talking to a man. The photo – Siobhan in the centre. It hadn't just been Matt there, but Siobhan's mum too. Sally recalled the image – the woman's hair blowing in the wind, partly covering her face. Sally's mind filled in the gaps now, the features those wind-blown strands of black hair had covered. Dark eyes. Sally saw them now.

Here was Robyn. A woman Sally had, unwittingly, confided everything in. A woman Sally had let into her heart because she was so desperate to find an ally, and answers.

The pub, Robyn, Sally's thoughts – they were all still there, but they were blurring.

'My ex, Matt set the account up, years ago,' Robyn said. 'He never used it, though. When he left me, it didn't seem worth setting up another.'

'But ... I don't get it. The support group ...' Then Sally

remembered – 'Matt' had been the one to suggest she should go. Robyn had obviously wanted to meet her.

'After we clicked online, I wanted a chance to get to know you, properly,' Robyn said. 'Then I did – and I was hooked. You were even better in person.'

Sally frowned. She was trying to weave together two realities that didn't fit. When she and Robyn had met at the support group, Sally had actively wanted to get away from her. How was it that when she'd spoken to her online she'd felt so differently – as if that person was a kindred spirit?

'Why didn't you tell me then who you really were?'

'Would you have carried on letting me in, if you'd known? Of course I'd hoped we'd hit it off when we met face to face, but it didn't really work out that way – I'm not always so great socially, and I could sense you backing away. I didn't want to lose you. I just wanted to get to know you. I like you. You intrigue me.'

'But this . . . ' Sally shook her head. 'This wasn't the right way to do it.'

'And you, coming here, that was right?' Robyn said, a cynical smile on her face.

'This is crazy,' Sally said. Her head was swimming. 'I can't do this.'

'But you wanted it.'

'I wanted something. But not this.' She felt sick to her stomach.

'There was a connection. We got each other.' Her eyes met Sally's.

Sally's cheeks were burning hot now. She felt a rush of shame. The shame of what she had wanted.

'Why are you here?' Robyn asked.

Sally wished she wasn't. She wanted to disappear.

'You see, I knew you'd think that, that was why I couldn't be honest. I thought: Robyn, you've let too many good things slip away. Give this one a chance to happen.'

'By lying to me about who you were?'

'By not telling you absolutely everything.'

Sally thought of everything she'd done, the advice she'd followed. If Matt had been a lie, had it all been a lie?

'I'm guessing now that this was a bad move,' Robyn said.

'Yes,' Sally said. 'You're right there.'

She thought of Matt – of what she'd imagined he could offer her, and what he had turned out to be. She'd compared Theo to this. Something that had never really existed. Talking with Robyn had offered her an escape, but it had also guided her.

'Before I go,' Sally said, with a flicker of panic, 'I need to know something.'

'Sure,' Robyn said.

'Was any of it true? The things you told me about Siobhan, the advice you gave me . . . ?'

'Yes,' Robyn said. 'Everything else was true.'

'The things you said about Riley?' Sally felt confused, dizzy. 'The things you told me to do.'

'I never told you to do anything,' Robyn said, shaking her head. 'The decisions you've made for your child – those came from you.'

On the journey home, regret flooded Sally's body and mind. How had she allowed herself to believe in Matt?

None of it had been real. Matt wasn't a safe haven. He hadn't even been a real person. She had wanted a place where she could feel safe, but that place had never existed. There was no way out from all this.

On her wedding day she'd been so sure that she and Theo would weather every storm together. But that hadn't happened. The pressure had come and they'd faltered. No, *she'd* faltered.

It was too late. It was all too late. Something had shifted. She'd hoped, earlier that evening, that she could feel like someone different, someone alive and free – and yet here she was coming home an empty shell. She felt crushingly stupid. It wasn't that easy. How could she ever have imagined it would be?

When Sally got home that night, she paid the babysitter and went to check on Riley. One of his legs was out of the cover and dangling over the edge of the bed, but he was breathing gently and deeply, fast asleep.

I told myself talking to Matt was a way to understand you better, Sally thought. *But maybe I just wanted something for me.*

Chapter 42

An hour a week. An hour where Theo's life was suspended, and he had to look at it. What was working, what wasn't – and why he was making the decisions that he was. Harriet listened and asked questions. It didn't feel entirely comfortable yet, talking about his feelings, his family, his parents. But slowly, he was starting to trust that looking inside for the answers he needed was the right thing.

There was enough judgement, enough anger, enough blame coming from the outside and directed at them. He had to find a way to support Riley. And in order to do that, he had to understand himself. He had to become a different kind of man.

On Sunday, Sally walked through the motions of the day. Riley's shoes on. Jacket on. Park. Walk back. Hands held. Zebra crossing. Keys in the lock. Laundry on. Dishwasher on. Kettle on. Play a game. All the while she felt numb. She'd almost thrown everything that mattered away. She'd wanted to walk out on the person she'd become, and be someone else with Matt. She hadn't wanted to walk out on Riley, or even on Theo. But she'd wanted to escape from the pressure. From herself.

Her day was punctuated by messages from Robyn. At first, she read them.

Give me a chance.

I could make you happy. I know I could.

She didn't reply. More came.

You're wrong to walk away from this.

You don't want to be alone.

Sally deleted them, then blocked Robyn's number. She couldn't bear to think of what she'd almost done. It wasn't Robyn's fault, but all the same, cutting her out made things easier.

In any case, Matt – the man she'd trusted and confided in – was long gone.

She missed him. She was, truly, on her own now.

She went through the motions. Spaghetti Bolognese. Laundry hung up. Dishwasher emptied. Toys tidied. Bath. Bedtime stories. This was it. All that there was now.

Stop.

Stop.

Just stop.

The house was silent. Sally went through to the bathroom. She looked at herself in the mirror and took out her hairgrips one by one, her dark-blonde hair falling loose around her shoulders. You could mistake her for the woman she'd been on her wedding day – full of lightness. It was an illusion, though. She wasn't that woman any more.

'You have such beautiful hair,' Theo used to say. 'But do you have to have so much of it?' He'd pull strands from his pillows, the plughole, laughing. The memory of his laugh, of them laughing together, felt distant.

She found a pair of scissors that she used to cut Riley's hair now, and her gaze fixed on her own eyes in the mirror. She lifted the scissors to her hair, about three inches up. She wanted to feel how it would be to do this. She took a breath and closed the blades of steel together. There was resistance at first – her hair thick and wiry where it was bunched together – but as she pressed the handles together hard, a curl fell onto the floor. In isolation, it looked pretty, that shiny hair. Like you might want to tie it with a ribbon and keep it.

She raised the scissors again and held them up by her shoulders. She opened them and they took a larger chunk of hair into their metal jaws. *Crrrrsh,* the scissors went, as they closed shut on the strands. Curls fell on to her kimono, on to the floorboards. Her eyes remained fixed with determination on her reflection as she cut off curl after curl after curl. It was gone.

Sally swept up the hair with a dustpan and brush, as if it was just another domestic chore – tidying the countertops, or putting away Riley's toys. But as she tipped her hair into the bin it felt like a release to let her old self go.

She stood up and caught sight of herself in the mirror, hair cut bluntly to her jaw. No softness in her. This was Sally now.

I am me.

On Monday morning, when she woke up, it took Sally a moment to remember. She reached a hand up to touch her hair and felt the place where it wasn't. She ran her fingers through her curls to the ghost of the tips. Phantom hair. The spectre of her past self. Sally, as she had once been, no longer existed.

'Mum,' came Riley's call from downstairs. 'Mum – it's breakfast time. Why are you still upstairs?'

She got up and went to the mirror hanging on her bedroom wall. Her hair stopped short by her jaw, the cut jagged in places. God, it looked terrible. She picked up a couple of hairgrips to tidy it as best as she could. At the breakfast table, Riley's jaw dropped.

When they arrived at the school gates, Riley said, 'Everyone's looking at us.'

Sally glanced around. The school mums looked away quickly, but it was clear they'd all been staring.

'Me, this time,' Sally said. 'My hair.' She touched it, the ends of it chin-length.

'I kind of like it,' Riley said.

Sally wasn't sure if she liked it herself or not. But she felt relieved that it was gone.

Riley squeezed her hand. 'Who cares what other people think, anyway?'

Theo and Freddie worked together in the café. When there was a brief lull, Freddie would fill it – with stories about Isabel, the flat, the excitement of being back in London after so long away. They didn't talk about their parents, or about Riley, and Theo liked it that way. They'd found a supplier whose cakes matched up to the standard of Gabi's, and word had got around – the customers were coming in crowds now.

Busy. Busy. Busy. It was easiest for Theo. One hour a week was enough to think about the fractures across their family.

What he might be losing. What he had already lost.

Sally went to see Isabel after school drop-off. They met on a park bench near Isabel's flat.

'Your hair, Sal. What in God's name were you thinking?' Isabel laughed, and then, surprising herself, Sally was laughing too.

'Let's not talk about my hair,' Sally said, shaking her head. 'Anything but that.'

'We can fix it. I mean, the length is good.' Isabel reached out and touched it. 'But seriously, you've made a total mess of the cut. I'll straighten it out for you.'

'Thanks. Can you fix the rest of me while you're at it?'

'Go on. I'll give it my best shot,' Isabel said.

Sally wondered if she could face it – telling Isabel about Robyn, what had happened. She didn't want to have to relive it. And it felt humiliating.

'I went out the other night.'

'Oh yeah?'

'Oh, Iz. I've been a real idiot.'

'OK, now you've got my interest,' Isabel said. 'Who did you go out with?'

'There's someone I've been talking to online, since this all started. Matt. We got talking through that forum you sent me the link to. We talked about the kids – he had a teenager – and what it's like trying to make a judgement call about all this.'

'Right . . . ' Isabel said.

'I got, I don't know. Attached, I guess. I felt like he understood me,' Sally said. 'And things with me and Theo have been so difficult lately . . . I wanted to meet him, to see what – if anything – was really there. Listen, believe me, anything bad you're thinking about me right now, I've thought it myself already.'

'It's not that,' Isabel said. 'It's just, I didn't realise things had got that bad with you and Theo.'

Tears sprung to her eyes. 'Neither did I.'

They were silent for a moment. Isabel waited for her to go on.

'I'm not trying to make excuses for what I did. But I just wanted to talk to someone who was going to get this – all of this with Riley. Understand what I'm trying to do.'

Isabel listened, calmly. 'So, what happened . . . ?'

'When I got to the pub, Matt wasn't there.'

'He didn't come?'

'He didn't exist. A woman was there, instead.'

'Sorry?' Isabel said, confused.

'I feel like such a fool. Robyn. That's her name. I know her from the real-life support group. She took on her ex's username. I didn't think to check.'

'Why would she do that?'

'I don't know. Maybe she finds her life difficult to cope with, just like I was starting to. I don't know if I can even blame her for that.'

'Has she contacted you again?'

'I've blocked her number. I won't go back to the support group. Our paths won't cross again.'

'You sure about that? She sounds pretty intense.'

'She only came into my life because I let her in. I hold my hands up to that. I needed someone. Now I'm closing that door. I'm doing this on my own.'

'Wow. Well, in a way, perhaps she did you a favour.'

'How?'

'Were you really ready to turn your back on Theo?'

Sally paused. 'I didn't want to. I don't want to. But I needed more than he could give.'

Theo was with Harriet, in her small consulting room. This place where talking was sometimes a release, other times a pressure. Today, his words weren't coming easily.

'I want to go back to last year. Back to before this happened. When we were happy.'

'What was it like then?'

'Riley was fine. Sally and I used to laugh – all the time. Sometimes she'd laugh so hard . . . ' He smiled at the memory. 'I loved seeing her like that. We'd be there giggling like kids, at some dumb YouTube video of sausage dogs dressed up or whatever. Sometimes we'd laugh about things Riley had said, sometimes we'd laugh about nothing.'

'And now?'

'It's all decisions. Blame. Recriminations. Worry. Even when we're working together to sort something out, it's like there's a distance between us. The way my parents have reacted has been difficult.' He'd already given Harriet the details and talked about it a little.

'How are things with your parents?' she enquired gently.

'I called Mum yesterday,' Theo said. 'We talked, but nothing's changed. They haven't said outright that they won't come and see Riley. They haven't gone that far. But they haven't come.'

'How is that for you?'

'Hard. And it's tough on Riley, of course. We haven't said anything, but she's smart – she knows something is up. She used to see them every week.'

'How does their standing back make you feel?'

'Frustrated. Angry, I guess, that Riley is the one missing out in all of this.'

'You feel angry because Riley is missing out on the time with her grandparents, because they can't understand her transition?'

'Yes,' he said.

Her words seemed to echo in the room. *Riley is missing out.*

Just like she was missing out on the time with him, because even when he had been there, he hadn't truly been there. He'd wanted to be, but every time he met with Riley he was willing his child to be different, to be the girl she didn't feel comfortable being.

If he was going to go back to his family, he had to forget about normal. See his own childhood for what it was – good, but not the only way to shape a family. His own dad had made the world easier to understand by showing him its unbreakable rules and boundaries. But he would parent Riley in a different way. Because the world Theo was living in, and Riley was growing up in, was one where doors were opening, and boundaries were being broken down. Theo couldn't be like his dad – and he didn't want to be.

The following morning, as she walked away from school, Sally thought about how things had changed. Riley didn't get invitations to play dates with other children these days. As Riley became more beautiful to her, others stepped away – not understanding, seeing a threat. Sally was left reading into the silence, unsure what the real reasons were.

She heard a voice call out behind her, interrupting her thoughts. 'Hey, hold up.'

Sally turned and saw Faye, Euan's mum. She was wearing leggings and trainers, with an oversized hoodie. She made her way towards Sally, and Sally instinctively tensed up. She wasn't in the mood for more judgement. She just wanted to go home.

She picked up on Sally's hesitation and raised her hands. 'Don't worry, I'm not about to tell you you're ruining my child's life. I promise you.'

Sally relaxed enough to return the smile. Her posture softened. 'Thank you.'

'I like your hair, by the way.'

Sally raised a hand to it, self-consciously. Isabel had tidied it, and made it look a lot better, but she still wasn't used to it.

'Listen. My exercise class got cancelled – which, I'll be honest with you, is a massive relief. Do you fancy a coffee?' She pointed towards the café on the high street.

Sally let her guard down a fraction, but not enough to say yes.

'No nosy questions,' Faye said. 'I promise.'

'OK, then,' Sally said.

At the café, they ordered and took a table in the corner. There was a group of other school mums on the far side and Sally saw them turn to each other and whisper when she came in.

'Ignore them,' Faye said, not attempting to lower her voice. 'They just need someone to talk about. And that awful interview Beth did has given them something for now. When Euan started reception and I was a single mum still, I was all they had. Now they've finally realised I haven't got designs on any of their husbands, I guess they needed someone else to get their claws into.'

As she and Faye sat down, Sally almost forgot that they'd barely spoken before. She felt comfortable with Faye. As if she didn't have to be someone different, as if she didn't have to prove herself.

'I feel for them, in a way,' Sally said, stirring a sugar into her coffee. 'Don't get me wrong – I hate that I can't drop my kid at school without the whispers and stares these days. But I know they're only thinking of what's best for their own children.'

'You're too generous,' Faye said. 'Not saying there aren't mothers like that – but just that those women aren't them. They're not scared for their little Johnny. What they care about is making it known that you are getting it wrong. Because then they can believe they're getting it right.'

Sally smiled. 'Maybe.'

'Trust me on this. Ignore them. A lot of us parents are with you. Maybe we should've been more vocal about that. And the kids couldn't care less. Euan's barely mentioned that Riley's a boy at school now. Nothing's changed for him.'

'Ms Bailey said most of the kids have taken it well,' Sally said. 'Which has been a big relief.'

'Exactly. Kids are resilient. It was completely wrong of Beth to escalate things like she did.'

'Thank you.'

'You know what,' Faye said. 'Euan loves hanging out with Riley. How about we go to the park together after school?'

'Yes,' Sally said. A glimmer of light. 'I'd like that.'

Later that day, Sally watched as the children disappeared into the long grass. To anyone passing, Riley and Euan were just two normal boys, playing in the field behind their school, Sally thought. That's how she hoped they'd be seen, at least. It was easier that way, to not have to explain, to justify. She watched as Riley collected pine cones and acorns, putting them in his pockets.

Sally had a child who was healthy, and becoming happier with each passing day. She knew how lucky that made her.

She watched Riley now, bending down to pick up more treasures and then holding them up with a look of pure glee. She wanted her child to run free like this for ever – wind in his hair, surrounded by oak trees and ponds, fresh air that left Riley's cheeks wind-whipped and sent him off to a sound sleep after his bath.

Euan's mother must have seen something in her expression. She reached out and touched Sally on the arm. 'You OK?' she asked.

'Yes. Yes, of course,' Sally said quickly. 'Just nice seeing them play together.'

'Riley's brilliant,' Faye said. 'You're doing a great job. You know that, right?'

Sally felt a lump rise in her throat. Then Riley smiled over at her and waved.

'Some days,' Sally said.

Theo shaved, looking at himself in the bathroom mirror in Gabi's flat.

This weekend, he told himself. This weekend he would talk to Sally.

He would tell her he loved her.

He would tell her he loved Riley.

He would tell her how much he'd missed them.

And he would tell her that he wanted them to be a family again.

Chapter 43

On Friday, Sally was at home with Riley and Euan. The two boys were playing out in the back garden, huddled over the sweet jar and putting some food out for Saturn. Faye barely got any time to herself, so Sally had offered to have Euan around to give her a break. It had felt good, getting to know Faye. There might be parents who couldn't accept Riley, but there were others, better ones, who would.

Perhaps this is how it would be now. Sally would be like Faye, running a household on her own. It wasn't what she wanted – she wanted Theo to come home.

But if this broke her and Theo up, Sally would manage. She would do it.

Her mobile vibrated on the kitchen counter: unknown number. She picked up.

'Hi. Is that Sally Pieterson?' a woman asked.

'Speaking.'

'Hello. My name is Karen.' The woman spoke gently and slowly. 'I'm calling with regard to your child, Riley. '

'Yes?' Sally said, glancing out at the boys playing in the garden.

'I work for social services. We've had an anonymous report.'

'I'm sorry?' Sally said. There must have been a mistake.

'There's been a suggestion that your child is in a situation they are not comfortable with. I have a duty to follow up.'

'Right,' Sally said. She felt sick. The ground was shifting beneath her feet. She found a chair and sat down.

'I appreciate that this will come as a shock for you. We will need to do an assessment, talk to Riley and see you all at home. I can talk to you about it in more detail then. Is Monday at four OK?'

An assessment.

She looked out at Riley again. This couldn't be happening to them. Numbly, she agreed to the appointment.

'When we get a report like this, it's our duty to make sure that everything is OK. To check if the parents might need some additional support. No one wants to take any chances with a child.'

Sally thought of the softness of her child's hand in hers. Riley's voice, full of laughter. They were wrong. Whoever it was who had done this, was wrong.

She knew she had to stay calm, but inside, she wanted to scream: *Just let us be.*

Sally called Theo, and he came around on his way back from work. He and Sally sat together in the living room and she told him about the phone call.

'It doesn't seem real,' Sally said. 'This. Riley. Us.'

'Who would do this?' Theo said, his brow furrowed.

The question had been running through Sally's mind, again and again, ever since the phone call. One name repeated itself: Beth.

'We can't get caught up in that,' she said. 'We just need to get through the assessment. What's done is done. Now we need to support Riley in this, and show social services that they've got nothing to worry about.'

'You're right,' he said. 'And we will.'

'You'll be here on Monday?' Sally asked.

Theo's eyes met hers. So close. He was so close. Almost close enough to step back into her life.

'I mean, I know it was me that made this happen at school. I pushed for it . . . ' Tears welled up in her eyes.

'Sal,' he said, stopping her. 'Riley's our child. Of course I'll be here.'

At bedtime, Riley fell asleep during the start of a story, his arm hanging limp over the edge of the bed. Sally brought it up and under the cover, and tucked the duvet around him. She smoothed back a lock of hair, her hand warmed by the skin on her child's face.

She couldn't start doubting herself. She couldn't. She had to trust that she was doing the right thing, and the ease with which Riley talked and moved each day reassured her that she was. They weren't committing to forever; neither of them were. They were just seeing how this all fitted. But someone, somewhere, disagreed with what she was doing, and it stung. She couldn't stand at the school gates without casting a glance at the other parents and questioning who had made the call. Who felt so threatened by her decision, or concerned about her child, that they had chosen to get the authorities involved? It hurt.

Sally stood for a moment in the doorway, looking at the outline of her sleeping child, lit by the dim glow of an Octonauts lamp. She couldn't bear to dwell on the thought that they might take Riley away from her. It was too cruel and unnatural to contemplate. At the very least, though, there'd be interviews, investigations, questions – things they wouldn't be able to hide from Riley. Their fragile new normal would be poked at, tampered with. She wasn't sure that their family, already fractured, would withstand any more strain. And Riley, taking his first steps in shoes he finally felt were the right ones, would be reminded again that to the outside world, he was different. That to some people, in fact, nothing about him was right.

It was 4 a.m. and Theo couldn't get to sleep, thoughts of the social services assessment crowding his head.

He should have been there. He should have been living with them. He should be with them now. He'd wanted to make everything right – tell Sally how he still felt about her, how much he still cared – and then this had come along and thrown everything up in the air.

He'd spoken to Freddie and his parents to let them know what was going on. They'd tried to be strong and reassuring, but Theo could tell they were as worried and upset as him and Sally.

He thought of Riley: the baby he'd held in his arms; rocked and hushed to sleep; bathed and fed; taken for her immunisations; bent over holding her small hands as she learned to walk; fixed stair gates that she learned to climb over; put plasters on her grazes. She was the child Sally and he had longed for, and so much more than that. They'd been there for her in every possible way, and now someone was saying they weren't doing enough.

It was worse than that. The realisation made him feel sick to his stomach: someone out there thought they were trying to harm her.

Tomorrow, a woman is coming to our house. Mum says she wants to know about our family.

Because we're special, Mum says. Because of me being a boy. And before, how everyone got that part wrong and thought I was a girl.

If you're different, people sometimes have questions, Mum says.

Chapter 44

After school on Monday, Theo was playing Connect 4 on the floor of the living room with Riley. Sally was pacing up and down, cradling a mug of tea. The scene – everything about it – was familiar. A slice of their old life. Apart from the fact they were waiting for the social worker to arrive.

'Sit down, Sal,' Theo said.

'I will, in a minute.'

She took a sip of tea. This didn't happen to parents who cared as much as they did. That's what she'd always thought. With one phone call that certainty had been torn from her.

'The woman's coming,' Riley called out, jumping up on the sofa for a better view through the window.

Sally saw a woman in her forties, in a trouser suit, walking up the path. She went around to open the door, while Theo and Riley followed closely behind.

'Hi, I'm Karen,' she said, holding out her hand for them to shake.

'Pleased to meet you,' Sally said. 'Come in,' she said, motioning for the social worker to step inside the house.

Sally told herself to take it one step at a time, as if this wasn't a stranger arriving to assess them, assess Riley, assess their parenting.

Riley dashed ahead into the living room.

'I know this can't be easy for you,' Karen said. 'But I'm sure you understand that we have to follow this up.'

'It's OK,' Sally said. Though it felt a long way from that. 'Do sit down,' she said, offering the armchair.

She and Theo sat side by side on the sofa. She could feel his leg against hers. The longing caught her heart. If they were holding hands, it would all feel a little easier.

'There are a few questions I'll need to ask you and Riley.'

I look out of my window. It's dark but I can't see the stars tonight. I'm looking hard but I can't see the big bear or the little bear.

I want to go and ask Mum which ones they are. But it's late.

I think she's tired. The woman today asked us a lot of questions. She said she helped mums and dads. That she visited lots of children. Not just me.

We drew three houses. One for good things. One for things I'm worried about. One for dreams. In the good things house I put Euan. And Pokémon. And my Transformers pants. In the dreams I drew a rocket. Karen said did I have anything to put in the worries house? I said no. Then I said baths. And Dad not being here. Then I got tired of the questions.

Mum gave me a biscuit with chocolate on it, and one for the woman too. My stomach hurt, though, and I didn't even want my biscuit.

When Mum and Dad thought I was eating dinner, I looked back into the hallway. Dad covered his eyes with his hand. Mum did too, and made a strange sound like she couldn't breathe. They hugged.

I think Mum is tired of questions too. Tonight at bedtime her eyes were red, and when she said good night and cuddled me, she held on for a really, really long time.

Chapter 45

The next morning Riley had slept later than usual. Sally hadn't wanted to wake him. The social worker had done her best to keep the atmosphere light, but Riley must have picked up on something about the seriousness of the visit.

She was glad of the distraction when Isabel arrived and hugged her at the front door.

'My flat is a bombsite with all Freddie's stuff, it's good to be out of there. And because I know you, I brought flapjacks,' Isabel said, passing Sally a brown bag. 'Home-made.'

'Thanks,' Sally said, taking the bag. They went through to the living room.

'How did it go yesterday?'

'OK, I think,' Sally said. 'She was nice enough. Theo was here. She spoke to us both separately and then talked with Riley. I told her about what's been going on at school, and about seeing the GP. She wanted to know about Theo, whether he was living with us or not.'

'So what's next?'

'They'll decide if they need to see Riley at school. Then, in the next four to five weeks they'll do a child and family assessment. God, Isabel. I feel sick just thinking about it.'

'Surely they'll see now that you guys are doing everything you can to support Riley.'

'Will they? I hope so, because the idea that we'd be doing this to Riley against his will? I can't believe anyone could think that.'

'It's insane. It's not fair at all that you guys should have to go through this. Listen, I know it's easy to say, and harder to do, but try and relax.'

'I know. I have to. We just have to go through the motions. Get through this.'

'And you will. You know that, right?'

The light. She had to keep focused on the light. But at times like this the dark threatened to creep in and overwhelm her.

'How have things been this week?' Harriet asked Theo.

'Going through this social services assessment has been really tough on Sally.'

'Just on Sally?'

'On both of us.' He found it easier to think about Sally's pain than to acknowledge his own.

'How has it been, being with her through this?'

'It's made me realise how much I want us to be a family again. I was getting there anyway – in fact I'd been planning to tell her how I felt, before we got the phonecall. But this has made it all so much clearer. Sally and I were sitting there talking to the social worker, and all I wanted was to reach out to her. Hold her hand. Feel close to her again. It wouldn't have fixed things, I know that. But it would have made everything easier.'

Harriet listened, waiting for him to continue.

'But at the same time, there's a distance there. I don't know if we can close it.' It pained him to acknowledge it. 'Maybe we've moved too far apart to be able to come back together.'

At school we're learning about volcanoes. We're making lava out of newspapers and painting it red and orange. I like using the big fat brush and putting a lot of paint on it.

Evie said, 'Give me the brush.' And I said no.

Her eyes went all small. Then she said it. The mean, mean thing.

'My mum says you're not really a boy. Everyone knows that really.'

I wanted to shout at her. But I didn't. I didn't want to get in trouble with Ms Bailey. So I broke my volcano. I got in trouble anyway.

Now my tummy hurts again.

Chapter 46

Sally looked at her To Do list. The waiting. Each hour that went by without a call from Karen seemed to last for ever.

She concentrated on preparing Riley's favourite pasta sauce, so that they could eat it together when he got home. The small things. She tried to keep focused on the small things.

As she was getting dinner ready, her phone rang: Isabel.

'Sal,' Isabel said.

'Hi. Aren't you at work?'

'I am. I am and I'm not. I just had to duck out of a meeting.'

'You OK?'

'Yes. I'm fine. Listen, when I came the other day, there was something I wanted to tell you, but you know, with everything going on with Riley, the time didn't seem right. But now I think I might burst if I don't.'

'Go ahead. I'm all ears.'

'I'm pregnant, Sal.'

'Sorry?'

The word, in connection with Isabel – it had thrown her.

'I'm pregnant. With child. "I'm a means, a stage, a cow in calf", as Sylvia Plath put it.'

Sally's heart swelled with pleasure, but she told

herself to take a breath. She couldn't assume that this was good news.

'Whoa,' she said. 'And that's . . . ?'

'Good. I'm starting to think,' Isabel said. 'Though the almost throwing up in a board meeting part, not so much.'

'Congratulations. I'm so happy for you. Wait – does Freddie know?'

'Yes. He's excited. In fact, he's really excited.'

'That's wonderful.'

'Come to ours this evening? Listen, I know things have been a bit awkward lately with the in-laws, to say the least – but Freddie really wants to tell the whole family together.'

Sally dropped Riley around at Faye's house that evening. He bounded up the front path, with his overnight bag on his back. Faye and Euan opened the front door. Euan was dressed in a Superman outfit.

'Sleepover!' Euan called out.

'Superman sleepover!' Riley called back. They ran together into the house and up the stairs.

'Thank you so much for this,' Sally said.

'It's my pleasure,' Faye said. 'Euan's pretty excited about it, as you can probably make out.'

'I could've taken Riley along tonight, but things have been sort of weird with his grandparents lately. I didn't want to force it.'

'It's fine,' Faye said. 'I've got *The Lego Movie* and popcorn all set up for them.'

'You're a star. Thank you. Any problems at all, just call me. I can get back here quickly. But Riley's usually OK at other people's houses. Better than ours, sometimes.'

'I'm sure it will be fine. Enjoy tonight. You deserve a night off, what with everything you guys have been going through.'

'Thank you,' Sally said, grateful to have Faye, a friend she could count on.

Sally arrived at Isabel's flat with a bottle of champagne and non-alcoholic wine. She tried not to think about whether her parents-in-law were already there. Isabel greeted her at the door and Sally gave her a really big, long hug.

'Such amazing news,' she said.

'Thanks, Sal. I hope you're good at bluffing. I didn't want to wait before telling you. Too impatient for that.'

Sally went inside. Theo was with Freddie in the kitchen, and she said hello to them both. Seeing Theo stirred up her emotions. It wasn't easy, being with him and yet not really being with him. And it was hard to be happy when their whole life was hanging in the balance, but she couldn't let that show. Tonight was about Isabel and Freddie.

'Riley settle OK at Euan's?' Theo said.

'Couldn't get away from me fast enough. I left Faye both our numbers, just in case.'

'Cool. Thanks for arranging it.'

'Riley's been wanting a sleepover for ever.'

It all felt a bit stilted and awkward. But they were talking. Talking was good.

'Listen, do you know what this is all about?' Theo asked her.

'No idea,' she said. She looked away quickly, knowing that Theo could always see right through her.

The doorbell rang. 'That must be your parents,' Isabel said as Freddie went off to open it.

'It'll be fine, you know,' Theo said. 'With my mum and dad.'

'I know,' Sally said. 'We don't need to talk about Riley tonight.'

'I think we have to try and be patient.'

'Maybe tonight could be the start of us rebuilding things with them.'

Saying hello to Elena and Stephen hadn't been entirely comfortable. It was there, in the room with them, how they'd reacted to the change with Riley. But once they were all sat around the table for dinner, the conversation flowed surprisingly easily. Freddie led the chat, full of energy and enthusiasm. Isabel talked to Stephen and Elena, politely asking questions. Sally found herself relaxing into the evening.

After dinner, Freddie chinked the side of his wine glass.

'Everyone,' he said. 'Isabel and I have an announcement.'

Intrigued, Elena looked at her husband, and then at Isabel, and then at Freddie.

'We're having a baby,' Freddie said excitedly.

Elena and Stephen's faces erupted into wide smiles. Everyone got to their feet; there was a chinking of glasses, heartfelt hugs. Theo looked so happy; he looked like the man she used to know.

Elena's eyes, large and brown like her sons', met everyone's. Everyone's except Sally's and Theo's. She didn't look them in the eye.

She *couldn't* look them in the eye.

Sally thought of the way Elena had been when they'd said hello – cold, distant.

Sally looked at Theo. She felt as if she couldn't breathe.

Elena. *Elena.*

A cog turned in Sally's mind, clicked into another and turned.

Time stopped.

She was sure of it. Elena had done this to them. It was her.

Chapter 47

At nine the following morning, Sally picked Riley up and took him back to their house. He was full of stories about the sleepover. At home, they built a den out of sofa cushions and Riley clambered inside, taking a box of Lego in with him.

Last night, she'd hidden her concerns and hadn't said a word to Theo. On the surface, it had been a perfect evening. Isabel was positive and happy about her pregnancy, and Freddie was almost unrecognisable from the commitment-phobe he'd once been, full of excitement about becoming a dad. Elena and Stephen were also delighted. They'd all agreed that while they wouldn't tell Riley yet, he'd be thrilled at the news he'd have a new baby cousin.

Sally had kept up the pretence that everything was OK, because it felt like the right thing to do. But the whole evening the thought had whirled in her mind. The person who'd reported them to social services. It hadn't been Beth. It hadn't been a teacher. It hadn't even been an embittered Robyn. The report had come from somewhere much, much closer than that.

She had no evidence, no proof. Nothing beyond her gut feeling. But she trusted it. Just as she'd had to that whole summer.

She left Riley in the living room and went into the kitchen to call Theo.

'I have nothing concrete, and I may be completely wrong. I hope I'm completely wrong. But is there any chance it could have been your mum who reported us?'

'No,' he said. 'There's no way.'

She waited for it to sink in, just as it had for her.

He paused. 'She wouldn't do that.'

On the journey to his parents' house, thoughts – recollections of the past few weeks – had rushed through his mind. He'd never seen his parents so upset by anything before. He couldn't rule it out. Even if he risked offending them, he had to know for sure.

Now the three of them were sitting in his parents' living room. He looked from his father to his mother, wishing with all his heart that Sally's suspicion was off. They'd talked through the news from the previous night, and Theo knew he couldn't put it off any longer.

'Mum, I know it hasn't been easy for you, Riley's transition. The decisions we've made.'

She shook her head and looked down. 'No,' she said.

'I'm sorry to even ask this. I can't believe I'm asking it.' He took a deep breath. 'Please tell me you didn't call social services and report us.'

She was quiet for a moment. 'I didn't,' she said at last.

Theo was relieved. But the atmosphere was still tense; he could feel it. Something wasn't right.

'Your mother has been very upset,' Stephen spoke up. 'It's not right what's happening. Even the teachers are involved now, the other children.'

'I saw what Sally was making you do to poor Riley, and it upset me a lot,' Elena said. 'I just want it to stop, Theo.'

Theo shook his head. 'Mum – how could you?'

'It wasn't your mother,' Stephen said.

Theo stopped, shocked. 'Dad?'

'I thought the authorities would know best,' Stephen said. 'They must have rules for this kind of thing. Regulations. It's out of control.'

His father's betrayal hit him like a punch to the stomach.

'I don't think what your dad did was right,' Elena said. 'I told him not to do it. But . . . '

'But you don't think that what is happening to Riley is right either?' Theo finished.

Elena nodded.

'Do you understand what that could mean for us? For Riley?' Theo said. 'It's within their power to take Riley away from us.'

'They can stop this madness,' Stephen said. 'They will put an end to it.'

'No, Dad. No,' Theo said.

For the first time in his life, he pushed back.

'This isn't madness. It's our life. We're Riley's parents. You're the one who has to stop.'

Theo and Sally met in the café later that afternoon.

'You were right,' Theo said. 'Well, almost right. It was my parents who reported us.' He shook his head. 'Only it wasn't my mum. It was my dad.'

Sally struggled to take it all in.

'Why would he do that?' she said. 'I know this has been difficult for them. But how could it come to this? Riley is his *grandchild.* How could he possibly think this was the right thing to do?'

'I know,' Theo said, shaking his head again. 'And I'm even more upset than you are, if you can believe that. I guess it was some kind of misguided attempt to protect Riley.'

'By breaking us up? By putting Riley's security on the line?'

'If it's any consolation, I think he's starting to get it now. He's called social services and withdrawn the report.'

'But it's too late, now, surely. That won't make this go away, will it?' Sally said.

He shrugged. 'I don't know.'

Sally's heart felt heavy. Their once-close family was splitting down the middle.

'He's seen how devastated Mum is. They find what's happening with Riley really difficult to understand.'

'We all find it difficult to understand, Theo,' Sally said. 'Not one of us knows, really, what it is for Riley to feel what he does each day, that his body is wrong. I don't get it either.'

He seemed startled. 'But you've been behind this from the start.'

'Do you think because I spoke with the school, bought the clothes, because I'm calling Riley he, I find this easy? Because I don't, Theo. I find it really hard to admit that our daughter is gone.'

Tears came to her eyes but she fought them back.

'I don't care about the flak from the other parents, the stares, the judgement. Not really. I can deal with that. But for your parents to suggest . . . ' Her voice faltered. 'If even Riley's grandparents aren't behind us on this – if they could turn on us to the extent that Riley could have been taken away – then what chance do we have? We're only at the start, Theo.' She bit her lip, determined not to cry.

'I told them,' Theo said. 'I told them they were wrong. Wrong to call social services. Wrong to interfere. But most of all . . . ' Theo paused. 'Wrong not to trust us that we were making the right decision.'

Sally paused, taking in what he'd just said.

'You said that?'

'Yes.' Theo nodded. 'If this is what Riley wants, we're doing this together.'

Chapter 48

Stepping into Harriet's consulting room the day after confronting his parents, Theo felt more at ease.

'I told Dad it wasn't his decision. That he needed to respect what we were doing, even if he didn't like it.'

'How did it feel to stand up to your father like that?'

Theo thought back to it. The rush of adrenalin. The way he'd seen no other way forward than to do something he'd never done before. He smiled. 'Really good. It felt really good, actually.'

He pictured his dad as he'd left his parents' house. Stephen had seemed smaller, somehow – diminished.

'I have a lot of respect for Dad,' Theo said. 'Don't get me wrong. I care about him. Freddie and I both do. He's always done whatever he could for us. He's a good man.'

Harriet listened, waiting for him to continue.

'But his way isn't the only way to be a father. Or a man.'

The next day, Sally walked Riley to school. Waiting for the social services assessment meant they were all still in limbo. The same streets, the same houses, the same shops. It was familiar, but Elena and Stephen's betrayal had left everything seeming different – her parents-in-law, there for them since Riley was born, had shown that, when it came to it, they didn't trust Sally and Theo to know their own child. But there was light, too – Theo's words meant she no longer felt alone.

They got to the playground and Riley dumped his scooter by the bike racks.

'Mum, there's the new boy! Arlo. He's my friend.'

Sally looked over to see a small blond child, playing with Euan.

'That's nice,' she said.

Faye made her way over. 'They seem to be a three these days,' she said. 'He's cute.'

'I haven't seen him before.'

'Just started. His mum's a good one. We should get her out for coffee before the others get her.' She smiled.

Sally tried to smile back.

'You haven't heard yet?' Faye asked.

'Is it that obvious?'

'Yes. Anyone would be the same.'

'Social services said they'd send the assessment around now, let us know what the next steps are going to be.'

'Fingers crossed,' Faye said. 'I hope they don't put you through any more of this.'

'Me too.'

Riley waved at Sally, and Sally waved back. Her child. Their family.

In somebody else's hands.

Later that evening, Sally met Isabel by the gates of Rosemount residential home. They pressed the buzzer and walked down the avenue of trees towards the large house.

'Thanks for coming with me today,' Isabel said. 'I'm sure Dad will be happy to see you again.'

'You and Freddie have already told him about the baby, then?'

'Yes,' she said. 'We went in last weekend. But now I have the scan photo to show him.' She pulled it out of her handbag and showed it to Sally.

'A lovely, tiny monkey,' Sally said. 'Congratulations.'

'Thanks,' Isabel said. 'I thought it looked more like a gummi bear, myself.'

'So he was happy to hear the news?' Sally said.

'Yes. But he won't remember. I guess one of the very few joys with dementia is that now I get to tell him all over again.' She was smiling, but there were tears in her eyes.

They went in through the front doors together and into the communal living room, where Noah was playing chess with another resident. He looked up when they came in.

'Isabel!' he called out. 'Sally!'

He gave them both a hug. He turned to Sally, his eyes bright.

'Did Isabel tell you?' Noah said, a big smile spreading across his face. 'I'm going to be a grandfather.'

Sally got the train home that afternoon. It had been wonderful seeing Noah and Isabel together, watching his face as he put on his reading glasses to take a closer look at her grainy scan photo, working out where the baby's head was. Isabel's face had relaxed and she'd smiled. In the last few months she'd looked happier and more content than Sally had seen her in years.

It had felt good to step out of her own world for a couple of hours.

Her mobile rang, and her heart rate picked up when she saw the name: Karen.

Theo had been thinking about Riley all day. Waiting for news. At four, he got a message on his phone: Sally.

I just had a chat with Karen. I have the assessment. Call me.

He left Freddie to run the café, got on his bike and went.

Standing in the hallway, Sally read to Theo from the report page. 'These parents are caring for their child as well as they can, in challenging circumstances. We are satisfied that Riley Pieterson is not at risk. There will be no further action.'

Sally's smiled. 'It's over, Theo.'

'Everything's OK?'

'Yes.'

He hugged her. As his arms wrapped around her she felt herself soften. She didn't have to be strong.

'It's over,' she whispered again. She pressed her face against his chest. 'It's over.'

Please come home now, Sally thought. I want you to come back home.

Dad was here tonight. I heard the door go click, so now he's gone.

I don't feel sleepy. I put all my animals in a line on my bed and they are straight. I put my shoes in a line and they are all straight. My pens too.

I get in bed and pull the blanket up. All straight.

If I can get everything back straight, it will all be better again.

Chapter 49

Stephen and Theo sat together in a booth at the café after closing, with the door locked, and Theo began to see traces of the father that he knew.

'Your mother and I have been talking,' he said. He gave an awkward cough, but carried on talking. 'It seems I may have been overly hasty.'

It was something, Theo thought. But not enough.

'I may have made a mistake.'

'And?' Theo prompted him.

'And I owe you an apology.'

'You know that you need to say this to Sally too, right?'

'Yes. And I will. When me and your mother come over to your house later. But I wanted to talk to you first.'

'I appreciate it,' Theo said. They sat there in silence for a moment.

'Have you, erm, heard anything?' Stephen said.

'Yes – we have the assessment report that they won't be taking any further action.'

Stephen let out a breath of relief. 'Thank heavens for that.'

'Dad, what you put us through . . . ' Theo said. He couldn't just dismiss it, the hurt, the worry, the feeling of betrayal. His father's apology didn't make any of that go away. 'It's been hell for Sally and me.'

'I made a very serious mistake,' Stephen said. 'I see that now. I thought they'd just give you and the school a talking-to. That they'd put things right.'

Put things right. It was how Theo had felt when this all began. But those words, in relation to Riley, didn't fit any more.

'Maybe there isn't just one way for things to be right, Dad.'

'It wasn't like this, when you and Freddie were children. This has been a lot for your mother and I to accept.'

'I know it's been difficult for you both.'

The edges of Stephen's mouth curled down, and Theo could see the hurt there. 'She's our grandchild, Theo. We love her. We don't want her to be singled out.'

'Nor do we, Dad. But it's as a girl that Riley feels uncomfortable. Believe me, I've struggled with this too. It's as a boy that Riley feels happiest.'

Theo put a hand on his father's arm. Stephen covered it with his own and held it firmly.

'Riley's strong, Dad. Riley's going to be OK.'

Sally made a cup of tea and drank it in the kitchen, waiting for Theo to arrive with his parents. It all felt raw still, but she had to take her fury and her pain and turn it into something constructive. She had to try to build a bridge out of the wreckage. If Elena and Stephen could take the first step and come over, if they would do that to try and rebuild their family for Riley's sake, then she could find it in her heart to forgive them. She could do this.

Riley dashed into the kitchen. 'They're here!'

She had to do this.

Together with Riley, she let Theo, Elena and Stephen inside.

Their eyes met in a shared understanding of what had happened, and what needed to happen now.

'We brought some daffodil bulbs,' Elena said. 'I know it's cold out there, but I thought we could plant them together. Give us all something to look forward to in the spring.'

'Great. Let's go out into the back garden,' Theo said.

'I'll get my spade,' Riley said. 'I've got a big spade. Granddad?'

'In a minute, love. I just need to talk to your mum about something.'

Sally and Stephen stood in the kitchen together.

Stephen's eyes willed her to make easier what he found so difficult to say, but Sally would not fill the silence, however tempting it was to do so. She needed to hear it – every word.

'I owe you an apology,' Stephen said, his voice gruff but clear. 'I made a grave misjudgement.'

If she accepted his apology now, she would have to let go of her anger. There would be no grudge held. If she was going to forgive him, it had to be completely.

'I thought I could keep things in order,' Stephen said. 'I wanted there to be order. It's what always helped my sons.'

He had wanted to help – she could see that now. Somewhere deep inside, he had had good intentions. He'd been misguided, but it had come from a place of love.

'Your family is very different from how ours was,' he said, without judgement.

'We have rules too,' Sally said. 'They just aren't the same ones you raised your children with.'

'I respect that.' He went quiet.

'Riley's missed you,' Sally said.

He looked away and then rubbed roughly at his eyes.

Sally reached out a hand and touched his arm. 'We've all missed you.'

He gave a brief nod. When he looked up his eyes were wet

with tears. 'Thank you, Sally. For accepting my apology. For taking us back.'

Theo stayed and cooked dinner that night, after his parents had left, back in the familiar territory of the kitchen after weeks away. Spaghetti and meatballs, with red wine for him and Sally. There was finally something to celebrate. It had been slow, and a little painful, but Riley had his grandparents back.

Riley squirmed excitedly in his seat as Theo served up the food. 'Lots, please,' he said. 'I'm really hungry.'

He ate quickly, strands of spaghetti flicking up and leaving tomato lines on his cheeks.

Theo caught Sally's eye, and the two of them smiled.

Being together, as a family, felt good. No one was there assessing them. No one was going to take their child away. And no one – no one that mattered – was going to try and divide them. It was more than that, though – it was Sally. Being back with Sally felt good.

The three of them talked – about Riley's space project, about Arlo, the new boy, about the café, about Sally's latest designs, about the five-a-side football club Freddie had joined.

When dinner was over, Theo and Riley carried through the plates to the kitchen area, and Sally loaded the dishwasher.

'Dad, will you stay tonight?' Riley asked.

Theo looked at Sally. It felt possible. Close.

'Not tonight,' he said. He directed the next part to Sally. 'But maybe soon.'

'Will you put me to bed?' Riley asked.

'Absolutely,' Theo said. 'I brought you a new book. It's an Asterix one with Cleopatra in it. One we haven't read—'

'Great,' Riley said impatiently. 'We can read that.'

They went upstairs to the bathroom and Theo turned the bath taps on while Riley got undressed. Perhaps soon this could be – would be – their everyday again. He'd felt a warmth from Sally downstairs, a sense that if he wanted to come home, the door would be open.

'Lots of bubbles this time,' Riley said, stripping off his T-shirt. He bent over the side of the bath and scooped out a handful of bubbles, then blew them at him.

Theo laughed. He remembered how Sally used to do the same thing.

This closeness. This everydayness. The routines, the habits, the private jokes. He'd missed it so much.

'Dad,' Riley said, looking him in the eye.

'Yes?'

'I want to be a girl again.'

Sally was sitting on the sofa with her laptop, catching up on some emails. She could hear Theo come back down the stairs, and she realised she was smiling to herself. Something had happened, just then, over dinner. She and Theo had become closer, and it felt right.

He put his head around the living room door.

'You were a while,' Sally said. 'Did Riley not want to go to bed?'

He came in and took a seat beside her. He was shaking his head, dazed. 'You're not going to believe this.'

'Go on.'

He rubbed his brow. 'Seriously. It's nuts.'

'Tell me.'

Sally wondered what, at this juncture, and after all they'd gone through, could cause Theo to be thrown.

'Riley's just told me she wants to be a girl again.'

Sally felt stunned. 'No way.'

'It's what she said.'

'That's not possible.'

Theo shrugged. 'Seems like anything's possible.'

Riley must be testing them. That was it. Maybe they should have anticipated this.

'What were hi exact words?'

If she was to make sense of this she needed to know them. Every one.

'"I want to be a girl again. I don't want to wear dresses. I don't want to play with dolls. I don't want pink things. But I'm a girl. I want to be a girl at school again."'

'You're serious about all this?'

'I wouldn't mess around with something like this, Sal. I'm telling you it exactly as she said it.'

Sally shook her head. 'My God.' She wanted to laugh – in a way, it felt like the only sensible reaction. 'What a mess.'

'A bit, yes.'

'Maybe she's testing us,' she said.

Theo's eyes met hers. 'Either way, where do we go from here?'

'See if Riley says it again.'

'And if she does?'

'Then we have to listen,' Sally said, not yet able to picture it.

'Reverse everything?'

'I don't know.'

'We go back to worrying about the stuff other parents do? Screen time, Haribo intake, washing behind their ears . . .' Theo said.

He was acting as if this was nothing. No big deal. She felt the intimacy they'd shared earlier that evening disappear.

'Do you want this to be happening?' Sally said.

'No,' Theo said, shaking his head.

'Are you sure?'

'Sally,' Theo said. 'Don't be like that. I don't care about being right.'

Sally felt churned up. 'God, this is confusing.'

My duvet's up high, almost to my chin, and my toy elephant is in bed with me. Everything is going to be all right now.

Everything is going to be just like it was before.

Dad listened to me, and now everything is going to be OK.

Star light, star bright . . .

Chapter 50

The next morning, Sally woke up, alone in bed, and thought for a moment that she'd imagined it all. Then the conversation with Theo came back to her – their awkward goodbye at the door when he left, as they arranged that he would come back the following day to spend some more time at the house.

Riley came into her room and climbed up into bed with her. Sally put an arm around her and held her close.

'Did Daddy tell you?' Riley said.

'He mentioned what you'd said at bathtime, yes.'

'I want to be a girl again – did he tell you that?'

'Yes,' Sally said. 'And is that how you still feel this morning?'

There had been no outward change; Riley looked just the same as she had the previous day, the previous weeks.

'Yes.'

'This seems a big change.'

'I know,' Riley said, curling in closer. 'But I've thought about it a lot.'

'Do you want to think about it a bit longer?'

'I don't really need to. But if you want me to, I will.'

Theo came around at ten.

'You OK?' he asked her. 'Do you want to take a break, go out for a walk?'

'Yes,' Sally said. 'Good idea. I think I just need to clear my head. A walk would be good.'

She left Theo and Riley playing Junior Monopoly and walked in the direction of the café. She looked at the paving stones, the tarmac that had melted towards the kerb.

Summer's heat had distorted everything, Sally thought. Made liquid out of what was once solid. And now it was setting again, in an unexpected shape.

She pictured Riley's body slipping into the clear blue water of the swimming pool in Italy.

The locks of hair cut from Riley's head; from her own.

Ribbons of dresses.

The whispers of strangers. Of family.

Sally. Theo. Riley. Separate people. Separate lives, each taking their own direction.

Be at peace with this, Sally thought.

If Riley is sure, then this is a good thing. Embrace it.

Your girl is back.

It was time to let it all go. The boy Riley. The teenage years, with their decisions and complications. The man she'd made herself picture Riley becoming. She could say goodbye to those things, and let her daughter back in.

And there was more. More that was coming unravelled right in front of her. The mother she thought she'd have to be – active in support groups, booking doctors' appointments, speaking up; that courage, the fearlessness, the conviction – she didn't have to be anymore. She could be softer again. Her world could shift back into a more conventional, socially acceptable shape.

Theo moved his piece, the silver race car, around the Monopoly board, and gave Riley the rent.

Sally had been right, at least partly. This, Riley accepting that she was a girl, *was* what he'd wanted all along.

But it didn't feel right.

They'd all changed. Each one of them.

And now the pieces of their family – which he'd hoped could slot back together, just as before, weren't doing that at all.

Chapter 51

The next day, Riley's school was closed for teacher training, and to Sally it felt like a stay of grace. They had some more time to think. The previous day had brought no fresh revelation, or U-turn. Riley, as far as they could make out, still felt like a girl.

Sally's dad and Catherine were due to visit, and she'd called them ahead to let them know what the situation was. When they arrived, Sally welcomed them, grateful for their company, and for the certainty that they would no sooner judge now than they had at the start.

Jules took Riley into the living room, leaving Catherine and Sally alone in the hallway.

'Thanks for making the trip,' Sally said. 'Riley's been looking forward to it.'

'You know we love coming down,' Catherine said.

'It's been a bit of a weird weekend.'

'I can imagine.'

'She announced it to Theo on Saturday night. I feel like it's come out of nowhere.'

'And she's sure?'

'She says she is.'

'Confusing business, this, isn't it?'

'Yes,' Sally said. All the emotions of the past days welled to the surface and threatened to spill over. 'It really is, yes.'

Catherine gave her a hug. Sally let herself sink into it, resting her head on Catherine's shoulder. Catherine touched her hair and something inside Sally gave way. Silently, a tear rolled down her cheek, and she didn't move to stop it. More tears came, until she felt they might not stop. There, in Catherine's arms, she felt safe.

'I should pull myself together,' she said, wiping her eyes. 'I don't want Riley to see me like this.'

Riley came rushing back into hallway, her cheeks flushed with excitement.

'We're going to set Saturn free,' Riley said. 'Granddad and I decided it's time. We're going to let him go into the wild.'

In the afternoon, Jules and Catherine took Riley out to the shops and the park, and they came back relaxed and happy. The question of gender hadn't come up, Jules said, and no one had forced it. Sally hoped the same would happen at school that week, so that there was no need for a decision to be immediate.

In the evening, she cooked chilli for them all. She'd thought about calling Theo, but held back – it all felt too muddled, too fragile. They seemed to upset each other without even meaning to, and she didn't want Riley to pick up on that.

Jules and Catherine stayed over, and the next morning they all ate breakfast together.

'I'm back to school today,' Riley said to her granddad. 'Will you take me?'

'We've got time, haven't we, Catherine?' Jules said.

'Yes, of course. We don't have to leave right away,' Catherine said. 'I could load up the car and get some shopping while you're gone.'

'So you can take me?' Riley said. 'Can he, Mum?'

Sally smiled. 'OK. Go on. Off you go and get ready, then.'

Chocolate sprinkles on the top. Chocolate sprinkles.

I look at Granddad Jules.

'I think Mum might be cross about this,' I say, looking around the café.

'I know. Hot chocolate with sprinkles is practically a crime in her book,' Granddad says. 'Though I definitely remember her having a few when she was your age.'

'It's nearly school time,' I say.

'You're right. And we'll go in a minute. But I don't get to see you often. I wanted to talk with you,' Granddad says.

'OK.' I scoop out some froth with chocolate on it and eat it. 'We can talk.'

'Your mum tells me you want to be a girl now.'

'Yes. I do.'

'What is it that makes you want to go back to being a girl?' Granddad asks.

I shrug. 'I just do.'

Granddad waits. It feels quiet.

'When I was a boy, I felt better. But everything went wrong,' I say.

'Wrong, how?'

'Dad stopped living with us. Mum got upset. Grandma Elephant and Granddad stopped coming.'

'That's not your fault. You know that, don't you?'

I shake my head. Tears come to my eyes.

'I miss Dad. I want him to come home. I made it all go wrong,' I say. 'And that must mean I can make it right again.'

'You didn't make it go wrong,' Granddad reassures me.

'I did.'

'Mums and dads disagree sometimes. They argue. Children don't make that happen, and it's not their job to stop it.'

I shuffle in my seat. 'I want things to be like before,' I say at last. 'Dad at home.'

'And you think if you're a girl again, that will happen?'

I look down at the table.

'To get Dad home again, I need to make myself all straight. Everyone was happy when I was a girl.'

'Everyone apart from you?' Granddad says.

I nod. 'Yes. Everyone apart from me.'

Chapter 52

Sally answered the doorbell, expecting it to be Catherine, home from doing the shopping.

Instead, it was Theo, looking flustered.

'Hi,' she said. 'What are you doing here?'

'I just got a call from school. They said Riley hadn't arrived. I tried you on your mobile but I couldn't get through.'

'What?' she said, puzzled. 'She should be there by now. My dad took her in this morning.'

She brought up her father's number on her phone and called it.

'Dad, are you with Riley?'

Sally breathed a sigh of relief at her dad's answer, and nodded to Theo to show that everything was OK. She returned to the phone call.

'Dad, where are you? You're in big trouble.'

Sally and Theo walked together to the café on the high street.

'I should have known he'd pull something like this,' Sally said. 'You'd think an ex-teacher would have more respect for punctuality. I'm really sorry if you were worried.'

'It was a long half hour,' Theo said. 'One of the longest. I'm just glad everything's OK.'

They found Jules and Riley sitting at a table inside. Sally sat down next to Riley and gave her a hug. She gave Jules a stern look.

'Are you cross about the sprinkles?' Riley said.

'No,' Sally said. 'I'm cross that your granddad hasn't got you to school, like he promised me he would. They called Theo, Dad. We've all been worried.'

Jules looked from Sally to Theo. His expression was serious. 'I'm sorry. Genuinely, I am. But what we were talking about seemed important.'

'And what was that?' Theo asked.

'I think it's up to Riley to tell you.'

'But Dad—' Sally began, checking her watch.

'Wait,' Jules said.

'Please don't be cross,' Riley said. 'With Granddad. Or with me.'

'We won't be,' Theo said.

'I still want to be a boy,' Riley said.

For Sally, the cloud of confusion of the last few days cleared. Here was the truth that, really, had never left her bones. Riley hadn't changed her mind.

'I just wanted things to go back to normal,' Riley continued. 'But lying is wrong, I know that.'

'You've told the truth now,' Theo said, 'and that's what matters.'

'Was there are reason you said it?' Sally asked Riley, gently. 'That you wanted to be a girl again?'

Riley bit her lip. 'Because I thought it would make everyone happier.'

Riley hadn't been testing them – she'd thought she was saving their family. *He* had. Sally's heart ached as she drew her child towards her and into a hug.

'I thought it would make you want to come home, Dad.'

*

Sally and Theo dropped Riley off at school, apologising for the lateness, and then walked back to the house together. They were silent for the first block, the events of the morning still settling for them both. Sally felt like an egg-timer, tipped over and back again, the sand of her thoughts running this way and that.

'Well, that was a wake-up call,' Theo said, sombrely.

'Yes,' Sally said. Of course Riley would have picked up on the problems between them. There were no excuses – they'd been wilfully blind. 'We really misjudged all this, didn't we?'

'I guess so,' Theo said. 'We should have talked with Riley properly about what was going on – me moving out. Been honest. He's smart enough to have realised that this was serious.'

'I didn't want it to be real,' Sally said. Regrets crowded in on her.

'I know, me either,' Theo said. It felt like the most honest conversation they'd had for a long time. 'But all the while, it *was* real. It was where we were. It's where we still are. Riley was old enough to know about it.'

'All the time we were arguing about the best way to keep Riley safe, and it was the tension between us that made him the most unhappy.'

Ultimately, it wasn't other people who'd done the damage, Sally thought. It was them, Riley's own parents, the people who loved him most in the world.

'It got so bad Riley felt he had to lie to us,' Theo said. 'About who he is. What he needs. It was hard, hearing that.'

'It really was. Whatever Riley decides, whatever twists and turns might come next, Theo – we have to make sure that we're all more honest, and that we work together, even if we're not together.'

Theo nodded. 'I'm in. It won't come to this again, we can't let it.'

Chapter 53

The next day, Sally was in her study. She lifted the garment she was sewing up to the light. A pair of newborn-sized trousers, for Isabel's baby. Riley's cousin. In the midst of all the upheaval with Riley, a new life was coming.

She snipped a loose thread as her phone rang. She smiled at the synchronicity – it was Isabel.

'Iz, hi,' she said brightly. 'I was just thinking of you.'

'Oh, really?' Her voice sounded unsteady.

'You OK?' Sally asked.

'Yes,' Isabel said. 'I don't know. Hormonal, I suppose. It's intense, this pregnancy thing, isn't it? My twenty-week scan is today.'

'That's exciting.'

'I know, it is. The thing is, Freddie won't be able to make it. He's out of London meeting with a supplier. He got the dates mixed up.' She gave an audible sigh. 'Listen, I know I can go on my own but . . . '

'You won't be on your own,' Sally said. 'I'm already on my way.'

Sally met Isabel at the hospital, and they waited on the hard plastic chairs near the ultrasound rooms. Isabel held Sally's hand tightly. They'd talked for the past fifteen minutes about what had happened over the weekend – how Riley had lied to smooth things over, and eventually confessed.

In Isabel's other hand she had a ticket with a printed number on it. A TV was playing out adverts for baby kit and gave breast-feeding advice.

'Twenty weeks,' Isabel said. 'It's taken for ever to get here.'

Sally remembered it – that day when she and Theo had thought they were finding out who the tiny baby inside her was.

'I don't know if it's the hormones,' Isabel said, 'but I freaked out a bit this morning. What if it's not that Freddie can't be here? What if he doesn't want to be here?'

'I'm sure that's not it,' Sally said, though she had to admit his past flakiness left her with a shred of doubt. 'Anyone can see he's happy about the baby.'

'He says he is. But Sal, it's a huge change for us. He's gone really quiet on me the last couple of days.'

Freddie, Sally thought. We've put our trust in you this time. Please be the man we all need you to be.

'He wants this,' she said. 'All of this. Try not to worry.' She took Isabel's hand.

143 flashed up on the noticeboard.

'You're up,' Sally said.

Isabel looked down at her ticket to check the number, then glanced around. One last look in case Freddie had arrived late.

'Let's do this,' Sally said.

Isabel winced in surprise as the cool gel went on her stomach, and the ultrasound technician spread it over her small bump.

'Bit cold, sorry,' she said.

Sally held her breath as they waited for the technician to take measurements. She kept her eyes fixed on her friend. Isabel didn't do nervous. Not usually – but now Sally could see it, the concern etched into her forehead even as she forced a smile.

The new life that Isabel had started to picture – so much rested on this moment.

The technician broke the tense silence. 'Everything looks fine.'

Isabel let out a relieved laugh. 'Amazing,' she said.

The door opened and they both looked up. Freddie – visibly sweating and dragging a suitcase behind him. A huge smile came over Isabel's face, and Sally's heart lifted. He'd done it.

He grabbed a seat and sat down, taking her hand in his. 'I cut the meeting short and got a cab back. I couldn't miss this.'

The technician smiled. 'Well, I'm happy to say everything's looking very good in there.'

'Brilliant,' Freddie said.

'Would you like to know the sex?' she asked.

Isabel looked at Freddie, who shrugged, and then at Sally. 'It didn't help you guys much, did it?' she said, with a smile. 'I can see our baby moving,' she said, looking at the screen. 'It's healthy. I don't think we need to know anything more than that.'

At home that evening, Sally looked at the framed family photos in the hallway. There was one of Riley as a toddler, hair in bunches, splashing in a puddle in a dress and Peppa Pig wellies. Sally flipped it over, turned the tiny latch and took out the print. She opened the drawer and put it away inside an envelope. There was the faintest tug at her heart.

From the shelf she took out an envelope of prints she'd had made after their summer holiday in Italy. She flicked through them and selected one of Riley standing by the pool in swimming trunks, shoulders tanned, short hair wet, beaming into the camera. She put it inside the frame.

She moved on to the next frame and did the same thing. She imagined for a moment that she was a stranger – viewing her child for the first time. Riley looked like any other boy. A son any parent would be proud to have. A son who filled her life with sunshine. A son Theo might finally be able to see.

That evening, Theo came around, and he and Sally ate together. And talked.

They both looked different than they had before. For Sally it was her hair, growing back slowly, long enough to carry a curl now, and the dark shadows, visible under the bright lights of the bathroom mirror when she did her make-up in the morning. With Theo, it was the lines on his brow.

She glanced down at his hand. He still wore his wedding ring, as she wore hers. Sally had only taken it off for one night. She didn't like to think about that night. But she wouldn't change it, either. There was no going back to where, and who, she'd once been.

Theo looked at her, with his eyes dark and round. Like Minstrels – that was what she'd thought when she first met him. The corners of her mouth lifted involuntarily, a memory of a better time. A time when loving each other had been easy.

Theo didn't look away. 'This was never about love. I never stopped loving you, Sally.'

Sally couldn't imagine the gap in her heart ever closing. But she knew now that she had to find a way to try.

'I know that,' she said. 'It became bigger than us.'

The faces that had dominated their lives that year – grandparents, teachers, doctors – retreated, until they vanished. Sally saw her husband clearly again. Theo. All she wanted was for them to find a way back together.

'Do you think we can do it?' he said. 'Go back to how we were?'

Their crossroads. Her answer would guide them into their future, apart or together. Opening up to the possibility of trying again was even more painful than shutting it out had been.

This wasn't about saving Riley. Riley didn't need saving.

This wasn't about Sally or Theo rescuing each other, either.

It was about building their family again, from the ground up. Taking risks.

It was Sally's move.

'No,' she said. 'I don't think we can. But I hope we can start again.'

In school, I'm painting a picture. The teacher is looking at my picture more than the others.

'That's my mum,' I say. 'And this is my dad.'

'That's your house?'

I nod. 'Oh, and that's Saturn. Our snail.' I had to draw Saturn there, even though he's free now. He's still kind of part of the family.

'And that's you, by the front door?'

'Yes.'

'What are you wearing?'

'Trousers. A top.'

'And this?'

'A . . . ' I forget the word for a second, and have to search for it in my head.

'A coat, because it's cold?' the teacher says.

'No.' I shake my head. That's not right. 'A cape.'

'A cape?'

Grown-ups really don't get it sometimes.

'Because I'm a superhero.'

Epilogue

SPRING

Almost a year had passed since Riley said the words that changed everything. Now, Sally sat in her deckchair in the back garden, watching her child climb through the upper branches of the apple tree. She leaned back. She knew, this time, that Riley wouldn't fall.

Riley had always been there – the same child, however you framed or reframed him. He was a boy, these days – at home, at school, in the park – and in all his grandparents' lives. Maybe it would always be that way. Perhaps it would change in a month. What happened next was Riley's choice. No one else's. Sally still found it hard some days, not knowing, but she had found a way to accept the uncertainty as a part of their life.

Finding Riley had been the easy part, Sally thought. Finding herself, finding Theo again, finding who they could be, together, in this new landscape – that had been harder. But it was happening, slowly. A couple of days before Christmas, Sally had taken Theo's hand in hers again. A week later, he had come back home.

Now Theo's shoes were on the rack beside Riley's trainers, his toothbrush by the sink next to Sally's. Each day, perfect or imperfect, was another day Sally and Theo had chosen to be together. There might be the flicker of a smile, a memory shared, a closeness on the sofa as they watched TV together in the evening. Sally tried not to think about it too much, what it meant. She didn't want to crush it. Because while these moments were all so small, and ordinary, they combined into something that was everything.

The transit of the seasons had marked Sally and Theo, but there was symmetry in their damage. They both knew what it was to falter, to walk through wreckage and keep looking for the light. They both knew what it was to love so deeply that you had no choice but to keep going through, even when it wasn't easy, to love so much that through was the only possible way out. They'd both had to keep believing, no matter what, that a better day would come. Sally thought, today, that perhaps it had come.

The question never went away: *Was this – Riley's transition – the right thing?* Sally knew that walking down a path with good intentions, your child's hand in yours, didn't make it the right path. She knew that the further they went with Riley, the harder it would be to turn back. It weighed heavy on them, some days, that in seeking to help, they might also unintentionally harm.

They did the only thing they, in their particular family, with their particular child, could. Together, they trod carefully. She and Theo were honest with each other. She thought. She hoped.

People in the street would occasionally cast glances at Riley, curious, confused or silently interrogating, searching Riley's face for an answer. Riley rarely noticed, and Sally and Theo wouldn't say anything.

Sometimes, though, Sally wanted to stop them. She wanted to say this:

Go ahead and look. It's OK to wonder, to question – we don't mind. Take in this blaze of light, this dynamo, this child of ours, and soon you'll forget what it was you were even asking.

A Letter from Sadie

Thank you for choosing to read *This Child of Ours.* I hope you've enjoyed it.

The novel started as the germ of an idea while I pushed my weeks-old daughter around in her pram. My second child would be an easier ride, I'd thought – a girl this time – and I'd know instinctively how to raise a girl, wouldn't I? Of course it wasn't, and isn't, like that at all! What do we expect of our children – and of ourselves – and why?

Riley's story was a real journey in the writing, and one where I've been lucky enough to meet some extraordinary people. I wanted to write a story that would reflect our complex, conflicted and fast-changing society – one that can be quick to judge – and allow you to form your own opinions.

If you've enjoyed *This Child of Ours*, I'd be really grateful if you could spread the word and leave a short review on Amazon or Goodreads. It needn't be long – a couple of lines is plenty – and your words have the power to open this book up to others.

With love,

Sadie x

Reading Group Questions

1. Did you enjoy *This Child of Ours*? What did you like best and least about the novel?

2. From just the cover and title, what did you expect the book to be about?

3. What do you imagine life holds for Sally and Theo? Do you think they will be able to rebuild their marriage?

4. What do you think the future holds for Riley? Do you imagine Riley continues identifying as a boy? How do you imagine things will be for Riley growing up?

5. What emotions did Riley's story evoke in you? Did *This Child of Ours* make you question your beliefs about gender?

6. How did Riley's age affect how you saw the situation?

7. Did you warm to Sally? Do you agree with the choices she made?

8. What was your perception of Theo? Did it change at all during the course of the novel?

9. If you got the chance to ask the author of this book one question, what would it be?

And finally, the million-dollar question …

10. What would you have done?

Loved this book? Sadie would love to hear from you!

Find her online at

@SadieBooks

facebook.com/SadiePearseBooks

Sadie has also written books as Vanessa Greene. Find out more about those books at

www.vanessagreene.co.uk

@VanessaGBooks

facebook.com/VanessaGreeneBooks

Sadie Pearse Q&A

Where did the idea for *This Child of Ours* come from? Why did it capture your imagination?

You can't really miss the conversations about gender these days, can you? The way boundaries are more fluid than ever – and young people have choices that simply didn't exist a decade or two ago. When I had my daughter, I thought about it a lot – how could I avoid putting my expectations of what a girl could be or 'should' be on her?

Society is changing, referrals to gender identity clinics are on the rise, and while some may take these changes in their stride, for others they are more challenging. They can call our whole perception of the world into question. When you put a child's welfare at the heart of the debate, it can get pretty heated.

I was struck by the huge weight of responsibility on the parents' (and medical professionals') shoulders – to get things right, which sometimes means having to be able to predict the future. Online parenting forums are full of judgements, of wrong and right, but it seems to me that there's a huge grey area in between. A lot of unknowns, still. What if your idea of 'right' was different from your partner's, and your child's wellbeing was at stake? Can romantic love really conquer all? These were the ideas in my head when I started to write.

***This Child of Ours* is about a family in turmoil. Did you find it difficult or exhilarating to write the more emotional scenes? What was the hardest scene to write?**

The whole book was a heart-wrecker! Once you start to really care about characters, you go through a lot of what they do, for good and bad – as a reader, and even more so as a writer. I decided to write this book freely, so that Theo, Sally and Riley led the action – I started off knowing not much more than that Riley would tell them she was a boy. I guessed the situation would put pressure on all of them, and their wider family, but I didn't expect the twist and turns that came. I found the scenes where Sally has to face up to the possibility of life without Theo very emotional to write. It's not what any of them want, but a sign that the conflict has become bigger than their love.

What kind of research did you do to paint such a vivid and nuanced picture of the Pieterson family's situation?

I put out a request to speak with parents of children and young people with gender identity issues. The interviews were eye-opening. I talked with nine mothers and one father, their children aged between five and eighteen, at various stages of transition. Some of their children were attending school with new names, some were taking puberty blockers or were starting hormones. Two of the young people were also on the autistic spectrum, so gender identity was only one aspect of what their particular families were dealing with. Anxiety and depression were present for some – in the child, or in their own lives. Some of the parents were straightforwardly accepting of their child's transition, others had found the loss of their child they thought they had very difficult. They were kind enough to share a lot about their personal journeys, their families, the prejudice they'd encountered, the judgement calls they'd had to make. They were extraordinary, and yet also very ordinary: parents who loved their kids, doing their best while juggling work, siblings, relationships, all the other parts of life. Dealing with more than most.

Sally and Theo's opposing views on what's best for Riley leave space for debate and give *This Child of Ours* a brilliant balance. Did you find it easy to not let your own views influences this book too much?

How best to support children with gender identity issues is a really complex topic, and my thoughts on it changed a lot during the interviews and during the writing. They continue to change. My job, as I see it, is to reflect what I see, and let readers form their own opinions, so I do what I can to ensure my voice and views aren't in there. If they sneak in, I generally see that as a shortcoming. The one place they have come in, though, I suppose, is in showing that the issue isn't cut and dried, that different approaches to dealing with Riley's situation can come from the same place of love.

What's the most difficult thing about writing characters from the opposite sex?

Argh, I find it really hard! Particularly bringing to life the details, the daily habits like shaving, say, that I'll never fully get. I found it easier to physically inhabit Sally and see things from her point of view, but I sometimes found I was looking at Theo from the outside. In redrafting I focused on getting inside his head, and the therapy scenes helped with that.

Can you tell us something you edited out of this book, and why you did that?

This book went through a lot of drafts, and I got quite attached to some of the plot points I eventually cut. In an early draft, Freddie was killed in an accident on his way back to England to be with Isabel. There was a crossover of work and life – a friend of mine had just died and it came through in my writing. I suppose I wanted to make some sense of how random and cruel these things can seem sometimes. But it really wasn't right for the story – and when I took it out, everything else fell into place. Bringing him back to life and giving him and Isabel a second chance was a lovely feeling! One of the best joys you can have as a writer. But nothing is wasted, and writing it out helped keep me on track for the rest of the rewrites. I was lucky enough to work with two honest, talented editors who both offered their own perspective on this novel, and they helped me improve it a lot.

It's great to see more conversations around gender in the media these days, but it's still a sensitive topic. While writing did you worry that you might offend people unintentionally?

Yes, definitely. I know something of the challenges and prejudices those in the trans community (and their families) face, and I would never want to add to those. But I also wanted to create a full picture, and in my view that means showing the unwieldy, sometimes unkind, nature of real-life reactions and emotions. In the novel people occasionally slip up on Riley's pronouns, using 'her' and 'she' when Riley has made it clear that doesn't feel right. These slips don't happen to hurt Riley particularly deeply, but in real life this kind of thing could be extremely upsetting and triggering to a transgender young person. Rather than present an idealised picture of acceptance, some characters struggle to accept what is going on for Riley, some disbelieve it, others make slips that are unintentional but still thoughtless. I wanted to show the way we, as a society, as individuals, are in an imperfect, messy kind of transition.

What other topics would you like to write about in the future?

There's a lot going on in our world at the moment – a lot of it divisive, and negative, but there is something energising happening too. There are conversations happening for the first time. It's incredibly fertile ground creatively. The human rights marches, the anti-gun student movements in the US, the MeToo and Black Lives Matter campaigns – there's a sense of rising up, of speaking out, and fighting back. I want to look at how the wider world can affect our own smaller, domestic ones. What are the new dilemmas that we as individuals, as parents, as friends, are facing in our lives?

What do you do to recharge and come up with the idea for your next novel?

In the past I've been guilty of rushing from one writing project to another, but after this one I knew needed some breathing space. I went to visit a uni friend in Bristol and we walked an art trail through the city's houses – that was a great way to recharge my creative batteries. Also – outdoor swimming! It's the best.

Did you enjoy the gripping and emotional rollercoaster that was *This Child of Ours*?

Keep your eyes peeled for Sadie's new book for more family drama, moral dilemmas, and ordinary people thrown into extraordinary situations.

Coming Summer 2019

Acknowledgements

Thank you (a huge thank you) to the mums and dads who spoke to me so honestly about their experiences of parenting a child or young person with gender-identity issues. I haven't told your stories – they are yours and only yours to tell – but your strength, humour, immense love and adaptability inspired this novel.

Thanks to the fantastic team at Sphere, in particular my editors, Manpreet Grewal and Viola Hayden – Manpreet, who worked with me in the early stages with calmness, creativity and skill, and Viola, who took the reins so ably and brought her own talent and vision to editing and publishing it. To Maddie and Cath, for all their support, and to Thalia Proctor and Liz Hatherell for the desk editing. Thanks also to my publicist, Millie Seaward, and to Amy Donegan in Marketing; to Tracey Winwood for the cover and Tom Webster in Production, plus the excellent Sales department.

To my agent, Maddy Milburn, for her editorial insights, kindness and support.

To my good friend Emma Stonex, who read the manuscript in its very early stages and offered advice and encouragement. To Caroline Hogg for the same. To Sophie Mumford, inspiration and light, who went through each stage of this book-pregnancy with me.

To Faye Talbott, who won a place in this novel at the Grenfell charity auction – I hope you enjoy being in it.

To Kelly Concannon, who helped me with the social work research.

Thank you to my mum, Sheelagh, for caring for my children over the past year so that I could write. Also to my kids themselves, because it was having them, and loving them, that got me asking all these questions.

Thank you, most of all, James. You are by my side on the brightest days and through the stormy weather. You never falter, and you never forget to buy the milk.*

*By which I mean wine, obviously.